A BLESSED EVENT

A BLESSED EVENT

Jean Reynolds Page

BALLANTINE BOOKS · NEW YORK

A Ballantine Book
Published by The Random House Publishing Group

www.ballantinebooks.com

Library of Congress Cataloging-in-Publication Data is available upon request from the publisher.

ISBN 0-345-46215-7

Book design by Susan Turner

Manufactured in the United States of America

First Edition: March 2004

1 3 5 7 9 10 8 6 4 2

With love, this book is dedicated to my mother, Grace,
and to my husband, Rick

ACKNOWLEDGMENTS

I HAVE MUCH GRATITUDE surrounding this book beginning with Colleen Murphy, who cared enough to point me toward those who could make this publication happen. I would like to thank my agent Susan Ginsburg (Agent doesn't quite cover it. Friend, editor, advisor . . . Those are the tip of the iceberg.) and the whole crew at Writers House. Also, many thanks to my editor at Ballantine, Charlotte Herscher, whose enthusiasm and excellent eye made this a better book. A common thread through all of these good souls is Victoria Skurnick, whose generosity still astounds me.

Other literary guardian angels include the exceptional Barbara Wedgwood, along with other folks at the SMU informal courses. Out of that wonderful experience I found a group of dear friends, extraordinary writers all, who shaped this book at every turn with careful readings and suggestions. They are Ian Pierce, Jeanne Skartsiaris, Mary Turner, Lou Tasciotti, and Chris Smith. Earlier workshop-mates, too many to name—although Roger Terk and Fanchon Knott must be singled out among them—offered wisdom and comments. More thanks than I can express, guys.

Before the good fortune of a book contract, Tim Page, Al Silverman, and Juris Jurjevics believed, and helped me to believe, it could happen. For this, I am blessed.

Others who offered expertise with great patience include Patrick Naylor, Eric Cromatie, and Katie Hendricks, who provided legal advice, and again to Mary Turner for the court dialogue. I would like to thank Karen Bradshaw and Christine Gleason who, among so many other things, gave medical advice, and Martin Curtin, OFM Cap., who sat through endless questions regarding the church and a life of service. Many thanks.

Much love to Joyce and Neil Ross, Ralph and Susan Reynolds, H. V. Massengill, and Ellis Page for more years of encouragement than I wish to count; to Lisa Wagner, Betsy Collins, Beth Franzblau, Marc Farre, Lynn Saunders, Lynne Griffith, and Jodie Hurwitz for listening as I talked it all out; and to Ellen Jacobs, for my home away from home in New York City.

And abiding gratitude to Hilda Lee for teaching me about rewrites (and then more about rewrites); and to Andy Ziskind for a delightful short-notice photo shoot.

Thanks also to the Durham Arts Council in North Carolina for the grant that helped validate those early years of writing.

Finally, all my love and appreciation to Rick, Franklin, Gillian, and Edward Page, and to Grace Reynolds Massengill and to the late Hubert Reynolds, for all the sacrifices that were necessary so that I could see this through (and with no complaints along the way).

*"Behold now, the Lord hath restrained me from bearing:
I pray thee, go in unto my maid; it may be that I may
obtain children by her."*

SARAI TO ABRAM, GENESIS 16:2

ONE

I WANTED A FAMILY. I wanted Joanne to be part of us, of our family. Cal, my husband, he wanted the same thing, at first. Somehow, all our reasons got lost. I was the last one to know that something had gone wrong with our plans. Once I found out, everything went to hell pretty fast.

By the time it all came clear to me, Joanne's 1980 Buick Le Sabre was down the hall in my bedroom, tipped headlong over my dresser. A steep embankment runs up beside our house to the highway. Joanne lost control of her car at the moment when her headlights would have flashed by our window. She was my closest friend. I don't remember a time before I knew her. She was as close as family. When she agreed to my plan, she became family. I still believe that.

The seconds after that accident were the most awful moments of my life, when Cal and I woke to the sounds of Jo's car crashing into our bedroom, crunching our wall like a Saltine cracker. Wood and paint sprayed everywhere, along with glass from the windows and picture frames. I had cuts in a dozen places on my body that I never felt.

My first thought was about the baby. Somehow I thought Joanne would be strong enough to get up and walk away. She'd stood up to her daddy for twenty-seven years; a car wreck shouldn't have been the end of it. But the baby, I didn't know if the baby could take something like that. Then I saw Joanne. I saw her bloody and broken through the car window and I just knew they were both lost.

I stayed in the room as long as I could, until the smell of gasoline and the sight of my friend turned my stomach inside out. I stayed while Cal went to get help and I tried to reach in and touch her, but warm blood was everywhere and I had to pull back. Every part of me was shaking.

After the police, the fire truck, and the ambulances all got to my house, I sat in my kitchen. I was trying to get away from the shouting, the thick air and, most of all, from the sight of Joanne. They said she was alive, but just barely. She probably wouldn't make it out of the car. It was more than I could handle. Sitting in my kitchen, I could block out everything else; only for a few seconds at a time, but just enough to hang on to my mind. I'd stare at my cigarette—the first I'd smoked in two years—like it was the most important object in the world, some treasure, and push all the other images away. It would come back to me in no time; but a moment here and there kept me going, like catching your breath when you're too winded to move on.

Cal stayed in there all morning, talking to the police. He came in the kitchen once with the deputy to answer some questions with me.

"When was the last time you saw her?" the deputy asked Cal. I could hear the medical people in our room, trying to get Joanne out of the car. "She been here recently?"

"Yesterday afternoon," I answered for him. "She came over here."

I thought of her then, standing in my house, troubled by something—both of us unaware of the terrible things that would come so soon.

"Yeah," Cal told the deputy. "She was here when I got in from work."

She'd been at the house for an hour before he got home, working hard to say something to me, looking for words that wouldn't fit into the thoughts she had in her head.

"Joanne," I said. "Just tell me, whatever it is."

I put my hand on her arm and she jumped. We'd been familiar as twins for twenty years of my life. She'd never flinched once before. Then Cal came in the front door. She took one look at him and I didn't need any words to know what she couldn't say. It was my fault. I'd put them together. She left without another word to me or to him.

"Was there anything that made you think she was upset or angry?" the deputy asked. He was looking at me.

"Yeah," I said. Cal looked at the floor. "She never quite got it out, but I knew she was upset."

I looked out the side window of the kitchen, saw the steep rise that led up to where our side yard met the asphalt, the curve in the road before you get to our driveway. I saw the tracks in the tall grass where she'd left the highway, gone airborne. She hit the curve like a straightaway, they told me, never touching the brake. They said the accelerator might have stuck or she might have hit the wrong pedal when she was trying to brake. I couldn't think otherwise of her. My soul couldn't hold any other explanation; but I knew what the deputy and the rest of them were thinking. They were thinking that those things never really happen and this was never really an accident.

"Can you tell me anything else?" the deputy asked me.

Cal looked at me, nodded at me to go ahead.

"She was having a baby for us," I said. The cigarette shook in my fingers. I couldn't make it stop. A smear of blood from a cut I hadn't bothered to wash covered my hand, or maybe it was Joanne's blood. I didn't know.

"It's Cal's baby," I said.

The deputy looked up from his notepad. His whole face was a question.

"We'd asked her to have a baby for us. With us. I can't, you see. I can't have a baby. I told her to have it for me, with Ca—with my husband. She'd be an aunt. A godparent."

The deputy looked down at his notepad again and scribbled. I couldn't see his face. Cal had walked to the den. He stood at the window with his back to me. A blinding sun, rising in the Texas sky, made him look dark, like a shadow standing alone.

The deputy got his voice back.

"Had something changed for her?" he asked. "When she talked to you. Was she thinking she didn't want to do it?"

"She'd changed her mind, I think. Not about the baby. She'd changed her mind about us, about Cal, I think."

Cal walked back to me. He rubbed his hand, light on my cheek, and I felt a tear I didn't know was there.

"You don't know what she was going to say," Cal told me.

"I can guess pretty well."

Cal looked as if he wanted to say more, but he stopped.

"We'd shared something, the three of us," he said, now talking to the deputy. "It was hard to figure out what we all felt. She didn't know what to do with it. Hell, I know I got confused. I think we all did."

Then he turned to me again.

"I love you," he said. "She loved you too. We didn't think about everything enough. How complicated the feelings would get."

His face was pulled in all different directions with pain—pain that I'd caused. In some ways, I might as well have been driving that Le Sabre this morning. I put it all in motion. Now I wanted her back, with or without that baby growing in her belly.

"How far along was she?" the deputy asked. "With the baby?"

"Almost five months," I said.

He looked almost sick, or disgusted, I couldn't read him that well.

"The accident," he managed, finally. He'd heard enough of our story. "Do you remember anything else about the accident?"

"The crashing noises seemed like they might have been a bad dream," I told him, "I woke up stunned and scared, my heart racing."

All I remembered was the hot exhaust, the smell of gas, all bearing in on my nose, choking me like a pillow pushed against my face. It took us both a second to collect our wits.

"Cal came around first. He scooted out of bed, out from in front of the car, and pulled me with him. The motor was still running and the car was lodged on my dresser. The motor kept running and running. It must have stopped sometime, but I don't remember when."

Cal started screaming. I didn't say this to the deputy, but I can hear it in my head if I listen. "Joanne! Oh Christ, Joanne!"

But Joanne was a mess and not in any shape to answer. Her face was mashed in on one side, no face at all, really, all blood and hair. And I stood there and looked at her like she was acting in a movie—frantic that the baby had gotten crushed, still hoping that Joanne would come to any minute. But she didn't come to. She didn't move.

"Cal tried to call for help, but the crash did something to our phone," I said. "He went to his work radio in the truck, got somebody at dispatch to call an ambulance."

I stayed in there as long as I could, until Cal got back. Then I had to leave, had to go to my normal-looking kitchen, a weak puppy hiding from thunder.

"Joanne never opened her eyes or anything. Not that I saw."

After I'd answered all of the officer's questions, one of the policemen, or maybe a paramedic, yelled for the deputy to come back down the hall. Cal ran after him. I stayed behind to think about everything we'd done. It sounded different, our story. Saying it all out loud to a stranger, all the details about the baby, made it sound wrong. I never saw it that way before.

I didn't want to think about what Joanne looked like as they pulled her out of the car. Like a coward, I left her there with them, the baby too. I left them both, sat at the breakfast table in my bathrobe staring at the yellow-colored wallpaper in my kitchen. That's when I knew I had to have a Salem Light. I went through every drawer in the kitchen to find the pack. Stale and wrong, it satisfied my fear.

Then I registered the solid ache of what it would mean to lose Joanne—Jo and the baby with her. She'd been with me nearly forever, lived behind me, almost all my years of growing up. Our backyards ran together like a playground and her room looked as familiar to me as my own. Her mama knew my favorite foods, my favorite colors, bought me clothes when she went shopping for Joanne. My mama French-braided Joanne's hair before school and taught her how to embroider on her jeans.

Joanne knew when Junior Evans kissed me and when Sean Latham first moved his hands to places that had been a secret to everyone, including me. Then there was Cal. She knew I wanted to marry him before I'd said it—to him or to myself.

When they brought her down the hall of my house on a stretcher, when they said she was still alive, I yelled out something, I don't know what, some kind of prayer, like some crazed Holy Roller. I don't know where it came from. I'm not somebody God counts on for attendance.

I ran to her, planned to tell her how sorry I was, but I stopped when I got a good look. Blood, some fresh and some dried, covered her bandages and the still-familiar features of at least half her face. The skin on her arms and shoulders looked like old wall paint, dull and matte. She looked dead. I couldn't help thinking she'd rather be.

Cal stood in the hall and cried. Loud crying, like a child.

It wasn't until the ambulance drove off, until the road dust behind it conjured ghost images in the heat, that I realized they hadn't said anything about the baby. If Joanne was alive, what about the baby?

"The baby," I said to Cal. "What'd they say about the baby?"

He walked into the den, sat on the arm of the couch.

"There's a heartbeat," he said, his voice hoarse and spent. "That's all they know."

THE DOCTOR AT THE HOSPITAL said that Joanne couldn't hear us, said she couldn't think or smell or feel as far as they could tell. Her face was bandaged all on one side, that whole side of her head, really. Tubes were taped to her face and her arm; they ran to machines with screens and alarms.

Orderlies moved her out of the emergency room, rolled her to the Intensive Care Unit where the neurologist could come and see her, run his tests. At first, the doctors wouldn't let me in. Then they told me I could sit with her behind the curtains that were supposed to be like walls. I was to get out of the way if the specialist came in.

"She doesn't seem to be responsive," they kept saying when I asked how she was.

Her chest moved in time with the machine. They covered up the hurt side of her head, so that the part of her face I could see looked bruised, but normal. Cal stayed until they got her settled, until I was sitting with her and he had nothing to do but wait in the hall. Then he went back to the house. The town borrowed a crane from some construction company to get Joanne's car out of our bedroom and he said he ought to be there while they worked.

I'd been with her when she bought the car, one afternoon the summer before. Hell, I loaned her money for the down payment. It was two years old, but had next to nothing in mileage. We drove it off the lot and went straight to the boat landing at Lake Riley. She had a couple of joints with her and we smoked until the water looked like it had changed color, then ate a grocery-sized bag of Cheetos and rinsed our orange fingers in the lake.

I pictured the machine dragging that car out of our house. They told Cal they would cover the hole with a big tarp to keep weather out for the time being.

"Miss?" The nurse's voice made me jump. "There's someone in the hall who would like to talk with you."

The deputy, the same one from our house, was standing outside the ICU. I got up and walked out to meet him.

"I'm sorry to bother you," he said.

"That's okay."

"How is she?" He shifted his weight, nodded toward the ICU doors.

It didn't seem like he ought to be at the hospital. The spectacle was over. It had become private—just me and Joanne.

"She's staying alive with tubes," I said. "They say she doesn't know anything. But I don't know."

He nodded.

"A real shame," he said, finally. "Young woman like that." I looked at him, tried to see if his face had any accusations in it, but he just looked sad.

"We've tried to reach her folks since early this morning, but couldn't find anybody home, then or now. That's still the right place, over on Willow Creek?"

"Yeah, that's right."

"You sure?"

"I ought to be sure," I told him. "I grew up next to that house, lived there about as much as I did at my own."

At least during the day, when her daddy wasn't home, I thought but didn't say.

"Well, we've been over there several times. It's locked up. Nobody comes to the door."

I pictured her house in my mind. My old house right behind it. My memory held every inch of the land, the yards, the houses, and the rooms. I missed it. Mom had sold our house seven years before, two months after my daddy died. I barely had time to clean out my old room.

"Do you have any idea where else the Timbros might be?" he asked.

"The hardware store. Did you try there?"

"Yeah, we checked there first. It was closed this afternoon. Nobody's been there today far as we can tell."

It wasn't like the Timbros to close up shop. Mr. Timbro hated to close even on holidays for fear he might miss out selling batteries or a lightbulb. Why should he sit around in his own living room when he could be selling things to everybody else.

"I don't know, then," I said. "If they're not at home or at the store."

Truth was, I wanted to put off seeing them face-to-face as long as possible.

The deputy stood there for a minute. Quiet, out of questions.

"I better run on," he said, finally. "Let me know if her people show up."

I watched him walk down the hall, felt relieved to be free of real talk. Then I went back in with Joanne, touched her hand. It felt warm, almost feverish. Her lavender nail polish was chipped and old. I laid my hand on the blanket over her belly; imagined the baby, all head and fingerlike limbs. I felt too tired to cry.

THE POLICE FOUND THE TIMBROS at a hardware convention in Houston.

"How much do her parents know?" I asked Cal after he talked with the deputy. He'd come back to the hospital, convinced me to go to the cafeteria with him.

"They know she's on life support. It's bad. They know that."

I reached for his hand across the table. He rubbed my fingers like you might pet a small animal. I noticed he hadn't touched his food.

"The baby?" I asked. "Do they know about that?"

"No. Nobody's told them anything yet. Unless Joanne said something to them before."

"I doubt that. She hasn't said more than a dozen civil words to her dad in over a year. Not a whole lot more to her mom."

Her parents—her dad, really, but her mom didn't stop it—told her to leave home when she got fired from the lumberyard. She got caught

sharing a joint with Andy Roman on her lunch break, and her dad
threw her out. She even spent the past Christmas with Cal and me.
She took her mama a present, but she didn't go in the house.

"She might have said something to her mama about the baby," I
told Cal, "but I don't think so."

It was mid-afternoon, quiet time for food services at the hospital.
The plump ladies running the cafeteria kept up a lively exchange between the clang of steel pans and the thud of oven doors as they
cleaned up lunch and started in on dinner. I had soup in front of me,
too hot to eat. Raising the spoon seemed such an effort anyway.

"It might actually make her folks feel better," I said. "At least her
mama."

"What?"

"A baby."

He looked at me like what I'd said didn't register.

"You know," I told him. "Something left of Joanne."

"What are you thinking, Darla?"

I didn't know what to say. What was I thinking?

"Darla? You don't figure she's still going to have that baby?"

His eyes, large and full on me, looked scared. He hadn't smiled in
so long, weeks it seemed. But I couldn't lie. Ever since I'd heard the
word *heartbeat* . . . My baby was alive.

"The doctors said the baby is fine. The baby's not dead, Cal. As
long as Joanne's on life support, the baby will grow. I won't take life
away from our baby. She wouldn't want that."

"Joanne drove off a hill. She's half-dead. How can you think she'll
have the baby?"

His loud voice silenced the cafeteria ladies. Only the hum of appliances and the low buzz of fluorescent lights still registered.

"You don't know her the way I do," I said, my voice barely there.
"It's what she would want."

"Sugar," he said, now calm and careful, "we fucked up. All of us.
Now we've lost Joanne because of it. We've got to let go."

He seemed so sure. How could he be so sure about something so
wrong?

"Cal. It's all we've got left. We can still take one good thing out of
this. You'll see. It's the right thing."

"I can't talk about this right now," he said. "This isn't the right time to settle it."

I couldn't imagine that he'd feel the same after things calmed down. We'd made so many plans. He got up, stood beside the booth.

"I need to get some air," he said, "I can't breathe in here."

"Okay," I said, not offering to go with him. I didn't want to hear him say it again, that it was wrong to still want the baby.

He took his tray to the conveyer belt that ran dirty plates and cups to the kitchen, then went out and walked through the double doors that led back into the hospital. I didn't know where he was going, but I didn't have the energy to worry about it.

My mind went back to Joanne. I knew her. She'd want to stay and bring the baby to life. I *knew* Joanne, better than anybody.

"You want me to take that?" A young black man dressed in white cafeteria clothes had his hand out, was offering to take my tray, my empty soup bowl. I couldn't recall eating the soup.

"You all finished?" he asked, prompting me again to respond.

I nodded, mumbled a "thank you" as I handed him the cluttered tray.

WHEN I GOT BACK TO JOANNE, my mother was sitting in the chair by the bed. The staff probably thought she was Joanne's mother. Not a bad assumption, all in all.

She looked small to me, my mother. Parents always seem big, larger than life, even when you get older. Then in a strange moment, it changes. You catch them out of context in the normal world.

She wasn't short, just average height. But her face, shoulders, arms—all her features were built on delicate bones. With smooth skin and carefully placed hair, even in her fifties, she looked like a girl. I'm not sure I'd noticed this before.

"Hi, Mom," I said, my voice low like I might wake a sleeping Joanne.

I could tell she'd been crying, probably on and off all day.

"Oh sweetheart," she said, rising to give me a hug. "I know how hard this is on you."

Her mint green blouse smelled like powder. Chanel or something.

It was her scent, mature and maternal. I wondered when I would get old enough to smell like that.

"Where's Cal?" she asked. "You shouldn't have to be here by yourself."

"He just went out for a walk or something. I think he needed to clear his head."

She walked over to the bed, wiped a speck of something crusty and dry in the corner of Joanne's eye. Only part of Jo's face could be seen. The rest of it lay under the respirator and the bandages.

"You sit," Mom said, nodding toward the chair she'd been in, the one comfortable place to rest in the curtained cubicle. It reclined back so you could try to doze if you planned to stay all day.

"That's okay," I told her, "I'll sit here with Jo."

I settled at the end of the hospital bed, propped my feet on the low rail support under the mattress. The side rails were down. No worries that she might stand up, hurt herself falling while trying to walk.

"I thought Larry and Arlene would be here," Mom said, moving back to the chair. "Have you seen them?"

"They were at a hardware convention in Houston. They're on the way back. It took the law a while to track them down."

I didn't want to think about Joanne's parents, about telling them everything, making them understand.

"They're both away?" she asked.

"Yeah. They closed up the store."

Jo's dad had coached football before his back started giving him trouble. He couldn't stand for so long at a time on the sidelines, so he left the high school and bought out Mr. Jenkins at the hardware store. But he stayed a coach inside, driven to one goal after another—selling more appliances than other regional stores, upgrading his register system, always something, an urgency you could feel whenever he was in the room.

"This is going to tear Arlene to pieces," Mom said, looking at Jo.

She was already in pieces. Joanne and I had both thought that for a while. Since they'd bought the store, Mrs. Timbro stayed there almost every day except Sunday. She'd never had a job before. To me, she looked tired all the time. I said this to Joanne once.

"I know," she told me, sounding sad. "She used to only have to worry about pleasing him at dinner. Now she's got to suit him all damn day. It wears me out to look at her."

Mom and I sat for a while without talking. The bandages that covered half Jo's face looked like some gruesome costume she might cook up for Halloween. The machine that kept her breathing made her sound angry; hard malignant breaths.

"You go on home, honey," Mom said. "I'll stay here."

She sounded like "home" might be a normal place and I started to remind her home wouldn't be home until we got the wall fixed. Then it hit me. She didn't know.

"How'd you hear about this, Mom?"

"Betty Sayers from the church called me. She said there had been some sort of car accident on your road. She had the scanner on early while she was up getting Bob off to work. She was afraid it was you or Cal, so she tried to call your house and just kept getting a busy signal. Finally, she decided to call up here to the hospital. Her cousin, who was a nurse on duty, told her the paramedics were working on getting Joanne Timbro out of her car so they could bring her in."

The window in the ICU faced the west, caught the afternoon sun as it moved toward late afternoon. It couldn't possibly be the same day we had woken up to, but it was. Driving in from Houston, the Timbros would be back any minute, would walk through the door, see Joanne and listen to the doctor as he told them about the accident, about the baby still growing in her belly.

"Mom, I need to talk to you," I said. The words snagged in my throat.

She looked up at me. I could feel Jo's leg against my back, half expected her to poke at me with her foot, grin and tell me to lighten up.

"Joanne didn't just have a wreck on our road."

"What do you mean, honey?"

"Her car ran off that high embankment near our house. It went airborne. Actually landed *in* our house, in our bedroom. The back end lodged on Granddaddy's oak dresser. The dresser stopped it from running over us, I guess."

My voice sounded flat, even to me. I felt numb, unable to reflect the drama and the horror of Joanne's flight. Mom looked at me as if I might order the words in a different fashion, add some inflection that would set them right so they made sense. I felt bad for her; she didn't know the story would get worse before I finished.

"Dear Lord. How in heaven's name did she do that?" she said, after the picture of what I'd said finally formed in her head.

"She never slowed down when she hit the curve."

"She didn't slow down?"

"Maybe the accelerator stuck or something. We don't know."

I looked at Jo. The eye that wasn't bandaged was closed. Her long lashes looked too fragile for the burden of her heavy mascara. Her skin was pale and smooth, no rouge left, but I could make out blue eye shadow.

Mom stayed quiet, shook her head.

"There's a baby, Mom."

"What do you mean?" Her question was soft as she looked up at me from the chair. "You?" She stopped, looked hopeful.

"Not me. That hasn't changed."

Jo's leg behind me still, reminded me of her presence. She was there, but not. For the first time, it occurred to me how empty days would be without her.

"Joanne's pregnant," I said, dreading the words to follow. "She's . . . she'd agreed to have a baby for us . . . with us."

"For you and Cal?"

I nodded. "Cal's the father."

"Cal?"

"I asked Joanne to have a baby for us. Cal and I asked her."

Mom went silent, looked at Joanne and then at the wall. Anywhere but at me. Still facing away from me she asked, finally.

"How could you afford it?"

"What?" I was buying time. We were heading toward words I didn't want to say, not to my mother.

"The doctors. What they have to do. Isn't it expensive?"

I didn't know how to tell her what we'd done. What Joanne and Cal had done, and how I'd asked them to do it.

"We didn't go to doctors, Mom."

"What do you mean?" She turned to look at me.

"We tried. Joanne tried. You know, on her own, to take Cal's . . . She tried to do it herself . . ."

Mom looked confused, then she looked away from me again. I could tell she was listening, waiting. I wasn't sure what she waited to hear, how much she wanted to know.

"And that's how?" she asked, finally.

"No. It didn't work. Joanne said she felt stupid. She wasn't sure she was doing it right. We . . . she tried like that for several months. Cal, well, he felt silly too. I don't know. After all that, it just seemed easier, better . . . Mom, I can't talk about this anymore. I told them to. I *asked* them to."

"They were . . . together? Like that?"

"Yes. It was my idea, Mom."

The air around us felt so still. I could hear the random noises outside our curtain walls; family members in mumbled conversations, beeps of machines, nurses' quiet shoes against the hard, slick floor.

"Why was she out driving?" Mom asked. "Why, at that time of the morning?" She was done talking about the other.

"I don't know what happened, why she was in the car in the middle of the night. She came to tell me something yesterday. But never got it out. She left when Cal got home."

"And the baby? How far along was she?"

"Nearly five months."

My voice broke, gave out, and Mom got up and came to me, put her arms around me and held me like she used to when my problems involved skinned knees.

"It must be hard, unbearable, really." She held me and I felt the words vibrating through her chest when she spoke. "You have to say good-bye to both a friend and a child, all at once. I'll stay here with you. Whatever you need."

I pulled away from her.

"Mom? The baby's still okay, they think."

She shook her head, as if to ask me why that would matter.

"Jo's body isn't gone. Only her brain was damaged."

"What do you mean?" She stepped back from me. Resolve faded in her eyes, made room for fear.

"Her body can still support a baby," I told her. "As long as they keep her breathing, give her food. It's what the doctors said."

"Oh God, Darla, no! You can't want that."

When she looked at me, I wished she hadn't. I'd finally gone too far, expected her to accept too much. Before I could talk, plead my case, and try to calm the panic in her voice, I heard Mr. Timbro, his steady growl outside the thin curtain that separated us. He addressed the doctor like a freshman who'd just made the team.

"There has to be some option," his cigarette-scratched voice pressed for some positive plan. "She's alive. That's what we've got to focus on."

"Mr. Timbro," the doctor started, "I've explained . . ."

"Who's the doctor in charge, because—"

"Larry," Mrs. Timbro interceded, "just let the doctor tell us . . ."

But as they drew back the curtain, the voices stopped. I saw Joanne all over again, felt myself staring through their eyes at the form on the bed, barely alive; someone so unlike my friend, their daughter.

"Oh Darla!" Mrs. Timbro cried out at me. I stood still, but she came, grabbed tightly on to my arms with her hands like she might shake me, but instead fell into sobs, free and full of tears. I was crying too, held on to her because he, her husband, wouldn't. Couldn't, I suppose.

He stood apart, just beside the bed, and for the first time in my life of watching him, fearing him, I saw him give in to something lost. His face, his body, all bold roundness and sturdy size, slumped, helpless in the only defeat I'd ever seen him accept.

TWO

— ❖ —

IT WAS ONLY APRIL AND already hot. Wind, straight out of Mexico, blew through the open classroom windows. I fought the urge to doze in English. Junior year covered British Lit, drawing rooms full of measured conversation and irony. Joanne had math just before lunch. I doubted she was faring any better. Both classes sat on the east side of the building, the windows large and in line with the morning sun.

After class, Joanne met me in the lunchroom, put her tray down across the table from mine.

"I can't take three more hours of this," she said, picking bits of pepperoni off of school-issue pizza. "Let's just leave, ride to the lake. We can sit on Jimmy Cagle's pier. Nobody's over there during the week. Might as well get a tan if we're gonna be hotter than hell anyway."

"Your daddy's gonna notice if my car's not in the parking lot," I told her.

Ever since we skipped the day before Christmas break, he'd started looking in the afternoon. He always marched some kind of team out to the field last period of the day, football players in the fall, baseball in the spring. Mrs. Gray, my eighth period Home Ec teacher, had liberal views on bathroom passes, giving me a chance to slip out to my car for a cigarette break. When the team filed by, I would duck low, watch him scan the lot for a blue El Camino. Smoke from my Virginia Slim trailed toward the open window of the car like some tribal signal.

"Daddy's not here," she said. She took a bite of pizza, then made a face and put it down. "He's on jury duty, got picked yesterday, so he's stuck there all week, probably."

"Okay. Do you know how to get to the Cagles' lake house? I've only been there by boat. Don't have a clue where to drive."

"Yup." She grinned at me. "I know how to get there."

She had pizza sauce on her hand and on her cheek. She looked like a kid with fingerpaint. I reached up with a thin napkin and wiped the side of her face.

She wanted me to ask how she knew, but I held out. I was reasonably sure she hadn't gone to the lake with him. Jimmy Cagle had been with a lot of girls, none of them any happier after being dumped. He'd asked me out once and I said yes, but Joanne convinced me to call him back and cancel.

"I don't want to listen to you moaning a month from now about what an asshole he is," Jo told me then.

After that, we made a promise to stay off of his list of priors.

Joanne sat across the table, just looking at me.

"All right, I'll ask, you little shit. How do you know the way to Jimmy Cagle's lake house?"

She laughed. She loved it when she won.

"My dad gave him a ride home when practice ran late one Friday. His folks were already at the lake for the weekend, so we took him out there."

"Did he hit on you?"

"With my dad in the car? Shit, no."

I wasn't sure I believed her. She looked too pleased with herself and she'd waited a long time to tell me about it. A car ride with Jimmy Cagle wasn't trivial, but I let it go.

"I've got to go to my locker before we leave," I told her. "Just meet me in the parking lot."

WE HAD TO RIDE with the windows down. My car, a used El Camino with a truck-bed in the back, didn't have working air when my folks bought it for me. Daddy thought it could be fixed, but he was wrong. Fixing it would have cost as much as he paid for the car. I didn't care. I liked to hang my elbow out the window when I drove. It felt like I was going fast, even when I wasn't.

Before we turned off the highway toward the lake, I kept the speedometer close to 70. Jo had her head back on the seat and her eyes closed, warm wind rushing over her. The air felt like summer, but it smelled like spring. The confusion in my senses gave me a strange sense of anticipation, offering endless possibilities. I wanted to tell Jo, ask her if she felt something too, but the air around us was too loud for talk.

She got us lost looking for the Cagles' place. We wound in and around the roads that ran parallel to the lake on the west side. That's all she really remembered. What the house looked like and that it sat on the west side near Darrell's Marina. When we finally found it, the first thing we recognized was Jimmy's red pickup in the driveway.

"Looks like I'm not the only one skipping while Daddy's on jury duty," Jo said. "Except Coach Garmon'll probably tell on him and he'll catch hell. Somebody other than me this time, at least."

The way she said it, her voice hard and faraway, I knew she was thinking of the times she'd told me about, the times her daddy took a belt to her. He hadn't done it in a while. We both figured she'd outgrown it, hoped she'd outgrown it—but you couldn't be sure. It didn't stop her from trying to piss him off.

I reached the dead end of the road and started to turn the car around.

"Wait a minute," she said. "Let's park here. We can walk up and see who he's got with him."

"Why do you think he's got somebody with him?"

"What else is he going to be doing out here? I bet I'm right, don't you?"

I pictured Jimmy Cagle, in his cabin with some freshman. By this time of year, he'd gone through most of the sophomore and junior girls and all the seniors who'd go out with a younger guy. The high school wasn't that big. You always knew someone had slept with him if they went out for more than two weeks.

"You want to spy on his cabin?" I could almost feel the blood in my veins, running steady through my arms, through my neck.

"Okay," I said, registering the familiar adrenaline sparked when Joanne dragged me into her schemes.

When Joanne had a thought she followed it, taking me along for the ride. She picked up the slack where my nerve left off.

I pulled the car off to the side of the road, but as it slowed to a stop, the moment became oddly accelerated. We walked along the lakefront. Wet leaves and fish gave the bank a familiar smell, ripe with memory.

In the summer, gas from the boats mixed with the lake smell. Then in the evening, charcoal grills joined in. I'd been on the lake, fishing with my dad in his boat, every summer when I was little; could tell you the time of day by the smells.

"There he is," Jo said. "In the window on the back corner of the house."

The blinds were open and Jimmy stood by the window. No shirt. Laughing at something. He had a great smile, too sincere to be the jerk we knew him to be. It made me wonder if there wasn't a nice person inside him somewhere. That was what made girls go out with him, the idea that they alone could save Jimmy Cagle from himself.

"Let's go around to the other side." Jo started toward the house.

"He's got the windows open," I said. "He'll see us."

"No. There are bushes on the other side near the house. Besides, I don't think he'll be looking out the window." She glanced back at me, raised her eyebrows.

The radio was on inside the house. Around the corner, the other window to his room was closed. Through the hedges that grew tall by the house, we could see into the room. Jimmy had Melissa Duncan on the bed. His shirt lay across a chair, but she still looked pretty much intact. Her shirt was unbuttoned down to her bra, but her shorts were still zipped and buttoned.

Jimmy stood looking down at her. He looked at her like she was the first girl he'd ever seen. He said something we couldn't hear. Whatever it was, it must have been special because she slid over and made room for him beside her on the bed. Melissa was another junior. I would have pegged her too smart for skipping and fooling around with Jimmy. She belonged to the Beta Club, entered French Club competitions.

"Melissa Duncan," Jo whispered. "How far you think he'll get?"

I shrugged. It didn't feel like a game we ought to be playing. I didn't even like watching, but I couldn't look away either.

Jimmy's hand moved on her, over her blouse and then inside. He didn't kiss her when he did this. He just looked at her, looked at her eyes.

Jo leaned closer to me trying to get a better view. She steadied herself with her hand on my waist. I could feel her breath on my ear.

"Damn," she muttered. "Can you believe this?" Melissa arched her head back. Her eyes were closed, but Jimmy's stayed open, on her.

Watching Jimmy with Melissa, Jo so close behind me, I began to feel overwhelmed by things I couldn't name. I wanted to stay and I wanted to go. I felt my heartbeat in my neck, in my ears. It was so loud I worried that Jo might hear it. I didn't want to look crazy, didn't want her to see me, standing there, losing my mind.

"We gotta go," I whispered, still not moving.

"Why?" she asked. Her words fell warm on my neck. The air around us stayed absolutely still.

Jimmy Cagle pulled back a corner of Melissa's shirt. Her breast, new and willing, slid from behind her bra, into open view. Jo, leaning over my shoulder, watched. Her lips parted. Jimmy lowered his mouth to Melissa's breast. I felt like I was falling, reached back and found Jo's arm to steady myself. Jo braced herself to support me. Something inside me was losing ground, scrambling for a foothold. Images flooded through me: vulnerable skin underneath blouses and bra, arms damp with humidity and breath warmer than the air.

"Jo," I said, my voice hoarse and low, "I've got to get out of here."

I turned and started walking. I took a deep breath, hoping to settle myself. She didn't follow for a second or two, then turned, finally, and came behind me.

WE DROVE BACK in the direction of town, stopped at the bait and tackle store near the highway to get a soda and kill time until school let out. She didn't ask what got into me at Jimmy's cabin, didn't ask why I wanted to leave.

"You think they did it?" She was drinking an RC Cola. She held it at the neck of the bottle, her hand almost a fist around the glass.

"They weren't slowing down," I said. My voice felt flat in my throat.

I wanted to lose the image of Jimmy and Melissa in my head. I felt like the four of us had done something, not just those two. Watching was somehow as wrong as doing.

"You got any change?" I asked Jo.

"Yeah," she said. "What you want?"

I wanted candy. Penny candy sat in jars on the counter, Mary Janes, peppermints, and caramels with white cream in the middle.

"Just a quarter," I told her. "I want a bag of candy."

She gave the waitress a dollar and we filled a brown sack with all the different kinds. On the drive back, wrappers littered my car, flew around in the rush of air from the open windows. I felt better. The fast air, the sugar in my teeth, and Jo laughing at some comment she'd overheard at lunch—things that put us back in our normal world.

When I got to our neighborhood, I drove around to her street to let her out in front. The sight hit both of us at the same time. Her dad—arms crossed, his face a mask of anger—stood waiting. He leaned against his truck, watched my car slow down at the curb.

"Shit," she said, and I slowed the car to a stop. "He knows."

He didn't move. Didn't speak.

"I'll get out with you," I told her. "I'll tell him you went with me to the doctor or something."

She watched him, squaring off with her eyes locked to his, and shook her head to tell me no. She got out of the car, pulled her book bag from the floorboard, and motioned with her hand for me to go on.

"Jo. Let me—"

She motioned again for me to go, closed the car door with a solid thump.

I turned the car and drove slowly. In my rearview, I watched the two of them, a foot apart from each other, with him in front, walking in measured paces up the driveway toward their house.

THREE

—— ◈ ——

ALLIANCE, TEXAS—JULY 1983

MOM AND I LEFT the Timbros in with Joanne. Her doctor, a short man with dark curls close to his head, asked us to stay in the family waiting area while he talked to them. He said he'd want to see me, and Cal too, if Cal got back.

"I think he must color his hair." My mother was talking about the doctor as we entered the small room down the hall. "A man his age doesn't keep dark hair like that without help."

"He's not old," I said.

"Not old, no. Heavens, he's younger than I am. I just mean a man in his late forties."

She didn't care about his age or his hair. She just wanted to make normal conversation—something to ease the dread of the conversation ahead of us. We had to talk about Joanne, about the baby.

Slick vinyl armchairs lined the walls around the waiting room. In the corner, a coffeemaker and a stack of Styrofoam cups sat on a pressed wood end table, ready for any takers. The coffee smelled strong, heavy with residue from days of serving anxious families. A television, mounted catercornered on the wall, showed the news, but there was no sound. Just pictures, flashing images of countries I would never care to visit.

Mom sat beside me, reached up and brushed hair from my face, tucked it behind my ear.

"Darla," she said. "What are you wanting to happen with this baby?"

She seemed like Mom again, centered, offering words we count on from our mothers. Joanne never had that, not really. She became stronger than her mother by the time she was twelve. After that, she was navigating life with her father all by herself.

"The only thing I've wanted all along is to raise a baby with Cal. It got messy. Messier than I'd realized, until yesterday."

Yesterday. Joanne at our house, trying to tell me about a problem that she needed to sort through. She tried to say it, but couldn't get it out. I called her after she left, but didn't get any answer.

"You couldn't have known this would happen," Mom said. How did she know? How did she know that part of me felt so responsible?

Watching Jo lie so still—tubes in her arm, in her mouth—I tried to imagine what she might have said if I'd convinced her to talk. Maybe she would have said that she couldn't reconcile new feelings for Cal with our friendship, with how this whole thing got started and where it had gone. I should have made her tell me when she was in my house. I had her there, had a chance, and I let her leave. It had been less than twenty-four hours since then. That couldn't be right.

"Why did Joanne . . ." Mom struggled to name it, then couldn't. "What was going on before this happened?"

"I don't know. I think she'd started to have feelings for Cal. She came to the house, tried to tell me something and couldn't."

Saying it out loud, the part about Cal, I felt my head floating, separate from my shoulders. The off-kilter sensation gave way to nausea. I leaned back against the wall, took in as much air as I could. The room, down the hall from the ICU and removed from any patients, still had the tainted smell of sickness. When my head felt normal again, I looked at Mom. She was still watching me, waiting for more.

"I really don't know what was going on in her head." I made myself go on. "She had strong feelings, about me, Cal, the baby. I don't know. So much of our lives . . . we've been together so long."

My voice was going, fading into nothing. I saw myself fading. Part of me had gone with Joanne.

"I know how close you were," Mom said, her eyes wet. "You shouldn't try to guess what she was thinking. She's always been one to speak her mind. If she didn't tell you, maybe she didn't know what to say. Maybe she didn't know how she felt."

"Mom? What if I started something that ended up killing her?"

I felt tears coming again. I wondered how long I would cry every time I talked about her.

"You weren't driving that car, Darla."

"I know, but she was out that night for a reason. It had something to do with me. She was on her way to my house."

Mom leaned into me. Stains from my tears left blotches on her blouse. She didn't tell me I was wrong. In an odd way, I was grateful for that. With so little left of my regular world, I needed to own the guilt. It kept me from fading closer to nothing.

"You can't torture yourself with questions forever," Mom said, finally getting to her point. "You and Cal have to build your life back. Try to move on from this."

The thought that she could be right moved through me like a memory, something familiar but just out of reach. But it passed, and the idea of the baby, Jo's baby, Cal's baby, my baby—that's what stayed strong. The baby was the only thing worth all the misery.

"I know I don't deserve that baby," I said. "But no one can love it more than I will."

Mom moved away from me, settled back against the chair. She closed her eyes and rested her head on the pale blue wall behind her. The pastels of her shirt, the wall, the beige-pink chairs, blended in a sherbet mix as I cried, not touching my mother.

I don't know how long we sat there. Time seemed like an irrational measure of the day. After a while, Cal came in. He'd gotten a ride home and had come back in his truck. He started toward me, but stopped in the middle of the room, as if he didn't know what was natural and what was odd. Even from a distance, he smelled like cigarettes. I'd gotten to him, I suppose, with my regression to Salem Lights. He'd quit before we were married, shamed me into giving it up myself. Now we were both miserable backsliders, dragging each other to lower ground.

"Hey, Liddy," he said to Mom.

She moved first, got up to hug him.

"Do you know about everything?" he asked her, pulling back.

Mom nodded and he looked away. Ashamed. He was ashamed. Not like me. I was sorry, but not ashamed.

"I'll admit I don't understand. I don't understand this at all. But that's not what we have to think about just now. Cal, what do you want?" Mom put her hand on his arm. "Have you thought about it? What you want to do about the baby?"

"I don't think it's up to us." He looked at me. It was a face I didn't know. "The doctor is talking out there with the Timbros. I think they want to take away life support."

Take away life support? They hadn't been there for Joanne in months, hadn't been decent parents for longer than that. Take away her life, the life inside her? I was her family, not them.

But I knew they could do it. I'd never thought of that part. They were her next of kin.

Oh Jo! Sit up and talk. Tell them how full of shit your parents are. Tell them I'm your family.

I got up, must have been talking, saying some of what I was thinking, because Cal answered with, "Stop, Darla." I didn't know what I should stop doing, but I had to get to them, to get to the hall. I had to get to Joanne before they took her away, took my baby away with her.

"Darla," I heard Mom say. She said it again, louder, and my name filled the pale blue waiting room. "You can't . . ."

The three of them—the Timbros and that doctor—stood just outside the ICU. They couldn't talk about their plans inside, in her presence.

"I understand," the doctor was saying. "It's complicated, I know, but she's not aware, not anymore."

"Stop talking them into something," I said. They looked startled, all three of them, as if I'd come at them spouting obscenities. "The baby's aware. The baby's healthy. You can't do this. Joanne planned to have the baby for us. You can't take it away."

"Darla." Mr. Timbro spoke my name sharply, as a reprimand.

"I'll take the blame for all of this." I cleared my throat, willed my voice to go more slowly, fall to a lower pitch. "It's my fault. All of it. But don't take it out on the baby."

"Honey." I heard Cal's voice. He was beside me, his arm around my waist, and I felt stronger.

Cal was the father. Cal could do something.

"You've got no say in this, Darla," Mr. Timbro told me. "You're the one who messed up her life. The doctor just filled us in on all this foolishness you cooked up. You've got no say in what happens now."

"She was having a baby for *us*. It's what she wanted."

He stepped toward me. I wanted to move back, but I didn't. I stood still as he leaned toward me.

"Did you think for one second about what it would do to her life, this scheme of yours?"

"I didn't turn her out of my house." I was talking too loud, words flying through tears. My throat felt like it was closing, like he was choking me. "One fuckup too many and she's not good enough to be your daughter anymore. Isn't that right? What do you think that did to her?"

I remembered Joanne pulling into my driveway, the day she got fired from the lumberyard for smoking a joint with Andy Roman on her lunch break; the day her daddy threw her out of the house.

"She didn't have a home anymore." I kept going, even though I was shaking, trembling. "No place to go for Christmas. No special dinner on her birthday."

He looked at me, his mouth set hard. His eyes frightened me.

"She came to me. I was her family." It took everything I had to speak.

"Is this how you think family gets treated?" He pointed toward the doors to the Intensive Care Unit.

He had me. Blood burned raw in my cheeks. All the anger, the energy I'd felt defying him shriveled to nothing. How had she done it all those years? How had Joanne kept his awful soul at bay? Mrs. Timbro stood mute beside him. Her eyes looked as sad as I felt.

"Darla," Cal was saying. "Let's go."

I felt lost, pressed by a crowd moving in the wrong direction.

"They have to listen to us, to our side," I said to Cal. "You're the father."

"Darla," Cal said again.

The air around me seemed scarce. I pulled in hard to get a full breath.

"Cal agrees with us," Mr. Timbro said.

Suddenly there was no air. I'd forgotten how to breathe, to live, it seemed.

"He thinks it's best to let her go quietly."

At least there was no pleasure on his face when he said it, no gloating. His hardness had faded. He was hurting. I had to give him that much.

"Cal thinks it's best," he said again. "Best for everybody."

In Cal's expression, there had to be something, something that called what Joanne's father said a lie. But he wasn't looking at Mr. Timbro, not in anger, not in denial. He was looking at me.

"Cal has agreed to respect the wishes of the parents," the doctor said, making pretty words out of Mr. Timbro's announcement.

"Cal?" I pulled away from him.

"She's their daughter, Darla."

In the dead ugly light of the hospital hall, I hated Cal, something I never imagined I could feel.

"Darla," he was saying, reaching again for me. "We've got to salvage our lives, somehow."

"And just pretend like we're normal? This isn't normal."

"It hasn't been from the start." Cal backed up a step.

"I know that," I snapped, "but the one innocent person in all of this is the baby. Your baby, *their grandchild.*" I looked at Mr. Timbro. Pain still softened his face, but he didn't have tears. What I said wasn't enough.

"We've made our decision," he said, closed his eyes to shut me out. His chest hiked up as he took a breath. The long exhale that followed was the only sound in the hall.

Then *she* spoke up.

"It's not my decision, Larry." Mrs. Timbro's voice came out so small, it might have been a child's.

He turned toward her, but didn't speak.

"Seeing her in there, Larry." Tears came down her face. "She's alive. There's something alive in her. Our flesh and blood, Larry."

It was probably the hardest thing she'd ever done. Years of silence broken in those tight little words that she barely got out of her mouth. Then she stopped talking. She'd run out of courage, or words, or both. It occurred to me that Joanne had stood up to him for both of them.

Mr. Timbro stared at his wife. He creased his forehead, looked puzzled but not concerned, or even annoyed. I wondered how long she would hold out. I was clinging to the hope of that baby by my finger-nails. Mrs. Timbro was my only chance. Seeing how he looked at her, how she lowered her eyes from him, I didn't figure my odds were all that good.

"We need to go, Arlene," he said, ignoring all that she had said before.

"Larry? I think—"

"We'll talk when we get out of here," he interrupted her. "We can't sort things out standing here. We'll be in touch, Dr. Wyman."

He acknowledged the doctor; left me, my mother and Cal without so much as eye contact. But Mrs. Timbro looked back. She looked at me and gave a slight nod before she turned and followed him down the hall.

FOUR

I FELT RELIEVED when the Timbros left the hospital. In the silence that followed their departure, the hall appeared to expand, as I, in turn, grew small. Walking away from the ICU with Mom and Cal, I didn't realize that the daylight was gone until we passed a window and I saw the black square of night framed inside it. It struck me as odd that time existed whether I was aware of it or not, moved on in a normal fashion.

"Are you okay?" Mom asked.

"I don't know. I don't know what okay is."

Cal looked awful. He gave us a numb regard that didn't show one way or the other what he might be thinking. If he was sorry for siding with Larry Timbro, I didn't see it.

"Cal?" Just saying his name, I felt my anger rise again.

"This is the worst thing I've ever gone through," he said. He spoke in a monotone, like the operator's voice when you leave the phone off the hook.

"Have you eaten anything all day, Cal?" Mom asked.

"I don't know," he said. "I don't think so. I stayed at the house while they moved Jo's car. They put a big tarp over the hole, but . . . well, the house is hot. The window unit keeps the den okay, but . . . I don't know."

He rambled. Mumbled to himself more than to us, all of it nonsense as far as I was concerned. I didn't give a damn about the house.

"Do you want to go home?" he asked me.

Part of me did. Part of me wanted to sit in my yellow kitchen with a cup of coffee and pretend that nothing had happened. No yawning hole in the wall. Jo apt to call any minute to tell me about something dumb on television. I'd have paid good money to slip into that fantasy for an hour. Give my head that much of a break.

"I don't think I can go home right now."

"You've gotta get some sleep, Darla," he said. "We both need sleep. We can pull out the couch in the den and it'll be comfortable. I closed off our room so you won't have to look at it at all."

"He's right, honey," Mom said.

She moved beside me. I was taller by an inch or two. She put her arm around my waist and I felt huge and awkward by comparison; wrong in every way I could name.

"I want to go to Jo's house." That much was clear to me all at once. "Rigsby's probably messed all over the place. He's been there all day by himself."

At the thought of Jo's dog, I felt something inside me break in half, some part of my soul that kept the sadness contained. The devastation passed beyond tears and deep into the place where there were sounds not quite my own. I heard them, those sounds, carried through my voice, as if I'd chosen them. I felt myself doubled over, sliding down. All of this seemed beyond my will, beyond my control. My shirt rode up as my back slid against the wall. The coolness pressed against my spine.

A group of people walked by, kept their eyes to themselves, their gait steady. In a hospital hall you aren't crazy if you moan and shrivel to the floor. Like ordinary streets caught in the middle of a war, hospitals play host to pain. Nobody judges you poorly for giving in.

The people receded down the hall and I felt overcome by a sudden gratitude for their indifference. My focus became indiscriminate. Small occurrences grew large as I shriveled to nothing.

"Darla?" It was Mom's voice. She and Cal bent over me. Mom had her hand on my arm.

"Honey. Come on."

One on either side, they lifted me, letting their weight take mine.

"I want to take you home," Cal said. He sounded more like himself, but I didn't trust it.

"I want to go to Joanne's." The words came out of me, wet and low in my chest. "Take me to Joanne's."

Mom nodded to Cal and they walked with me, each holding one of my arms. As we stepped into the elevator, I regretted leaving Joanne behind. I was abandoning her, it seemed, for nothing more than sleep. I thought of her, bandaged and still, and I wanted to go back, to sit in the chair near her bed and doze to the sound of the machine taking breath in and out of her body. But I left her, made a silent promise to protect her, to protect the baby, as long as I could.

WE LEFT MY CAR at the hospital. Visiting hours had ended and the lot was nearly empty. My station wagon seemed small and strange sitting under a streetlight. Cal drove me in his truck and Mom followed in her car. We didn't talk the entire ride.

Joanne's house was half of a rented duplex. All the lights were on next door where two kids ran in front of the window, playing some sort of game. I saw the mom, more girl than woman, really, come scoop up the smallest shadow as it fell. Her name was Evie. I'd met her a few times. She lived there with her husband and kids. Joanne liked her, said her husband was a nice guy too. I figured they probably hadn't heard about Joanne, but I didn't have the energy to knock on the door and tell them.

The only light on at Jo's place came from her bedroom. It was a small light, maybe from her closet. I could see it through the curtains.

"Let's just get the dog," Cal told me. "We'll take him back to our place."

I didn't answer him, didn't tell him that I couldn't go back with him. Couldn't or wouldn't, I didn't know which. It didn't matter anyway. I fumbled in the shadows to get my key in Joanne's front door.

It was quiet inside. *Just how she left it.* I had the urge to hold my breath, to change nothing, not even the air in the room. But I knew the dog should have been greeting us. Maybe he knew somehow, was crouching in a corner alone and scared.

"Rigsby?" I called out. "Here boy."

Nothing.

"Was he with her?" Mom asked. "Did they say anything about a dog?"

"I never saw a dog," Cal said, turning on lights. He walked toward Jo's bedroom for a look.

"Rigsby!" I opened up the back door and called out. Maybe she'd left him outside by accident. That would have been rough on him in the heat of the day. He wasn't a puppy anymore.

"Excuse me," a voice called from next door. Evie stood on her back stoop, the light from her kitchen framed her in the doorway. "Are you lookin' for the dog?"

"Yeah," I said. "Have you seen him?"

"He's over here," she said. "Joanne left me a note on my door this morning. Must have been early, because I found it when I went out to get the paper. She asked if I would get Rigsby and keep him here for her. She said she might be gone a while and she'd call and let me know."

She walked into her yard and came over to the fence. I met her halfway on Jo's side.

"She left you a note this morning?"

"Yeah. You know where she went?"

I didn't want to say it, didn't want to tell her that Joanne never got there, wherever she was headed. But she waited for an answer and I had no choice.

"She's in the hospital," I said.

"Oh my God!" she said.

I saw Rigsby at her screened door. His paws scraped at the metal on the lower section, wanting to get out.

"Hold on a second," she said to me. "Let me get him outside."

When she came back, the dog followed her, jumped and barked by way of greeting as Evie tried to get the details of Joanne's accident.

"She's not conscious?" she asked for the second or third time.

A stream of light came from Jo's kitchen as Cal opened the back door.

"Did you find him?" he asked me, squinting to see who was with me.

"Yeah," I answered. "Evie had him. Jo left her a note to look after him for a while."

"A while?"

"I don't know for how long," she told Cal, sounding defensive. "Do you want me to keep him for her until she gets better?"

"No," I said, a little too quickly. "I'll look after him."

"Okay." She seemed disappointed, but opened the gate between the two yards and let him come to me.

He came immediately, sniffed my hand as I reached to pet him, then smelled my clothes.

"Hey, fella," I said. His fur felt soft as I touched him. He had mats near his body because he hated to be brushed and Joanne never forced him to sit still for it.

I wondered if he recognized Jo's smell, underneath all the hospital odors. He adored Joanne. Tan and black with half a tail, the shaggy mutt had attached himself to her that summer at the lumberyard, the summer she'd lost her job and broken ties with her family. He'd been a stray.

"Let me know if there's anything I can do," Evie was saying. "If she gets to feeling better and needs clothes or somethin' . . ."

For a second, I let myself think that might happen. Joanne could wake up, start asking for her stuff, and I'd have to call Evie and say, "Could you throw a few things together . . ."

"Thanks, Evie," I said.

I walked into the house with Rigsby, let him sniff through the rooms to see what had gone on while he was next door.

Mom came out and stood by me in the kitchen.

"Why was he over there?" she asked.

"Jo left her a note," I said. "Asked her to keep him for a while."

The same questions in my head were on her face, but she looked too tired to ask them.

"I don't know why," I answered before she said anything more.

She took in a deep breath. The kitchen door was closed, but I could hear Cal moving around in the den.

"I don't want to be around him right now," I said. "I can't believe he took *their* side."

"That's not right, Darla. You can't punish him for how he feels."

"I can't change how I feel either."

She shook her head, turned to go into the den, and I followed her.

"So what do we do now?" Cal asked. He'd settled on the couch. He looked like hell.

"I want to stay here tonight."

Cal looked up at me, shook his head but didn't argue. It was Mom who spoke up.

"Honey, the last thing you need is to be alone in this place tonight."

"I do need to be here," I said. It wasn't an argument. It was a fact. "I'll be all right. I promise."

"Cal can stay with you here," she told me, "or you both can come back home with me if it's just your house you can't face."

"I really want to be alone. I appreciate everything, Mom, but I've got to have some time to myself. Cal, you go to Mom's. You shouldn't go back to our place tonight either. Mom can feed you something. That's the best thing both of you can do for me. Just look out for each other and give me a little time alone."

They didn't try to argue. No one had much fight left after the long day. I sat in a chair opposite the two of them on the couch.

"What do you think will happen with the Timbros?" I asked neither one in particular. "Can they really take away life support while there's a baby alive?"

"I don't know," Mom said. "I think they can, but I imagine they both have to sign legal papers for it. I just don't know.

"Darla," she said. "This can't possibly work out. With the baby, I mean. I won't go into how I feel about it, what the three of you got yourselves into. But it can't be like you planned it. Not after all that's happened."

"That's all I was saying," Cal said. "Back there at the hospital. Everything's gone too far to turn out like we planned it, Darla."

"I'm trying to sort out what we have left."

"Even if it's not what's best for *us*?"

I didn't answer. I didn't know how to answer. Mom got up.

"You two need to talk," she said. "And I've got a phone call to make."

"Come on," Cal said, standing up. "I'll make some coffee."

WE SAT AT THE KITCHEN TABLE, both silent, steaming mugs in front of us. We acted like we didn't know each other very well. Cal gave in finally, broke the silence.

"I know you don't agree with me."

His words left me staring, wondering what he wanted me to say.

"This whole thing seems so wrong," he went on, his hands cupped around his coffee mug. "I don't know how I could have ever thought it was okay. I haven't said anything to my folks. I'm ashamed to tell them what we've done—and that was before the accident."

"Look at your parents, Cal. They can't judge anybody."

His mom and dad were divorced, barely speaking and still fighting over money. His dad, an insurance salesman, was living in Seattle with the woman he'd been seeing for years while he was married. Cal's mother stayed in Portland, where Cal grew up, telling anyone who'd listen what a piece of crap her ex-husband had turned out to be. Cal avoided them. Even on holidays, we made excuses not to go up there, had only been twice in the six years I'd known them. They'd each visited separately a couple of times since we married.

"I know I don't have much to go on when it comes to family," he said, "but we made a mess, Darla. You've gotta admit that much. Things have been weird ever since we started this."

"I didn't see it that way," I told him.

"Come on, Darla. I slept with your best friend. Hell, it was your idea." He dropped his voice so my mother wouldn't hear us.

"I can't go over this any more right now." I felt shaky and weak.

We fell quiet again. I heard Mom's voice in the other room, still talking on the phone. After a while—minutes, maybe more, I don't know—I felt as if I could breathe.

"Maybe . . ." I tried to order the words but they came out jumbled, ideas stumbling into the air. ". . . maybe if I'd talked to her more, asked her how she felt, maybe she could have told me what was happening. We could have worked it out and it wouldn't have gone so far, made her so conflicted."

"What are you talking about?" he asked.

"Joanne. I don't understand why she was coming to our place in the middle of the night."

He looked down, stared at his coffee, cream gathering at the surface as it cooled. Then he sat back, braced his hands against the edge of the table.

"She didn't fall in love with me. I know that's what you think she was going to say, but it's not."

He said it and stopped. I waited for more. There had to be more. But he stared down again, not speaking.

"She didn't what?"

"She didn't love me."

He looked at me as though this would explain something, make everything clear.

"What do you mean?"

"I was the one who changed," he said. I could see that with every word, he hoped it would be enough, that he wouldn't have to say any more.

"Cal, I don't know what you're trying to tell me."

"I started to have feelings, to get confused." His voice snagged when he said *feelings*.

"You?"

"Yeah."

"I don't understand. Did she know?"

"I told her, and I told her it was making me miserable. That I loved you, as much as ever. That I couldn't put all the feelings together."

He looked at me, again. His face, his expression, begging me to guess the rest of it, save him from the words. I shook my head.

"When was all this?" I didn't know what to ask, what to say. I tried to imagine what I should be feeling, hearing him say this, but I was numb to all the normal responses. "When did this happen?" It was all I could think to say.

"I don't know." He stood up, walked to the sink and then halfway back. "I can't do this, Darla. I can't talk about this anymore."

He left the kitchen, walked into the living room but still didn't sit down. A small lamp by the couch gave the only light, so I couldn't see his face.

I walked to the living room. His words settled in my brain, a confusing heap of sounds that gave me more questions than answers.

"Darla, I'm sorry," he said, his face turned away from me.

I still didn't know exactly what he'd told me, what he'd meant to say.

"Cal?"

"I'm too exhausted to do this tonight," he said. "Can we talk about this tomorrow? Please?"

I started to say more, to ask more, but I heard Mom saying her good-byes on the phone. She came out of the bedroom, stopped when she saw us standing there.

"Are you two okay?" she asked.

We stood silent as if we'd been caught at something unseemly.

"I'm fine," I said. "Cal, go with Mom. Please, just let me stay here."

He nodded, any resistance in him long spent.

"I don't feel right, leaving you," Mom said.

"I'll be okay. It's really what I need. Please."

She gave in, finally, said she'd make sure Cal ate something, would put sheets on the guest bed and look after him for the night. He followed as if he'd been drugged. They went in her car. He left me the truck.

RIGSBY SAT ON THE COUCH BESIDE ME, his head on my lap. At least for a time, I was numbed by some blessed power. Maybe God came even when you didn't ask, like all the old folks said; took pity when the pain became too great.

I tried to narrow my emotions down to one or two. Despair sort of summed it up, but even that wasn't right. Jealousy? It had to be in there somewhere, but Cal's feelings for Joanne folded neatly into my own, seemed of one piece, somehow. Or maybe not. Jo was almost dead, and that changed everything.

Rigsby made grunting noises, sweet sounds from inside his sleep. My muscles were restless, but I didn't want to move my legs and disturb the dog's comfort. He deserved time anchored safe against a human body, time before the confusion of Joanne's absence set in.

The table by her couch was a round cardboard table, the kind from Kmart. The last people to live in the duplex before Joanne had left it,

along with a charred-out Hibachi grill. We'd dressed the table up with
a cloth that matched her curtains, then fancied ourselves decorators
after we put it beside her secondhand couch.

As I sat with Rigsby, I looked at the stack of books she'd left on it,
a half a dozen library books sitting under the lamp. There were books
on nutrition and pregnancy, prenatal precautions, labor and childbirth,
a travel book on Santa Fe and one on New Mexico. I picked up a book
on nutrition. She'd dog-eared pages on vitamins and supplements like
calcium and iron.

Looking through the books, I forced thoughts of Cal out of my
mind, felt comforted by the evidence that Joanne was looking after the
baby, that she worried and cared, as if she'd planned to be a mother.

"What am I gonna do?" I said to the quiet air.

Rigsby picked up his ears, just barely opened his eyes.

The weight of the day settled on me, the questions running an endless reel in my head as I felt sleep coming on. Half-awake, my troubled
thoughts scraped raw against the images of bent metal, broken glass,
and blood; scraped until I saw myself crying, lost inside the sadness. As
I gave in to the fatigue, the images grew more furious, more exaggerated. The awful frenzy brought me around to the thought, "I need to
talk to Jo." Joanne, whose off-kilter sense had calmed my fears before.

Then I was fully awake. The flood of loss came at me, worse than
anything I'd dreamed or imagined. I remembered the pain of seeing
Daddy, dressed and painted in a casket, and I couldn't bring myself to
think of Joanne buried. My world without her eyes on it would change
who I was. It was a selfish thought, but all I could claim.

I thought of her last morning. She got up, probably showered, took
her pills, got dressed. Put on mascara and eye shadow and lived her
morning like someone who expected to have an afternoon. My
thoughts stayed on her morning, willed it to take a different turn. *God,
give me time back. Please, just one day to make it different, different
from . . .*

I hadn't talked to God in years, but this request, real as I'd ever
prayed, would have bought God a disciple to rival any story in the
Bible.

I waited, not breathing, earnestly hoping for some strange turn of the natural order to untangle my world; but the time on Jo's clock moved forward, not back. God hadn't given me a solid break in years.

The twisting hurt that was in me spread deep into muscle and bone and I thought it might be better if I died too. *But the baby is alive.* That small thought held me in the world.

I moved Rigsby to the side, went to look for something that would bring the numbness back. Jo had a cabinet full of answers in the bathroom. I picked one that said it would help me sleep and took two when it said take one. I thought of pouring a drink for good measure, but by the time I got to the kitchen, found the bottle and a glass, the pills had started to smooth the edges, so I went to the bedroom, crawled into Jo's unmade bed. The pillow smelled like hair spray, and the sheets, like Jo. I never knew she had a particular smell until I recognized it in her absence.

I drew the covers to me, pulled them in a heap to my face, and breathed Jo deeply into my lungs. I braced for pain, but instead felt an odd comfort. Grateful for that much, I gave in to the dull sleep the pills offered. The last thing I felt was Rigsby on top of the bedspread beside me, curling around himself and settling warm and tight against my leg.

FIVE

I HEARD JOANNE'S DADDY drive off in his truck. It had been less than an hour since I put her off at her driveway, her daddy standing there, his face full of hard judgment. I felt scared for her, wished I could have told him it was all my idea, leaving school early. My car. My idea.

He'd tell my parents, but that's all he could do to me. They'd take the car away for a while and tell me how I disappointed them with stunts like that. But their feelings wouldn't change. They wouldn't look at me with empty eyes the way he looked at her.

I dialed her house and her mom answered, said Joanne was home but couldn't come to the phone.

"Can I take a message?" she asked.

No message, I told her, but could I come by?

Joanne's mom was quiet when I asked this. I could almost see her looking out the window, trying to figure how long it would take him to go and get back from wherever he went.

"Maybe just for a minute," she told me. "You can only stay a few minutes."

"Thanks, Mrs. T.," I told her, and hung up the phone.

No fence separated the Timbros' yard from ours, but it was easy to tell when you crossed the line. The grass in their backyard stayed cropped, as neat as his football field at school. Flowers grew inside flower beds, circles of bricks with potting soil inside. Several of these beds decorated the yard, always full of whatever flowers were right for the season.

My daddy kept our front yard neat, but mowed the back when the spirit moved him. Mom had a long, haphazard flower bed off to one side full of green plants most of the time and daffodils in the early spring.

As I went the short distance from my house to hers, my bare feet felt the passage from our long, soft grass to her crew-cut yard. My naked toes looked small and exposed as I crossed to her side. Mrs. Timbro stood near the kitchen door and opened it before I walked up the three steps to the top of the stoop.

"She's in her room," she said, and nodded in that direction as if I might not know the way.

"Darla," Mrs. Timbro said before I got to Jo's door.

I turned to see what she wanted. She held out a plate with some kind of cobbler, apple, I think.

"See if you can get her to eat a little something."

Food was all she knew how to offer. I took the plate from her.

Joanne didn't answer when I knocked.

"It's me," I said.

"Come on in," she told me. Her voice sounded small.

"Hey," I said, and put the cobbler down on her desk.

She was on the bed, sitting cross-legged with a pillow on her lap. Her hair fell in dark strands all around her face. She looked up at me with eyes puffy and red, all the expression used up.

"You okay?"

She just shrugged.

I sat on the edge of the bed, looked around the room, anywhere but at her. I could give her that much.

Her room wasn't like the rest of the house. All the other rooms reminded me of my grandmother's house fixed up for company—old furniture, used but kept nice, with pillows in place and no dust anywhere.

Walking into Jo's room was like switching from black-and-white TV to color. Pale yellow shag carpet, a lime green bedspread, beads instead of a door to her closet. Her room had been the same since we were thirteen. She'd argued with her dad about it, begged for the carpet and stopped eating for a day or two in protest. He finally said okay, gave in to her out of sheer exhaustion, I think. It was the only time I remember that happening.

By the time everything was ordered and in place, she was already starting to outgrow it. But she'd never say that. Never give him the satisfaction of asking for something different.

"He took Pony away," she said, finally. Her voice registered flat and calm.

I tried to sort through the words.

"What do you mean? He took Pony? Where?"

Pony was her dog, the one she'd picked from a mix-and-match litter at her uncle's farm three years before. The puppy had been skinny, long legs out of proportion to his head, with thin ears that stood up like little teepees on his head. She thought he looked like a colt, named him Pony on the spot.

"To the dog pound," she answered, and her voice broke midsentence. "He said I was a hateful ingrate, nothing like he raised me to be. Said I didn't deserve a dog or anything that loved me 'cause I'd just turn it to trash, any love I got."

She cried. Hard sobs that were too big for the room around us. I felt closed in by the sound, didn't know what to do to make it right. I knew her mother could hear Jo's cries. I wished that she would come in, tell us we'd all go get the dog back together. She was a nice woman, Jo's mom, just too weak to be of any use.

"He took Pony away from you just because you skipped school?"

It seemed extreme, even for him.

Joanne tried to take a deep breath, inhaled with choppy hiccuping sounds.

"He's full of shit," she said, her voice hard again. "What he's think-ing is all full of shit."

"Like what?"

"He thinks I was off with Jimmy Cagle."

"Jimmy Cagle? Why? I brought you home."

I couldn't see where Jimmy Cagle fit into anything.

"He heard from Coach Garmon that Jimmy skipped. Somebody saw him driving off with a girl. My dad, the genius, decided the girl was me. Figured you were a cover, picked me up somewhere to make it look like a normal day."

"Did you tell him you weren't with Jimmy?"

"Oh yeah," she said, her words shrill. "That made everything all better."

"I mean, you could have told him about Melissa."

"Yeah right. Tell him we were at Jimmy's lake house, but it was Melissa who was actually screwing him. That would make sense. Just get her suspended from school or something, wouldn't do a damn thing for me," Jo said. "He wouldn't believe me anyway. He thinks I'm a liar to start with and he's already made up his mind that I slept with that asshole. Said he's heard those boys talking. *He knows what goes on.*"

She mimicked his voice, low and righteous. She was so dead-on, I could just hear him.

I saw my house through Jo's back window. The light was on in my room. Even on a bad day, my house played by the rules. I'd never have to watch while one of my parents carted off my cat as a punishment. The horror of his act crept through my skin, causing it to tighten and chill with fleshy bumps.

"Okay," I said, trying to shake the feeling. "Let's think about what happens now. Can you go get Pony back? I'll take you to the pound."

"They won't let me have him when I get there. I'm not eighteen and they know my dad."

"How about your mom?"

She looked at me, her eyes half-open like she'd just gotten up from sleeping. Then she just shook her head no, her mother wouldn't be any help. I knew that before I said it.

"What will happen to him, to Pony?" I asked her.

In the brightness of her room, Jo's face seemed exaggerated, eyes and lips raw from crying.

"He'll be scared," she said, almost in a whisper. "He's never been anywhere but here, so he'll be confused and really scared. Then, if nobody gets him, they'll put him to sleep."

Her dad couldn't be that hard. I couldn't imagine any anger that sure of itself. Jo lay down on her side, her legs tucked under her, arms still firm around the pillow. On her arm, where her sleeve rode up, I saw a bruise, spread across the entire back, up to her shoulder. Still fresh, the reds and blues mingled just under the skin. It disappeared behind her shirt so that I wasn't sure how far it went.

"Did he hit you?"

I almost wished he had, offered some concrete stain of anger, something clear and open to the world.

"No." She looked at her arm, regarded it with impassive eyes. "I was going after Pony. I tried to stop him, and when he shoved me away I slammed into the dresser."

"What'd he do then?"

"He went on past me, left me screaming, clawing at him like a maniac while he took my dog."

I kept thinking of her mother. How could her mother stand by and watch this happen, even just listen to it?

"Come here," I said.

I sat by her on the bed, scooted back with my legs out straight, put my back against the wall beside the window. She moved her head over to my lap, stared out at the room at nothing in particular. I wanted to straighten her hair, run a cool cloth over her face, do all the things my mother did to ease a fever or coax away my nausea. I did touch her hair, pulled tangled strands away from her eyes and off her forehead. She didn't seem to mind.

"We'll think of something," I said.

"Pony's at that place now," she said, mumbling, not even talking to me, really. "I know he's scared." She sounded scared.

"They're nice people at the shelter. They like animals or else they wouldn't work there. They'll take care of him. Nothing bad will happen to him today. We'll figure out something."

After that, she seemed to let go a little. I felt the added weight on my leg as her head relaxed. I even thought she might be dozing, so I stayed quiet. Her arm lay exposed, the colors of the bruise turning thick. I pulled an afghan over her shoulders. We stayed like that for a while. Out the window, the day started to change. Clouds covered the clear sky and made it seem later than it was.

When I heard the truck, I must have tensed, because she jerked her head, sat up.

"You oughtta go," she said. "He'll get pissed at anybody trying to make me feel better."

"Let me tell him about today. He might believe me."

"It won't do any good," she told me. "He's already mad at you too. Remember? You helped me try and pull it off. That's all he'll say."

She stood up, anxious, almost twitching.

"Just go," she said. "I'll get in more trouble if you stay."

I opened her window, crawled out over the edge, and stepped down onto the fence that went around the air-conditioning unit. It was an easy out, one we'd used since we were little. I heard the door slam on the other side of the house, imagined him walking in, sure of himself, conscience easy with what he'd done.

BACK HOME, my house smelled like pork roast. The hot comfort carried me to a better place in my mind, made me believe that it might work out all right for Joanne. Maybe her dad changed his mind; cooled off and brought Pony home.

"You need to wash up pretty soon," Mom said when I walked through the kitchen.

"Mom?" It was an afterthought, but as I started, it seemed necessary, almost urgent. "Jo and I skipped our afternoon classes today. Rode to the lake. It was so hot and miserable in the school."

She leaned back on the counter, looked irritated. Looked like a parent ought to look when a kid skips school. No more, no less.

"Darla, you're not in elementary school anymore. You can't just up and leave because you're hot or you want to go shopping. Your grades will suffer if you do this sort of thing. It's not the first time."

"I know, Mom. I won't do it again. I promise. It's just . . ." Just what? I couldn't think. Couldn't get my mind off Joanne.

"Listen," she said, her tone even. She let out a long breath. "We'll talk to your dad when he gets home, sort out what we're going to do. We can't just let it slide this time without consequences, but . . . I appreciate the fact that you told me." She stopped, her face softened. It was a face I never thought about, mostly, but counted on like air.

"I really do appreciate your honesty," she said again, and it was done until Dad got home.

She turned back to the counter, went back to stirring gravy.

SIX

◈

ALLIANCE, TEXAS—JULY 1983

THE MEMORY SEEMS LIKE A DREAM, *the dream is a memory. It's a Sunday in July when I am nine. The windows are open but there is no air in the church. Joanne is wearing a dress, has come with my family to the Sunday service. She asked to come. Her family is Methodist, but they never go except at Easter when Mrs. Timbro makes them. Not even at Christmas do they go. "He didn't choose to be born," she says, talking about Jesus, "but He chose to die. We need to show we are grateful for that." It's funny to me that she believes, but never goes.*

I am falling asleep but Joanne is fully alert, listening. "Your father in heaven loves you," the preacher says. "He will forgive you over and over if you just ask. But you have to ask, 'cause He won't go beggin' you to love him back. You got to make the effort. He'll take you in His arms every time."

As the heat folds around my brain, pushing my eyelids down, I look over at Joanne. She has tears on her face. My eyes go wide.

"What's wrong?" I whisper.

She shakes her head, looks away and drags the back of her hand across her cheeks to get the wetness off.

"Joanne!" I whisper shout. My mom looks over and makes a "shush" with her lips. She doesn't see Joanne or she'd be asking too. My mama knows as well as I do that Joanne never cries.

The sermon is over and the piano starts in on the invitational hymn. Over the easy lengths of the piano chords, the preacher talks, inviting all who feel the call, the solid pull, in their hearts, to walk forward and profess openly before God and His people. This is where I get nervous. I feel the call, have felt it for a while. Feel God's big hand pushing at my heart. Almost every Sunday I feel it now. But I don't step out. I can't imagine walking down to the altar in front of all those people. I'm afraid it's something I will never do. Maybe the push will become so strong, I tell myself, that I will not be able to stand still. I will move onto that stretch of carpet that is as long as a whole summer day.

While I am thinking about all this, I see Joanne move. I see her out of the corner of my eye even though I'm supposed to be praying. She steps away from me into the aisle and walks with big strides toward where the preacher stands. Without thinking, I step out to follow. It will never be easier than it is with Joanne walking ahead of me. I keep moving, my eyes on her, not the people around me. Her chin is high. She looks up at the preacher, nods when he whispers something to her.

He whispers the same to me when I get to him.

"In the name of our Lord Jesus Christ, God receives you today as His own."

Afterward, I feel strange, standing in line beside Joanne to shake hands with all the church people who have lined up to congratulate me on my decision. They hesitate more with Joanne, but welcome her all the same.

After church, the preacher talks to us. He asks, how did we come to make this decision? "Because I believe what you said," she tells him.

"Me too," I say because I can't very well tell him it was because I just followed Joanne.

He says Baptism Sunday will be in two weeks, can we both be there? Joanne nods, so I do too.

She eats lunch with us at the Town's End restaurant after church.

While I chew soft green beans and fried chicken, I listen as my parents go on and on about how proud they are that we followed our hearts.

"It's not an easy thing to do, profess your faith," my mother says. "I remember."

Joanne barely eats at all. She just stares out the big window beside her, watching cars go by on the road that leads out of town. When we drop her off at home, she gets out of the car, then leans back in to thank my daddy for food that was still sitting on the table when we all got up to leave.

RIGSBY WOKE BEFORE I DID, started to walk around on the bed. I saw a thin strip of light between the curtains. Daylight didn't seem possible; sleep had been too short. I'd dreamed about Joanne when we were kids. She seemed so close.

Before I got up, the phone rang. I looked at the clock by the bed; it was after nine. Probably Cal, calling to check on me. I needed to get to the hospital.

"Hello."

"Hey. You're home. I was worried about you."

He thought I was Joanne. I didn't recognize the voice. Jo didn't talk about anybody she'd been dating. Whoever it was, I hated to be the one to tell him.

"This isn't Jo," I said, trying out words in my head before I said them. "This is Darla, her friend."

There was a long silence before he said, "Darla?"

"Yes?" I had no clue.

"How've you been doing? It's Sean. Sean Latham."

The name, the suddenly remembered voice, brought feelings to the surface that surprised me. Sean Latham—a big grin on his face and a body too skinny for his clothes. Forever, it seemed, he'd taken up all of the space in my thoughts.

"Sean? Where are you?"

We'd gone out senior year, before I went off to college in Austin. By the time I quit school, came back home a year later, he'd moved out west with his parents.

"I'm here," he said. "I've been back in Texas about eight months now. I'd really like to see you, catch up and all. You sound good."

He stopped talking and I didn't know where to start, how to tell him, especially since I had no idea why he'd be calling Jo. He spoke up again before I did.

"Is Jo around? I couldn't get her all day yesterday."

"Jo's in the hospital. She was in a bad accident."

The line was quiet, so I said, "Yesterday. It happened yesterday."

Finally, he spoke again. "How bad?"

"She's not conscious, Sean." My own tears started again. I wanted her here. "They don't think she'll recover," I finally got out.

"Oh no," he said.

The way he said it, with genuine sadness . . . he'd known her again. They'd been friends, maybe more.

"I'm sorry, Darla. Really sorry. Listen, I'm not far from Jo's place. Can I come over?"

"That's really nice but . . . I need to get to the hospital."

"I won't stay long," he said. "I want to talk to you, if I can."

Rigsby was scratching at the door to get out. I needed to shower, figure out what I was going to put on. It would take a while for me to leave anyway.

"Okay," I told him. "I'll be here. I'm gonna shower, so if I don't answer, just come on in."

"I'll be there in about half an hour. Will that be okay?"

"Yeah," I told him. "That's fine."

He hung up.

Rigsby barked and I went to let him out, stepped out to watch him sniff around. The air felt hot already and the grass, left too long without a mowing, drooped over.

Next door, the neighbor kids, a boy and a girl, just little guys, splashed in a round blow-up pool while Evie sat on the back stoop and watched, looking bored. They climbed in and out of the pool; grass and dirt stuck to their little legs then floated free in the water when they got back in.

A real wooden fence enclosed the yard on both sides of the duplex. A chain-link fence down the middle separated Jo's half from Evie's.

Evie waved at me and I waved back. Taking my cue from her, I sat on the steps, watched Rigsby do his business in the back corner of the yard. He had trouble supporting himself on his back left leg, a weakness left over from the awful mess he was in when Jo brought him home a year before from the lumberyard.

I remember all of that so clearly, that summer. I'd quit my job in the accounting department at the courthouse, and Jo had been working for about six months at the lumberyard. Cal and I had moved into our house and I was home every day, fixing it up.

By then, all I wanted was a baby of my own, but Jo wasn't thinking about babies. Mine or anybody else's. She liked all the guys at the lumberyard. "Regular guys" she called them. Not smooth-hand boys like the ones who'd worked in the office with me. She was sick to death of boys.

"Have you heard anything about Joanne this morning?" Evie's voice came from the other yard.

She was standing at the fence and I got up to meet her. Her kids still giggled and splashed behind her.

"No," I told her. "I'm going to the hospital to check on her soon. I stayed here last night."

If she thought the last part was odd, she didn't say it.

"If she comes to at all, will you tell her I'm thinkin' about her. I'll get over there when I can."

"I'll tell her."

Extra pounds, weight she probably never lost after the babies, settled on Evie's arms and around her hips, but she moved liked the smaller person she'd been before.

"It's just awful, what happened to her. God, you never know what's gonna come."

Cries and screeches stopped us from talking. Behind her, things had gotten ugly in the pool. The little boy, who looked about three, had a handful of his older sister's hair and was putting most of his weight into pulling it out.

"Cut it out! I'll whup both of you!" Evie yelled.

The boy let go and the girl slapped his arm before he got it out of the way. He sat in the water crying, but the mother ignored him, turned back to me.

"I remember when Joanne moved in. I was glad to have another girl around."

"Joanne talked about your kids," I said. "She liked watching them play in the yard."

"Yeah," she said, looking back at the two, who were getting along again, "everybody likes my kids. Fella who lived here before Joanne loved 'em too. He was a homosexual."

I didn't know what to say to that. She didn't look to be waiting for any response. Evie talked to fill silent spaces in the air.

"Nicest guy you'll ever meet. He took me to the hospital when my water broke with Anthony, the youngest there, on account of Michael, my husband, was at work. Looked after Lana for me in the waiting room until Mike got to the hospital. Said since he'd never have a wife to take to the hospital with a baby, he liked having the experience with us."

Sweat rolled down the side of her face. July heat had already started to settle in on the day.

"I'm sorry," she said. "Joanne's hurt real bad and I'm running on with nonsense like a mynah bird. I can't believe she's in a coma. That's just terrible. And she's so pretty too."

Pretty. Not nice. No one ever called Joanne nice. I don't think anybody but me knew about her soft side.

"Is there anything I can do that would help?" she asked.

"That's real sweet of you, but I can't think of anything right now. I do have to go shower though. Another friend of hers is coming over."

"Is it her preacher friend?"

"Preacher?"

"Yeah, she's got a preacher friend, a priest, she calls him, 'cause he's a Catholic. Comes over a lot. I thought he was her boyfriend who just wore those funny shirts all the time, but she said no, that's just what priests wear. She said Catholic preachers don't date or marry."

Evie was always sitting at the window, watching Joanne's life like a soap opera.

"No, this is a friend of ours from high school. An old boyfriend of mine, actually."

"Yeah, I bet that's him," she said. "The priest. Went to high school with y'all. The last couple of months, he's been here a lot."

I tried to picture Sean standing in a pulpit, but all I could think about was the Sean who sat on the couch with me, flushed and eager, all lips and hands.

"I haven't seen him in a while," I said. "So I don't know. But I don't think so."

The shower washed away the sticky moisture that had settled on my skin while I was outside. I thought about Sean Latham; his voice, deep, but still recognizable to me. He must have changed in so many ways, but a priest? He was thoughtful, kind, but I didn't remember any religion.

Smooth water ran down my back, down my front, over all the places he'd touched when we were up in the den over the garage at his house. He played music on the stereo, "Fire and Rain" . . . "A Song for Adam" . . . Songs about the clutter left behind by tortured souls. I understood those songs, finally. Thick inside Joanne's clutter with no music to ease me, I understood.

The phone rang. I heard it through the warm rush of water. It was Cal, I knew, calling to see how I was. I could see him at my mother's kitchen table. Full from a breakfast she made him eat. I didn't want to talk to him. Talking would mean deciding how I felt about what he'd said. It was too much, on top of everything else. I just let it ring.

"HELLO!" SEAN CALLED from the other room. I'd finished bathing, was getting out of the shower.

"Just a minute!" I yelled back.

I felt my heart, beating in my throat, heard it inside my ears. I had to settle down. Breathing in, air full in my lungs, I willed myself to calm; then pulled on Joanne's robe that hung on the closet door.

Sean had filled out, wasn't skinny anymore, and there was the collar. Jesus, Evie had been right. Sean Latham, a priest. He'd grown tall, still blond, but darker, closer to brown than I remembered.

"You are a priest."

"Yeah, figure that one out." He smiled, shrugged. "That's what I am." Then his face went serious. "Tell me about Joanne."

Wet hair stuck to my neck, dampened the collar of Joanne's terry robe. I pulled it tighter around me; felt her close. With that feeling, I forgot about Sean, thought only of her in that hospital bed and the tears started again. They came without warning, had to run their course. I felt so helpless.

Sean moved toward me, came and held me. He was solid and new, not a memory anymore, but with a kindness still familiar to me.

"I'm sorry," I said, pulling away. "I'm a mess. I don't know if I'll ever feel right again. I miss her. Sometimes I can't breathe."

"I know," he said.

I looked at his face. He was near tears too. I moved away from him, needed distance. He was so much the same, but everything was different.

"Can I get you anything?" I asked as I opened a nearby drawer.

Joanne had smoked close to a pack a day before she got pregnant. She'd had cigarettes all over the house. I looked in the cubby of her desk by the wall. Found a pack near the back.

"No. I'm fine. Just tell me what happened?" he asked, settling beside me on the couch. He watched me light a Marlboro Menthol. The cool rush in my lungs offered relief to something unbearable, something I couldn't even name.

"Just start with yesterday," he said.

I told him. Talked like I'd relied on him all my life. Most of it he knew already. The baby. He knew about that. I was glad to skip the explanations.

"Why didn't she tell me you were here?" I asked him when I was done. "Why *are* you here?"

"We ran into each other by accident," he said. "Jo was walking Rigsby. I was at St. Elizabeth's down the street. I'm working at a retreat center about twenty miles from here. I come back to the old parish to visit and help every chance I get. Anyway, Jo talked to me about all the stuff going on."

"But why didn't she tell me about you?"

"I don't know, Darla. Things started getting complicated, more complicated, right after I saw her for the first time. She actually came to the parish and left a message for me. She said she needed somebody outside the situation. Somebody she could talk to."

"Was she upset about something? About the baby? Or . . ." I added, "about Cal?"

He looked at me, his eyes direct.

"It's not that simple. It's not really for me to say."

"Who else can tell me?" I was tired of merry-go-round conversations. "She's in a coma, Sean. She can't talk to me, and she wanted to. I know that. She came to my house yesterday—I mean, the day before that. God, time is all messed up."

I took a deep drag of the cigarette, held it until I could think again.

"They want to take her off life support. Well, he does, anyway." I said it so calmly. I wondered if I'd already given up.

"Who wants to do that?"

"Her dad."

"But you said the baby's okay?"

I felt a wave of gratitude. The idea that he understood why that mattered, it meant I wasn't crazy.

"The baby's fine," I said. "I think Jo would want the baby to live."

"I'm sure of it." He nodded.

I wanted him to tell me everything. Every word she'd spoken to him, about me, about Cal and the baby.

"She tried to tell me something, the night before the crash," I said. "But she couldn't say it, couldn't get it out."

"I know. I knew she was going to your place. I didn't get a chance to talk to her after she got back."

"You know, don't you?"

"She came to me for help, Darla. For advice."

"What could she tell you that she couldn't say to me? Standing right in front of me, she couldn't say it. She's never been like that before. Not with me. Cal told me he'd started having *feelings* for her. He couldn't get out any more than that. What was going on?"

"She had reason to worry about you. She wanted to be careful, careful not to mess up anything in your life. That's really all I can say, Darla. As for talking with me, the collar makes it easier for people to get it out sometimes. Sets up ground rules, like with doctors and lawyers. She needed somebody removed from what was happening."

"What could mess up my life worse than this?"

"She didn't mean for this to happen," he said.

"I know," I said.

Rigsby barked to get in and I went to the back door. The dog was on Sean immediately. Licking, jumping. He knew him well. Sean must have been around a lot. So they were friends, Jo and Sean. Good friends. Did Jo have a whole existence she kept from me?

"She wanted to do right by you, Darla," he said, bending down to rub the dog's head.

The past tense. He used the past tense. *She wanted . . .*

"Sean, what do you mean *do right by me*?" I sat back down beside him.

"You need to talk to your husband."

"What the hell does that mean? Dammit, Sean, my life is in a bunch of pieces right now."

The edge seemed so close, I sensed the drop just inches away, a fall that could kill me, and I wasn't sure I cared. Had Joanne gotten there, that close?

I must have been shaking, because I felt my body, my skin, go still when Sean put his arm around me again.

There was an easy place with him that I remembered, back before I got scared and left him without explaining why. I couldn't confuse that place from before with my present life. Everything was different. But it felt right to give my weight over to him. He was even stronger than before.

"I'm sorry," I said, sitting back, but not wanting to. "Please tell me if you know anything that can help make sense out of the last twenty-four hours."

"Talk to your husband."

He was close to saying it. I could read his face. He wanted to. But then he'd regret it. He always hated not living up to his own standards. Funny thing, back in high school he was the one with the conscience, but I was the one who ran.

"I need to go to the hospital," I told him.

"I'll ride with you, if you don't mind."

"That'd be good."

I went back into Jo's room, made myself go to her closet to look for clothes I could wear. It wasn't even noon yet and my nerves were worn clear through.

SEVEN

——— ◈ ———

J O DROVE MY CAR while I sat next to her and struggled to wrap a
birthday present for my cousin, Peggy. Paper and tape cluttered the
seat around me. The present was a brass bong we'd found at a garage
sale across town. The mom who sold it to us had a son five years older
than we were. She thought it had something to do with incense and
let us have it for a quarter. Giving it to Peggy, there was a reasonable
chance that we'd make use of it ourselves.

"How does that thing work anyway?" Jo asked me, cigarette smoke
streaming out of the crack in her window.

It was January and the sliver of cold air from outside rattled my
wrapping paper, making it hard to secure the tape.

"I don't know," I said. "Peggy'll show us."

Peggy lived by herself on twelve acres of land outside McCabe.
Twenty-three and the only grandchild on her dad's side, she'd inher-
ited her grandmother's house. My mom's sister, Aunt Gracie, lived
with Uncle Roger in Austin, where he worked at the university's main
library. Peggy grew up acting like a little adult in a house with her very

adult parents. Out of college and on her own, she'd just started to realize how young she was.

"You're low on gas," Jo told me.

"I know," I said, taping an awkward scrunch of paper over the pipe section of the bong. "That's because I'm low on money. I was gonna bum a few dollars from Peggy."

"I've got some money," Jo said. "I'll put some gas in tomorrow before we head home."

Peggy had been looking after Pony for almost a year. The day after Jo's daddy took him to the pound, I talked her into going over and adopting him. Since Peggy lived fifteen miles outside of Alliance toward Austin, Jo and I figured that was our best shot at keeping Pony away from Mr. Timbro.

At first, Joanne and I drove over every week or so to check on Pony; but on one of our early visits, Peggy treated us to her homemade cactus jelly and her homegrown pot. It was the first time we'd tried either one. After the pot, the cactus jelly tasted like ambrosia. By senior year, Jo and I were spending more time at Peggy's than at home.

"You going out with Sean again this weekend?" Jo asked me, cracking her window a little more to flick her ashes, then closing it back to where it had been before.

"Yeah. He asked me during social studies today if I wanted to do something tomorrow night," I said. "I don't know where we're going though."

She drew in deeply from her Marlboro then handed it to me. Her cigarettes were too strong for me, but I'd finished off my pack at lunch and didn't have any money to get more. I took a drag and handed it back.

She didn't ask any more about Sean. I couldn't get a read on what she thought of him.

"I gotta tell you something," she said.

"What?"

"Don't be mad at me."

I looked over, tried to read her face. I hated conflict with Jo.

"Has Sean started flirting with you?" I didn't believe he'd do that, but I didn't want to hear I was wrong.

"No, dumb-ass." She laughed and I felt the muscles in my face soften. "He's stupid over you. Relax."

She stopped talking. The heel of her hand rested on top of the steering wheel and she moved her cigarette around between her two front fingers.

"So what'd you do?" I asked.

"You're not gonna like it. I haven't told you before because I didn't want you to be mad at me."

Jo had been a little strange lately, but nothing her usual mood swings couldn't account for.

"Just tell me, you jerk," I said. "I won't be mad."

She took in a breath, glanced over at me.

"I did it," she said. "Actually, a bunch of times. I've done it."

"It?"

"I'm not a virgin anymore."

I felt a weird collapse inside myself, something in my belly sliding down to my knees. I wasn't mad. I couldn't say exactly what I was.

"Who?" I asked. "When?"

"The last couple of weeks," she told me. "At the end of Christmas vacation, it started."

"Jesus, Joanne! With who? I didn't know you'd been out with anybody."

She looked at me, just for a second, then turned her face back to the road. The *who* was the hard part. The *who* was why she hadn't told me before.

"We haven't been out anywhere much," she said. "Just to his lake house."

"Jimmy Cagle?"

She nodded.

My face flushed hot. Warm air from the car vent began to feel like flames. I saw Jimmy Cagle again, at the lake with Melissa. In my mind, I made Melissa into Jo. My heartbeat quickened; I felt my ears go hot. It wasn't anger I felt, one of the very few times Jo called it wrong. But I couldn't name it, the feeling I had.

"I thought we said we wouldn't go out with Jimmy?" I covered with the response she expected, but my heart wasn't in it.

"I know. I'm a shithead," she said. Having confessed, her voice was easy again. "We said we wouldn't let him get to us. Dump us, like everybody else. But that's just it. I don't give a shit about him. I just wanted to do it. Get it over with. It's not a big deal. Not really."

"You don't like him?"

"He's okay," she said. "Kind of an asshole, but really nice sometimes. He's as pissed at my dad as I am. Dad sat him out of games after all that shit last spring. Didn't treat him right during football season either. That's how we started talking, ragging on my dad."

"How is it?" I asked. I didn't want to hear about her dad. "What's it like?"

A big grin came on her face.

"That's why I wanted to tell you—that, and I couldn't stand keeping a secret." She turned off onto the road that led to Peggy's house. "After the first couple of times, it's pretty good. Sometimes better than good. Especially when you've got a buzz on."

When she talked about it, everything about her—her eyes, her skin—seemed to take on an enhanced quality, an energy you could almost see.

The sensation in my belly, in my legs, got stronger, as my muscles got weaker. Sometimes listening to Jo talk about her experiences was more intense than actually *living* my own. I was afraid I couldn't stand up if it didn't go away by the time we got to Peggy's.

"I can't believe you didn't tell me before. I ought to be really pissed."

"You oughta," she said. "But you aren't, are you?" The last question came in a little girl's voice. Pleading.

"No," I said. "Just don't keep stuff from me, and I want you to be okay if he pulls a Jimmy, drops you for some cheerleader. You know how he is."

"That's just it," she said. "I pulled a Joanne before he could get around to it."

"What?" I was grinning by now.

"I dumped him."

"Shit. You didn't?"

"Yeah," she told me. "Fuckin' dumped him." She nodded her head, as if it sealed the deal. Smiled as she stared ahead at the road.

"Shit," I said again.

We turned off of the main highway. Peggy's driveway of graveled dirt gave up clouds of dust as we bumped our way toward the house. Rectangular patches of garden soil made her yard look like an earth-tone quilt. Most of the patches were empty. A few had hearty winter plants. Peggy supported herself by selling organic herbs. She sold them herself at farmers' markets and supplied grocery stores.

"Hey, guys!" Peggy was standing in the yard as we drove up.

I wanted to ask Jo more questions about Jimmy, but Peggy came to the car as soon as we stopped.

"Happy birthday!" I said as I got out of the car, grabbing the oddly wrapped present off of the seat beside me. My coat was on the floor-board, but I didn't bother getting it.

"We got you a present," Joanne said, coming around the car. "Cost us a bundle, so you better like it."

"Aw, that's sweet of you. Come on in," Peggy said, turning toward the house. "I swear Pony knows when you're coming. He's been excited all afternoon."

I saw the large greenhouse on her back property. It kept her going in the colder months, lush rows of basil and sage. Tucked in the middle toward the back was her winter crop of cannabis. In the spring, a larger patch grew outside, hidden deep in the green that stretched to the back and side of her house. College students around Austin and San Antonio proved a steady supply of customers.

"Ya'll hungry?" she asked. "I've got some muffins left over from breakfast and soup from last night I can heat."

She opened the door and I felt the buttery air of the kitchen around me. Mom called Peggy "ample," a word that described both her size and her spirit. She loved to feed people, make them laugh, then offer blankets and pillows for the night. We shared the same loose, dark hair that our mothers had. I was tall, but she was taller. Just shy of overweight, she carried her flesh with easy movements, a natural grace that caught people off guard.

"What kind of muffins do you have?" Jo was hungry. Lately, she'd been hanging on to her lunch money for makeup and cigarettes.

"Banana and apple," Peggy answered her.

"Could I have both?" Jo asked, petting Pony, who was jumping up and down at her side.

"You bet."

She wrapped a bunch of muffins in tin foil to heat them, got out glasses to pour sweet tea for us.

The kitchen had remained a grandmother's kitchen in spite of passing to younger hands. The woodstove sat beside a newer electric one. Peggy kept a fire in it for the heat, and cooked on it most of the time. We gathered there to get warm. Wooden floor planks, a century old and slightly bowed, looked as smooth as chocolate milk.

"So what's this present?" Peggy asked. She took the taped-up mess of paper from Joanne. "Damn! Looks like Pony wrapped it."

She pulled the wrapping from around the bong.

"Where the hell'd you get this? This is great!"

"A yard sale," I told her. "The mom sold us incense she thought went with it. It's in the car if you want it."

"Cool," Peggy said, turning the bong over in her hands before putting it on the counter. "I love it. We'll try it out in a little while. You guys staying over tonight?"

"Yeah," I said. "I told Mom and Dad we were celebrating with you. Since your folks can't see you till tomorrow, I said we'd just stay the night. It's cool with Jo's folks too."

"Great," Peggy said, taking the muffins out of the oven.

The smoky wood smell, mixed with the fruity scent of the muffins, made me feel little, knee-high in my own grandmother's kitchen years before. That kitchen was long gone, my grandmother in a nursing home, all my other grandparents dead. Still, Peggy's house was close enough to make the memories real in my head.

Jo sat beside me, her face blank. No grandmother memories stirred in her mind. She had grandparents, three still living, just no warm recollections. She told me once that her best times from first grade on had been with me.

Peggy put the basket of warm muffins on the table.

"Dig in," she said. "We'll scrounge up a late dinner when we're hungry again."

I ate an apple muffin, watched Jo go through three of them. She'd take a bite, then tear a piece off and give it to Pony. Peggy set up the bong and we took turns taking hits. The spent matches on the table became an endless fascination for me as the air around me lifted and held my body in mellow suspension.

I smiled at Jo and she answered with a giggle that tumbled around me and got me tickled with her. Peggy, more used to the effects of the strong, home-styled weed, presided, spoke to us like the silly children we were.

We never got around to dinner exactly, but ate can after can of Vienna sausages with crackers. Peggy poured from an endless pitcher of sweet tea and opened two bags of Fig Newtons that were gone before we were full.

We all sat until the early winter dark took over the room; until the only light was the hard glow that came through the edges of the wood-stove door.

PEGGY'S GRANDMOTHER had left a double closet full of quilts. All hand-made. Some she'd made herself, some she'd gotten from her mother. They were probably worth a fortune, but Peggy used them as if they were no more than Kmart blankets.

"She made them to keep people warm," Peggy said.

She threw a heap of them onto the floor of the largest bedroom, where she slept. We made pallets four or five quilts thick on top of the bare wooden floor, and still had plenty left to pull over us for sleeping.

A woodstove, smaller than the one in the kitchen, sat in the corner of the room. Shaped like a barrel, it gave fierce, uneven heat, so we made our beds close by it to stay warm. Peggy had space heaters she could plug in if it got too cold, but winters in Texas very rarely called for more than the barest efforts.

"So what's new?" Peggy asked.

She sat on her wrought-iron bed, her flannel gown identical in style to the two she'd loaned us for the night. Jo and I sat cross-legged on our floor beds, Pony in Jo's lap, already dozing.

"Jo had sex," I said, still stoned enough to be blunt and silly.

"Really?" Peggy said.

Jo made a face at me, but I could tell she wasn't mad.

"Yeah," Jo said. "What the hell."

"So are you all in love now?" Peggy asked her.

"Nah. That love stuff's more Darla's thing. I just wanted to do something different."

"Darla?" Peggy said. I felt my face go hot. I didn't want the conversation to veer toward me, but it was too late. "How is the handsome Sean? Have you two gotten serious yet?"

I wasn't sure what she was getting at.

"We're coming along," I said, shooting Joanne a look.

"He's felt her up," Jo said. "And working his way down. Same road, just stickin' to the speed limit."

"It's not like that," I said, both wanting to explain myself and change the subject at the same time.

"It's okay, Darla. I know how much you like him," Peggy said.

I felt grateful to Peggy for not turning my feelings into a punch line. Most of the time I could count on Joanne, but when it came to Sean, I couldn't predict her.

"Yeah. I do. I like him a lot and he really cares about me."

Joanne made a small, huffing sound. "They always do," she said.

"Shut up, Joanne!" I didn't know why she was being so awful and I hated that I let it get to me. I almost never blew up at her.

"What crawled up your ass?" She looked more hurt than mad.

"It's just that not all guys are assholes, that's all."

What she'd said put bright, ugly colors on the feelings I had about Sean. She knew that. She knew it would hurt me.

"Hey," Peggy said. "We don't have to talk about this now. Listen, I've got some news too."

I looked at her, glad to shift my attention away from Jo.

"I've applied to law school at UT," she said. "I actually applied a while back, but I find out soon if I got in. Looks pretty good, with my scores and all."

"That's great, Peggy," I said. I had trouble imagining Peggy wearing a suit. "Would you still live here and drive, or move to Austin?"

"Little of both," she said. "I'd stay with my folks some there, come back here on weekends."

"Good deal," Jo said. "Would you still be able to keep Pony?"

She tried to sound casual, but I could tell she was worried.

"Oh Pony'll go wherever I go. Don't worry about him. We're buddies. He likes Mom and Dad's place."

After that the evening settled out into rambling talk, until yawns took over and words became scarce. When we pulled our covers up to sleep, I could hear by her breathing that Jo was awake with me, even after Peggy had fallen into long snorelike sounds.

After a while I heard Jo shift over in my direction.

"Darla?" she whispered.

Her breath smelled like pot and Clove gum.

"Yeah?"

"I'm sorry," she said.

Something in her voice made me tear up. She sounded small.

"Me too," I answered.

That said, sleep came easy and lasted all night.

I COULD HEAR SEAN'S FATHER in the garage below us. He had the radio on—some station playing Lawrence Welk music—while he worked on his Mustang.

"Does he always work on the car this late?" I asked Sean.

"Sometimes, on the weekends when he doesn't have to get up early for work," he said. "It's probably the only way he can get any time to himself."

Sean's arm felt solid around my shoulder. We were watching TV in the upstairs den, over the garage at Sean's house. The couch sagged on one end and Sean sat on the low side so that I fell slightly into him. He always sat there. He didn't know that I'd figured it out. Or maybe he did.

"How come your brothers aren't bugging us?" I asked.

There were five kids in the Latham family, four boys and a girl. Sean was the oldest. We were almost never alone at his house.

"I called the room tonight," he said.

"Called it?"

"Yeah. It's a new thing we worked out, signing up in advance for the room. We figured it was the only way any of us could work out privacy for ourselves."

"How'd you get your little brother to go along with it?"

I couldn't see Colin, the seven-year-old, worrying too much about privacy.

"That's where bribery comes in." Sean grinned. "He's asleep by now anyway."

Something dropped in the garage, something metal—large and heavy by the sound of it. It made me jump.

"He's not gonna come up here," Sean said, tightening his arm. "Nobody is."

He looked at me for a second, waiting for me to respond. He was gentle that way, always waiting, giving me a chance to pull back if I didn't want us to go on. But I did want to. He had to know that by now.

His breath on my cheek was short, whisper thin.

"Darla," he said. That's all. Just my name. As if he liked the sound of it in the slight air between us.

I moved toward him and we started. Our mouths, his hands, in all the seamless minutes that followed. I liked it better in his house, inside a room with walls rather than in his car with the dark unknown so close outside.

His hand went to my shirt, buttons sliding open as easily as petals coming off a flower. Inside my clothes, the tips of his fingers found tender parts of me, and when his attention moved down, with a single-handed struggle against the button on my jeans, I stopped him, suddenly aware of the wetness he would find, afraid that there was something wrong with me, something he wouldn't like. It had happened before, but not so much.

"What?" he asked. His eyes looked almost frantic and I felt confused.

A small contraction inside me gave both pleasure and pain, but more pleasure.

"What, Darla?"

"I'm . . ." What? What was I?

"I don't know," I said. "It's just . . ."

"What's wrong?"

"It's wet," I said, low and embarrassed, as if the word itself was ugly. "A lot. I don't know why. I'm sorry. I didn't do anything."

He smiled, the look on his face both sweet and relieved.

"That's a good thing," he said, and moved gently against me. "I don't know everything. But I know that much." His words sounded thick, almost a moan.

I helped him with the button on my pants, braced my leg against his urgent pushing while his hand slipped underneath my jeans to touch between my legs. I don't know how he knew, or even *if* he knew, what to do. Maybe blind luck led his fingers to places I'd never imagined were part of my body. But the pleasure, tinged with a slight, sweet pain brought me moaning against him, my sound joining with his, reaching the same note as he pushed warm against my thigh.

I felt myself go limp against him, but he pulled away from me, his insistence gone. And when he fell back against the couch, spent, looking wounded somehow, I was worried that I'd failed him.

"Are you okay?" I asked, suddenly aware that my clothes were open and undone, while his had stayed zipped and modest.

"Yeah," he said. "I'm okay—I think. I just need to go for a minute. I'll be right back."

He left and went down the hall and I heard the bathroom door close. I tucked my legs up underneath me on the couch, felt a low hum, a fine vibration, running over my skin. I hoped he was okay. I worried that he'd left, wondered why.

The answer to that, whatever it was, seemed trivial when he came back. Acting himself again, he pulled me next to him, hugged me as if I'd saved him from something terrible.

"I love you," he said.

Something swelled inside me, emotion that threatened to push tears out of my eyes.

"I love you too," I told him. We sat for a while, the television flashing pictures we barely saw, making sounds we ignored. There were no more noises from the garage below.

"I better get home," I said, when there was no time to spare before my curfew.

He seemed reluctant to move his arms. But he did, and we tiptoed through the dark rooms in his house, slipped outside, and he drove me home.

EIGHT

SEAN WENT OUT ahead of me and I locked up Joanne's house. Evie waved at us through her living-room window, then ran to the door.

"Hey, Preacher, how ya been?" she asked Sean as she stepped out onto the porch.

Sean smiled, gave her a shy wave.

"Listen, Darla," Evie said. "Let me know if there's anything I can do for you here. Joanne gave me a key for times when she locked herself out, so I can get in if I need to."

The kids flanked her on either side. Still damp in their bathing suits, they huddled inside big towels.

"Maybe just check on Rigsby, if you don't mind," I said. "Let him out a couple of times. I already left food for him."

"I sure will," she said.

Then she stood and waved good-bye, as if we were guests going home after a visit.

I went to the passenger side of the truck to get in, even though the keys were in my hand. It hit me, standing there, Sean looking at me, wondering what I was doing. For a fraction of a moment, I felt us again, as we were—Sean driving me to the movies, Sean taking up nearly all the space in my world. Joanne was fine back then, walking and laughing, sleeping with boys she barely knew. I wanted to be there.

"Darla?" Sean stood on the curb, looked at me.

I started to cry. Standing on the street in front of the place Joanne had lived; the place she'd never go again, I cried from so many places inside me, I didn't know where the sorrow started, or where it could possibly go.

"Come here," Sean said as he walked toward me. "Come here."

He put his hand on my arm. All the muscles in my legs felt like string. I wasn't sure how many times I could break down before I finally got too weak to come back. When I could see again, breathe a little, Sean opened the door to the truck and helped me in. Evie was still standing on her porch, watching.

Sean took the keys from me and drove, while I used the rearview mirror to put on concealer and some lipstick. It didn't help the blotches on my face, but it made me feel better.

"Can you please tell me something about why Joanne came to my house?" I tried again.

In high school, Sean would have told me anything, just because I asked. But he wasn't a kid anymore and I wasn't the center of his life. He was stronger, and if possible, even kinder than he had been before.

"Darla," he said. "If I told you every word she said to me, it still wouldn't answer your questions. I don't know why this happened. Even when I put everything I know together, I can't say why she was driving to your house like a bat out of hell in the middle of the night."

"Why would she get in her car at four A.M.? What couldn't wait?"

He shook his head, looked at the road and didn't say anything. His light brown hair, shorter than I'd ever seen it, absorbed some of the brightness coming through the window. The hair and his collar gave him a divine quality, a creature touched by God. I envied what God had claimed and I hadn't, all those years ago, then felt embarrassed at the thought.

"What did she tell you, Sean? What did she say the last time she talked with you?"

He glanced over at me, his eyes wet.

"The last time I talked with her, before she came to your house, she was calm, really okay. But I didn't see her after she left you. I don't know everything that happened. She was excited about the baby, about doing this for you. I know that much. She was worried about some things. Like I said, you need to have a talk with Cal."

Cal's name hung in the air between us. It was the first time Sean had said it, called him anything other than my *husband*. Cal seemed far away. Over the course of one day, our recent life had faded, become less real to me than memories of Jo and even Sean, more than a decade before.

"Sean?"

He looked over at me.

"If I hadn't just checked out of our relationship the way I did," I was halfway through the question before I realized I'd said it out loud, "if we'd stayed together then, where do you think we'd be now?"

I had to believe that everything with Joanne, the awful pain laid bare, paved the way for a question like that. A question I would have never asked on a normal day.

"We would have had more," he said, as if I had the right to ask after all. "More time. I believe that."

The clarity of his voice amazed me, the sureness of the sound. He wasn't self-conscious, not even a little.

"But different roads would have led me to the same place. I know that I am where I belong."

That thought offered little but resentment. God was industrious, using my mistakes to hasten His ends. But I tried to rethink it, tried to believe that any sort of divine plan seemed better than relying on chance. If God had mapped out Sean's life even before my exit, then maybe more than random horror explained the twenty-four hours of hell I'd lived.

"You haven't asked me why I started avoiding you back then, why I stopped answering your calls," I said.

"You said you'd changed your mind about us, about everything."

"Did you believe me?" I asked.

"No, but I couldn't do much about it. Do you want to tell me what happened?"

"Yeah, sometime. I do want to tell you, sometime," I said. "But not now."

He nodded, looked at the road. I couldn't read him. I wanted to see something, curiosity, something more in his face. Flirting with divine property wasn't cool, and I knew it. I wasn't anything more than a gnat to God, but it wasn't fair to Sean.

"Can I ask you something?" I said, changing the subject.

"Sure."

"What does the church say," I asked. "About life support, when there's a baby?"

He seemed relieved to be moving on. Ethical questions had much firmer ground than the place we'd been heading.

"It's complicated," he said. "Life is sacred. Any life. But the surrogate thing, the church isn't in favor of that."

He didn't mention the adultery part of the surrogate thing. I wasn't sure he knew, although it would be just like Jo to tell him, for the shock factor if nothing else.

"But I have to consider it from the standpoint of what's done. Nothing that's happened is the child's fault."

"Can you tell them that?"

"Tell who?"

"Joanne's parents. Can you tell them it's wrong to end her life? To end the baby's life."

We were passing through the east end of town, near the lumberyard. A Quick Mart sat just ahead of us on my side, and when we got to it, Sean pulled in and drove to the side of the gas pumps. He put the truck in neutral. The air-conditioning still blew cool in my face while I waited for him to talk.

"This is hard for me, Darla."

"What?"

"Everything. Being who I was. Being who I am."

It sounded like a riddle, a play on words that would make some clever sense when he was done with it. But it didn't. It didn't make any sense to me. So I stayed quiet.

"I want to do anything I can to help you deal with this. Joanne told me how much you want a baby. She told me about how long you've tried. How they told you . . . well . . . I know your condition isn't getting better."

Did she tell him all of it, I wondered? Did she tell him how the same damn problem made me run off, just when I thought I'd be with him for the long haul? It's funny how Sean made a beeline for the church the minute I ran away from God—and him. I couldn't ask him if she'd told him, couldn't make myself say it out loud.

"I want to help," he went on, "but those people aren't Catholic. *You're* not even Catholic. If they ask me, I'll tell them what I think. I'll even tell them what I think Joanne wanted. But I can't be a prop in your drama with the Timbros."

He sounded irritated, almost angry. If I'd thought less of him, I would have guessed he wanted to get back at me for all the hurt I'd laid on him way back when. But that wasn't Sean. Not then. Not now. He was telling me the truth.

I nodded. Words wouldn't come. I felt gutted, as empty as skins left from a carcass. At least everything hurt less when I felt so slight of substance.

"Are you all right?" he asked.

"I'm hangin' in there," I told him.

He let out a long breath. I rolled down the window a little, lit a Marlboro from the pack I had taken from Joanne's desk.

"I'll try to help you, you know that." Even wavering a little bit pained him, I could tell. "But even if I talked to them . . . it's just . . . I don't know . . . there are limits to what I can say, what I should do."

"No, Sean. That's not what I want. I'm not trying to get you to do that, to go against yourself. I wouldn't ask that. I appreciate the honesty. That's all I want from you. Joanne never gave me any bullshit. Please, don't you start."

He rested his elbow against the window of the truck, supported his forehead with his hand.

"I mean that. Joanne told me what she thought. Always. Until that last visit anyway. I need that from you. A friend, not a prop, or a mouthpiece. Just be honest with me, that's all."

"I can do that," he said.

Yes. He could do that. He had always done that. He'd been a lot more honest with me than I'd been with him.

"Do you still have any of the feelings, like we had before?" I don't know why I said it, but it didn't seem out of line, given the moment. "I mean, what happens with all that, when you . . . you know . . ."

He didn't flinch, and while I didn't exactly deserve an answer, he gave me one.

"Those feelings get channeled into something different now," he said, his voice earnest and real. "I still care about you, if that's what you're asking. I always have."

I didn't know what I was asking. I was glad when he went on.

"I'm happy that what we were is a part of me. It was real. I'm not sorry about that."

He didn't ask how I felt, which was just as well. I didn't know. He put the car in gear and we got back on the road to the hospital.

I SAW THE TIMBROS through the windows of the ICU when we got to the hospital. I stood out of sight for a second, glanced long enough to see Joanne beyond the open curtain of her cubicle. I needed to satisfy myself she was still alive, but I didn't go in, didn't want to face them. Sean stood beside me, followed when I headed toward Mom and Cal, who were standing down the hall. As we got closer, a question formed on Cal's face. He hadn't seen the collar yet.

"Sean Latham!" Mom said, and she went to hug him like he was still seventeen.

"Hey, Mrs. Andrews!"

Then she saw his collar.

"What in the world have you gone and done?" she asked.

"I've become a priest."

"A real one?"

I wondered what other kinds there were, but Sean didn't seem to take offense.

"Ordained for two years now," he said.

Cal still hadn't said anything. I stood between them, caught their two images in my peripheral vision on either side. Out of focus like that, they could have been brothers, the height, the coloring . . . So much was the same, and so much was different.

"Hi," Cal said, extending his hand, "I'm Cal Stevens."

"Sean Latham," Sean answered, putting his hand in Cal's. "How's Joanne? Has anything changed?"

"No," Mom answered. "Her parents are with her now. The doctor hasn't been in yet."

"I was worried about you," Cal said to me. "I tried you this morning and you didn't answer."

He glanced over at Sean and I felt a thread of guilt work through me: for not answering his call, for my thoughts about Sean, for breathing on my own when Joanne couldn't . . . a full-service menu of guilt.

"I must have been in the shower. I'm sorry."

A machine in one of the rooms started beeping, and a nurse hurried in. Two doctors, the oldest I recognized as a high school friend's father, looked over a chart together down the hall. Other families huddled like ours, people standing around holding coffee, looking worried. I thought of the television display at Sears, all the TVs muted, showing a different drama. It was like that in the hospital. So many stories clustered together, room after room.

"Why don't you two go to the cafeteria," Mom said. She was looking at Cal and me. "I'll catch up with Sean."

"I want to check on Jo first," I said.

"I'll wait here," Cal said.

Jo LOOKED SMALLER and, except for her growing belly, thinner than I'd ever seen her. Her arms and face. It flashed through my mind that she'd like that, getting skinny without trying. She used to joke that the flu got her in shape for bikini season. I imagined a conversation we could have, normal, joking. I knew her well enough to make up all her parts.

"Darla?"

It was Mrs. Timbro. I was standing in the middle of the room, not moving toward Jo's bed. I was so lost that I didn't notice Jo's mom coming toward me.

"You look exhausted, honey. Did you sleep at all?" she asked.

"A little. I stayed at Joanne's," I said. "I went to let Rigsby out, and just didn't want to leave."

Quiet tears came down the sides of her face.

As I followed her over to Joanne's bed, Mr. Timbro got up from the chair, motioned for me to take his seat.

"That's okay," I said. "I'm just checking in for a minute."

Since I wouldn't sit, we all stood.

"Listen, honey," Mrs. Timbro said, finally. "We've talked." She looked at her husband. "We've decided that we should keep Joanne on life support, at least for now."

I couldn't believe I'd heard her say it, couldn't believe he'd given in. He stood back, hands in his pockets. He didn't stop her from talking, didn't say she was wrong, so I fashioned it must be real.

"The chances are slight that anything will change," she said. "One doctor says there's no hope at all. Another one says he sees a small amount of brain activity, he believes. He said he's seen it before, once or twice. A little bit of recovery from something like this. But there's the baby, of course. So we've decided not to do anything for the time being."

Her words said one thing, but her face said another. Her eyes still apologized. Maybe she'd spent so much of her life looking that way, she didn't know how to change her expression.

"That's great, Mrs. Timbro. It's the right thing. Honestly, it is."

She nodded, walked away from me. It was gray outside. I could see through the windows at the end of the big room. Clouds had come over.

Mr. Timbro still stood by the chair. He didn't move toward me, didn't say anything at all.

"Mr. Timbro," I said, "I know we don't get along. But I'd just as soon not fight anymore. There were a lot of things said yesterday . . ." I didn't know how to end what I'd started to say. I didn't want to apologize. Joanne wouldn't have wanted me to.

"It was a rough day for all of us," he said, finally, without any real emotion in his voice.

That's all. *A rough day.*

I went over to Jo. A single sheet covered her and with her body so small, the small mound of her belly became more obvious. I took her hand, closed my eyes, and tried to feel for some response. A finger moving, a flinch or turn. But there was nothing.

I'd seen her like that once before, passed out in my dorm room in

Austin. She'd gotten too drunk to get up the stairs, so my roommate and two other girls helped me drag her up to the second floor. We put her on my bed near the wall. I'd squeezed in tight beside her, kept checking her on and off all night to make sure she was still breathing.

"She's still pretty, isn't she?" Mrs. Timbro was beside me, looking down at Jo.

"She's beautiful." My voice didn't want to cooperate. I was afraid I'd cry again, so I stepped back away from the bed.

"I'm going to the cafeteria," I managed to get out. "Do you want anything to eat?"

"No, honey," she said. "You go on. We're going to be sitting here a while with Joanne. The doctor's going to come in soon. He said they'd do some more tests today, but I don't know what kind."

I started to leave, when Mr. Timbro spoke up.

"I wouldn't mind," he said, "a cup of coffee, if you think about it on your way back up."

Arlene Timbro looked at her husband like he'd spoken in Portuguese. I was surprised too, that he'd softened up enough to ask for anything. But I just said sure. I'd be glad to get a cup. How'd he like it?

"Black's all right," he said.

Then I left the room.

CAL WAITED IN THE HALL ALONE. Mom and Sean had gone off somewhere, probably to the waiting room to sit and catch up—all of it a ruse to get me talking with my husband. I wondered what they'd talked about, Mom and Cal, all last night and this morning.

"You hungry?" he asked.

"A little."

We got into a crowded elevator. Pressed up next to Cal, I realized how far we'd gotten from each other in just a couple of days, how strange it felt to be that near him. But maybe it hadn't been all that fast. The last weeks, he'd been busy with work, late and tired at night. And I'd been thinking about the baby. Spending time with Jo after she got off work.

Just four days before the accident, Jo and I had sat on my back porch and watched the sun go down over the small hills behind my house. When only a thread of orange singed the side of one hill, Jo motioned to me with her hand.

"Come over closer," she said, keeping her belly as still as she could.

I scooted my chair over and she pulled my hand onto her abdomen. I felt what she'd told me about, flutter bumps of my baby's foot or hand. I envied her and adored her in equal measure. Cal wasn't home. I don't remember if I ever told him about it.

"The Timbros aren't talking about taking Jo off life support anymore," I said, as we sat down in a booth with our muffins and coffee between us.

"I know," he said. "I talked to them earlier, before you and . . . your friend . . . before the two of you came in."

"You remember me telling you about Sean. I went out with him in high school," I said, sounding more defensive than I wanted to. "I haven't seen him since then. But he's a Catholic priest now, assigned to a retreat center around here. He and Jo ran into each other a few weeks back, and they've gotten together a few times to catch up."

"Did she tell you about it before?"

"No," I said. "She never said anything."

"That's weird. Don't you think?"

I'd never seen him act like that before. Suspicious. Questioning. How the hell was I to blame if an old boyfriend, turned celibate priest, showed up in town again.

"Cal, we've got enough going on without talking about Sean. He and Joanne were friends. I think he'd been counseling her some. She had some problems that she didn't know how to handle. What were they, Cal? I think I'm the only one who doesn't know."

"Does *he* know?" His face looked white.

"Cal, talk to *me*. Forget about Sean. What was going on that I didn't know about?"

He pushed away from the table, away from me, and laid his head back on the vinyl booth. An old woman with a walker worked her way past our table. She smelled of cigarettes and antiseptic wash. It took her forever to pass and the pungent odor lingered after her. Cal's words, when he finally spoke, seemed part of the smell, the moments mixed forever in my head.

"I went back to Joanne," he said. "I wanted to be with her again."

"What? When?"

"More than once." He slumped in the booth, his arms in his lap. The muffin in front of him sat whole and untouched. "I wasn't thinking, really. It was a kind of, I don't know, obsession. An impulse. I thought about being with her and I'd be there at her door, asking her to let me in. After a while, I didn't even like her all that much, but I couldn't stop thinking about touching her. Her touching me."

I felt sick. I could see them, picture them together, like I knew they'd been before. Only, behind my back, it was different. Very different.

"She . . . ? How could you? My God, Cal. How could she?"

"No, wait, Darla . . ." His hands were across the table. He had my wrists. "Darla, look at me."

Sweat, or tears, maybe both, covered his cheeks, so shiny and pink they looked sunburned. This had been in him, hurting him for weeks. And Jo? I thought again of the afternoon with the sunset and the baby kicking inside her. How could she have sat with me?

"She didn't, Darla," he said, still holding my wrists. "She wouldn't. I kept going back. Every time she told me to leave her alone. She said I didn't deserve you, or the baby."

"You didn't sleep with her again?"

"She told me to go to hell."

Someone working in the back dropped a tray full of dishes. The crashing made me jump. I startled and began to cry all at once, as if the sound had hit me.

"Why, Cal?"

"Why what? Why did I go to her?"

I didn't know clearly what I was asking, but I nodded anyway. That gave us a place to start.

"She was different. Different from anything I'd ever known."

"You mean different from me," I said, feeling guilt and anger in equal parts.

He didn't answer me. He didn't have to. I'd seen Jo with someone before. In Austin, one of the times she came to visit me there that year. Just a guy I knew from my Biology class. I'd gone to a Spanish tutoring session and left Jo in my room. When I got back, he was there with her. Had come by to drop off some notes, and stayed when he saw Jo. They were in the bathroom when I came in. They never heard me. I sat on my bed, saw glimpses of them through the crack in the door, listened to it all. I should have left, but I didn't. She was amazing. Pure skin and nerves, no emotion. All pleasure. The next day, she couldn't even remember his name. I asked if she wanted to see him again.

"No," she said. "I'm here to visit you."

She'd been that way with Cal, I knew. Pure skin, no emotion. All with my permission. He never knew what hit him. Especially with such a contrast to me and my problems—sometimes struggling more to keep pain at bay than to experience pleasure. They'd been together twice before she was pregnant. Compared to me, Joanne must have seemed like a carnival ride. Only, without my permission, Joanne had turned into a concrete wall. I almost felt sorry for him.

He was still trying to explain when I interrupted him.

"She wanted to tell me," I said.

He nodded.

"By the end," he said, "I think she hated me."

I could see that. How that could happen. Then it hit me too. What she'd been going through. Should she tell me and mess up my marriage, my picture of a family with the baby she was giving us? Or should she keep quiet? Keeping things from me, over time it hurt her. She couldn't hold secrets in, especially secrets that would injure me. It must have been terrible.

I didn't want to be near Cal.

"Let's go home," he was saying to me. "We need to work this out, Darla. I messed up. But I feel better, getting it out. We can . . ."

"Better than she got to feel."

"What do you mean?"

"She was struggling with this mess when she was driving that night, Cal. I can't even think about that."

"Darla? We have to . . ."

"I'm staying here, Cal. I want you to leave."

"Dammit, Darla!" His voice rose and several women looked our way.

"I want you to leave."

"You started all of this, you know," he said. "All of this damn mess."

I got up, put my tray on the conveyer belt, the food untouched. Then I left, went back upstairs through the stairwell so I wouldn't have to stand at the elevator and wait. So Cal wouldn't have a chance to catch up with me.

When I got to the third floor, Mom and Sean were standing near the ICU, talking with the Timbros. Cal had gotten off the elevator and was coming down the hall. Everyone looked at Cal, then over at me, our separate entrances saying as much as words.

"I'm sorry, Mr. Timbro," I said. "I forgot your coffee. We—"

"Darla," Cal said as he walked up to us. "We need to—"

"I meant what I said, Cal."

He stared at me with hard eyes. He was angry! How the hell could he be angry with me? I didn't care anyway. I just wanted to be in the room with Jo, sitting near her. Feeling that as long as she was alive I could hope for something, if not for her, then for the baby. There'd be part of Jo in the baby. I knew that much.

"Darla?"

"Not now." I was looking at the floor.

He stepped back. Gave up, I guess. "I need to check in at work," he said. "I'll come back later."

No one said anything. Not even Mom. The space around us, ripe with tension, felt small.

"I need my keys," Cal said, talking to me.

I started to go into my purse and then remembered, looked at Sean. Sean reached in his pocket and pulled out the keys to Cal's truck.

Cal looked over at me again, then took the keys from Sean and left without saying anything more.

NINE

◈

I T WAS A WALK-IN CLINIC, Peggy had told me. I didn't need an appointment. The name of the place, The Healthy Woman, seemed ironic, since women went there for a reason—and it wasn't because they were healthy.

"It's easy to find," Peggy said. "Just a few streets over from the university. A few of my friends have volunteered there. It's a good place."

Joanne made the drive with me to Austin on a Friday afternoon. We got excused from our afternoon classes for a "college visit," a senior scam everybody played as much as possible.

"You okay?" Jo asked. "You look kinda pale."

My hands were sweaty on the steering wheel and when we passed the road to Peggy's house, I was tempted to turn off, forget the whole thing and hang out in her house all afternoon. But I had to do something about the pain, low in my back and all through my right side. My periods had gotten weird as hell, never coming when they were supposed to and killing me when they did.

"I'm all right," I said. "Just nervous."

"Maybe it's just really bad cramps," Joanne said.

She raised her voice so I could hear her over the wind coming through our open windows. Even with all the air rushing in, I felt barely able to breathe.

"It's not cramps. It's not only when I'm having my period that I get it, it's before too. And it's been happening when I'm, you know—with Sean."

"Does he know?"

"I don't think so," I told her. "I hope not."

"And you're sure it's not just your period?"

"It hurts too much for cramps—plus I'm two weeks overdue this month and it's still happening some."

The last part scared me the most. It would kill my parents if I'd let myself get pregnant.

"You started having pain before you stopped having periods, right? So it's not because you're pregnant," she said, answering my thoughts.

"No, but I'm still late."

She shrugged her shoulders, gave me a sympathetic smile.

It was hotter than hell outside already, and only the middle of May. Jo had on shorts. She propped her bare legs up on the dashboard toward me and she settled back against the door of the car. Her shirt was wet down the front from sweat and I imagined what a ragged picture we were going to make, walking into the doctor's office.

I wasn't sure I could tell a stranger about the whole thing. The pain itself wasn't so hard to talk about—but the late cycle, the fact that it happened some when I was with Sean. How could anybody understand? It didn't feel wrong, being with him that way, but the last thing I wanted was for some doctor to call my parents.

"You oughta talk to Sean, you know," Joanne said.

We were at a gas station, waiting for some guy to finish pumping our gas. He ran a squeegee over the windshield and the shrill sound brought my nerves to the edge of my skin.

"I can't tell him."

"Why? He loves you, Darla." That last part sounded grudging. I couldn't figure out what she didn't like about him.

"I know. It's just that . . . what if . . . what if what we're doing—me and Sean—what if that's the reason?"

"Darla," she said, cutting her eyes sideways at me. "If screwing around caused that kind of pain, I'd be in traction."

I laughed. Joanne could make me laugh. I'd never been more grateful.

Maybe she was right. Maybe it had nothing to do with Sean. I'd replayed my time with him in my head, over and over—when I was in class, eating dinner, sitting in church. It never seemed anything but right. But lately the pleasure had gotten confused with the hurting. Sometimes when I was with him, I felt almost no pain. Other times, I thought it would slice me into halves. Not between my legs, but in my side. Like Jesus, speared as a final injury.

I'd started wondering if it was God punishing me. I couldn't bring myself to share that thought with Joanne, much less Sean. The consequences of it being true ran so far beyond physical pain, it terrified me. I'd gone to church almost every Sunday of my life. Memorized half the New Testament Bible verses at one time or another. But I'd never really thought much about the wrath-of-God business, the Old Testament fury; had never done anything to make myself a target—until lately.

"What'd you tell your mom?" Jo asked.

"I said I wanted to check out the campus and find my dorm. That way, I won't feel like a complete dork when I get there in August."

"She buy it?"

"Mom never assumes I'm lying. Makes me feel like a real shit sometimes. She wanted to come with me, bring Dad and make it a family outing."

"What'd you say?"

"I told her that it'd be an adventure with you, that I had to figure out my way around sometime. She said I was right, that we'd go later as a family and get together with Aunt Gracie and Uncle Roger."

"Peggy's folks?"

"Yeah."

"So your mom's cool?" Jo asked again.

"Yep. She even gave me spending money so we could get some food, have fun. Why are you so worried about her?"

She shook her head, looked out the window at the large fields that stretched along the side of the road.

"I don't know," she answered without looking at me. "She's just always nice to me. I didn't want you to hurt her feelings."

"Well, I feel bad about lying too. But she's really okay with the two of us going, and I'm glad she gave me money. I don't know how much this clinic is going to cost."

"I've got some money too if you're short," Jo said, sounding like herself again. "And let's do that with the dorm. Then we won't be lying. I'd like to see where you're gonna live anyway."

Jo surprised me sometimes. It seemed funny that she still could.

"Okay. We'll go to the dorm."

I hoped I had a dorm room in the fall, instead of maternity clothes and more doctors' visits, but I couldn't bring myself to say that—to Jo or anybody else.

"What'd you tell your parents?" I asked her.

"Nothing."

"Jo. Your dad's gonna know."

"I got a pass from the counselor, told her I was looking at the business management program at the community college, the one in Racine. The old bastard can't say I didn't get permission. Just two more weeks of school—ever. Then no more getting passes from a certified moron so that I can decide what I do with my day. I can't wait until it's over."

She didn't sound excited. She sounded tired.

"EASY TO FIND, my ass," Jo said, as for the third time we circled the block where the clinic was supposed to be.

Finally, she saw it. The entrance faced into a small alley between buildings, rather than onto the street itself. A small shingle was visible driving by, but it was easier to miss than to see. The phrase *back-alley abortions* came to mind, got stuck in my head and pestered me, taunted me with shame.

Inside the building, the wallpaper was covered with flowers, all varieties indigenous to Texas. Names were printed near each one, calligraphy-like letters that were prettier than the pictures.

The receptionist gave me a sheet to fill out, to explain the problem. *I'm sleeping with my boyfriend and something is wrong.* I wrote down the part about the pain. I didn't write about sex, or about a late period. I wasn't sure how I'd gone so quickly from being Liddy and Hal's good child to just some teenager filling out forms at a community health clinic. Even worse, I wasn't sure I could ever go back to who I'd been. I finished as much as I could answer and turned in the sheet at the desk.

"I'm gonna go to the bathroom," Joanne said. "You be okay?"

"Yeah. I'm fine," I lied.

A young woman dressed in nurse's pants, short with an extra fifteen pounds or so on her hips, kept going in and out of a door behind the receptionist, calling patients back. After we'd been there for about twenty-five minutes, she called me.

"Darla Smith."

Jo, back from the ladies' room and going through magazines, rolled her eyes at me. "Smith," she muttered under her breath. The false name idea had occurred to me only after I started filling out the sheet. I didn't have time to come up with anything more creative. The nurse stood there with a clipboard in her hands and waited, so I got up. My legs felt like solid wood.

Dr. Adams didn't look like any doctor I'd ever seen. She had the hair and dark eyes of a black person, but skin nearly as light as mine. A small mole, just to the side of her nose, added an exotic quality to her face. After asking a question, she waited for me to answer, looked at me while she waited, and didn't busy herself with papers or any other distraction.

"You left some places blank on the sheet," she said. "About your last period."

"I can't really remember. I'm bad at keeping up."

"What's your best guess," she asked.

"I haven't been all that regular, but I know I'm over this time. A couple of weeks over." I tried to sound casual.

The short nurse moved around near the counter, clanging metal implements that would have something to do with my exam. I knew she could hear us talking, but it was her job to pretend she couldn't.

"Darla?" Dr. Adams asked. "Do you have a boyfriend?"

I felt cold and naked when she asked me that. The thin gown on me, the cotton sheet over my legs, fell loose around me, leaving air from the room all over my body.

"It's okay," she said. "I'm not asking personal questions so I can judge you or lecture you. Sometimes when young girls come here, it's because they don't want to talk to their parents. I need to know something about your sexual activity so that I can make good decisions about taking care of you."

"Is that why I'm hurting?" I managed to ask. "Because of what I do with my boyfriend?"

"No," she said. "That's not it at all. It's just that, if you have the condition I think you have, the symptoms can come up when you're intimate. The pain can feel worse during those times. Does it?"

I didn't answer, just stared at the baseboards where beige linoleum met the cool blue paint of the wall.

"Darla? Does it hurt when you're intimate with your boyfriend?"

The skin on my cheeks flared hot. My eyes stung with the arrival of tears. I didn't understand why she was asking. If being with Sean didn't cause the problem, then why did it *make things worse.* She wasn't telling me the truth. She talked around the truth, glossed it over with all the proper words.

"Darla?" she said gently, still waiting for an answer.

"Yes," I answered, still not looking up at her. "It does. Sometimes."

I couldn't bring myself to add anything to the admission. I felt as if I'd gotten my answer anyway. What I'd done was wrong. No matter how right it felt, God wasn't going to let me get away with it.

"I have a pretty good idea of what we're up against," she said. "But let's get this exam over with and then we'll talk some more, okay?"

HER HANDS WERE SMALL AND COOL, even inside the rubber gloves she wore. No amount of careful handling could make what her hands were doing feel normal. Then came the feel of cold metal and I closed my eyes, worked hard to get my mind away. I thought of being on the lake with my daddy when I was little, before he sold our boat. I imagined sitting at the front, leaning over and watching the water rush under, like a flat waterfall running underneath us.

When Dr. Adams finished, she told me to put on my clothes, said she'd come talk with me after I got dressed.

I WAITED FOR HER in the chair. I felt cold and sticky where she'd examined me. She'd had something on her hands. Some gel. The paper on the exam table looked crinkled and torn from my squirming.

Waiting, I tried to work up my nerve. I had to ask the question. She would come in and this was my one chance. I wondered how far God planned to go in punishing me. I made the promise then, before I talked with her. I made the promise to leave Sean alone, if He'd just let me off the hook with nothing but that miserable pain. When she came in the room, the words felt huge inside me, but sounded small when they found open air.

"Am I pregnant, Dr. Adams?"

I blurted it out before she even sat down.

She smiled at me. Her eyes were kind.

"No, honey, I don't think so," she said. "I ordered the blood work, that's just standard with a late period. I'll need you to run by the lab and have that done before you leave. You can call us for the results in a couple of days. But I'm almost sure you're not, so don't worry about that. In fact, one complication of your problem—especially with it showing up early in your life and so severely—is that you may have trouble getting pregnant when you want to. But that's down the road a ways, huh?"

I nodded. The relief of her words set me to trembling. I hadn't even realized I was holding my breath. A momentary wave of near-euphoria went through me. *Not pregnant.*

"What you do have is endometriosis," she said, sitting down in the chair opposite me. Her face looked serious. "You're awfully young to have such a severe case, but I'm almost certain that's what we've got going on here."

"What happens with that?"

"Nothing much worse than what you've already described—at least for now. Later, there may be problems with fertility. But maybe not. These things aren't predictable."

"So I just live with it, it's not like cancer or something?"

"No. No. Nothing like cancer. We try to control the pain; that's our goal," she said.

She pulled out a little packet about the size of a pack of cigarettes, only thinner.

"We've had some luck with birth-control pills."

The words, said clearly, no faltering or shame, startled me. *Birth-control pills. Back-alley abortions.* They occupied the same shadowy alcove in my mind.

"Dr. Adams, we're careful when . . ." I stammered. "He uses . . ."

Oh God, I couldn't say it out loud. I wanted to run out, back to my car, back to my house, to my room. I wanted an open window with ample air and smells of barbeque grills and cut grass. I'd gotten in way over my head.

"No, Darla," she stopped me. Just as well. The sounds coming out of my mouth weren't words anyway. "For the endometriosis. We've had luck with the pill in controlling the pain."

She went into an explanation of tissue from inside the uterus getting outside of it, attaching itself to other parts of my insides.

"The tissue gets active, irritated when you have a period—or intercourse—and sometimes for no reason at all," she said, "and causes the pain."

I felt dirty, my insides splattered and messy.

"You've turned eighteen already, right?" She was looking at the sheet I'd filled out.

"Yeah," I said. "In March."

"For real?" One of her eyebrows raised higher than the other. "This is important."

I figured she'd seen a lot of Smiths come through the office.

"For real," I said. "I turned eighteen in March."

"I can prescribe these, then, without talking with your parents. But I think you ought to let them know what's going on. At the very least, talk to them about the pain."

"Sure," I said.

Sure, I thought. Tell my parents. That notion came and went pretty fast. I took the sample pills from her and the prescription she held out to me.

"There's a pharmacy down the street from here," she said. "They give discounts to our patients."

"Thank you," I said, and left the room without looking back at her.

After they took a tube full of my blood, I went back to the waiting room and checked out. The bill was less than I'd thought it would be, which explained why the waiting room had filled to standing-room-only since I'd gone in; women getting off work with little money to spare.

Joanne sat on the floor, had some little boy on her lap, reading him a book. She nudged him up and stood when she saw I was ready, then guided him back to a woman who looked as if she would give him a brother or a sister any minute.

"Thank you," the woman said, looking grateful. "He's a handful for me these days."

Joanne just smiled.

"What's going on?" she asked me as we were leaving.

"They gave me birth-control pills." I held up the sample packet.

"Damn." She opened it, looked inside. The pills looked like tiny rocks from a fishbowl.

"The doctor said it would help the pain."

"Damn," she said again.

We crossed the street, walked toward campus to find my dorm.

SEAN'S TRUCK WAS IN MY DRIVEWAY when I got home. Mom's car wasn't in the carport, but she'd left the door unlocked. He was sitting at the kitchen table, looking pretty wrung-out.

"What's wrong?" I asked.

I thought of the pills in my bag. Just having them made me feel strange, secretive. I thought of going to him, all pledges to the Almighty put aside just one more time. I would suggest we go off somewhere. Then I remembered how I looked—my hair, my clothes, limp from the hot drive home.

"Hold on a second," I said.

I walked to the sink, turned the water on cold, and splashed my face, then dried it with a damp dish towel.

"Okay. What's up?" I asked.

"My dad laid a bombshell on us today," he told me as I walked over to sit down with him.

I couldn't imagine Mr. Latham doing anything to upset his family. He was the nicest man alive, or at least ran a close second to my dad.

"He's moving us to Albuquerque."

"New Mexico?"

"Yeah. His job's being phased out here. He's got an offer out there. He's got to have a job."

Mr. Latham was some kind of soil analyst. He worked for the county at the Ag Center.

"But you're all set for A&M this fall, right? So you'll still be in Texas."

He shook his head. "When we move, I lose in-state status. We can't afford out-of-state tuition. He's all torn up about it, but he says he can't turn it down."

"What are you gonna do?"

"Go with them, I guess. See if I can get in some school out there."

He was sitting, but he kept moving in his chair, leaning forward on his knees then sitting back again. He might have expected more from me. Crying or something. I felt so battered by the day, Sean's news found me already numb and broken.

"Let's go somewhere," I said.

WE DROVE TO LAKE RILEY, over to Northside where old men, mostly Mexicans, gathered to fish in the muddy shallows. No one we knew ever went there. We parked on the road and, without talking at all, went into the woods behind the shore. Sean had an old stadium blanket, plaid with worn patches of wool eaten bare by moths.

He stretched the blanket out on top of dead leaves. Below my shorts the wool felt raw on my bare legs. Sean lay down beside me, his arms around me, more clutching than holding. I knew I'd bargained with God; I shouldn't be with Sean. But He had to give me some time. I couldn't give Sean up all at once.

The pain rose again inside me, and I must have let out a small cry because Sean looked at me, understanding my sound to be sorrow. He put his finger to his lips. I needed to be quiet, careful.

The hard wool beneath me, Sean's sadness, and my jagged pain all seemed of one piece with what was happening—with what was to come. I had to end everything with him. I'd gotten in too deep, scared myself, and God had bailed me out. It occurred to me that I couldn't do it. Promise or no promise, I was part of Sean.

So close to him, I could feel his absence all the more clearly. He was too good to be taken from my life. Maybe God didn't mean for it to happen. Maybe God would forgive.

We went back by Sean's house. He needed to pick up something he'd bought for me, he said; something he'd left in the pocket of his jacket.

When we walked in the entryway, his mom came rushing over.

"Darla," she said. "Your mom called here. You need to get over to the hospital."

"What's wrong?"

"It's your dad. He's had some sort of episode with his heart. I don't know the details. It's not exactly a heart attack, something else, but your mom wants you to come right away. I spoke with her about fifteen minutes ago."

"Is he okay?"

"I don't know, honey," she said.

Sean had his arm around my waist. He gave me a quick squeeze.

"Let's go," he said.

He grabbed his jean jacket off the coatrack and we hurried out to his truck.

DAD WAS SLEEPING when I got to his room. They'd moved him from the emergency room already. He was okay, Mom said. A real scare, but he was okay.

"It's a rhythm problem," Mom said, as we stood outside his door. "The beats started going haywire, they said, and he collapsed. Lucky for us, he had stopped at the church to pick up a deposit for Preacher Lewis. With the hospital just across the street, they got him in here fast enough to shock him right away. He's fine, honey. He's fine."

Sean stood behind me, had his arms around my waist. Mom had her hand on my face, brushing my tears.

MY DADDY WASN'T A SMALL MAN, but he looked it, lying there, his skin a gray-white color that belonged more to death than to life. It was a cheap shot on God's part, taking it out on my daddy. He had me though, had me locked and sealed inside a promise I'd been bound to break again and again.

"Let's sit down somewhere," Sean said. "You're shaking."

We were still standing in the hall.

"I'm okay. You go on. I'm going to stay with Mom."

"You sure?" he asked.

I was hurting him, not letting him help. I knew it, could see it in his expression.

"I'm sure," I said.

He stood for a minute, stood beside me fidgeting, trying to make up his mind about something.

"I've got something for you," he said, his hand was in the pocket of his jeans jacket. "Now's not the time. But I want to give it to you soon. It's important. I'll call you later tonight, maybe come over if everything's okay."

I nodded. He kissed me light and proper, gave my mom a hug, and left.

I imagined the lengths I would have to go to in order to avoid him—two more weeks of school, where he would be at my side after every class, all the phone calls and trips by my house that were sure to follow my show of distance. The real hurt inside me lingered, mixed with the other pain from my head, from my heart. I envied my daddy, so deep in sleep.

I never wanted to see what Sean had in his pocket. If I saw it—a ring, I imagined, likely small and symbolic, but real all the same—I'd let the world go to hell before I'd keep him away from me.

I went in Daddy's room with my mother. We sat in straight-backed chairs by his bed, side by side like an audience. I leaned back against the hard, wooden slats, exhausted from the day; but she sat on the edge of the seat, her back rigid, eyes keeping vigil, strong with love.

TEN

———— ◈ ————

AFTER CAL LEFT, I stayed with Jo through the early afternoon. The Timbros had gone. They had a meeting, a personal matter, they said. I was happy to have Joanne to myself.

A deputy, some new guy I hadn't seen before, came by asking questions I'd already answered. He said they would likely rule Joanne's crash an accident. An accident, by default. As if it wasn't really, but they couldn't come up with anything better.

It didn't matter. I knew. Joanne was carrying a baby so that I could be a mother. She wouldn't have chosen to break that promise, no matter what happened that night. I knew that. I had to know. Otherwise, the world was someplace I didn't want to be either. "You need to get some fresh air." Mom tried to get me to leave, but there was nowhere else I thought I should be. She finally gave up and went home.

After she left, I closed off the curtain and pulled the chair up as close to Jo's bed as it would go. I leaned in with my elbow, my arm flush against her side. She was warm, alive, a state at odds with the past-tense language of coping we had all taken to using.

I talked to her. Explained to her that Cal had told me, that I understood how she'd felt, how torn up she'd been, trying to decide what to say to me. It was the first time since the accident that I'd sat down and said what was on my mind. I had a gut feeling she was listening, somehow, from wherever she was.

After a particularly involved monologue, I turned around to see Sean standing behind me, just at the opening in the curtain.

"You think I'm crazy?" I asked.

"I spend a good chunk of my day talking to someone I can't see. Faith in the listener is a particularly sane experience in my line of work."

He was smiling, but not joking.

"How is she?" he asked.

"Quiet for the first time in her life," I said. "Settled. Not like Joanne at all. I want her back."

He walked in and stood by her bed. I could smell the incense in his clothes.

"Have you been here all this time?"

"No. Your mom gave me a ride to Mass at St. Elizabeth's. I just got back."

He stood by my chair. I realized that after all the years, silence still wasn't awkward with Sean. The only sounds were muted beeps and rushing sounds from the machines behind all the curtains. Even the phones at the nurses' desk rang in lower tones, as if they, too, felt the need to whisper.

"She'd hate this place," I said. "All the dreary colors. I might bring a pillow or two in from her house to make it brighter."

Jo's breathing machine continued, but I barely noticed it anymore. I looked at her. The unbandaged side of her face stayed relaxed. A couple of short eyebrow hairs had started to grow in where she'd plucked them before. She wouldn't have let that slide. I made a mental note to bring tweezers with me when I came back.

"You have to be careful, Darla. Don't start hoping for improvements that won't likely come."

"I know. It's just that . . . we still have to respect her, what she would want. I don't know. She's here but she's not. Where do you think she is, Sean?"

He looked at me; the tension at the corners of his mouth told me he was barely holding it together. He rubbed his hand over his mouth, took in a quick breath.

"Feel free to give me the party line," I told him. "I need the comfort, all the pretty pictures."

"I don't know where she is," he said, looking at Joanne. "I'm just the messenger, working on a need-to-know basis."

"Wrong answer." It came out hard, accusing. I knew I shouldn't take it out on him, but I didn't know how to stop. "If your whole deal is right—that washed-in-the-blood, soul-saving business I bought for so long—where does that leave her? She's gone but not dead. Even while she was alive, she screwed around, smoked dope, had sex with my husband so she could have a baby for me . . . She swore like a construction worker—"

"And had the heart of an angel." He said it so quietly that my thoughts, my anger stopped, just inches from an edge I didn't want to find. "You've seen all along. I used to wonder what made you two close. You were so different. But I saw it too, spending time with her these last few weeks."

"And is that supposed to save her?"

"No," he said. "But all the other stuff won't condemn her either. She was going through something before the accident, Darla. Changing. When I met her again two months ago, I saw how different she was. Different from high school. Then when she talked to me . . . she sat for hours, talking and listening . . . I realized she was in the thick of reinventing her life. I don't agree with what you did, all of you . . . honestly, I can't even begin to comprehend it, but somehow, it set her in a different direction."

He was right. She was different, but so was I. The baby was changing both of us. Maybe that's why I hadn't noticed it so much in her.

"Waiting for the baby made us both better people, thinking about how we *ought* to be. We were changing together, I guess."

"What about Cal? Where did he fit into everything?"

I started to say what seemed right, that Cal was the father and his role was clear; but that wasn't the answer, not the true one. Joanne had started to shut Cal out of the equation and I had followed her lead, without thinking, without asking why. I'd always followed her lead.

Cal's confession had come to me too late to settle the conflict she was feeling. But what *about* Cal? I wanted to blame Cal, but that was wrong. It wasn't his fault. Not really. I wondered if it was mine.

"I don't know where he fits in," I said, avoiding the answer. "Cal's been working a lot more. He wasn't around much when Joanne was there. That makes some sense now."

The nurse came in with a perky "Hello," more to announce herself than to offer a greeting. She carried a bag of fluid in her hand, smiled at us and went about her business with Joanne's IV.

"Her color's better," she said. "I'd love to have that hair, I tell you."

Her cheerfulness shed stark light on our serious talk, exposed it by contrast and made me self-conscious. In the awkward quiet of the nurse's presence, fatigue settled in on me. The sleeping pills from the night before had left me with a headache, and I suddenly felt as if I couldn't sit up.

"You need to take a break from here," Sean said, standing up. He rubbed my slumped shoulder with his hand. "And I need to check in at the retreat center. Why don't you come with me? It's pretty out there. Lots of ducks and deer, the occasional armadillo . . ."

"I don't think so." I shook my head, tried not to look at him. "I don't want to leave her."

"Oh come on. Think about it. What would she tell you to do?" He nodded toward Joanne.

"She'd tell me to get the hell out of here."

The nurse glanced over at me.

"I'd leave if they'd let me," she said, adjusting a knob on the IV.

"Where's your car?" I asked Sean.

"It's here. I drove back over after Mass."

"My car's still here from last night," I said. "I'll follow you out of town. Just let me go to the bathroom first."

I said good-bye to Joanne and walked down the hall to the bathroom. Smells of a hospital collect in the bathrooms, intensify. Harsh soaps and cleansing residue mask the pungent odors of illness. I saw myself in the mirror, my skin washed in the gray-green light. On me, Jo's red peasant blouse looked like a costume, a fitting disguise since I didn't know who I'd become, or who I'd be, finally, when the ordeal had passed.

"IT'S SO GREEN HERE," I said to Sean.

We were sitting in the dining hall at the retreat center, the two of us small among the long tables. The Franciscan facility served a whole chunk of South Texas, Sean had explained when we arrived. The simplicity of the buildings, the density of the trees around them gave the place the feel of another time—time borne not in history, but in the imagination, like a fairy tale.

"It doesn't really fit with all the stereotypes about Texas, does it?" he said. "You know, tumbleweeds and cow pastures."

One of the Catholic brothers put sandwiches in front of us. Lettuce, some turkey, and cheese. I ate without noticing the taste in my mouth. We were the only people in the room. I could hear a couple of brothers working in the kitchen, but there wasn't a whole lot to do. The grounds, the cabins were empty, between sessions.

"Summer's a slow time here because of the heat," Sean said. "We've got a small group coming in this weekend, but nothing until then."

Industrial-sized fans moved air through the room. Windows, open to the screens, were shielded from the sun by shade trees, giving the room a cloistered feel.

"When did you decide you wanted to be a priest?"

I took a sip of lemonade. The tart coolness made my tongue shrink inside my mouth.

"I started thinking about the priesthood in New Mexico. My first year there, when I was waiting to get into a college, I spent a lot of time with my dad while he was working. He went around, helped people—people in these dirt-poor villages.

"He'd give them advice on their land, their water, their gardens. Try to help them support themselves and scrape some money out of what little they had. But all around these ramshackle communities, the land was amazing. Behind some mobile home park, a huge mesa would tower over everything, coming right up out of the flat desert."

He spread out his hands, his fingers in the air, trying to illustrate the size of the mesa. The expression on his face told me he could see it all, the desert, the villages. I almost expected to see it too, reflected in his eyes.

"There was something there, a presence, around those mesas and in the huge sky. The sky is so big. I decided I wanted to strip life down to the essentials—God, people, land . . . The whole idea of choosing poverty, it seemed simple. There wasn't one thing in the world I cared to own."

"Sounds like *Death Comes to the Archbishop*."

"Yeah, I guess so. The place helped me reconnect with all the spiritual feelings I had when I was younger and getting confirmed."

"I didn't even know you were Catholic."

"I wasn't exactly advertising my religion in high school. My hormones were running the show pretty much back then."

"I remember."

This stopped both of us. I heard someone moving around in the large kitchen behind the swinging doors at the back of the dining hall. Sounds of metal on metal echoed throughout the building.

"It wasn't all hormones," he said. "I don't want you to think that."

"I know."

It was time to tell him. He deserved to know the reason I'd turned away from him. Why I told him I didn't want to see him anymore. Why I spent the last two weeks of high school avoiding him, making excuses, pretending to be sick. Why I'd never answered his letters.

"Sean . . ." I started. Then I didn't know where to go from there. "I didn't want to do what I did, back then."

He watched me, didn't respond or try to help me along. That was fair. I deserved to make the effort.

"The day my dad went to the hospital with his heart, I'd come back from Austin . . ."

He nodded.

"I remember," he said. That was all. Then he waited.

"I'd been to a clinic. I'd had some problems, a lot of pain. My period was late . . ."

His face softened. I told him the story, everything I could remember. How scared I was. How embarrassed and ashamed, scared that God was punishing me.

"I wish you'd told me," he said. "You could have let me help."

"But I thought *we* were the problem. I left you, in part, because I thought it was some bargain with God, especially after I got home and found my dad in the hospital. I wanted to keep my dad alive. It was all mixed up with guilt over what we were doing and the pain that my illness was causing. But then, after everything, I was stuck with the illness, and you were gone. I dropped out of college after that first year."

"I didn't know that," he said.

"It was the right thing at the time. I felt out of place, unhappy. I missed you so much. And I missed Joanne. So I came back home. A year or so later, when my dad died anyway, it hit me then that I had no control over anything in life. Bargain or no bargain with God. I felt stupid. I'd either been duped or I was just really confused. By then, I didn't know how to find you. What I'd say if I did."

I sounded bitter. That wasn't what I wanted at all. I'd made a life. I'd been satisfied, building a home with Cal. Spending time with Joanne.

"It hasn't been as rotten as I'm making it sound. It just took me a while to get settled and to figure out what I wanted."

"What did you want?" he asked.

There was an edge of bitterness in him too. I'd given him scars. We could compare sometime.

"A family. A family as good as the one I had growing up, only bigger. I envied your house, all the noise, the fun. Cal and I tried. I even had a small surgery, but it didn't help. That's when I talked to Joanne. I wanted her to stay part of it all, to be in our family. At the time, it seemed like a perfect solution. She always said she'd make a better aunt than a mother. I wanted the mom job. That was our chance."

A breeze came through, ruffled loose napkins stacked on a table by the door. Several drifted off onto the floor. They looked delicate, like huge butterflies.

"And what do you want now?" he asked. His voice had gone gentle again. He leaned toward me on the table.

"First off, I want the impossible. I want Joanne to stand up and tell that nurse to take her perky little ass to some other room."

He laughed. It's what she would do if she could talk. We both knew it.

"And I want the baby. I want to raise the baby; I can almost feel myself holding it. I want to be a mother and tell the kid all about Joanne."

"What about Cal?"

I shook my head, couldn't think of words.

"I don't know." I didn't want to think about Cal.

"He's the baby's father, Darla. You've got to deal with that one way or the other."

"I don't think he wants the baby anymore," I said. "He agreed with the Timbros before they changed their minds about life support. And this stuff with him and Joanne . . . And I'm not sure what I want from him. He put her in such an awful position."

"Who?"

"Joanne. Coming to her the way he did. Giving her a guilty secret she wrestled with. That may be the reason she was out driving that night like a madwoman."

"I talked with her about Cal," he told me. "More than once. I don't think she suddenly went off the deep end that night."

"I know, but . . ."

"Why are you trying to find reasons to shut him out?" he asked.

"This is pretty weird coming from you."

"Yeah, well, you got that right." He laughed. "But think about it. Walk it from his perspective."

"Stop counseling me," I said, in harder tones than I intended. "I'm sorry. This is just all too much right now. I'm still so confused about Joanne, what she was doing."

He sat back, put some distance between us as if he knew I needed air, a little more space.

"She wanted to have the baby," he said. "She wanted to give you the chance to raise a child. That's the one thing I'm sure of. And I know that she was starting to think of what kind of person she should be, in the baby's eyes."

"Yeah, after she felt the baby kick for the first time, it was real— to both of us. She didn't want to have kids of her own. Ever. She used to tell me that all the time. But she wanted to have this one for me. It's amazing, really."

"She told you she never wanted kids?" he asked.

I remembered my conversations with her, loads of them, sitting out by the lake with the car windows down.

"She said kids would interfere with real living."

"You think she believed that?" he asked.

"At the time she did."

He shook his head. So much about him was the same as it had been before. His gestures. His quiet way of disagreeing.

"Well? What do you think?" I asked.

"That she thought she wasn't a good enough person to be a mother. She didn't deserve it."

A fly moved around my arm, tickled my wrist and made me flinch.

"And you think this because . . . ?" I wasn't sure I wanted to know.

"Something she said, once. She said you'd be a great mom, that you were wired for it. Not like her. Of all the good people in the world, she said, a kid shouldn't get stuck with somebody as damaged as she was for a mom."

Another breeze gave a quick burst of air, then died. It seemed a re-action to Sean's words, God's irritated sigh. Everyone, even God, had the same exasperated response to Jo from time to time.

"She said that?"

"Yeah," he said. "She did. But the idea that there was a baby grow-ing. Even if she didn't plan to be a mother, it made her want to be a better person."

"She was a good person. She didn't need to be better."

The past tense again. Even I had given in to the idea that she was gone.

"Sean?"

"Yes."

"The police, they sound like they think she meant to do it." I hated even saying it.

"Crash the car into your house?"

"Yeah. They're ruling it an accident, just to close the case, but they don't believe it. Not from what I've heard them say."

"Joanne? Doing that on purpose? Not a chance," he said.

I felt myself breathe, full and easy for the first time all day. I wanted to hug him. He sounded so confident, as confident as I needed to feel.

"She wanted to make herself, her life, better. She didn't want to end it. I'm sure of that. She thought being around you helped make her into a better person."

"Me?"

He nodded. "You saw the best things in her. She wanted, no, she *needed* for you to see the best in her."

I had the impulse to run to the hospital, somehow will her to get up and talk to me. We could make the best of ourselves together. We'd come so much closer already. I wanted it so badly I could see it in my mind. But just outside the shelter of that fantasy, the truth waited. The sadness of it should have stopped my heart, my breathing. It bore down again as I sat there with Sean, bore down beyond feeling, beyond hope. Still, my eyes stayed dry. Maybe the drought of sorrow followed the flood.

It must have been only seconds after Sean spoke, but it seemed to last forever, the resurfacing of all the hurt. I felt myself rocking, existing somewhere inside the pain. Then there was a sound inside my head. My own low moaning, I think, but I didn't know for sure. I didn't even know if it was real or not. In the middle of my confusion, I was somehow aware of Sean's hand on my arm. He stayed near me until the panic subsided, until I could breathe without thinking of taking a breath.

"Come on," he said, finally, when I felt almost normal again. "Let's take a walk. I'll show you the lake."

"It looks like a forest out of *Sleeping Beauty* or something," I said. "How long has it been here, the retreat center, I mean?"

We walked away from the main complex of buildings into a stretch of woods by the small lake that bordered the property.

"An old fellow, really eccentric—rich from oil and lumber, I think—left the land to the church more than twenty years ago. It's a great place to sort out your thoughts. I wanted to stay in New Mexico after I was ordained but they sent me here. It's only been a few months, but I already love it."

I still felt jumpy. I wished I'd brought my pocketbook. There was a pack of menthols I'd bought at the hospital gift shop with at least one, maybe two cigarettes left. One long drag would have settled me in my skin a little better.

"Who's that in the boat out there?" I asked.

A woman, my mother's age, maybe older, sat in a rowboat, fishing in the late-afternoon sun.

"That's Harriet. She's out here almost every day, lives across the lake. She's a cousin, six times removed from the old man or something. He never married, so his land got parceled out to a weird collection of relatives."

Ahead of us, by the water, a man sat on a bare patch of fallen leaves beside the water. He had on one of the long brown robes I'd seen some of the others wearing at the main buildings, like Friar Tuck. His presence only added to the fairy tale mystique of the forest.

"Are the rest of the Merry Men hiding in hollow trees?"

"That's Father Jerome. He's in charge here."

Father Jerome's full head of white hair contrasted with the deep tan of his face, but he had a youthful quality, even though he was older.

"So you are both priests here?" I asked. "And those other guys in the kitchen, they're called *brothers?*"

"That's right. You're catching on."

"Do you wear one of those robes?"

"A *habit,* it's called. Yeah, I do. Sometimes."

A few *bad habit* jokes ran through my mind, but I figured he'd heard them all.

"FATHER SEAN!" the old man called to us as we came near. He spoke loudly, used Sean's name as a greeting. "How are things with your friend?"

I thought he meant me at first, was afraid he'd seen me freaking out in the dining hall, then I realized he was talking about Joanne.

"About the same when we left," Sean answered. "This is Darla, Joanne's friend and an old friend of mine from high school."

"Oh yes," the older man said, "I remember you mentioning Darla here."

I blushed, wondering about the context of that conversation.

"Nice to meet you." He extended his hand. "I would be polite and stand, but my back has been giving me a hard time lately. So forgive me."

Father Jerome was a short man, ample in the waist. He sat like a kid, legs crossed Indian style underneath his habit. He had a cigarette in one hand and a Bible in the other. A Walkman sat on his lap, connected to headphones that were loose around his neck. We settled on the grass beside him. Earthy smells of mud and leaf decay mixed with the harsh scent of smoke from Father Jerome's cigarette.

"Could I bum one of those from you?" I asked. "If you have an extra."

"I assume you don't mean the Bible." He smiled at me, pulled a pack of unfiltered Camels from the recesses of his robe.

"Hard-core," I said, reaching for the pack. I took one out and gave it back to him.

"Nasty habit. All of them, but especially these." He held them up as an exhibit. "You should quit while you're young."

I nodded in agreement, tried to light the cigarette with one of his matches, but the wind kept blowing out the flame. Finally, he handed me his cigarette and I took a drag on mine and lit it with the end of his. Sean just shook his head, perplexed, I think, by all the effort.

"Here you go," I said, handing his back.

I SAT QUIETLY while Sean filled Father Jerome in on Joanne. They had talked on the phone, so her accident wasn't news.

"Is there any hope she'll recover?" he asked Sean.

"Very little. We're thinking more about the baby coming to term at this point."

Father Jerome's forehead creased as he listened.

"God bless the innocent little thing," he said. "Boy or girl. Which is it?"

He looked at me.

"I don't know. We told Dr. Adams a while back that we wanted it to be a surprise."

He smiled.

Out on the lake, Harriet had stowed her fishing gear and had begun rowing in our direction.

"Any luck out there?" Sean asked.

"Not much," she called back, her accent a thick Irish brogue. "The Spirit is quiet today, not calling the creatures to move about."

"Another day, then," he said.

"If the good Lord wills." She turned and started to row away from us, toward her property.

I watched her and felt something move inside me, a faint stirring of something. A memory, maybe. One just shy of clarity, but so familiar.

"She thinks that her success with the fish depends on God's mood?" I asked.

"She feels everything depends on God's will," Father Jerome corrected me. "Especially as it relates to the lake here. Said she never feels Him more strongly than when she's out there, alone but not alone. I've got to say, that's why I'm so often here. I think God has favorite places, and this one's got to be in the top third of His list."

I looked out again. Harriet's form became smaller and, after a moment or two, I could barely hear her oars as they slid in and out of the water. The sun had moved below the trees behind us, and the play of shadow and light on the lake's surface near the shore gave the water an animated quality of life and movement. There *was* a sense of something—something present and unseen.

"What's on the playlist now?" I heard Sean asking Father Jerome.

When the older priest looked confused, Sean said, "Your Walkman. What're you listening to today? Tom Waits? Johnny Cash?"

I shot Sean a surprised look and he explained, "Father Jerome is an old West Texas boy. He likes to stay in touch with the sinful appeals of the secular world."

"Know thy enemy," Father Jerome added, raising his eyebrows.

"So what is it?" Sean prompted him again.

"Something different today. Some group called Air . . . smith? I think that's it."

"Aerosmith?" I couldn't believe he was listening to Steven Tyler's screeching rants.

"That's impressive," Sean put in with a grin on his face. "Why Aerosmith?"

"Brother Patrick is bringing the St. Agnes kids out today. One of them gave me this tape the last time, wanted me to see if I liked it." Then he turned to me. "These young boys think they can shock an old man. They don't know the depths to which I have traveled with Mr. Waits and Mr. Cash."

"Who are the St. Agnes kids?" I asked.

"The St. Agnes facility works with juvenile offenders," Sean said. "Those kids push you away every chance they get. They want to find out how much you'll take before you give up on them like everybody else."

I wasn't listening all of the sudden. I'd become distracted by the lake. A vivid ray of sun, slim and dazzling, shot through a break in the trees and fell across the water. The narrow, brilliant reflection seemed too startling to ignore, like a flashlight beam cutting through the dark night.

Along the path where the light hit the water, the intermingling appeared to shed sparkles of some new element. Spiritual fairy dust off the shore of a monastic retreat. A slight breeze touched the hair on my arms and I felt my nerves quicken. I turned to Sean and Father Jerome, hoping to share some comment on the sight in front of us, but they didn't seem to notice.

"My limits show themselves from time to time." Father Jerome was still talking about the kids, "But Brother Patrick, God bless him, has endless reserves for those boys."

In a second's time, the sun had shifted and the vision on the lake had passed, but it lived in my mind, down to the smallest detail.

BY THE TIME SEAN WALKED me back to my car, the evening had begun to set in.

"Will you call my mom?" I asked. "I left a message earlier today that I was riding out in the country, but she might be worried."

"Sure," he said. "How about Cal?"

He stood beside the car, braced himself on the side as he bent over to look at me through the open window.

"Tell Mom to call him if you want."

"You need to make an effort to talk to him. You know that."

My mouth was in a hard line. I could feel it, but I couldn't change my expression.

"I'll call him tomorrow," I said. "I'm going back to Jo's tonight." I sounded so sure, unrelenting, but thoughts of Cal were getting to me.

I wanted so much to stay angry. Anger kept me from blaming myself. Even I knew that much; I felt certain Sean knew it too. I won-

dered what other parts of my psyche Sean understood, even before
I did.

"I'll call him when I get home," I said.

He just nodded, didn't push any further.

Before I backed out, I saw Brother Patrick heading for the retreat-
center van. He had five or six of the St. Agnes kids walking with him.
I'd seen them from a distance on and off all afternoon, a rangy bunch
of adolescents helping with chores, talking with the brothers. They
didn't strike me as kids. Their faces, more than their bodies, gave them
the look of adults.

In the parking lot, one boy stopped, as the group walked on. He
looked at me, his eyes large and unblinking. Brown curls of longish
hair fell around a face that was tanned with pleasant, almost pretty,
features. But as he kept his gaze steady with mine, I started to shake,
a small, nervous tremble that ran from my shoulders clear through to
my fingers. It looked like a younger incarnation of Jo, staring at me
from inside the boy's eyes.

Then his eyes changed and the glare came at me, hard and accusing. I'd seen Jo give her father that look, but I was never on that end
of her contempt. In the boy's dead-accurate sights, I felt reduced to
nothing more than the gravel on the parking lot around me. He was
just a kid who'd been wounded beyond all reason. But he seemed
powerful, all the same. I looked away, put the car in reverse. In my agitated state, I hit the gas too abruptly and sent dust and rocks flying
around my car.

"Easy there!" Sean called out.

I looked back as I drove out of the parking lot. The retreat buildings were a shadow behind a line of trees. The boys, including the one
who had lagged behind, had gotten into the van and Sean stood alone
in the gravel lot. I saw him wave, put my arm out the window to return the gesture. Then I drove ahead. I looked in my rearview in time
to see the van pulling out onto the highway, heading away from me and
fading in the early-evening light.

ELEVEN

"WHERE THE HELL have you been?"

Cal was sitting on the front steps of Jo's porch when I got back from the retreat center. There were no lights on, at Jo's or at Evie's, so I didn't see him as I stepped out of the car, didn't notice his truck parked with all the other cars along the street. When he spoke, it startled me.

"I've been worried about you," he said when I didn't answer. "I thought something might have happened."

"Like what?" I didn't know what to say to him. He sounded genuinely frightened and I felt bad that I hadn't called.

"I don't know, Darla." He stood up to come toward me, met me halfway on the brick walkway that led to Jo's porch. "I'm just glad you're okay."

"I told Mom to call you," I said. I couldn't animate my voice beyond a flat, perfunctory tone. "I didn't mean to scare you."

"She called this morning. Maybe I missed her later, if she tried again. I've been sitting here for more than two hours."

"Jesus, Cal."

We had stopped walking. It was as if some barrier kept us from going onto the porch together. He wanted permission to go with me, I think.

"Cal," I said. "I'm sorry I scared you. It's really late. I'm exhausted."

"So come home."

As my eyes adjusted to the dark, I saw the two identical porches of the duplex, identical windows and doors; twin sisters with such different inner lives. Since Jo's accident, her space had become my sanctuary. Cal's shadow seemed oddly placed amid these images.

"I know you don't understand," I said. "I don't even understand. I need to stay here a little longer, Cal. I need to sort through some things by myself. I'm not trying to shut you out, honestly. I just don't know how to let you in at the moment."

"You're just avoiding things that have to be said, Darla. We've both been avoiding them, even before the accident. You can't go on pretending that we don't have a life together. That's not going to bring Jo back."

He didn't know. He really didn't know how much easier it seemed to go on without him, without anyone. To shut down feeling altogether. How was he supposed to get it when I couldn't even put the words together in my own head?

"Darla, I'm here. I'm willing to work our way back, but you've got to help me."

We'd been good together, up until I decided it wasn't enough. Until I brought in Joanne, manipulated fate. Now I was blaming him for the unnatural turns our lives had taken.

"I know we need to talk, Cal. I want for us to talk."

He seemed relieved. We walked together up the steps of the porch. On the other side, I saw the blinds on the far bedroom window move a little. Evie, keeping watch.

It reminded me of Mom's apartment; Mom waiting for me to come in when Cal and I were going out. Mom slipping off to her room, so that he could come over for a "date." I cooked him dinners there—homemade rolls and brewed iced tea. "You need to go home," I'd whisper when it was getting late. "You are my home," he'd say. Mom stayed out of sight, hoping for us to fall in love. We did fall in love. I'd almost forgotten.

"Just let me get some sleep tonight," I said, reaching out, touching his arm. "I promise, we'll sit down tomorrow and sort some things out."

He stood by me, didn't move or respond for the longest time. When he lifted his hand to touch my hair, instinct pulled me toward him. He moved his fingers through my hair, touching my neck. He felt familiar for the first time in . . . maybe weeks? Longer? Even before the accident, he'd started to become a stranger to me; subtle shifts in intimacy I'd chosen to ignore.

"I miss you, Darla. We ought to be dealing with this together and I feel like we're on opposite teams."

It felt good to be touched. Almost good enough to forget the anger over all that had happened—his siding with the Timbros on that awful first day, his secret pursuit of Joanne. I'd betrayed him first, his very nature, brought all of that on by asking him to go along with my plan. Even when he'd resisted, at first, I'd pleaded. And he'd given in.

"I'm not trying to put you off, Cal. Honest, I'm not. I'm just tired and I can't face our house. Not tonight. You've been back. You've seen it since . . ." I couldn't think too much about the crash, our room, Jo's blood. "You've been there. I haven't. Please just let me get some sleep here tonight. I'll come over tomorrow, I promise."

He pulled back and I felt his absence. I had missed him. My neck still registered the coarse skin of his hand, tough from his days outside.

"Do you have to work tomorrow?"

"I can call in," he said. "Trade off one of the weekend days."

The game wardens rotated through a seven-day workweek. Flexible hours, odd days off—I liked it when he was home during the day in the middle of the week. He'd grill steaks and I'd bake potatoes. Dinner for breakfast. We'd even have wine, find a movie on television. "You're just crazy enough for this to seem normal," he'd say. It thrilled me to be seen as crazy, exotic. Normal had been my curse in life. There were so many nice things I'd forgotten about life with Cal.

"I'll come to the house tomorrow," I said again. "I promise."

Part of me almost followed. Part of me knew that I should.

Ten or fifteen minutes after I'd gone in the house—after I'd gotten a soda from the kitchen and let the dog out the back door, after I'd settled on the couch with the TV—I heard Cal's truck start up. I wondered what he'd done all that time, sitting in the dark outside.

Did he drop his keys? Or did he just sit and look at the dark street and the small light in the window of the place where his wife had chosen to stay?

I had found the part of me that missed what Cal and I had. Way back, before all my plans with Joanne. I felt too tired and confused to think about what might happen, but held the feeling. I knew I would need it when I went to face the house again.

IT WAS STILL EARLY, the morning sun barely showing over the trees. Only minutes outside brought a film of moisture to my skin. July in Texas. Rigsby stayed at my heel as I walked down the sidewalk to Mr. Romeros' house. I'd called the hospital to check on Jo. The nurse told me about the beautiful flowers that Joanne's landlord had sent.

"They take up the whole room," the nurse said. "Wish my landlord was this nice."

Mr. Romeros lived down the street from Jo. He owned the duplex, plus a few other rental houses on the same block. He was always in and out, fixing the sink and the air conditioner. He was a widower and I suspected he had a bit of a crush on *Jo-ann-a.*

"Darla," he said. His accent made my name sound musical. *Dire-laa.* "I'm so sorry about *Joanna.*" Just barely my height, he wore khaki work pants and a plaid shirt, long-sleeved, even in the July heat.

He was a sweet man, Mr. Romeros. I wanted to talk with him, to ask him if he would give me some time to get Jo's things together. The flowers reminded me that I needed to let him know I'd been staying at Jo's, so he didn't think somebody had broken in.

"I have been sad ever since I heard what happened," he said.

He opened the door wider for me to come in, ushering Rigsby in behind me. He produced a dog treat from the kitchen, even though I didn't see any pets around his place.

"You want a coffee or maybe juice or something?" he asked.

"I'm fine, thank you."

"Well, sit down." He motioned toward an olive brown couch that faced the television. He sat to the side of me, in the recliner. Rigsby settled at my feet.

"Mr. Romeros," I said. "I've been at Joanne's the last couple of nights."

"I saw the lights," he said. "I called Evie to make sure everything was okay. Evie doesn't miss much."

We both smiled at the understatement.

"We don't know what's going to happen with Joanne, but it doesn't look very good for her." I didn't mention the baby, although I suspected Evie had filled him in on that too. "I was wondering if I could be in and out of there for a while. I want to look after Rigsby for the time being and Jo has so much stuff."

"It's true, then," he said. "She's not going to be getting better?"

I shook my head. "Probably not."

He closed his eyes for a moment, then crossed himself in a small gesture before giving me his attention once again.

"She is paid up for now," he said. "So you have time. Of course, if you need longer, that will be fine too. And I will return any rental money that is left if you close her contract early. Whatever you need to do. She paid me through August."

"August?" Jo was always talking about being behind on her rent, Mr. Romeros giving her an extra day or two for her paycheck to clear. "Why is she paid through next month already?"

"A note was in my box. It was the day of the accident that I found it. The note said that she would be gone, but she would let me know what she planned to do in the fall. She left a check with the note, a check for the rent while she was away."

He got up from the recliner, went to a desk just inside the kitchen door. He took the note from the drawer and brought it to me, nodded as he gave it to me, as if to say, "Look for yourself."

Joanne's high school scrawl hadn't changed; had never evolved into the adult script we cultivate for signing titles of ownership and cashier's checks.

Dear Mr. Romeros,

I need to go away for a while, so don't worry if the place looks empty. Here's a check to cover August and I'll be in touch about what I'm planning to do after that.

Thanks a bunch for everything.

Joanne

My hand looked disconnected, holding the paper. I read it twice, hoping to see something I'd missed, some explanation of what she meant. *I need to go away . . .*

"Probably the last thing she did before getting in the car," he said, standing over me, looking down at the words in my hand. "You keep. Okay? The last words from your friend."

He gave my shoulder a tentative pat with his hand, barely touching me in the awkwardness of the gesture. It seemed an unbearable kindness.

WHEN I GOT BACK to the duplex, before I reached the brick walkway, I saw the Timbros' truck coming up the street. The note Mr. Romeros had given me was in the pocket of my jeans, Jo's jeans. *I need to go away . . .* It was a riddle, but one that I would sort out on my own. I decided not to show it to them. It seemed private somehow and I couldn't bring myself to share that last little bit of her with her parents.

But it wasn't *them.* Mrs. Timbro was driving alone. I watched her slow down by the curb and stop the truck. Her small arm raised nearly above her head as she moved the gearshift into park. She looked like a kid, pretending to drive. I walked over to meet her.

"Hey, hon," she said, climbing down out of the seat. "I hate driving this thing. The Buick's in the shop today."

Rigsby walked over and sniffed at the leg of her pantsuit. Her knee-highs made her ankles a different color from the rest of her skin.

"You holdin' up okay?" she asked, taking my arm as we walked to the house.

"I guess," I said. She was acting too eager, too energetic. It frightened me a little. But then, she was always different when she was away from her husband, as if she had a whole personality that she had to create in his absence.

I hadn't bothered to lock up when I left for Mr. Romeros'. When I opened the front door, Mrs. Timbro stood at the threshold—even after I'd walked in. The place smelled like my morning coffee, the overripe smell of a pot that's been sitting too long on the warmer. But everything else in the house was Jo. Nothing of mine cluttered the essence of her daughter. She stood frozen in the doorway. An involuntary sound snagged in her throat, only partially finding air, and she began to cry.

"Mrs. Timbro," I said, walking to her, closing the door behind her.

"I'm sorry. I forgot you hadn't been in here since the accident. Come on. Sit down."

I led her through the room to the couch, guided her to sit, and when I moved away from her, she kept hold of my hand, squeezing it like a frightened child. I sat beside her to wait out the wave of grief that seized her. It was familiar to me by then; I was seconds away from it myself, all the time, but I knew it would pass.

"Do you want some water or something?" I asked when she had settled a little.

She nodded and I went and poured a glass. Jo had no ice trays in the freezer, only a bag of ice frozen into one solid block, so I'd taken to keeping a pitcher of water in the fridge.

"I'm sorry there's no ice," I said, handing her the glass, "but this is cold."

I sat while she took small sips. A Kleenex she'd taken from her pocketbook to wipe her cheeks had left tissue lint near her eyes. I brushed it away and she looked at me, smiled a little.

"That's so like Joanne," she said. "She was always fixing my face, my collar or something. She wanted me to take more pride in myself. She told me to stop letting the world bully me. What she really meant was Larry. She just didn't understand us. She never understood him."

I didn't know how to comfort Mrs. Timbro. Most of what I knew of her centered around her flaws, her weaknesses. They ran deep and had become almost endearing over time, but they crippled her now. I didn't have Jo's strength to offer.

"I miss her so much that sometimes I get lost in thinking about her. I forget to breathe," she said, staring at nothing across the room. "I wonder if I'd just die if I didn't think about taking a breath. I know that's silly, but it feels like everything is so hard."

"I know," I said. "I don't understand how I can be without her. I've never been without her."

She nodded, leaned into me, and put her hand up to the side of my face.

"I know." She repeated my words.

When she sat back, her eyes had cleared a little. She took in a deep breath, pulling her chin up high, and let it out slowly into the still air of the room.

"Darla, I have to talk to you. Larry wanted me to wait, but I didn't think it was right. He's not gonna be happy, but . . ." She let that thought go, focused again on what she had to say. "We've talked about what's going to happen. It's not easy any way you look at it."

"Please don't take her off life support yet, Mrs. Timbro. The baby's healthy and—"

"I know," she interrupted me. She put her hand on my arm. "I know, Darla. That's what I'm talking about. The baby."

"Is something wrong?"

"No. We saw an ultrasound late yesterday. The baby is growing. Everything looks good."

"Pictures?" I asked. I thought of seeing the baby's form, real arms and legs, curled and snuggled inside Jo's body.

"They're amazing," she said. "I've never seen anything like that before. Have they told you what she's having?"

"I don't want to know," I said. "Please don't tell me. I didn't want to know even before all this, but especially now. If anything should happen, I'd rather not . . ."

Then she was quiet again. Something, some suspended notion, hung in the air between us. She didn't come to tell me about the pictures. I tried to think of what there was to say. What was left for either of us to say?

"Given the circumstances, Darla . . ." she started. "It's been such a confusing time since the accident, but I know you and Cal are having some trouble. I haven't pried, you understand, it's just I couldn't help but see it."

"It's okay, Mrs. Timbro. I know it's been pretty obvious."

"Well, honey. I know what your plans were, but you're not in any position right now to take on a child."

She spoke quickly, but her words formed a slow, articulated echo in my head. I didn't say anything, couldn't think of a single word that would make sense.

"You've got so many things you need to be working out and Larry and I, well, honey, we think it would be best if we took the child to raise."

If we took the child . . . took the child . . . My heart started racing. Fear, outrage, and panic took rapid turns in my head. No . . . no . . . no . . . ! I was thinking it, saying it too, I guess. She put her hand on my arm again and I slapped it away, grazing her shoulder so that she flinched. She looked at me, her eyes wide. She'd lived with rages through her married life. She'd learned resilience, how to ride them out.

"Joanne was having that baby for *me*! She went through everything so that I could have a child of my own."

"Things have changed, Darla. The accident changed everything. We've spoken with the hospital. As her closest blood relatives—"

"You won't take the baby away from me. You don't know how hard I'll fight you on this, Arlene." I'd never used her first name before, but I needed to meet her on equal ground.

"You just need some time to think this through," she said. "I know this is a lot to take in."

Her hand was on the coffee table, light fingers steadying her. She wouldn't hold up. But he would, and she wouldn't go against him this time. Not like before. She wanted this too. I should have seen it coming. I felt stupid to have missed it, to let myself get caught unaware, vulnerable. What did I have? What did I have to fight with? The answer made me even more uncertain of my chances.

"Cal's the father," I said, trying to steady my voice. "Joanne was having the baby for *us*."

"Honey," she said, "Cal doesn't know what he wants. You know that. And you haven't been home with him since this whole thing started. How can you say you plan to make a home for a baby with him? He thinks we might be right in taking responsibility. In some ways it would be a relief."

"You've talked to Cal about this?" My breath went shallow. I worked to take air full into my lungs. I couldn't lose my edge.

"Larry spoke with him last night."

"You stay away from my husband. Both of you. And please leave here now."

I had to get to Cal. I had to talk to him before he did something I couldn't make right. Joanne would never let Larry Timbro raise that baby. She couldn't fight him now. But I could.

"Darla. I know you're upset—"

"You don't know what I am. I mean it. I need for you to leave."

I sat on the couch and watched her get up and walk to the door. She turned once as if she might say something else, even opened her mouth, but then changed her mind and let herself out the door. Within seconds, my body gave in to the trembling I'd fought to control. But it was okay. No one but Rigsby could see how destroyed I felt by the moment. And it wouldn't last. I'd pull myself together and talk to Cal. I had to focus on the next step. I had to talk to Cal.

THE SIDE OF THE HOUSE where Joanne crashed through had been covered. It looked wounded, held together by makeshift bandages and good intentions.

Cal was standing outside, hosing down his truck when I drove up. The mud-crusted wheels sent rivers of brown water streaming down our driveway. I felt like a visitor, thinking I should have called before coming over.

"Hey!" he said as he headed behind the house to turn off the water. He looked genuinely glad to see me. "I'll be right back."

I got out of my car and waited for him to reappear. I was relieved to see him outside, it kept me from deciding whether I should just walk in the house or ring the bell first: a strange dilemma I'd thought about on the way over.

"They need to pave that damn river frontage road," he said as he came back around the house. "I come home with more mud than rubber on those tires."

I couldn't work my way through small talk. Mrs. Timbro's words kept playing in my head.

"Can we go inside?" I asked.

"Sure. What's happened?" He looked bewildered. Why wouldn't he? I was on a different page from where we'd left off the night before.

"I'm sorry, Cal. I'm all mixed up right now."

"Let's go in and sit down."

Walking into my house felt like going to a funeral. All the memories from before the accident had become subordinate to the horror of that day. We went in at the kitchen door and the bright yellow walls, once so cheerful in my mind, almost made me queasy. Cal's dishes sat piled in the sink. Newspapers, a couple of days' worth from the looks

of it, lay scattered on the table. I fished through my pocketbook and
got out a cigarette.

"Darla," he said, pushing aside the newspaper and pulling a chair
back for me. "Sit down. For God's sake, you look like you're falling apart."

"I feel like I'm already there."

I sat down and he pulled a chair close to me, sat where his elbow
touched mine as we leaned on the table. A long drag on my menthol
gave me space to think.

"Arlene Timbro came to Jo's today. She said they want the baby. I
know they've talked to you."

He let out a sigh. He was relieved I'd said it, that he didn't have to
tell me.

"Don't let them do that, Cal. Please don't let them do that."

I looked at him, at his eyes. I usually knew where I stood in our
relationship, held a firm stance that left me my pride. I'd lost all that
in one pleading phrase. I didn't care. He had to know how much I
wanted him to stand behind me on this one.

"Cal, I know we've got problems, but we can work to sort things
out. Don't let them take the baby. Jo grew up in that house and she
wouldn't allow any baby of hers to go through that. You don't know all
that she went through."

He wasn't looking at me. I put my hand on his arm, leaned in so
that my cheek touched his shirt. His clothes felt damp, water from the
hose and sweat mixed into the soft laundered cotton of his T-shirt.

"Cal, please. You really don't know how it was for her. We can't let
another kid go through that."

He put his hand on mine where I still touched his arm.

"Darla, I love you. I've loved you almost from the start. You know
that. But I don't know if I can be a father to this baby. I don't know if
we can build a life around this kind of mistake. We'd be reminded of
it every single day."

How could he see it that way? How could he see a baby as something wrong?

"I need to get back to *you*," he said, squeezing my hand to em-
phasize his words. "We need to get back to *us*. Back to stupid notes
pinned to my boxers and you bringing chili dogs to me at work. Re-

member how we were? I want that. We haven't been that way since all of this started. Since I . . ."

"Slept with Jo."

He looked away from me. He still couldn't think about her and look at me.

"The baby would remind me over and over what an awful person I am," he said. "You may be able to forgive what I did, Darla, or at least forget it so you can have the baby here. But I grew up with a father who screwed around on his wife—*all the time.*"

He took the cigarette from my fingers, pulled the smoke deep into his chest.

"I've always known one thing," he said. "That I'm *not* my father. Then look at me with Jo. I turned into the same fucking bastard who raised me. The baby's part of that. Don't you see?"

What could I say? There had to be words, the right words to show him how different this was from his father's life; how wrong it was to let go of our family. The baby was part of our family.

"You're not your father. I promise you, Cal. You're kind and wonderful in ways he never could have been. And I'm not your mother. She loved being a victim. You know that. In some ways, they were perfect for each other. I put you in a terrible position. You've been so good about my problems with the endometriosis over the years. So gentle when I had pain and understanding when I didn't feel like making love. That hasn't been easy. Your dad wouldn't have lived with any of that for a minute. Not faithfully anyway."

"That doesn't excuse anything," he said.

"I know, but your feelings for Jo . . . They're not your fault, Cal. They're not the baby's fault either. Don't throw it all together. The baby's a person, a person who needs us. And I need you."

As I said it, I knew it was true. Our marriage, at least over the last year, hadn't always been what I'd imagined it would be, but it was good. He was good. And a baby was what I'd always needed to make it complete, to take us from being a *couple* to becoming a *family.*

"Cal, give us a chance. Please. At least don't make any decisions now that we can't fix later."

He kept his face down and his hair fell across the side of his cheek. I couldn't see his eyes. I put my hand on his shoulder, rubbed across his back. He smelled like rain.

"I wanted the baby to make us stronger, more solid even," he said. "I knew over time it would get worse and worse for you, without a child. But what we've done . . . This isn't the way, Darla."

"We've gone beyond the point where that matters," I told him. "The baby is here now, right or wrong. It doesn't deserve to grow up in that house. Regardless of what *I* need. We've got to consider what the baby needs."

"You couldn't forgive me if I let this baby go. Am I right about that?"

I didn't answer. But we both knew.

"Do you still have feelings for that guy, that preacher?"

That question, out of the blue, almost made me laugh.

"He's a priest. And I have old feelings, good memories, that are exactly where they should be, in the past. He's a good person, but he's not part of my heart anymore."

I didn't think about what I said for too long. I didn't want to really know if it was true or not. It's what ought to be true, the only thing that could be true in the world that we wanted.

Cal sat back, nodded a little. He didn't want to know any more than that either. It was our one solid agreement of the afternoon.

"I don't know if I can do this," he said. "I'm telling you that up front. It's a fight we might lose anyway."

"I know. I'm just asking you to try."

"And I've already signed something saying that I won't contest their custody."

This hit me like concrete. He said it so casually.

"My God! Cal, no!"

He turned to me. His shoulders hung loose and defeated. I realized that I, more than anyone, had beaten him down, worn him out so that he looked only half alive.

"I can fix it, I think," he said. "It's only been a day. I can change it if we move right away. It's gonna be okay."

He put his arms around me, and I put my head on his shoulder like a little girl. I held him, held on. Truth was, I hung on for my very life.

TWELVE

---◆---

"I WANT TO SEE a real college classroom," Jo said, flipping through albums.

We were in a used record shop on Sixth Street.

"Why? There aren't any classes on Saturdays. It'll just be a bunch of empty rooms."

She shrugged her shoulders, didn't even look up from the records. The smell of dusty album covers had a thickness to it, a film of sorts that felt as if it would stay on my skin long after we left.

"It's no big deal," she said, walking to the counter with a copy of Jethro Tull's *Thick as a Brick*. The jacket looked shiny, nearly new.

This idea of a field trip to a "real" classroom, it meant something to her. I didn't know what was on her mind, but it wasn't worth trying to sort out. I figured I'd take her to the room where I had English Lit. We'd pass the building on the way back to my dorm anyway.

Outside on Sixth Street, cold wind blew leaves across the sidewalk. We cut a diagonal across the road and walked back to campus. The side door where I usually went in to get to English was locked, so we went down some cement stairs to a basement entrance and found it propped open with a doorstop. I took Jo up the three flights of stairs to my classroom.

"There aren't any books or anything," she said, puzzled.

"Different classes meet here. We bring our books, everything we need."

Jo looked around the room; a desk and chair for the instructor, rows of desks where students sat. The blackboard still had study notes on eighteenth-century French literature.

"That from your class?" She nodded toward the board.

"God, no," I told her.

"Who teaches here?"

"He's a grad student. Those guys teach a lot of the freshman courses."

My instructor was Arnie—Mr. Gladstone on the first day, Arnie after that. He didn't have more than five or six years on us.

"Is it hard?" she asked me. She stood to the side looking at the desks, not coming fully into the room.

I took off my coat and sat down at my regular desk.

"Not really. Not English anyway. We're studying *Beowulf*."

"But we already had that last year," she said.

I could hear Mrs. Minelli's scratchy cigarette voice butchering the cadence of old-English phrases.

"Yeah, but that took a couple of days. We're spending half the semester on it."

"It's a poem, for God's sake. How can it take up half a semester?"

"I don't know. He's made it pretty interesting so far."

"What's your hardest course?" she asked. She listened while she walked around, threaded her way through the desks, putting her hand on each one.

"Calculus," I said. "I'm not sure I'm even passing. What's up with you? You want to go to college now?"

"No," she said, coming around beside me. She laid the thin paper bag holding her album on a desk next to mine and sat down. "I just try to picture you in my mind sometimes. With most of the other places you've been, the stuff you've done, I've been there too. Now I'll be sitting in the office, typing, and I'll think about you, and there's a blank spot because I don't know what all this is like. What does your teacher look like?"

"Like somebody who just thumbed a ride here from Woodstock."

Joanne's face broke into a grin.

"No shit?"

"Seriously," I said. "Almost all the grad-student teachers are like that."

"Has he hit on you yet?"

She already knew. I could tell by the tone of her voice.

"Yeah," I told her. "A little. But I don't want to go out with him."

"Why?"

"I don't know. Something about him isn't right. He laughs too long at his own jokes. It bugs me."

She just nodded.

I stretched my arms out over the top of the desk. The Formica felt cool against my skin. Footsteps, distant and shallow, faded down one of the halls near us. I wanted Joanne to see the room full and the halls crowded. Not because it was better that way. I just wanted her picture to be real.

"It feels like a dream sometimes," I said. "Being here."

Joanne looked over at me, but she didn't say anything.

"Not like a good dream, a dream come true or anything. But like the real me is asleep somewhere and this is some picture in my mind that I'm moving through. I don't know anybody here yet, not really."

I'd been waiting one full semester to feel settled, to feel as if my mind had finally caught up with a body that was going through the motions of living. But it hadn't happened.

"When I got here yesterday," Joanne interrupted my thoughts, "when you were introducing me to all those girls on your hall, you seemed a little strange. Are you friends with any of those people?"

"Some of them are nice."

"That's not what I asked you."

"It's like I don't have the patience to start all over with friendship, answer all the stupid questions, tell all the stories."

The day before, I'd watched out the window until Joanne drove into the dorm parking lot. She'd called from the gas station two blocks away, lost and wanting directions. I saw her get out of the car. She stopped and looked around before she came to the door and I followed her eyes, tried to see what she was seeing. The campus filled in with color and dimension before my eyes. It startled me, frightened me a little, how I saw it for the first time when she did. I wondered if some part of me was missing, unplugged. Some part that worked only when she was around.

"I've missed you a lot at home," she said, like she'd heard my thoughts. Her voice stayed quiet, sounded small inside the empty room. She didn't look at me.

I waited, but she didn't go on.

"What's wrong?"

Her eyes had a sad, helpless look.

"Jo? What is it?"

"Nothing," she said. In an instant, she seemed okay again. But I knew she wasn't. Underneath the forced calm, there was something.

"Like I said, I missed you." Her voice had gone flat, monotonous, as if she was reciting a mantra.

"Joanne? What's up with you?"

"I'm fine," she said. She stood up. She was done. I wouldn't find out what was bothering her anytime soon, if at all.

She looked around, ready to leave, the snapshot of my place in the classroom certain in her mind.

BACK IN MY ROOM, we napped for most of the afternoon. My roommate was visiting her boyfriend in San Antonio for the weekend, so we had all the space to ourselves. Noise from the steam heater, the hissing and clanging, rattled the scenes in my dozing mind, and when I woke up, Jo was standing at the window in her T-shirt and panties. The thin winter light fell on her hair and I had to strain to see the colors of copper and rust that announced themselves boldly on brighter days.

"What time is it?" I asked.

"It's three o'clock. I'm starving already," she said.

"Well, Peggy's supposed to pick us up at six to go to dinner. I've got some Fritos in that cabinet under the hot plate."

She reached under, pulled out the bag, ate them slowly while she stared out the window.

"Where's Peggy taking us?" she asked.

"Some Mexican place. She gave the owner legal advice about getting a green card for one of his cousins. She said she eats there free now. They won't take her money."

"How the hell does she know about legal stuff yet? She just started this fall."

"Peggy was born knowing everything. Her childhood was a modified college curriculum. You ought to meet my aunt and uncle. Scrabble's like an Olympic event at their house."

"I'll pass," she said.

Somebody knocked on the door. I looked at Joanne, all panties and leg from the waist down.

"Hold on," I said.

"It's okay." She shrugged her shoulders, didn't move to cover herself.

When I opened the door I saw Francine from down the hall, her jagged shag haircut hung loose around the small, catlike features of her face. She had on a Led Zepplin T-shirt with patched-up jeans.

"You wanna get high?" she asked me before she saw Joanne. "Diane's got some shit her brother gave her."

Joanne came over beside me and Francine shifted back a little, surprised by someone in earshot, I guessed.

"Sorry," Francine said. "I didn't know you had company."

Her pronunciation of *company* took on more emphasis than it should have and I got tickled. Jo looked at me like I'd lost all good sense.

"Joanne's my best friend from home. She's here for the weekend. Are you gonna be in Diane's room?"

"Yeah," she said, still eyeing Jo. "Ya'll come down if you want."

"What's up with her?" Jo asked when I'd closed the door.

"She's like the head lesbian on campus. Does all the marches and rallies and shit. She thinks we're all just kidding ourselves about liking guys. You want to go smoke with them?"

"Shit no," she said, sitting down on the bed and looking tired again. "She kind of freaked me out, you know, with that Grace Slick thing goin'."

"She's pretty nice, actually. Really smart. She's helped me with math a couple of times."

"Yeah? Well, I should pass anyway. Besides, smoking's been all there is at home—except work. Gets kinda old, you know?"

"I'll trade places," I said, only half joking.

"Oh shut the hell up." She sounded seriously irritated. It took me by surprise. "You're lucky here, you know. You've still got something ahead of you. I'm flat out of choices. I've dated everybody who's even remotely attractive, or at least slept with them if they were too boring to actually talk to. I've smoked enough pot to light a bonfire. And now—"

She cut her sentence short. I was getting angry, all the talking in half sentences and riddles.

"Now what!" I snapped at her.

"Nothing." She sounded timid, so unlike herself.

"You're acting really weird," I told her.

She shrugged her shoulders, looked out the window at the gray afternoon.

I decided to let it slide. She'd tell me eventually what was bothering her, or else it would just go away. You never knew with Joanne.

"What's going on with Lindy and Conner. They're still around, right?" I asked.

She hesitated again. "Why'd you ask about them?"

"What is wrong with you? I'm just making conversation here. Are you still hanging out with them?"

Conner and Lindy were a couple of the other wild creatures in high school. I'd been vaguely jealous of Joanne's camaraderie with them, never feeling like I fit in when they were around.

"Not really," she said.

She looked conflicted. Maybe she thought I'd be jealous if she said she was spending her time with them.

"They're getting into some weird shit with needles that gets you really fucked up—and broke," she said.

"Have you *done* that stuff?" I asked. I wasn't sure I wanted to know.

She shrugged. "A couple of times." She wouldn't look at me.

"Shit, Joanne!"

"I know!" She turned to me, her eyes glaring hard at my judgment.

"Just shut up. I know. That's the last thing I need. I figured that part out. I don't hang out with them anymore."

"Okay," I said. "I'm sorry."

"No, no. You're right. That stuff's fucked up. Trouble is, now I spend most of my time arguing with Larry, 'cause there's nothing else to do."

She'd taken to calling her father by his first name, like he was a hateful teacher or an overbearing boss. I didn't want to talk about him. Mentioning Larry was like pushing Joanne's crazy button just to see the spectacle that followed, but I didn't see any way out.

"He's not any better now that you're working?"

She made a huffing noise, shook her head. She was still waiting for me to ask.

"What'd he do?" I finally obliged. It was like the big hill on the roller coaster. The ride wasn't done until you'd gone over it.

"He made me put him on my checking account. On *my* own god-damn checking account, where I put *my* paycheck."

"Why?"

"Just to piss me off, best I can tell. He came up with it after I stayed out all night a couple of times."

"What's that got to do with your paycheck?"

"My roof, my rules, that whole crock. It's just another way to keep tabs on me." She shook her head. "Touching, all the parental concern, isn't it?"

Her mouth was set in a hard line, but her eyes gave her away. After all this time, he could still hurt her. I thought she'd outgrow it, but she hadn't yet.

"Why didn't you tell him where to get off?"

"I can't afford my own place yet. I had to buy new clothes and everything to go to work in and I've got to get myself a car so I'm not using Mom's every day. There's some other stuff going on too."

She stopped, waited for me to ask, I guessed, but I was getting tired of the Larry game.

"Anyway, he's got me stuck for a while," she said when I didn't bite.

She sat down on the bed, leaned back on her elbows.

"It's weird," she said. "While I was in school, I felt like it was my house too. Now, all of a sudden, I feel like he's letting me live in *his* house."

"What does your mom say?"

"She says, 'You're not eating enough, honey.' She never talks about him. It's like if we don't mention what a bastard he is, maybe he will wake up nice one morning and it'll all be over. We're a real Hallmark family, don't you think?"

She looked exhausted and I knew she was done, had gone through the weightless free fall she needed to get back to her real self, to crawl back into her own skin. I tried to imagine hating my father. The very idea was like trying to speak Chinese or fly an airplane. It was so far outside anything I could understand.

"I'm sorry, Jo." I didn't know what else to say.

"Hell," she said, with forced resolve. "We've seen worse. Right?"

She picked up her pants off the floor and put them on, then pulled her hair back in a thick ponytail.

"We've got some time before Peggy comes. We might as well go down the hall to your friend's room. What the hell. Maybe I'll come on to the lesbian. It'll be something different."

I knew Joanne too well to rule out the possibility, but without her father around to provoke, I doubted if she had the incentive to go through with it.

She threw her brush down on the bed and went across the hall to the bathroom. My room seemed instantly hollow in her absence. It still surprised me how thoroughly she filled any space. I stood in front of the mirror and brushed my hair, felt the bristles move through tangled strands. Working with small sections, bit by bit, I brushed until it all felt smooth again.

PEGGY DROVE her mom's old station wagon, a land-boat of a car that doubled as a guest bedroom in the summer when too many people needed to crash at her place for the night.

She parked in the dirt lot in back of the restaurant, pulling up beside the "Employees Only" sign.

I was still buzzing slightly from the visit to Diane's room. After one joint, Jo had slipped into her party persona and was presiding over my hallmates as if she'd known them all her life. With her hands behind her back, she flipped a lit joint through one full rotation inside her mouth without burning her tongue. She told them about the time we stole a cheerleader's uniform out of Macy Lynn's car and dressed up one of the goats in the Ag barn. By association alone, I had actually acquired something of a personality by the time we left—and I hadn't spoken more than five words.

"Hello, my friend Peggy!" A small man, older than my father, greeted us at the door of the restaurant. His deep, Latin voice, thick with movie star cadence, seemed at odds with his small stature. "And you have nice friends with you."

"This is my cousin Darla and her friend Jo."

"Lovely," he said, and he led us to a large booth near the back of the room.

The slick vinyl felt warm, as if just vacated moments before. The spicy smell of refried beans and mole sauce that traveled from the next table over made me aware of the yawning hunger in my stomach.

"You two looked pretty messed up," Peggy said.

"Yeah," Joanne told her. "Darla's lesbo friend turned us on to some good stuff."

I saw Peggy grinning at me and I started laughing, as much from the pot as the humor.

"What?" Joanne asked, sounding defensive. "The friend? I'm just kidding. You were right, Darla. She's nice."

I looked at Peggy. Nodded for her to speak up.

"Some of us are," Peggy said, a small smile playing at the corners of her mouth.

Joanne sat for a second, her eyes glazed and squinting. She looked as if she might be translating a foreign phrase in her head.

"You?" she said to Peggy. "You're a . . . a . . . ?"

"A *lesbo*," Peggy said.

I felt myself giggling.

"Shit!" Jo was grinning now. "I'll be damned. Shit, I'm sorry, Peggy."

Jo was actually embarrassed. I hadn't seen her that way more than once or twice in my life.

"It's okay," Peggy kept saying, until finally the subject was dropped altogether.

Food and beer arrived in massive quantities before we even placed an order. Homemade tortillas and chile relleno, chicken with mole sauce and tamales with sauces of every color. With the exception of Christmas dinner, food hadn't tasted so good in months and I felt the relief of belonging in the place where I actually was. That was a natural state for Peggy and I envied her. The consistency of her satisfaction baffled me.

"Do you really like law school that much?" I asked her after the plates had been cleared for the arrival of flan.

"I *love* law school," she said, lighting a cigarette and waving away the custard dessert. "There's a place inside the law to do everything that needs to be done."

Jo sat back and listened. Her eyes were fixed on Peggy.

"There is always an answer," Peggy went on. "You just have to find it. It's like a perfect riddle that seems impossible. Then there's that moment when it becomes so logical, that moment when you know the solution. And it's not like the answer to some abstract science formula. It's an answer that you can take to the street. You can change a life with one answer."

Soft sounds of a Spanish guitar came from speakers hidden in the pageant of color that decorated the room. Mr. Martinez came back to our table. He asked us if there was anything else he could get for us.

"We're fine," Peggy said.

Some answer that Peggy had found in her law books had changed his life, the life of his cousin. His happiness, his gratitude seemed like something tangible that hovered near him.

"You're sure? Anything at all?" he asked again.

"No, but thank you," Peggy said, again. "This has been perfect." I closed my eyes and held the moment, memorized it so I could retrieve it later, when I would find myself once again breathing air that seemed strange, alien to all I knew.

THIRTEEN

"L ISTEN," PEGGY SAID. "We've filed the papers saying that Cal changed his mind about contesting their actions. That's the first step and that's the only thing that has to be done right away. Try to relax. Nothing is going to happen fast. The baby's not even born yet."

I'd called Peggy in a panic the night before. She left work early in the afternoon, drove to Alliance so that we could get Cal's new papers filed.

"Who's in charge of the baby now?" I asked.

"He or she is a ward of the state and both sides are petitioning for custody. Legally, they have the upper hand at the moment as Jo's next of kin. And any decision in your favor would be pending a paternity test after the baby's born. No problem there, right?"

Peggy stopped and looked at me. It wasn't a rhetorical question. With Joanne you couldn't take anything for granted and Peggy the lawyer was a lot different from Peggy the friend. I didn't mind. Lawyer Peggy was the one I needed.

"Joanne wasn't with anybody else, not since we started this. She wanted everything to be right. I promise."

Cal nodded. "We were all clear on that," he said.

"Good," Peggy said, draining the last of her beer from an amber-colored iced tea glass. "Did Joanne ever give you anything in writing? Even a note or something that might refer to your agreement?"

I shook my head.

"Okay. You'll be arguing on the basis of an oral agreement, then. We'll get people who knew about your plans, heard Joanne talk about them, to testify for us. But the next thing I have to do is to hook you up with my friend Janet. She does domestic cases, knows worlds more about custody disputes than I ever will. I'll call her tonight when I get back to Austin."

We sat in my living room, the three of us. I pulled hard on my Salem Light, taking menthol deep into my chest, then reached down to scratch Rigsby, who was nuzzling at my leg. He wasn't used to my house yet, stuck to me like gum everywhere I walked. But he liked Peggy. All animals liked Peggy. He nosed her for attention after I pulled my hand away.

"You both need to settle down," she said. "This'll all be okay."

Outside the construction workers were finishing up for the day, repairing the side of the house where Joanne had crashed. I heard their metal ladders rattling as they closed them up and loaded them onto the truck.

"I don't know about another lawyer," I told her. "I trust you, Peg."

Cal sat on the couch, hunched forward with his elbows on his knees.

"She's right," he said. "Plus, we may have to pay bit by bit. I don't know if somebody else will work with us on that."

"Janet's group works with low-income clients. Anything you pay them will be more than they get most of the time. They count on state funding more than earned income. Plus, she's a good friend of mine and she's one hell of a lawyer. You don't want me feeling my way along on this. I do environmental law. You got a toxic dump in your backyard, call me and I'm all over it. A custody case? You want Janet. I'd just be going to her for advice anyway."

"Will you stick around?" I asked. I felt shaky, a jumble of nerves. "Just until we get to know her?"

"Honey, I'll be here start to finish. You know that."

Peggy moved from her chair to sit beside me on the couch. She combed strands of hair away from my face with her fingers, laid her flat hand on my cheek.

"Look at me, Darla," she said. "You're gonna watch this baby grow up. You're gonna come running when it calls for 'Mommy.' You got that?"

I nodded.

"I'm not just doing this for you two. I'm doing it for that baby and for Jo. I know what she went through with her dad. We won't let a baby start that cycle all over again."

I could feel Cal behind me. I wondered if he understood why it was so important to keep the baby away from Larry Timbro. Peggy had seen it up close, how awful the man could be. So had I. But Cal had only heard it from us. How could he know? How could I make him know?

Peggy looked so calm, her face open and sure. I could breathe when she looked at me like that, said it was all going to work out okay. Peggy could make things right. She'd spent her whole life making things right.

"I'm not perfect," I said. "*We're* not perfect and neither is our marriage right now. That's not a big secret."

I looked at Cal. He put his hand on top of mine in a gesture of solidarity. I felt suddenly grateful, hopeful even.

"They'll bring all that up," I said.

"That's why you need Janet," Peggy said, sitting back against the arm of the couch. She gestured for my cigarette, took a drag, and gave it back. "We're going to hell and back and I want her driving, 'cause, honey, she knows the roads better than I do. Okay?"

"Okay." Cal and I spoke together. It sounded like vows, sworn and repeated.

Outside, the workmen drove away. Rigsby's ears perked up as they turned around in the driveway. I wondered if the house would ever look the same as before, if new paint could cover all the damage and make it right again.

THE TRUCK DROVE UP as I was getting out of the shower.

I'd wanted to take a bath, but the only bathtub in the house was off of our bedroom and the dust from the construction still covered everything on that side of the house. I had to use the shower in the hall bathroom.

When I heard the deep sound of the pickup, I thought the painters must have come back for something. Then I heard voices outside the bathroom window, Cal's voice and someone else familiar: Mr. Timbro. I felt naked at the sound of them, and put a towel around myself even though I was standing alone.

"Listen, Cal," Mr. Timbro started. "We wanted to come out and talk with you about what you did today. Our lawyer called, said he got a notice that you'd changed your mind. I know it's damn confusing, but you had it right the first time, son."

"Larry," Cal said. "I know you mean well, but I'm working things out with my wife right now."

I'd never heard him call Mr. Timbro Larry before. I wondered if he was trying to relate man to man, or if he wanted to show some sign of friendship, familiarity. Did he still agree with the Timbros? Did he just want to appease me? I had to stop being suspicious. I couldn't go through this peeking into every dark corner for hidden motives.

"I know women," Mr. Timbro said. "Especially the pretty ones. They'll scramble your brain right quick."

He chuckled as if he'd just given the punch line to a familiar joke. I looked between the slats of the blinds. The door on the driver's side of the truck stood open. Mrs. Timbro sat in the truck with her door closed. As usual, she let her husband talk for her. She sat with her head turned the other way. Rigsby was nosing around the front tires, but he stayed clear of the men.

"You gotta consider what all this means, Cal. You're taking on responsibility for that child. I'm not proud to say it, but you don't know for certain it's even your flesh and blood. One thing I know for damn sure is that it's my flesh and blood. Let me and Arlene do the right thing here. Give that baby a stable home."

"I agreed to the responsibility for the baby when Joanne got pregnant," Cal said, ignoring the remark about paternity. "It's what Darla and I wanted. A family. It's what Joanne wanted for us."

Mr. Timbro still had his good ol' boy face on. He hadn't given up on the two of them coming to terms over the issue like men ought to.

"You know as well as I do that them two girls cooked up this scheme and I don't blame you for gettin' caught up in it. Goin' along. But it's gone wrong now. My girl's never gonna wake up. There's a baby to think of, son, and you're in over your head. Hell, you're not even sure whether you got a marriage left or not. We're tore up over this, Cal. Plumb tore up. We gotta have a settled place for that baby by the time it gets here."

"That's what we're working on, Larry."

Cal stood in the T-shirt and jeans he'd changed into after work. His hands were on his hips in that mock-adult stance that teenagers adopt to look tough. He was trying. He was trying so very hard to stand up to Larry Timbro. Mrs. Timbro hadn't moved to get out of the truck. Her head was still turned away from her husband, from Cal.

"Listen, Cal, we talked about this. Mrs. Timbro and I are at a settled point in life. We got a good business, everything to offer a baby."

With the towel still around me I opened the shutters and raised the window to the screens. Cal looked my way.

"A baby doesn't need the strap end of a belt, Mr. Timbro," I said. My arms were shaking and I fought to keep the sound of my voice steady. Larry Timbro squinted to see me at the window, but his eyes just caught my general direction. I could tell he was surprised that I was at the house. I must have been a dark shadow from where he stood in the late sun.

"That baby doesn't need your rules and your disapproval," I went on, emboldened by my cover. "You weren't good at it the first time. You don't get another chance. Not with *my* baby."

"So she's back now," he said to Cal, not even addressing me directly. He shook his head, gave up looking for me, and stared at the ground.

"We've got a lawyer, Mr. Timbro," I said. "Go away. I don't want you in my driveway."

Cal turned in my direction, gave me something of a pleading look.

Maybe he was telling me that I was overstepping. Maybe he just wanted to handle it himself.

"You don't know what you're in for, Darla," Mr. Timbro spoke up.

His voice was controlled, but a chilling edge in his tone made me pull the towel tighter around me, even when I was sure he couldn't see where I stood.

"That child has Joanne's blood," he said. "Think about that."

"With all due respect, Larry," Cal spoke quietly, so quietly I almost couldn't make out his words, "from what I've been hearing, that's all the more reason for us to give it a shot, not you."

He stared hard at Cal, eyes that implied a cross between hate and disgust. We'd played on his last raw nerve. I felt the warm breeze from the window push against the cold air-conditioning of the room where I stood. My damp skin, sensitive to the contrast, felt the dueling swirl around me—separate currents, not mixing to a comfortable medium.

"You don't know what it's like," Mr. Timbro said, addressing Cal again. "You can't imagine raising a child like Joanne."

"I think it's best for you to leave," Cal said. He still looked like a boy, a small boy standing toe-to-toe with the playground bully.

"Think of how this baby came to be. Are you proud of that? Is that the way responsible parents live? Tell me, Cal, are you proud of your whole life?" Larry Timbro asked him. "Is your wife?" His tone made my skin prickle. " 'Cause when these lawyers get involved, it gets ugly. Is that what you want? It's not what I want, but I'll be damned if I'll walk away from it."

"Come on, Larry." Arlene Timbro had rolled down her window enough to speak to her husband. "It's time for us to go."

He turned and walked back around to the driver's side. His door still stood open, waiting for him to return. He got in and closed it and the hard sound made me startle. I listened as the truck shifted gears, whined a little with the effort of getting up the ridge that led to the highway. They drove away, over the blacktop. Rigsby, who had wandered over to explore the far side of the yard, stopped to watch the truck ride away.

Cal didn't move to come in the house. He stood, his hands still on his hips, his chest moving large as he methodically pulled the hot air into his lungs, then let it out again. Then I watched him, shaky legs taking him to the edge of the yard, where he bent over, hands flat on his knees for support. He vomited into the tall weeds and when I realized what was happening I turned away to offer him the privacy I would have wanted. Sitting on the top of the toilet seat I could hear him. We'd barely started the fight for our baby and it was already too much.

When I couldn't hear him anymore, I put my clothes on and walked outside. He was standing near his truck, looking at the land behind our house. A brilliant slice of orange sun broke between two clouds low on the horizon,

"It's pretty, huh?" Cal said, reaching back for me but not taking his eyes off the light. "The colors are almost more than you can stand to look at, you know?"

I slipped under his arm and leaned into him, looked where he looked and tried to think of what I should say. He was too gentle for the world I'd thrown him into. The best things about him were the hardest to watch when he was hurting.

"We're just feeling our way, Darla. I know that. I'll try. I promise you, I'll try."

"I know," I said.

I tried to think of what would ease him. What, in my limited power, could help. I reached under his T-shirt, rubbed the soft skin, the tiny hairs just above the waist of his jeans. I kissed his neck.

"Darla," he said, his voice throaty and coarse.

The piece of the sun slipped behind the lowest cloud; but the warm light, softened by the cloud's hazy mask, fell around us, changing the color of the day. I took his hand, motioned with my head back toward the house. He smiled. We walked together, leaving thoughts of Larry Timbro to another day.

I WOKE UP hours after I'd gone to sleep. Cal and I were on the pullout in the living room, but when I first woke with Rigsby curled at my feet, I thought I was still at Jo's. I squinted through the dark to find her dresser, the window in her room. Then I heard Cal breathing and remembered. I'd come home.

Cal mumbled, but didn't wake. I felt a panic, an urgency to be at the hospital, to check on Joanne. I needed to feel her breathing, keeping the baby alive. I'd left her to go with Sean two days before and since then had been tumbled and thrown into events I never imagined. I looked at Cal, wondered for a moment if I should wake him, but he'd been so tired, I didn't want to disturb his sleep. I wrote him a note and left as quietly as I could.

THE ROADS WERE EMPTY at two A.M. and I made good time, but when I drove into the hospital parking lot I realized the doors would be locked, so I circled around, trying to think of a story the security guard would buy. People knew me. I couldn't say I was a relative. Even so, they'd want to know what was urgent in the middle of the night. I didn't know the answer to that, although the feeling was very real.

Around back, two orderlies, brown-skinned men in their twenties, stood outside the emergency room entrance smoking. Farther back, a custodian carried bags of trash to the Dumpster, then turned to go back in a door at the top of a delivery ramp. A doorstop propped the door open as he went back in. He left it there, probably to get more trash.

I parked at the far end of the Emergency lot. The orderlies barely looked up as I slipped out of the car and walked to the delivery entrance.

Inside the basement hall, I could hear the custodian moving plastic bags, but he was far enough away that I didn't have to hurry. I found the elevator and pushed the button to go up.

THE ICU WAS BUSY. For people who work with sickness, night hours are as hectic as the afternoon. I slipped into Joanne's curtained cubicle without raising a second glance from anyone.

Jo looked smaller than I ever remembered seeing her. But her belly had grown, at least I believed it had. Except for the bandages and the tube taking air in and out of her lungs, her face looked peaceful. I tried to imagine the foul litanies that ought to be coming out of her mouth. The cracks to the nurses and pleas for me to sneak in some cigarettes.

"I miss you," I whispered, lying down and settling in on the bed beside her. "I know I'm supposed to always bail your ass out of trouble, but I can't fix it this time, Jo. I'm sorry. I'm looking after the baby though. I am doing that much."

The tears felt good, as if pressure pushing against me had suddenly eased. The blanket grew damp under my face and I rubbed against it, let the rough fibers keep me in the present tense. I was with her and she was alive. I wouldn't have that for so much longer.

"What were you doing, Jo? I know you didn't mean for this to happen, but what were you doing out there?"

Then I pulled the blanket away from her, put my cheek against the thin cotton gown that covered her small, round belly. The surface of her abdomen was taut, strong. Even unconscious, she protected the baby. As the rest of her body became smaller, her belly grew, accommodated my need for a family.

I pressed my cheek against her stomach and felt worn cotton and slight skin between me and the baby she carried. I half-expected a miracle that would lead Jo to respond, but the steady cadence of the respirator dulled my hopes.

The flutter against my cheek seemed too slight to be real, almost like a twitch of my own muscle. But then it happened again. Another movement, stronger this time. A foot, or maybe an elbow, some small part of a healthy baby straining against Jo's skin. I reached under her gown and put my hands on her warm belly. The movement, intermittent and playful, brought me away from the desperate place I'd gone.

I looked at Jo's face, so passive, so unlike her to have no expression. Jo's moods lived openly on her face.

"Thank you," I said to her, my hands still flat against her. But the baby had settled again.

I pulled up the blanket again over her body. An overwhelming fatigue washed over me, and I let myself go loose with it. Nodding off, I allowed the disjointed images from early dreams to take the sounds of her various machines and put them to other uses. I followed the pictures in my head. Curled on her bed, I made myself small and let sleep come.

FOURTEEN

*I*T COMES TO ME AGAIN *like it is new. I am nine, Joanne the same. She rises up through the slow water. The preacher has lowered her and brought her back. The stream is deep out where they are, deep enough to reach her shoulders when she's standing again. She looks the same to me and I wonder how she feels. I will know soon. I am next.*

She can't come to me when she emerges from the water. She has to go with the women who wrap her in towels. They want her to go away with them, to dry and change, but she won't. She wants to watch me and they don't argue.

The preacher calls my full name and I move through the sandy dirt bank into the water. The sun is hot, and in my white baptismal robe I feel myself shining. The water takes the robe, gives it weight as I move deeper. The deep pool of the stream should feel cold, but it doesn't. It feels like part of me.

I make note of the preacher's hands, one flat on my shoulder blades, the other on my forehead.

"I baptize you in the name of the Father, the Son, and the Holy Ghost," he says.

I close my lips and give myself to his hands. As my head goes under, I open my eyes, still squinting, but enough to see the light spread over the water. For a second, I change from flesh to light, and the water goes through my skin as if I am nothing and everything at once. When he brings me to the surface again, I wonder if I'm glowing. I look to the sky to see if something is there. Only scarce clouds and brilliant sun, and I think maybe that's been it all along.

I look to Joanne. She smiles at me. She is smiling and crying all at once and I know that she's felt it too, flesh to light and back again. Twins, born on the same day.

"I'M SORRY, but you have to get up."

I opened my eyes, my cheek lay warm against Joanne's arm.

"You're not supposed to be here, ma'am."

I'd become a ma'am. How old do you have to be to cross over to "ma'am"-hood? The nurse was young; she looked barely out of college. In my cross, just-waking daze, I wanted to do something juvenile, stick my tongue out or tell her to go to hell, but good sense prevailed. I sat up, pulled my hair out of my face.

"I'm her friend," I said, thinking how casual that sounded. "I just needed to see her."

"Have you been drinking?" the girl asked me.

I shook my head. "I wish," I said, straightening my shirt.

"There's a phone call at the desk," she said, ignoring my remark. "I think it's your husband looking for you. Go let him know you're okay and then you have to leave," she said.

I looked around for my keys while she checked the breathing machine, turned a knob or two on the IV.

"You can clear it with the desk next time if you plan to come and stay the night with her."

I nodded. She'd taken the high road but kept an attitude. She had the parental tone down pretty well for such a kid, and I had no recourse but to go along with her.

After she left, I smoothed Jo's hair, kissed her forehead, then walked out to the desk to see how frantic Cal was.

"Hello?"

"God, Darla! What are you doing there? It's four o'clock in the morning!" He sounded raw and irritated.

"I couldn't sleep. I just needed to see Jo, be near the baby. I left a note for you. I didn't mean to worry you."

"I know." He sounded calmer. "I just woke up and you weren't here. I called Jo's before I found the note, and when no one answered . . ." His voice trailed off. I'd really scared him. "I just don't know what to expect anymore."

"I'll be home in a few minutes," I told him. "They're kicking me out of the room here."

"You feel okay to drive? It's pretty late."

"I'm okay."

I hung up the phone and walked over to take one more look at Joanne. The dream still clung to me, felt close and real, settling easily at the edge of my thoughts like a recent memory. It was as if she'd been there.

"Where are you, Jo?" I heard myself asking, and I felt the hollowness of waiting.

Through the distorted vision of tears, Joanne's body gave the illusion of shifting, moving. Even the visual fantasy made my senses tighten and I blinked to clear my eyes, hoping it would go on when my sight had focused, the slow shifting of limbs and torso. But she was still, the same as before.

Standing over Jo, I felt a touch on my arm. Hope washed over my skin. Every nerve came alive. But Jo hadn't moved, and I took a breath and came to myself again, saw the young nurse beside me.

"I've got a best friend," she said, looking at Joanne while she spoke. "She won't let me pull a single piece of crap. Not even on myself."

She looked up at me and I nodded.

"Not a single piece of crap," she said again.

She laid her hand on my arm for a second, then turned to leave. I followed her out and she closed the curtain behind us.

I'D DRIVEN THE CAR a mile or so before I realized that my gas needle was flush with the line that said empty. I moved over, drove near the edge of the road in case I needed to roll to the side and get off the highway before the car died. It seemed okay, no sputtering or complaining from the engine.

Seven miles separated my house from the hospital, with an all-night Quick Mart positioned midway between, near the interstate.

I turned off the air-conditioning to save gas and turned up the radio to keep sanity. I willed the car forward. In my worry, my preoccupation with the gas predicament, I had the fleeting, mindless thought that I'd feel better if Jo were with me. Then I got mad at myself for forgetting. It hurt to forget and then remember. It hurt too much to keep doing it.

Mick Jagger screamed at me from the console. His coarse rant found something in me, a kindred rage that satisfied the empty spaces, if only for a moment.

"SHOOP-SHE-DOO-BE, SHATTERED, SHATTERED . . ." I screamed along with Mick, sang like a lunatic over the wind and the static and with every sound felt better than I had the second before.

In my grand catharsis I almost missed the neon Quik Mart light off to my right. I pulled a U-turn off the shoulder and bumped my car back onto the interstate service road that led to the store.

"HEY, DARLA!"

Tommy Wells, a boy I knew from high school, looked too awake and cheerful to be pulling the overnight shift at the convenience store.

"Hey, Tommy," I said. "I'm glad I got here. My car's sitting on empty."

"Damn," he said. "I'm glad too. There's nobody awake but crazy people this time of night. 'Cept us, of course."

I returned his goofy grin, felt at a loss to respond.

"How much gas you want?" he asked, finally. Up close, he smelled like cigarettes and motor oil.

"Do you take credit cards?" I asked.

"Naw." He looked apologetic. "We're s'posed to get the machines in for that but they haven't come yet. I'll loan you some money though, if you need it."

"That's okay," I said. "I've got some money. But thanks."

I fished in my pocketbook for cash, found seven dollars.

"Six dollars' worth, then," I said, walking over to get myself a Tab out of the case. "And this."

Tommy rang up the gas and the drink, gave me some coins back and walked around from behind the counter.

"There ain't nobody in here," he said. "I'll come out and pump it for you."

He walked ahead of me, skinny arms tan inside a plaid, button-up shirt that had been ripped sleeveless—on purpose, I assumed.

"You don't need no diet drink, Darla," he said. He smiled and his mouth was a mess of crooked teeth.

"That's what I always tell Joanne when she comes in here," he went on. "Same thing. She gets a diet soda, like her figure was anything but perfect—ever. Am I right?"

His drawl made normal words sound like lyrics to a country song.

"You're right," I said, smiling at the thought of his open admiration for Joanne and her figure—going back all the way to junior high. He'd been two years ahead of us, but failed a couple of grades and ended up graduating with our class.

The faint beginnings of daylight were showing beyond the interstate. Tommy fit the nozzle into the tank, then clicked it onto automatic and leaned against the pump to light up a cigarette. A sign above him warned against smoking while pumping gas, but his dangerous disregard for safety appealed to me, so I put my can on top of the car and lit one of my own.

"I seen her, you know." His face was serious. "That night."

"Who?" A small breeze blew his smoke my way. It mingled with mine and I felt a curious intimacy between us.

"Joanne," he answered, and something in me went still.

"That same night," he went on. "Just before she had that accident. 'Bout this same time, I guess, she come in here for gas, told me about how she's goin' out to pick you up."

His voice stayed casual, as if his words held no more significance than conversation.

"What did she say, Tommy?" I tried to sound calm.

"Damn!" He lunged for the gas nozzle. "I done rung up eight dollars instead of six. I hadn't got a bit of sense."

"Tommy?"

"Yeah?" He put the nozzle back in place. "Listen, don't worry 'bout that two dollars, I—"

"Tommy!" I couldn't stop the urgency in my voice. "What did Joanne say when she was here that night?"

He stopped moving, stared at me for a second. Another breeze came and I felt sweat on my neck and face.

"She said she's pickin' you up." He spoke carefully, looked uncertain about whether or not to go on. "Said the two of you was gonna take a road trip. Be like old times, drivin' together."

"Where'd she say we were going?" I felt all my senses pushed to the extreme. The cold surface of the soda can hurt my fingers.

"Are you okay?" he asked.

I wanted to scream at him to go on, to tell me every word Joanne spoke. Everybody in town had a "last time I talked to Joanne" story they were dying to tell. But here was a story that mattered, something I needed, and I could barely pull it out of him.

"I'm fine, Tommy. Really. Just, please . . . Please tell me what Joanne said. Where'd she say we were going?"

"Out West. New Mexico, she said."

New Mexico?

"Why?" I asked.

He looked confused, as if he didn't understand the question.

"What do you mean, 'why'?"

"Why were we going to New Mexico?"

"Hell, I don't know, Darla. You'd know more about that than I do. I just figured ya'll's bein' crazy like you always were. Why're you askin' me all this stuff?"

He acted nervous, like he'd done something wrong. I'd pounded him with my questions, left him frazzled. Maybe I *was* crazy. Nothing he told me made sense.

"How did she seem?" I kept my voice low, tried to sound normal. "What kind of mood was she in?"

He relaxed a little, put out his cigarette on the cement under his foot.

"I don't know," he said, still wary, but less freaked than before. "She's kind of edgy but, well . . . shit Darla, you know Joanne. She was always kind of edgy. Know what I mean?"

"Yeah. I know what you mean."

"Anyways," he said, "if it was somebody else, I'd a thought they was nuts. You know, leavin' at five in the morning for some crazy ride to New Mexico. But with you two . . . Especially Joanne. Shit. Didn't seem like nothin' new. Hey, you think she's gonna be all right?"

"Joanne?"

"Yeah. I heard she's still in a bad way, but if she's alive this long . . . well, she'll come out of it, won't she? Don't you think?"

"I don't think so, Tommy. I don't think she's going to wake up."

It was hard to read the look on his face. He seemed lost. A man without a map staring at miles of road.

"Her brain had a lot of damage. She's not really there anymore. At least that's what they say."

We were still standing by the pumps. On the rise above us, cars went by on the interstate. "Crazy" people out riding before the sun was even in the sky. I wanted to be one of them, going somewhere—with Joanne, just like she planned. It wouldn't have mattered why she wanted me to go. I probably would have just up and gone. But the *why* mattered a lot all of a sudden.

"I heard somethin'," Tommy said. "I heard she was *pregnant*."

He said the last word as a whisper, as if crowds around had pressed in to overhear.

"Yeah. It was for me," I told him. "She was having a baby for me."

"Damn," he said. "Really?"

"Yeah."

"Damn," he said again. He seemed to have lost all other words.

"I gotta get home," I said.

I moved into my car, settled the cold drink between my legs while Tommy stood at the door, holding it open. I put my hand on the handle to close it, but he stopped me.

"I'm awfully sorry, Darla. 'Bout everything. Ya'll's like sisters, I know."

"Thanks, Tommy," I said. I'd cried enough. I didn't want to start again.

"You'd of been a good mama," he said. "I know that much."

I looked up at him, grateful, tears starting on my cheeks. He closed the door for me and I made my way back onto the road that led

home. I turned the radio off, suddenly needing quiet more than
catharsis.

New Mexico. That was a place. A plan. Joanne had a plan and
driving off that bank wasn't part of it. Police or no police, I didn't need
any more than that to believe what I'd known from the start. It was an
accident, a terrible accident. Whether her foot slipped or a dog ran
across the road, it didn't matter. The only questions left were the ones
somebody else could answer. Why was she coming to get me? Why
was she leaving town? But who would know?

CAL WAS IN THE KITCHEN when I drove down from the highway onto
our drive. I could see him through the kitchen window, standing at the
stove.

When I got in the door, I saw that he had just finished scrambling
a pan of eggs. He'd put cheese on top. They looked good.

"I thought you might be hungry. We never really ate dinner last
night, what with Peggy here and then the Timbros."

I put my pocketbook on the counter, sat down at the table with my
Tab. He was trying so hard, even after I scared the bejesus out of him.
I resolved to do more for us, for him.

"Had anything changed at the hospital?" he asked, sitting down
with me.

"No. She's about the same. Her stomach is growing, I think."

Just mentioning the baby in a roundabout way brought a look of
discomfort to his face. I wasn't sure how we were going to get through
the custody fight if he couldn't even talk about the baby.

"Did you ever hear Joanne talk about New Mexico," I asked,
changing the subject.

"No. I don't think so."

He handed me a fork, motioned for me to start eating. I took a bite
of the eggs and immediately realized I had been hungry. They tasted
wonderful.

"She never had much to say to me one way or the other," he went
on, getting a bite of eggs on his fork. "And after she got so upset with
me . . ." He stopped. "I don't remember anything about New Mexico."

She had all those library books by her couch. *Santa Fe, Traveling
in the Southwest* . . . Sean. It had to have something to do with Sean.

I decided I'd call him as soon as the hour had gone from absurd to just early.

Cal had stopped eating. He sat watching me and I realized I'd consumed nearly the whole platter by myself.

"I'm sorry," I said.

"It's okay, I made them for you."

I looked at his face, how kind he was by nature. He didn't deserve the shitty situation I'd handed him; any of it. In spite of anything he'd done, he was a better person inside than I was. He didn't deserve the subject I was going to dig up next either, but we had to talk. I had to ask.

"I saw Tommy Wells when I stopped to get gas," I said, choosing the words carefully. "He said Joanne came in before the accident. She said she was going to New Mexico."

Cal's face was a blank. He didn't know where the conversation was coming from or where it was going.

"Did anything happen that you think would have set her off like that, made her want to run off?" I asked.

"What are you asking me, Darla?"

"I don't know. I'm just trying to sort out why she'd be leaving for New Mexico in the middle of the night." I stopped, making the decision not to go on, not to ask if he knew why she'd be coming to get me to go with her.

He shook his head. The trip was news to him. I tried again to imagine what would have gotten her in that car, made her write notes to her landlord, turn Rigsby over to Evie. Her office at work hadn't heard anything from her. I'd already asked. I needed to put the puzzle together. Had she been trying to get me away from Cal? The question still nagged at me.

"Did something happen, Cal? Something that would have set her off?"

"All you had to do was blow air in her face to set her off." He sounded irritated, tired of my attempts at solving all the riddles, of getting the answers that Joanne took with her into that coma.

"I hadn't seen Joanne—at our place or hers—for nearly two weeks. Until I came home and she was here. A lot happened, like I told you. I was a real ass. But none of it recent. Nothing to *set her off*. I prom-

ise. I'd tell you if there was anything else. Hell, Darla, I told you everything." He was at the end of his patience.

"I know. I know. I'm sorry."

I stood up and moved near him, pulled his head against my belly
and hugged him. "I'm sorry," I said. "I didn't mean to push. I'm just
tired and so much of this doesn't make any sense to me."

"Well, I don't have the answers you're looking for." His tone put
distance between us.

"Let's forget about it now," I said. "I'm going to try and get some
sleep."

"I'll go with you. I've been up since three-thirty."

"Cal, I really didn't mean to get you so worried. Are you working
today?" I asked him.

Part of me was worried about how tired he would be on the job.
Part of me wanted to figure out when I could reasonably leave the
house, go looking for some answers. I hated the person I was becoming.

"I've got to go in at two o'clock, then I'm on till eight. What are you
doing today?"

"I'm supposed to meet Peggy in town this afternoon, to talk some
more. I have some errands to run before that, try to find out what Jo
was up to that night."

He didn't ask any more questions. I suspected part of him didn't
want to know any more than he already did.

We went to the pullout couch, which was still rumpled from our
first attempts at rest for the night. I didn't even wash my face, but
crawled into the bed, felt the other half sag as Cal lay down beside me.
Rigsby made a sighing noise, curled up on the floor near my side. My
eyes made note of sunrise coming through the window. I rolled over,
away from the light, tucked my knees inside of Cal's bent legs.

"Thank you," I whispered to him.

"For what?" he asked over his shoulder.

I didn't know exactly, so I just said, "For everything today. Today
and tonight." He moved his hand behind him and I took it with mine.
Still holding his fingers slightly, I slipped into a long morning of dream-
less sleep.

FIFTEEN

GALVESTON, TEXAS—MID-OCTOBER 1975

I T WAS HARD TO SEE the color of the houses at night, so I looked for the widow's walk while trying to keep an eye on the road. Joanne saw the cottage before I did.

"That's it," she said. "There's the widow's walk and I remember that area jutting out on the porch."

We parked in a bare sandy area beside the house that looked to be the driveway. The water was one street over and I could smell the salt air when I got out of the car. The house was dark—a good sign—as were the other houses along the street. Summer people owned these places and they were snug inland now that the season had ended.

"What if they've got somebody watching the place?" I asked, while Joanne rooted around behind a scraggly shrub for the brick with the key underneath.

"I doubt it," she said, brushing the sand and straw from her pants, the key in one hand, "but we can move the car over there if it makes you feel better."

The house next to us had an empty lot beside it. A worn-looking sign that read "Beach Parking" tilted drunkenly near the road. Jo got our stuff out of the car, not even a handful of belongings between us, and I moved to the lot. The El Camino sat beside a couple of other nondescript sedans, putting me more at ease.

Joanne waited in the yard, then turned for me to follow her. Erratic wind jerked her hair in every direction at once and sand scraped under her boots as she went up the steps, then crossed the porch to the front door. Porch shadows and the absence of streetlights calmed my nerves. All the streetside shutters were closed, ready for any bad weather in the winter season, so I figured that once we were inside, small lights wouldn't be noticed from the street.

"Where'd you meet this guy again?" I asked.

"Houston. Last fall while you were away at school. I was partying with Conner and Lindy, but they passed out in the car before we even had dinner. Jack—Riker I think was his last name—he started talking to me in this bar, convinced me to ride here with him—after about fifty drinks."

"His cousin owns the house?"

"His aunt," Jo told me as she struggled to jiggle the key into the lock. "It's empty most of the time, he said. We crashed for the night and nobody bothered us."

"Lindy and Conner, too?"

"No." She shot me a look that said I was about one brainwave shy of average. "I left them in the car in Houston with a note taped to the steering wheel. Jack gave me a ride back to Alliance the next day."

The lock finally turned and she opened the door.

"I don't know about this, Jo. Breaking and entering is kind of illegal."

What had seemed like a good idea after splitting a six-pack at home became a bizarre reality as I walked in through the front door of a stranger's house.

"Relax," she said, walking ahead of me. "If anybody comes in I'll tell them I'm a friend of Jack's, that he's supposed to meet us here. I'll bet he'd back us up."

Vague shapes of furniture emerged in the room as my eyes adjusted. Sheets covered the sofa and chairs; a rug lay rolled against the wall on the far side of the room.

"There's a space heater in the hall," she said. "We used it before. We can put it in that front bedroom and sleep with blankets on top of the mattress. Nobody'll ever know we were here."

I told Mom and Dad I was staying at Jo's. Jo's folks had long ago stopped asking about her comings and goings. Half-drunk and totally bored, we'd left Alliance about nine o'clock in the evening, figured we'd get a few hours' sleep at this beach house she knew about, then mess around at the beach all morning and be back in Alliance before my afternoon shift started at the print shop. Jo called in sick before we left, put a message on the answering machine at the insurance office.

"Rachel will cover for me," she'd said.

The bed was huge, a high wrought-iron antique. The mattress sat well off the floor and was protected with a vinyl cover. From studying the bed alone, I could just see the aunt, gray hair and skin as thin as Kleenex. I turned off my imaginings when the old lady was flanked by a couple of police officers in my mind's eye.

"Hold on," Jo said. "I'll be right back."

First, she hauled out the space heater and plugged it in. Then I heard her open a closet door in the hall and she came back with an armful of blankets. After dumping them on a sheet-covered armchair, she grabbed a pale blue chenille spread off the top and covered the mattress. Then she sprawled across the bed with her coat still on. She looked happy.

I was impressed with her ease in the midst of our little felony. Something sparked inside me, the switch that always got tripped when I gave in to one of Jo's insane ideas. It took me close to the source, made me more alive.

A lamp on the bedside table and the glow from the space heater gave low light to the room.

"You hungry?" she asked. "I bet they have cans of stuff in the kitchen."

"No, not really." It was late; I was wide-awake.

"How about thirsty?" She pulled a bottle of bourbon from her backpack, which lay on the floor by the bed. "Courtesy of Larry."

"You took his bourbon?" I didn't want to see her dad's face when he found his liquor missing.

"He's got like four bottles in the cabinet. I'll put another one in before he notices."

She motioned me over and I sat beside her on the bed. After struggling with the wrapper that sealed the unopened bottle, she pulled the stopper and we drank without glasses. Passing the bottle between us, we slipped into easy talk, gradually peeling off coats and sweaters as the space heater and the alcohol wound us down to a simmering glow, warmed the room.

"You're just the best," I heard Jo say through the happy fog that made the strange bed into a place I thought I knew. Curled up at the end of the mattress, I felt the soft patterns of the chenille against my face until Jo's hand lifted my head and slid a pillow underneath. I was vaguely aware of the weight of a blanket pulled over my legs. I wanted to be rid of the confinement of my jeans, but my body was in no shape to cooperate, so I abandoned the idea.

On and off through the night I shifted and dreamed, feeling an arm under me when I rolled over, or a leg against the small of my back. I dreamed of someone, tender and hesitant, trailing fingers against the soft parts of my neck, brushing lips from my cheek across my mouth. I wondered if Sean had found me; then, even in the hazy dream, knew better than to hope.

"HI, MOM."

My mother looked like a kid in her turtleneck and sweatsuit. She knelt in the yard, arranging pumpkins around a small bale of hay by our front steps. With the sun high, it had been almost warm at the beach, but with sky beginning to darken, the air had a certain chill.

"Hey, honey." She smiled, barely glanced up from her work.

Sand peppered the dark blue wool of my peacoat. I hoped she wouldn't notice.

"Aren't you late for work?" she said, still intent on her pumpkins.

"I'm not due until four o'clock. I have to work until ten. I switched this week with Robert. Remember?"

"Right. I remember."

Mom and Dad had talked at length with me over the summer. I told them I didn't want to go back to school. They objected, felt strongly that I ought to try another year, but I held my ground. After it had been decided, they never made me feel bad about dropping out.

"You'll figure out what you want," Dad had said, finally. "Just take some time. You can always go back."

I saw their disappointment, but even that wasn't enough to get me back to Austin. As usual, they offered to support me.

When I got a job at the newspaper, working in the printing shop in the back, Dad opened a beer for each of us and sat with me on the porch. It was the first time he'd ever done that. We sat sipping out of cold cans on a warm September night. I thought of all the dorm mixers and class schedules that I didn't regret missing, not even a little.

"There are clothes in the dryer if you're running low," Mom called out just as I got inside the front door. She had all the windows open to let in the fresh air.

I'd have to change, put on some older clothes. Ink stains and printing smells ended up in everything at work. But I liked the job. That was the bonus I hadn't counted on. I didn't want to do it for years on end, but as a time-biding fill-in, it was pretty good. Every week we put out the newspaper, then on off days ran jobs for local businesses. Triplicate forms, merchandise labels . . .

But it was Tuesday, newspaper day. That was the best. Newsprint rolling out, fresh on the page. Local stories, just one step up from barbershop conversation, satisfied the town's curiosity. If you got married, arrested, or anything in between, the paper gave validity to the words that had been only gossip until the presses ran.

"I made some chili," Mom added. "Be sure to eat something before you leave."

Standing in the hall, I slipped off my shoes and checked for sand. There was plenty. I'd have to wash everything, including my hair, before Mom got close enough to look. I was headed toward my room when the telephone rang.

"Could you get that, honey," Mom called out to me.

I detoured toward the kitchen, balling my coat up and throwing it on the closet floor as I went by.

"Liddy?"

I recognized Carolyn's voice, my dad's secretary at the bank.

"No, Carolyn. It's Darla. You want Mom?"

"That'd be good, honey." She sounded agitated, out of breath.

"Are you okay?" I asked.

"I just need your mom. Right now!" She nearly barked the words in my ear, a real departure from arguably the sweetest woman alive.

"Mom!" I called out, adopting Carolyn's urgent tone. "Mom! Come to the phone. Hurry. It's Carolyn. I think something's wrong."

Mom was already on her way in the door. She quickened her pace and took the phone.

"Carolyn?"

She didn't talk after that, only listened for less than a second or two and dropped the phone, screaming for me to follow.

"It's your daddy," she said when we were under way in the car.

"What's wrong? Is there—"

"I don't know!" she cut me off, and I saw tears on her face, her eyes intent on the road ahead of her. "I don't know anything yet," she went on, softening her tone.

All the way on the drive to the bank, I kept thinking that she hadn't washed the dirt off of her hands, out from under her perfect fingernails. Soil and straws of hay clung to her gray sweatshirt. I'd never seen her arrive at the bank so unkempt before. I couldn't begin to think of my father, couldn't let myself wonder what was happening, what had already passed. So I focused on what I could see, the odd sadness of my mother's compromised dignity. It frightened me in ways I couldn't name.

JOANNE SHOWED UP at our house that evening. She stayed with me while my mother went to the funeral home with Aunt Gracie and Uncle Roger; she made Chef Boyardee Spaghetti, which we ate without talking.

Later, Jo's mom brought a casserole and Peggy arrived with fresh bread from an Austin bakery. There is so little to offer when someone dies too young. Food and quiet company have most likely been the only choices through all time. When older people pass on, stories, small anecdotes seem to help, evidence of a life lived thoroughly. But at fifty-one, my father's stories would have only emphasized the seasons he should have passed through before leaving us.

"Did he come to at all after you got to the bank?" Mrs. Timbro asked as she sat in the living room with me, Joanne, and Peggy.

"No." I shook my head. "He passed out, just like before. He'd been taking medicine for his heart, but I guess it didn't work. He died before the ambulance got there this time."

After her question, after my answer, the silence became distracting. I wanted Mrs. Timbro to go home so that I could stop trying to sit up straight. I wanted to curl up on the couch and listen to Joanne and Peggy talking to each other while I slept. I craved sleep, had no trouble nodding off in just seconds when I didn't have some task at hand. I kept expecting to break down and cry, to feel hysteria or a searing pain that ran through my very core. Instead I had a numb fatigue that wouldn't leave me.

"Do you want some more coffee?" Peggy asked Mrs. Timbro.

"No, honey," she said. "I'm going to get on back to Larry." Then she turned to me. "Will you call me if you need anything?"

I nodded.

"Are you staying here, Joanne?" she asked Jo.

"Yeah," Jo said, walking her mom to the door.

As soon as the door closed behind her, I lowered my head onto the embroidered pillow that decorated the couch. I gave up my "company face"—that's what Mom called it—and put myself in the care of the only two people I trusted to keep watch. Mom had her sister. I had Jo and Peggy. That would have to be enough for a while.

"Here," Peggy said, and pulled an afghan over my legs. "Jo and I are going to straighten up the kitchen so your mom doesn't start in when she gets home."

I just nodded, my eyelids already falling.

The town paper would run the weekly edition overnight. Uncle Roger had thought to call the newspaper office. He gave them all the information for my father's obituary so my mother wouldn't have to think about it. But I wouldn't be there to see the fresh ink hit the paper. I wouldn't be there when my father's death became news.

"THAT'S NOT HIM." I stood by the casket in the low light of the funeral parlor. The life-sized form in the casket had no hint of my father's true face. It was as if an amateur artist had drawn him, and from that source someone had made an effigy, cartoonish almost in its distortions.

"It's him, Darla," Jo said, thinking I was in some kind of denial. "They wouldn't make that kind of mistake."

"I know that. I just mean he's not there. What happened to the way he really looks?"

She just shook her head. I didn't expect her to answer, really. I still hadn't cried. Like a freak, I'd become some robot unable to manufacture human tears. Standing by the coffin, I knew in my mind that the body they'd fixed up and laid out was the same one that gave me piggyback rides, built my swing set, and drove me to school. But he wasn't there. I'd know it if he were.

"I'm feeling kind of sick," I said, suddenly overcome by the smells. "It's the flowers . . . something."

Jo had my arm, walked me outside, where the bright morning took me by surprise. The day should have moved hours ahead of where it was. Mom had said I needed to go see the body, before the family visitation that evening. She said I should get over the shock of seeing him like that before I had to deal with other people all around.

Seeing him once, or twenty times, I'd never begin to believe that it was my daddy there. Jo and I stood in the yard in front of the funeral home; the fall air felt cool and new. The sick feeling had passed, but a damp film covered my face and neck, reminding me that I could turn at any moment.

"I don't want to go back in," I said.

"Let's go home, then."

"I don't want to go there either. Can we just drive somewhere? You pick."

She took the keys I handed her and I followed her to my car.

WE HAD TO WALK DOWN an open path through the woods to get to the church. In years past, the path had been a road.

"A church?" I'd asked her in the car when she told me where we were going. "Which one?"

"A place I go sometimes. You don't know this one," she said.

I couldn't imagine a church in town I hadn't seen. There weren't that many.

As I turned to the left behind Joanne, both of us still following the path, I saw the clearing and then the church, or the parts of it that still stood. Only one corner remained intact with a part of the roof shading several pews. Three partial walls had the charred scars of a fire from long ago, and a center aisle led to the altar.

"What happened to it?" I asked.

"It burned a long time ago, just before Christmas one year. Probably a candle."

The pulpit, weathered and falling, stood on a strong marble base, and the exposed pews were splintered, but appeared strong enough to hold the congregation that no longer came to Sunday service.

"How'd you find it?" I asked.

"A friend of Lindy's brought us here one night last spring. Thomas, you've met him."

"Black guy, real low voice?"

"Yeah. That's him," she said, stepping over a low section of wall "into" the church. "Lindy was real messed up, and Thomas knew the church was out here, said his grandpa used to preach here before it burned down. We hung out until she started acting halfway normal again."

"Why'd you bring her here?" It seemed wrong to use a church as a place to come down from some excessive high.

"The grandpa still lives near here. We figured if Lindy got in a bad way, he could get us some help. Besides, nobody ever comes out here."

I stepped over the wall, walked up near the altar. I took the cool air full into my lungs. Dad would have loved the day—no sweating. Plenty of fish would be biting. The world was new without him, and so much less than it had been. I didn't know what to feel or expect. I didn't want to know.

"I come out here sometimes, when I need to work through something, or especially if I need to think and just be by myself," Joanne said. "Today, well . . . you know. I thought it might be a good place for you."

I followed her back to the covered area, sat down beside her on a pew and pulled my sweater around me. The breeze felt good. Through the trees, sun reflected off of something; it looked like water.

"Is that a creek back there?"

"Yeah," she said. "That's where they used to baptize people. Thomas told me that he remembered it from when he was really little."

Through the high grass between the church and the woods, I could make out tombstones. There must have been a couple of dozen.

"A cemetery," I said, almost to myself.

"It's pretty wild," Jo told me. "Some of those people must have been slaves. The dates go back before the Civil War."

I wondered how often she'd been out here, looking at the graves, sitting in the pews. It bothered me a little, this part of her life that I hadn't seen.

"If you want to be by yourself," she said, "I'll wait in the car."

"Why?"

"Well, if you want to . . . I don't know. Maybe you want to pray or something." I waited for the punch line, some slash of sarcasm. But she seemed sincere.

I remembered her firm posture when she went down the church aisle ahead of me as a kid, the look on her face as I came up out of the water at our baptism. I thought all that was long gone with her, a phase in her ongoing war with her father. The wild binges of dope and boys that defined the last couple of years didn't seem to have anything to do with that person, or the person sitting in the pew beside me telling me to pray.

"I don't know what you need right now," she said when I didn't respond. "I don't know what to do for you."

"I don't know what to ask for," I told her. "I'm okay, I think. I don't want to pray. I want God to forget I'm here, just ignore me."

"Why?"

"I want Him to leave all the people I love alone. Sean, my dad . . . you might be next. You might get sent off to the other side of the world, or maybe you'll get polio or some other disease that hasn't shown up for twenty years. God's just full of surprises."

I felt the anger, deep in my muscles, in my chest, and in the air I let out when I breathed. I was done with it, with Him, once and for all.

"Darla . . ." Joanne said, but I didn't want to hear any more. "You shouldn't—"

"Let it go, Joanne. This comfort business is a bunch of crap. Talking about it's not going to make it all better."

"It's just that . . . Darla, when I went through a really rough time while you were at school, it helped me to come here."

"Well, that's you," I said. "Not me."

She sat back, looked away from me. She wanted me to believe it all again. The blessings, the forgiveness. Part of me wanted to go along with her. I wanted to feel full and right, the way I had when we stood in our white robes by the side of the stream.

She reached around and felt under the seat. I looked down and saw several narrow cubbies attached to the pews underneath. The backs of the pews had no place for Bibles or hymnals. They must have used the cubbies to hold them. Joanne pulled out a plastic bag. Inside, a book was covered in Saran wrap. She unwrapped it on her lap and I saw that it was a Bible—a kid's version, the kind with big letters and pictures inside. I had one like it somewhere at home.

"Your mom gave me this, when we got baptized."

I looked at the Bible, felt a stronger yearning to give in to all the Sunday School memories, the simple feelings I'd left behind as I grew.

"Why do you even have that here?" I asked Jo, trying to shake free of the images she'd stirred.

She shrugged.

"I don't know," she said. "Ever since he made me stop going to church with you, I figured he'd take this away if he found it."

There was no question about who *he* was—her father was the overwhelming *he* in all of her miseries.

"You know how he is," she said.

A stained-glass Jesus held a lamb in the window beside us, the only one left intact. The movement of tree branches caused shadows to shift behind the colors of the glass. Jesus looked as if He were moving, rocking the baby lamb in His arms. It seemed so easy, all the promises, all the fairy tales. But the anger in me stayed firm. It was something I could own, something I could name. My daddy was dead and Bible verses were words, as lovely and empty as balloons.

"I didn't mean to yell at you," I said. I heard the flatness in my own voice. "We're just not on the same page."

"Well," she said, still holding the picture Bible. "You can have this if you want it."

I shook my head.

"Leave it here," I said. My voice stopped in my throat. "It's better if you leave it where it is."

The words began as clear sounds, but twisted into sobs before I finished, my eyes tearing up without warning. The moment tore open in front of me and I was helpless to stop it; every emotion I knew grew large, all the feelings swollen and sore. I cried then, finally, and Jo seemed relieved. Whatever she believed, it would have to be enough for both of us.

She pulled me over and I leaned against her, lost in the sadness that seemed to come out of me, but also from all around—from outside the damaged walls and the sheltering trees. Maybe from outside the light and air itself, reaching dark places where senses are rendered useless against the pain.

SIXTEEN

M R. ROMEROS APOLOGIZED. He'd probably been dreading our conversation for days.

"As the landlord, I must legally go by the wishes of her parents," he said, his Spanish accent softening the consonants in his words. "I'm so sorry. I know what friends you were. She would not want this."

I'd gone to Joanne's apartment, had planned to meet Sean there to begin boxing up some of her things. I didn't know what would eventually be done with everything, but I thought if I went through what was there, I might get some clue about that night, about New Mexico. The problem was, my key wouldn't open the door.

"It was the father who spoke with me," Mr. Romeros said. "I think it is all his idea. The mother, she seemed sad that this has to happen for you."

"It's okay, Mr. Romeros," I told him. "I know you didn't have a choice."

He walked me to the corner on my way back to my car at Jo's.

"I'm so sorry," he said again, shaking his head. He was still standing there when I turned the corner to the duplex.

Sean had the retreat van out front when I got back. I saw the boxes he'd brought. They were piled high in the back.

"We won't be needing those," I said when I reached him.

It had taken me several days to get ahold of him at the retreat center, because he'd been away in Austin. During that time, Tommy Wells' words grew in my mind until I couldn't sit still, couldn't think of anything else. I'd tried several times to reach Evie. At first, no one was home. Finally, Michael answered and said she was visiting her mother with the kids. She'd be gone for a couple of weeks.

I'd tried to keep my mind on the big issues, mending my life with Cal, the coming battle with the Timbros, but I couldn't let go of what happened that night; what it had to do with me. Cal acted alternately sympathetic and impatient. I'd noticed him staying at work longer and longer, just as he had before the accident. My energy felt scattered minute to minute.

"What's going on?" Sean asked when I reached him. "I saw your car and got a little worried when I couldn't find you."

"I'm locked out. Courtesy of Larry Timbro. Sorry you hauled all those boxes here for nothing."

"He locked you out? How?"

"He had Mr. Romeros change the locks," I said.

"Why would he do that?" Sean asked.

"Maybe he thought I'd steal something."

"Seriously, why?" he asked, shaking his head.

"Just to piss me off, probably. It's this custody dispute. You don't know Larry Timbro. He's got this control thing going. He'll get to me any way he can."

We moved into the shade of a tree and sat on the grass. The still, humid air closed in around me. A strange part of me envied Jo. She didn't have to worry about any of this mess.

"Look on the bright side," Sean said.

"I don't believe I've found that one yet."

"All that stuff inside just became somebody else's problem."

He was right. It should come as a relief, this unexpected exile from Jo's. I was glad I'd taken Rigsby to my house before they closed the drawbridge. The dog was the only part of Jo's world that really mattered now that she was absent from it. I glanced at the duplex, thought of her belongings inside. She'd planned to leave it all anyway. Why? I wanted to bring it up with Sean, but not in Jo's front yard; not sweating in the sauna that was Alliance in August.

"Where to now, boss?" Sean asked, when I stood up.

His tone, young and familiar, sent me reeling again to an earlier time. I could almost always see him as Sean the priest now, someone I'd met just recently. But every so often, a gesture or something in his voice would snap me back a full decade, back to the other Sean. I had to stop myself when that happened; stop myself from reaching for him in ways that would embarrass both of us.

"I don't know," I said, stumbling a little over my words, "I'd like to go somewhere and talk. I don't care where."

"St. Elizabeth's is down the street. There's a parlor there where we can sit."

St. Elizabeth's. Nothing like Sean in the parish parlor to jerk me into the right decade.

"That's good," I said.

St. Elizabeth's existed in a different season. The huge trees around the grounds and the stone walls of the church and the rectory made it several degrees cooler than it was just a couple of blocks away.

Sean pulled on the heavy door that opened into the parish hall and I followed him down various corridors to the parlor. After we were settled, I told him about Tommy Wells, leaving out the part about falling asleep on Jo's bed in the ICU. No need to secure my appointment at the loony bin so soon.

"She was coming to *get* you?" Sean sounded as perplexed as I felt. I'd hoped he would know more.

We sat together on a red velvet couch. The dark paneling and the smell of wood oil gave the room the feel of a gothic novel. I could almost hear the cloistered, insane relative, bumping around in the adjacent room.

"So who did she say all this to again?" he asked, as if it might make more sense with just a little more information.

"Tommy Wells. You remember him. Skinny guy, always hung out at the mound."

The mound was a pothead hangout just off school property. It occurred to me that Sean had probably never actually been there.

"Yeah," he said, passing on the judgmental comments, "I remember him. Did she say anything else?"

"No. Just the part about getting me and going to New Mexico. I thought since it was New Mexico, you might know something."

He sat back on the couch, leaned his head back, and closed his eyes. I wondered if he was delivering an impromptu prayer. Ignorant of the habits of priests, I just watched him, didn't speak. His kind face had stayed so familiar to me, even through a decade of absence. I hated the idea that I had hurt him, left him sad and doubtful about how much I cared. With the different paths our lives had taken, it was a wonder that we'd ended up in the same room again.

"It's not my place to go into this," he began, and I realized he did know something. He'd been wrestling with what he should say. The very integrity that I counted on made me feel like strangling him sometimes.

"What?" I prompted.

His mouth was open, but the words stopped short of sound. He was thinking. Editing.

"Dammit, Sean, just tell me," I said. "Stop thinking about what you're going to say. Jo wouldn't want me going crazy like this. What do you know?"

I was right about Jo. He knew it. He turned, looked me in the eye when he spoke.

"I don't know the answer to your questions," he said. "I really don't. I don't know why she was coming to get you."

"Sean—"

"Listen to me," he said. Then he took a full breath, let his shoulders relax, and he put his hand on my arm. "I'll tell you everything I know."

I could see Joanne while he was talking. She'd been in the parlor too, had sat on the same couch with him while she explained our tangled-up lives.

"She thought that if you stayed with Cal," he said, "it would be hard for her to be here, knowing how he'd come to her at her apartment those times. She was really wrestling with what to tell you, Darla. She didn't want to wreck your marriage, but she didn't want to live with a huge lie either."

"What did you tell her to do?"

"I didn't give her any answers."

"Of course not." The counselor's code.

"I just tried to help her sort it out. It was weird for me too, because it was *you, your marriage* we were talking about. I'm a priest and I'm very happy with my choices, but I'm not entirely impartial in all this. You have to know that."

He stopped, looked away from me, and I felt his effort to put some distance between the moment and that comment. The emotional connection between us had always been visceral. For my part, it was an effort not to move toward him.

"I told her that I thought you could handle it, if she decided to tell you," he continued, "that you would understand the extreme circumstances that fed into Cal's mistakes. I told her that I've seen marriages come out strong from situations like this one."

"Like this one?" I asked.

"Well, not *exactly* like this one," he said, smiling. "This is pretty weird stuff."

"That's an understatement," I said.

The light moment gave me a chance to breathe, to think about what he'd said.

"Darla," he said, finally. "You can't doubt where her heart was in this."

He leaned toward me, strong now in his resolve to be who he was, not who he had been—even with me.

"She wanted you to be happy. She wanted you to raise the baby. And doing that without the father is never the best choice for a kid."

"Is that your perspective, or hers? She'd probably rather have grown up without her father," I said.

"I wouldn't be so sure," he said. "But Joanne was thinking about all that. She also knew that the way she presented this to you—if she told you at all—would go a long way toward helping you to salvage your life with Cal."

"Is that what she wanted?"

"She didn't know what she wanted. She was trying to do the right thing, whatever that might be."

His words were measured, and I had time to see Jo in them. I wanted to touch her, to ease her conflict, but it was too late for that.

"What about New Mexico?" I asked. "Why was she coming to get me if this is what you talked about?"

"I don't know," he said. "She asked me about life in New Mexico, about the parish where I trained."

He stopped. The questions were all in my head, but I couldn't fashion them into words.

"She was thinking that after the baby came," he continued, "she might go there. Try to live there. Give you and Cal space to work it out."

"Oh my God, she was going to leave because of me?"

"Because of a lot of things. She thought it would be better for you, and for the baby, if she went somewhere else. She had me talk to Brother Garrick at the parish there about finding work for her."

"Did he?"

"He talked with some people, sent word to me that he was sure they could find a job for her in the parish office or maybe at the school as an aide."

The words settled on me, but seemed a jumble. The air-conditioning in the parlor felt too cold and I drew my arms closer to myself to get warm. I tried to imagine Joanne, knowing so much and never talking with me. It didn't make me angry, exactly, just sad; sad to have been excluded, sad to have been useless to her.

"She hadn't decided exactly what to say the last time we talked about it," Sean told me. "She wanted to sort out her options, but she had decided she had to talk with you. She wanted to find a way for everything to be right."

"Right? With her driven out of town because of what I asked her to do in the first place?"

"It's not that simple and you know it. She had other things going on."

"She's my family, Sean. Even now. *Especially* now. She's barely alive and she can't tell me anymore. Tell me what you know."

Again, I saw the conflict on his face, and still I pressed him with what I knew to be true.

"She wants me to be at peace, Sean. I have to know the answers so I can get on with my life. Cal and I are trying; we have a shot at getting close again, but my brain keeps going somewhere else. Back to Jo and what happened. I want to know why."

"I don't *have* those answers!" His voice rose, echoed off the paneled walls. We were talking in circles.

"Just tell me what you do know."

He nodded. "For some time," he said, "even before I came back to town, she'd been struggling with questions about her life. She'd gone through some bad things, I think. I honestly don't know what they were, but she wanted something more than the days she had before the baby. She didn't want to go back to the way life had been."

"She went through a lot with her dad," I said. "I know that much. What did she want to do to try to change things?"

"I don't know, neither did she, but she thought she might find it at the parish. She wanted to see what a life of service would be like."

"Service?" I asked. "What do you mean?"

"Being part of a holy order."

"Like being a nun?" *That* picture just wouldn't sort itself out in my head.

I felt like laughing and crying all at once. And the thought of Sean's priesthood with Joanne following to the convent . . . It was ironic, really. I'd driven the two people closest to me to consider full-time religion—a strange gift for someone with such failed spirituality.

"Like I said, I don't know what she would have done. She wanted a change, I know that much," he said.

"And what about me? She planned to just cut me out of her life?"

"Stop it, Darla," he said. "You know why she even considered it."

"I know," I said. "That was a selfish way to see it."

I looked at Sean. We were both exhausted from all the talking. As for me, every fresh piece of information made the puzzle more confusing.

I left him at the parish with the van full of empty boxes still sitting in the parking lot as I drove away. Whatever the plans Joanne had for us, I had to make my own future now—without her. That very thought broke my heart a dozen times a day.

Cal was right; I had to concentrate more on the future than the past, concentrate on the meeting we would have with Peggy and Janet the next day. They wanted to grill us one more time on what to say at the custody hearing, how to say it—as if the simple truth wouldn't get us anywhere.

All the questions about Joanne were leading to circles and dead ends. I needed to think about what she was trying to do, not why she did it. I'd get home and call Cal at work. Let him know that he could count on us again, that I was ready to move ahead.

The court date would be set soon, they said. Family Relations Court. It sounded so friendly. I could hear Jo chuckling at that one. I could hear her almost all the time if I tried; and I sometimes wondered which thoughts would have been hers, and which ones were truly mine.

SEVENTEEN

THE COURTROOM had a raised bench where the judge presided, but nothing else about it was as I expected. Straight-backed chairs and makeshift tables served the lawyers and witnesses. A little rearranging and the room could have been a church hall, spare and multipurpose, but without notable character. There wasn't a jury for these proceedings, Janet had explained. She said that it might work in our favor, given the provincial nature of small towns. This way we had one person to convince, winner take all.

"Is it hot in here?" Cal asked no one in particular.

He sat down at our designated table, pulled at his tie.

"It's not that bad," I said. "You're just not used to the suit."

We were taking a break. Mom and Sean had gone out to get a soda, and Peggy was talking with Janet. The Timbros sat stone-faced, refusing to relax at all, while their lawyer, a short dark-haired fellow, rifled through some papers as if he were in a big hurry. His mustache and his arrogance were equally thick. He made me nervous. Every

once in a while Mrs. Timbro would look my way. I had trouble reading her expression. It fell somewhere between frightened and sad.

She was probably thinking what I was—that Joanne would hate
this. I had stayed with Jo until visiting hours were over the night before. Whether she heard or not, I felt I should tell her about everything
that was happening.

Joanne wasn't in the courtroom, but I could feel her. She even had
a lawyer appointed to represent her interests. Off to the side, a thin
young woman wore a gray suit and a sour expression. She sat in a seat
that had a desk attached, like in a schoolroom, with her papers all
stacked and ready for class. They called her a *guardian ad litem*.

"Since Joanne is still alive," Janet explained, "she has to be represented."

This offended me, the mere assumption that my interests and
Joanne's could be at odds. Janet said it was a formality. She would have
little to do with the outcome of anything.

I'd held together pretty well through the morning, but the waiting
made me anxious. Before the break, Judge Wheeler had listened while
the lawyers laid everything out. Since we were the ones petitioning for
custody, the proceeding began with our witnesses. Marilyn Adams, our
obstetrician, had given the first part of her testimony. She told the
judge that she had been monitoring Joanne for the last four months,
ever since Joanne's home pregnancy test had come back positive. She
testified that she understood the paternity of the baby and the agreement Joanne had with me that Cal and I would raise the baby.

"Darla has come to all the visits with her," Marilyn said. "It's been
clear all along that although the fetus was conceived from Joanne's
egg, she had agreed to have the baby for her friend."

"How long have you known Miss Timbro and Mrs. Stevens?" Janet
asked.

"I run a clinic in Austin and I've been seeing both of them for eight
years now, since Mrs. Stevens was a student in Austin."

She didn't say that I'd first come to her—frightened, lying about
my name, and thinking I was pregnant. Cal didn't even know about
that mess. As a doctor, Marilyn was as discreet as she was good. She'd
become a good friend to me and to Joanne over the years.

She'd done her best to help with my fertility problems, but with limited money and the scarce treatment for my condition, the emphasis had to be on controlling the pain. She didn't offer much hope for me to get pregnant—though she tried everything we could afford and then some.

"We don't know what causes infertility with endometriosis," she told me early on, "so we don't know how to fix it."

Then when we came to her, Joanne and I—when we told her what we'd done, with Cal's help—she'd just shaken her head, smiled, and tossed an exam robe to Joanne.

"Okay," she said. "You know the drill. Put that on and let's see how this baby is doing."

That seemed so long ago.

"All rise," the bailiff said as the judge entered the room.

We all stood while he made his way to the bench. We settled at our respective tables and I looked back to see Mom sitting with Sean and Peggy a few rows behind Cal and me.

"Let's get going," the judge said, after he'd checked the papers in front of him. "Dr. Adams, I believe we continue with you."

The judge was younger than I'd thought he would be, older than I was, but at least ten years younger than Mom. He was known to be conservative. Janet said she didn't know whether that would help us or hurt us. Usually courts side with the natural parents, but in this case that was just one of us, and the methods by which it had all happened weren't exactly "Ozzie and Harriet" material.

"We have some of Mrs. Stevens' medical records here we'd like to discuss." Mr. Jackson, the Timbros' lawyer, had a folder in his hand. Janet had finished and it was his turn.

"What's he going to talk about?" I whispered to Janet.

She shrugged. Told me not to worry.

Janet said my infertility would show our actions to be a reasonable, albeit unusual, response; so I'd signed off on the release of my records. It seemed strange though, having people in suits talk about my infertility as if I were a livestock specimen that had failed to breed.

"Why do they want to go over this again?" I pressed her.

"Relax," she said.

Mr. Jackson, their lawyer, positioned himself to the side, so that we could all see his face as he asked his questions. He went through Marilyn's credentials and every so often would stop and say to her, "Is that right, Dr. Adams?" as if she needed to prove she had really gone to medical school.

He reviewed the records on Jo's pregnancy and the history of my illness as she saw it. Then he paused. When he spoke again, he addressed Marilyn Adams, but he was looking at me.

"Dr. Adams," he said. "Can you tell us what *r/o pg* means?"

Marilyn looked surprised. She hesitated, opening her mouth but not speaking.

"You wrote it here in the records," the lawyer prompted her, " 'r/o pg.' What does that mean?"

Janet made a little face and I got a bad feeling in my gut. Marilyn looked at me with an apology in her eyes.

"How far do they go back?" I whispered to Janet. "The records."

"As long as you've been seeing Dr. Adams," she whispered back. "Darla, have you ever *been* pregnant?"

"No," I said. A damp sweat chilled my neck and arms. I was waiting for Marilyn to speak. Her silence had gotten awkward. I turned to Janet again. "What's r/o pg?"

Cal was looking at me. The question on his face was clear, and I felt myself go weak.

"Rule out pregnancy," Janet said in a tone even lower than we'd been using before. "Is there something I missed?"

I wanted to die.

"When I first saw Dr. Adams," I said. "Just before I went to college. I thought . . ."

"Is there a problem, Counsel?" the judge asked Janet, giving Marilyn a small reprieve from her answer.

"Not really, Your Honor," she said. "But I do need a moment with my clients. Could we have a brief recess?"

"Ms. Burdette." The judge looked annoyed. "We just came in from a recess. Unless it's really urgent, I'd rather go on."

"It's okay," I whispered to her. I didn't want to cause a scene and make things worse—if that was even possible.

Mr. Jackson was standing beside Marilyn . . . waiting . . . looking a little too smug.

"As I was saying, could you tell us, Dr. Adams, what does *r/o pg* stand for?" he asked again, after Judge Wheeler nodded for him to continue. "It must be clear to you. You wrote it here in the notes. Granted, it was a while back. When Mrs. Stevens was in high school, I believe. But surely you remember what it means."

Marilyn let her shoulders relax, then put on her coldest expression.

"Rule out pregnancy," she answered. To her credit, she looked him in the eye, kept a professional tone of voice.

I started shaking, felt my cold skin turn flushed and hot. I wanted to stand up and explain. *It's not like that. It wasn't like that.* I glanced at the judge and he was watching Marilyn. His face gave away nothing of his thoughts—not the smallest hint.

"And what were the circumstances of Mrs. Stevens, *then* Miss Darla Andrews, or actually, Miss Darla *Smith,* it says here on the record. *Smith.* That's interesting. This was on her first visit here, I believe—what were the circumstances of her visit?"

I could hear Joanne. *I told you that name thing was stupid.* I should have known they'd find that visit in the records. I should have thought.

Behind me, I could feel all the eyes staring at me. I glanced over my shoulder at Sean. He nodded, looked calmer than he could have possibly been. Thank God I'd at least told him about it at the retreat center that day. But then there was Cal . . . I didn't dare look over at my husband. And Mom. *Oh, Mom. I'm sorry. You shouldn't have to listen to this.*

"So an eighteen-year-old Darla *Smith* comes to you with the concern that she might be pregnant? This was your first encounter with the current Mrs. Stevens?"

As Marilyn spoke, I watched as the court recorder typed up the secrets of my past, making one of the worst days of my youth an official part of the court record.

"WE EXPECTED IT TO GET BAD," Janet said after court had adjourned early for the day. Something to do with the judge's schedule. Marilyn would be up again to finish the following morning. "We knew they would attack your character, your morals, any way they could, but I am sorry I didn't see this one coming."

She looked more upset than she sounded.

"I know," I said. "I should have told you. I honestly hadn't thought about it being part of this. It was such ancient history. My God, I was only eighteen."

"Yeah, I was thinking more about your recent records, your infertility. But in the big picture, this is nothing. They just want to rattle you and it's not going to be that damaging as testimony," she said. "It's really not. The judge will not take a ten-year-old indiscretion and let it sway this child's custody. They're trying to establish a history of risky behavior, but in fact, it's just embarrassing, that's all. On the embarrassment scale, it's going to get worse before it gets better. You know that, don't you?"

"What are you expecting?"

"Testimony from your doctor about *how* Joanne got pregnant and your sanctioning of it."

I knew that part would come, but thinking about it made my thoughts shut down, refuse to move beyond the moment.

Mom had gone out to lunch with Peggy and Sean, but Janet said she needed to go over some things with Cal and me before we left for the day, so Cal had run out to get sandwiches for us. I hadn't had a chance to say anything to him yet. I'd avoided his eyes during Marilyn's testimony; next would come his questions. The Timbros' lawyer had twisted everything to make it look like I'd been some sleazy teenager, hopping from backseat to backseat at the drive-in.

Cal knew better. He couldn't hold it against me. He *wouldn't*. I knew him well enough to know that. But with Sean sitting there and Cal's recent baggage about his being back in town . . . It was just so awful. And Mom. I couldn't even think about Mom. She was just coming to terms with the baby, what the three of us had done. In some ways I was glad Dad never had to hear what she heard in court, what she *would* hear later on.

"What's on for tomorrow?" I asked Janet.

"We continue establishing Joanne's intent to have the baby for the two of you. That, and the presumed paternity, will be the cornerstone of our argument. Sean will go up after Marilyn finishes. It's a little tricky because of his ethical constraints with counseling, but he has no problem saying that he understood what she wanted for the baby. He knew you guys way back when, so he can testify to the longevity, the closeness of your friendship. Then we'll move on to Peggy's testimony. The nice thing for Sean is that he can opt out of any questions about Joanne that make him feel conflicted. The judge, Mr. Bible Belt, won't touch that one."

"Do you think they'll get into the other stuff with Sean? Could they?" I asked, voicing my worst fear of the moment. "That would be the hardest thing to sit through. Impossible for Cal."

"What other stuff?" she asked.

"About us. You know, the whole thing from this morning."

Janet looked at me, still drawing a blank. I thought she knew. I figured Peggy had filled her in on all of that.

"Why would he know anything about the doctor's testimony?" she asked. Her voice held a tension I could feel.

"We were together then," I answered, almost wishing I hadn't. "Sean and I dated in high school."

"Your boyfriend was . . . he was your—Jesus! The father of that potential baby . . . he was the priest? I'm sorry . . . it's just—Jesus, Darla. We need to go over this. Right now."

She looked like a smell hound, hot on a trail.

"He wasn't a priest then," I said, lost for other words.

"No. I know that," she said, her voice moving down an octave. "I didn't mean to jump on you. It's just that in terms of the assault on your character, this is great. Something they thought could hurt you might actually backfire. I mean, he's a priest. You fell in love with a man who became a priest. That's a totally different picture from the one they're painting. Obviously, you didn't hang around with dope fiends."

I wondered if she'd ever talked with Peggy about her former career.

"Anyway, do they know?" she continued. "The Timbros. Do they know who Sean is?"

"I don't know. I don't think so. Unless Mom said something at the hospital or they happened to remember. At the point when I was seeing Sean, they weren't real concerned with my boyfriends. They were too busy trying to keep tabs on Joanne."

"Perfect," she said, rocking back on her heels.

"You can't talk to him about that in front of everybody," I said.

"Who? Sean?"

"Yeah," I said. "You can't make him talk about that."

"Honey, we don't have a choice. It's not that big a deal, really, but if we don't tackle it and they find out, then it looks like there's something to hide. If we bring it out, we can work it to our advantage."

"But you have to think about him, and about Cal. This would be really hard on both of them."

"Darla, nothing about this fight is going to be easy. You and Cal knew that, so did Sean when he agreed to testify on our behalf."

I didn't think I could feel any worse, any more humiliated than I felt in the courtroom before. But getting Sean up to talk about us . . . My stomach had turned inside out.

"Let me talk to them," I said. "Just give me a chance to talk with both of them."

"You've got fifteen minutes with Cal," she said. "I'm going to see if I can track down Sean. I want to sit down with him this afternoon to prepare for tomorrow."

She took off, moving quickly toward the courthouse door. Cal was coming up the hall with a bag of sandwiches from a diner across the street. He tried to stop Janet so he could hand her one, but she waved him off and disappeared around the corner.

By the time he got to me, I'd rehearsed at least three opening lines that would ease us into the discussion we had to have. He saw my face and bypassed the necessity for any of them.

"It's gonna get worse, isn't it?" he asked.

"Let me tell you how much worse."

We sat down together on a long bench that ran along the corridor wall. He pulled two sandwiches and two cans of Coke out of the brown paper sack.

"Let me hear it," he said, holding his sandwich, but not taking a bite. He put his other hand on my knee. "I can handle it. I promise. I just need to see it coming."

It occurred to me how wonderful he could be. In spite of all our mistakes, he was a very good man.

EIGHTEEN

ALLIANCE, TEXAS—FEBRUARY 1977

JOANNE PUSHED the metal fishing boat out of the shed and we
hooked the trailer up to the hitch on my El Camino.

"Your daddy's gonna be so pissed," I told her, the unbroken chorus
of my days with Joanne, it seemed.

It was the middle of the morning on a Wednesday and we were
supposed to be in class at the community college. But we skipped out
because it was 67 degrees in February—one of those days that arrives
out of season, comes full-blown and without apology. We had until
four o'clock to get to the newspaper where Jo had gotten a job with me
on the evening shift. That was nearly a whole day on the lake.

"Daddy won't find out," she said, getting in the car.

"I hope to hell you're right."

We drove through town with one eye out for his black pickup, but
relaxed by the time we got to the highway. Bare trees along the road
seemed oddly naked against the warm sky.

"Look at that," Jo said, as we turned into the boat landing. She
stretched her arm out toward the water. "All to ourselves."

Only two other cars and one lone truck sat with empty trailers in the boat-landing lot. I saw one boat out on the lake. The other two had likely slipped into backwater coves where fish gather near stumps to feed.

Jo got out and stood to the side while I maneuvered the trailer back to the ramp. Her hair was down, wavy and long past her shoulders. The sun hitting that brown-red color made her look like a model in a shampoo commercial. I leaned out of the open car window so I could see to back the trailer straight into the water, then stayed there to talk while she worked with the boat.

She rolled up her pants and waded in.

"Shit! This is cold." She made a face and moved in deep enough to reach the towrope.

Three ducks flapped and moved closer to Joanne, hoping she had food to throw, no doubt.

"Besides," she grinned at me, cranking the towrope to lower the boat into the water, "if he throws me out of the house, we can just get a place together at those new duplex apartments."

It took me a second to figure out she was talking about her dad again. She did that all the time, popped up with some comment as if we'd been talking about him all along. She was afraid of him, but acted fearless. I'd never figured out how she could do that.

"Hold on a second," she said, unhooking the towline. Still knee-deep in water, she walked the boat to the dock and sat down on it with her feet dangling. I started to drive away and she yelled out, "Bring my visor and my cigarettes!"

I listened to the boat trailer behind me, bumping light on the rough gravel. It recalled days with my dad, was the happiest of sounds for me.

I walked down to the dock and after a few frustrating moments with the sputtering motor, we got it started and headed the boat toward the middle of Lake Riley.

The sun reflected bright off the silver insides of the fishing boat, making us squint. The low drone of the other boat sounded at the far end of the lake, near the dam, but the rest of the day around us had only muted noises of birds and water.

"What have we got?" she asked, looking at the bags I'd packed before I left.

"Deviled-ham sandwiches and chips," I said.

"Well, I'm not hungry yet, but look what I packed."

She opened the built-in cooler at the back of the boat and showed me cans of beer and soda buried thick in ice.

"Damn!" I said. "That looks pretty good."

Settling in, we drank cans of Budweiser and talked about accounting degrees we hoped we'd never use. Small motions of the lake rocked us in time with a gentle breeze. I couldn't imagine feeling better.

"What about it?" she asked after talk lulled for a minute or two. "You want to think about getting an apartment, one of those new duplexes?"

"Were you serious about that?" I asked. "I don't think we make enough."

I stretched my legs out across the boat and leaned my head against the side. She sat on the other side, her legs opposite mine.

"It's only two-fifty a month," she said. "We could come up with that and still afford school."

"Two-fifty?"

She nodded.

I hadn't thought living on my own was something remotely in reach, and I'd never considered whether I wanted to or not. It seemed unthinkable that I had a job that would pay for me to have that option.

"I don't know," I said, feeling the small excitement even as I hesitated. "I guess the only thing I have to think about is my mom. She'd be in the apartment alone if I moved out."

"She'd be alone if you were still in college," she said. "I mean, she sold the house so that she'd feel comfortable by herself. Right?"

She was right. There was no reason not to consider it. It had been more than a year since Daddy died. Mom and I both had to move on sometime.

"Do you like living with your mom?" she said. "I mean, is she okay? You don't talk about her much."

"I guess. It's different now with the two of us. She seems to be handling it better than I am. While he was alive, even though I wasn't a kid anymore, we still felt like a whole family. Maybe if I had brothers or sisters it would still be that way. But with just the two of us . . ."

I tried to think of what I was saying, what I wanted to say, but there weren't real words for the feelings. "I want it to be like it was," I said, finally. "I want to feel like a family again. It's really selfish. I mean, all that she's gone through. I guess it's wrong for me to think about it like that."

Jo put her hand out and I took it, like shaking hands only not, a sweeter gesture that held us suspended for a moment. Then it passed.

"Anyway, I want to get out on my own. At least I think I do," I said. "Just let me ease into the idea with Mom and see if she's cool or if she totally freaks."

"Your mom's still young, Darla. Ever think about that?"

I knew what she was getting at.

"I don't want to think about that," I said.

WE SWITCHED FROM BEER TO SODAS, so that we could coax our minds into clarity before work, and we ate sandwiches that tasted better than potted meat should.

"This is great," she said. "Can we figure out how to get paid to do this?"

"Yeah," I said. "Get on the Bass Pro tour."

It was only two o'clock, at least another hour before we'd have to head back. The motor of the other boat whined into a faster gear across the lake. I could hear it getting louder, closer.

"That other boat's coming this way," she said, stretching her neck to see behind her.

I saw one guy. He was standing in the boat, steering in our direction.

"Just cover up those empty cans with a towel," I said when it became clear that he planned to check us out.

She shoved the beer cans into the corner and threw a stained fishing towel over the pile.

"Who is it?" she asked.

"Game warden, I think."

The boat came closer and I saw the Wildlife Service seal on the side. The guy driving looked too young to be much of a hard-ass.

"You girls okay?" he asked us as he pulled alongside us in his boat.

"Yeah," I told him. "We're fine."

Jo usually took over when we got in trouble, talked us through or out of any messes we got into. But I knew the lake better and she deferred to me with the "Wildlife Officer."

"You've been sitting here for a while," he said. "I thought maybe your boat broke down or you'd run out of gas or something."

"No," Joanne piped in. "We're just enjoying the sun, is all."

In his uniform the officer looked like an Eagle Scout, all dressed for a meeting. His hair, light brown and fine as thread, kept getting picked up and blown in his face by the breeze coming across the lake.

"I hate to tell you this," he said. "But your registration's not up-to-date. You need a new sticker."

"Oh," Joanne said. I could see her mind working for some angle. "My daddy's been sick. He must've forgot. I'm sure when he gets out of the hospital, he'll take care of it right away."

"I'm sorry," the officer said. "What's wrong with him?"

It was clear that he was half on to her, but she planned to forge ahead with her story, was about to invent some tropical disease when I blurted out the truth.

"Her daddy's not in the hospital, but he might put us there if he finds out we took his boat. It was just such a pretty day."

I waited. This was the test, the defining moment. Did we get busted, or did he like me? He grinned and I stopped holding my breath. When he smiled, his features stayed even—symmetrical. Nothing lopsided or fake registered on his face. I liked him from the start.

"I'll give you a warning," he said, talking to Jo, but looking at me. "But you shouldn't bring the boat out again before the sticker's up-to-date."

He asked us both for an ID.

"Why do you need to see both of our licenses?" Joanne teased him.

"If you run off and get in trouble," he shot back, "I need to be able to ID both of you."

"Oh, right," she said, looking slightly annoyed.

"I get off at three," he went on. For a minute I thought he was going to suggest we meet him somewhere, then he finished his thought. "The next guy on duty probably won't be a pushover like me. You'll want to get in before that."

I STOOD IN THE WATER, felt like I was standing in a loaded ice chest. The rolled-up edges of my pants were wet from small waves lapping onto the landing and my toes were entirely numb. As I guided the boat onto the trailer, Joanne put the car in park and got out.

"Well," she said. "I guess we can put that apartment idea on hold."

"What do you mean?"

"Oh, come on." She was smiling, but her tone had an edge that put me on guard. "I can see the writing on the wall with this guy."

"What are you talking about?" I said, hoping my voice didn't sound too false, too loud. "I don't even know his name."

"But he knows yours. And let's see, whose type is he? Blondish-brown hair, tall, polite to a fault . . . Whose type is that? Hmm, let me see . . . Darla, I think."

"Are you mad or something?" I asked as we got into the car.

She got in the driver's seat and I didn't argue with her.

"No, not really," she said. "I'm just being a jerk. He seems really nice. That's the problem. I can guess where this will go."

"He probably won't even find me," I said.

We rode in silence back along the highway to town. She turned to take the back road to her house, so we wouldn't go anywhere near the high school, since her daddy would be out on the field for afternoon practice.

When we got to her driveway, she backed up the trailer to the shed door and I started to get out to open it.

Before I opened my car door, she said, "Cal Stevens."

"What?"

"His name is Cal Stevens." She held the warning he'd given us in her hand.

"Okay," I said, and got out to unhook the boat.

It was a nice name, one that suited him. Even Jo's lousy mood couldn't spoil the idea of him.

I opened the shed and together we pushed the boat inside. She went toward her house without saying good-bye.

"I'll pick you up in half an hour for work," I called out.

She turned and nodded, and the sad look in her eyes made the smallest of tugs at my conscience. I drove away, pushed all thoughts of Joanne out of my mind as I pictured the light-haired man standing easy in his boat. Cal Stevens.

NINETEEN

I WANTED TO BE ANYWHERE but the courtroom.

Marilyn was back on the stand. Even after a night of sleep, she looked exhausted. Medical school had prepared her to attend to birth and death, but it hadn't prepared her for Family Relations Court. And for her second day of testimony, Jackson skipped the amiable prelude and jumped right in.

"According to your records, who is the father of the baby carried by Joanne Timbro?" he asked.

"It's my understanding from my conversations with Ms. Timbro that Cal Stevens is the father."

"Did you assist Mr. Stevens and Ms. Timbro in any sort of procedure by which she could become pregnant?"

"No."

"To the best of your knowledge, did anyone else assist them with these procedures?"

Marilyn sighed, squinted at branches moving outside the courtroom windows, then turned back to the lawyer.

"To the best of my knowledge, they did not receive any medical assistance in achieving the pregnancy."

What followed caused my cheeks, my ears to burn, flare red, I was sure, in the bright morning light of the courtroom.

"Did Ms. Timbro and Mrs. Stevens discuss with you the method by which Ms. Timbro became pregnant with Mr. Stevens' child?"

"Yes." Marilyn wasn't giving him an ounce more than he asked for.

"And what method was this, according to what they shared with you?" If he was going on a hunch that we'd confided in Marilyn, it was a good hunch.

"As far as I know, they tried a couple of methods," she said.

"Could you elaborate? Or better yet, to save the court's time, let me ask a more direct question. Did any of these methods result in sexual intercourse between Ms. Timbro and Mr. Stevens?"

Marilyn paused and took a breath. "From what I was told, I believe it did. Yes."

"According to your conversations with Ms. Timbro and Mrs. Stevens, did Mrs. Stevens initiate these sexual encounters between her closest friend and her husband?"

"Objection," Janet piped in weakly.

"Overruled." The judge never took his eyes off Marilyn.

My head was down; I could only imagine Marilyn's discomfort. She hedged, kept the terms clinical, as sterile as possible given the subject, and said she didn't know how it came about, but that I had been in agreement with the arrangement. By the time the lawyer finished, the psychologist's assessment of "manipulative" didn't begin to cover the depth of pathology in my actions.

The judge asked Janet if she cared to "redirect." She tried, but the territory was established beyond her ability to reclaim it.

Then Sean was up.

I shouldn't have asked Sean to testify in the first place, but this latest business Janet wanted him to cover was a lot more than either of us bargained on. I didn't know if Cal would get through it in one piece or not. Everything seemed wrong.

Janet started with conversational stuff. Getting Sean to give his background, his holy credentials. No rumblings of what she planned to get into with him. But he knew it was coming. I could see the tension in his neck, his shoulders. He was bracing himself.

Just after she got through a play-by-play of his high school career as captain of the tennis team, really wholesome stuff, she moved into questions about Joanne.

"Now, Father Sean, how well did you know Ms. Timbro? It's on the record that you attended high school together, is that correct?"

"Yes."

"How well did you know her then?"

"Not well. She was close to a friend of mine, my girlfriend."

"Oh, right. It's hard to believe looking at a collar, but before the priesthood, guys are just regular teenaged boys—football, the prom. Who was your girlfriend in high school?"

"Objection, Your Honor." Jackson, their lawyer, stood up. "As much as I love hearing about the secret life and times of a priest, this is wasting the court's time."

"This has relevance, Your Honor," Janet said without missing beat.

"Continue."

Sean looked my way. I looked over at Cal, saw his eyes dead on Sean. I wanted to hide.

"My girlfriend was Darla Andrews. She's now Darla Stevens."

I don't think Jo's parents understood what the big deal was. They registered only mild surprise. But Mr. Jackson got it, put it together immediately with the doctor's testimony. In an awful way, he almost smiled. Nodded a brief touché to Janet. Janet went on with her questions, eventually got around to the dirt.

"Father Sean, I know it's been a few years, but would you mind telling us about your relationship with Mrs. Stevens when the two of you were in high school?" Janet asked.

"We dated," he said. "She was my girlfriend. We went to movies, football games. All the usual stuff."

From the look on Janet's face, I guessed she had coached him to answer with a little more enthusiasm.

"And how did you feel about each other? Would you say the two of you were in love?"

"What does this have to do with a custody trial?" Sean's jaw was set hard, his eyes stayed on Janet. I wasn't sure she'd filled him in on this turn of questioning.

"Please just answer me, Father Latham," she said, smiling. "I assure you, it's important."

"I cared about her very much," he answered. "You'd have to ask *her* about her feelings."

Janet raised an eyebrow, inclined her head. Lawyer body language, and it didn't take much to crack the code. She waited, kept her eyes on him.

"I believe that she felt the same," he said, his words measured and hard.

She was taking us back there, back to feelings that were hard enough to leave the first time around. Then she planned to rip us apart again, in front of everyone we loved, and some we hated.

I had argued with her to let this go, argued for nearly the entire night after we left the courthouse the afternoon before. I was fighting my own lawyer as much as I was fighting the Timbros.

"And, being in love, your relationship, like many teenagers', became physical?"

"Yes."

I despised her at that moment, almost as much as I despised myself for letting her go on with her questions. Sean's face mirrored my feelings.

"Were you her first?"

"All right! That's enough!" Sean said, his voice finally giving way to anger. He looked to the judge for some response, but the older man didn't speak.

I felt the urge to crawl over the table, to physically do her harm. How could we possibly get through the crap they planned to throw at us if I couldn't even sit through my own lawyer's questions? Then I thought of Cal. It had to be hell on him.

It was an effort to look in his direction. He leaned forward onto his elbows, stared down at the table. I tried to touch his hand, but he pulled away, shook his head, still not looking at me.

"I know this is difficult, but please answer the question, Father Latham," the judge said, finally.

I wondered if I should just let the baby go. Call the whole thing off. I was hurting everybody around me. What Janet was doing was unthinkable and we hadn't even gotten to *their* witnesses yet. I reminded myself of the baby, that everything we were doing was for the child.

"In your opinion," Janet restated, "were you the first person to have a physical relationship with Darla Andrews?"

"This is going too far," Sean responded in lower tones, as if appealing to Janet one-on-one would persuade her to stop. Still, he was barely keeping his voice civil. "This has nothing to do with Darla today."

"I would agree, Your Honor." Mr. Jackson stood up. "I object."

"Bear with me, Your Honor." Janet used her sweetest voice.

"I'll give you a little leeway, Ms. Burdette," the judge said, "but I expect you to get to the point soon."

"Thank you," she said.

Sean looked at me. I wondered what he was thinking. Was he sorry for me, or angry that I'd brought this on him? I couldn't tell.

"To your knowledge, were you the first person with which the then Miss Andrews had had this sort of relationship?"

"Yes." He barely opened his mouth when he spoke.

"In your opinion, was Mrs. Stevens, even then, the kind of person capable of making a commitment that grew out of love?"

"Objection," Mr. Jackson managed again, although he was trying to look as disdainful as possible.

"I have to say I agree with Mr. Jackson," the judge interjected. "I don't see where this is going, Ms. Burdette."

"Your Honor," she said, not missing a beat, "Mr. Jackson has attempted to portray Mrs. Stevens as a person of questionable morals. I am trying to establish that the behavior she engaged in was not taken lightly, by her or by—"

"This is just wrong!" Sean interjected, cutting her off mid-sentence. All eyes in the room turned to the priest. "You're all just playing a game here. Check. Checkmate. There are lives involved. Real people who have to sit and listen to this. People who are hurt by this." He glared at Janet.

"Father Latham—," the judge began.

"If you don't mind, sir," Janet said, "let him go on. It's all right." The judge nodded and she turned to Sean.

"Go ahead." Her voice took on a bitchy tone. She had changed into someone I'd never known her to be in our short, intense acquaintance. "What is it that bothers you, Father Latham?"

"Your Honor, I have to object!" Mr. Jackson stood up, as if he were above what Janet was pulling with Sean on the stand.

"Overruled. Sit down, Mr. Jackson. Your objections are taking more time than the testimony." The judge was not happy as he turned back to Sean.

"Please continue," Janet nearly taunted him. "Tell us what's on your mind, Father."

Sean's face flushed red. I hoped he never had occasion to look at me the way he looked at her.

"They may be trying to paint Darla as some kind of streetwalker, but you're worse. Coaching me, trying to manipulate me into making her into . . . into some innocent little Sandra Dee. She's a woman, a real person, who, like the rest of us, makes decisions. Some good, some bad.

"But there's a baby at stake here. A baby. A baby who needs a family. And whatever happened ten years ago has nothing to do with that. Our high school relationship isn't some hand of cards you can use to bluff your way to an advantage."

"Objection, Your Honor." Mr. Jackson was on his feet again. "You can't possibly let this go on."

"Overruled." There went those eyebrows again. He didn't want anyone telling him what he could or could not do in his own courtroom. "I can decide quite nicely what will go on here, Mr. Jackson. Sit down. Go on, Father Latham."

"I don't know what you're getting at with these questions about things that happened a decade ago. Darla was a faithful girlfriend. She's a faithful wife now. And as a mother she'd be . . ." He stopped, looked at me, and I felt my heartbeat in my throat, in my ears. "As a mother she'd be a gift to any child. That's the bottom line. That's what I believe. The rest of all this is just drama and I don't want any part of it."

Everything stopped except the court reporter typing Sean's words. Eventually, she stopped too and the room went still.

"That's all, Your Honor," Janet said, finally.

"We have no questions," the Timbros' lawyer said with a bluntness that broke the spell. He shook his head as if to say he wouldn't dignify Janet's shenanigans with any questions of his own. I suspected that he didn't want to touch a priest on a mission. I didn't blame him.

I looked at Janet, hoped to hell she felt chastised, embarrassed by Sean's assessment of her piece of theater. It took a few minutes before I realized what had happened. Janet had set him up. The whole scene, start to finish. She'd set him up, baited him until he broke through with his heart, raw and open. I felt sick. But even through my disgust, I registered some warped admiration for her accomplishment.

As Sean stepped down from the stand, Janet touched him lightly on the shoulder. A gentle gesture, an apology—almost. His expression changed as he looked at her, realized the same things I had. He looked helpless, gutted and helpless.

"I'm sorry," I said in a low voice as he walked by. My voice was shaking. He gave me a weak smile, went down the aisle, and sat beside my mother.

It occurred to me that we might win this thing, but the cost would be high, higher than I'd imagined it could be.

"THEY'VE GOT ONLY TWO WITNESSES," Janet said, a paper cup full of soup in one hand and a plastic spoon in the other. "So after Peggy goes for us and then Dr. Akers, they'll present, probably today through tomorrow morning. Then it's a matter of how long the judge takes to decide."

We were sitting in a small conference room in the courthouse. Peggy had brought in lunch, but no one except Janet seemed to be eating. Cal sat mute beside me, a whole burrito lay unwrapped on the table in front of him. I hadn't bothered to take the paper off mine either, and I felt too shaken by the morning to concentrate on what she was saying, to think about the afternoon ahead of us.

"Darla." Janet was looking at me. "Hang in there. We don't have much more to get through, but we've got a couple of rough spots ahead today and tomorrow. You've got to hold yourself together for the baby. You hear?"

I nodded.

"Cal?" she said. "You doing all right?"

"Yeah," he said, but I knew he was lying.

As Peggy walked up to take the stand, the afternoon sun shot blinding shafts of light into our faces from the side of the room. Peggy was sworn in. She squinted and put her hand up to shield the brightness as Janet asked her first question. The bailiff asked an officer to help him lower the shades of the large windows.

The change from sunlight to shadows took the mood of the room down to a pensive lull. All murmuring conversation ceased. There weren't more than a dozen people in the room, but we seemed to share closer quarters without the light.

"That's better," the judge said. "Please continue."

"When did you first learn of Mr. Timbro's behavior toward his daughter?" Janet asked.

The story of Pony had grown old, archival in my mind over the years, but hearing Peggy go through it again, her words brought fresh images of Joanne, crying in her room, too sad to move and frantic about her dog.

I missed her. God, I missed her.

The judge furrowed his forehead as he listened—perplexed, I hoped, by the extreme degree of cruelty in a father who said he loved his child.

"She was devastated," Peggy said. "Absolutely hysterical over the possibility that they might put her dog to sleep. Darla called me. So I went and got him, the dog. I adopted him."

"Did Joanne see him again?"

"All the time. At my house. In fact, when Pony—that was his name—got sick two years ago and had to be put down, I called her. She went with me to the vet. She said good-bye, rubbed his head as he went to sleep."

"No more questions, Your Honor," Janet said.

The saga of Pony the Dog had gotten to nearly everybody.

I felt like crying. The God-fearing judge looked shaken. Even Mrs. Timbro raised a Kleenex to her eyes. Larry and that bastard lawyer of his seemed to be the only dry eyes in the room. They had their heads together, mumbled, and talked for a few minutes before Mr. Jackson got up to ask Peggy his questions.

"Did you have any contact at all with the animal shelter after you adopted Pony?" he said.

The dog's name coming out of the lawyer's mouth sounded ridiculous.

"Yes," she answered.

I wondered what he was getting at.

"What did they say to you?"

"They said that the owner had called, was interested in getting the dog back."

"Was it Ms. Timbro, Joanne Timbro, who requested the dog back?"

"No."

"Mrs. Timbro, her mother?"

"No."

"Who was it?"

"Her father, Mr. Timbro. He'd gone back to see if Pony was still there."

Weak sensations ran through the blood in my arms, in my chest. He'd gone back? Did Joanne know she could have had Pony back? Peggy didn't look surprised by the questions, neither did Janet.

"Did we know this?" I whispered to Janet.

She nodded. "We're only trying to show his extreme actions when angry. It's okay, really." She gave my arm a pat.

"So you called Ms. Timbro, Joanne Timbro?"

"Yes," Peggy answered.

"And what did she say?"

"She said to keep the dog, to tell them that I didn't want to give him back. He signed papers waiving all rights to the animal and—"

"That's fine," the lawyer cut her off. "Why do you believe Ms. Timbro would give up the opportunity to have her dog back? Obviously, her father was feeling regret over the incident. Did she want to make him suffer?"

"Objection. Speculation," Janet stood up and announced.

"Stick to your questions, Mr. Jackson," the judge said, but he didn't sound irritated, only weary of the whole dysfunctional business.

"I'll end here," the lawyer said. "Thank you," he directed toward Peggy.

"Is that all for you too?" the judge asked Janet.

Janet stood up.

"If I may, I'd like to have the witness answer Mr. Jackson's last question."

"All right," the judge said.

"Did Joanne give you any reason for leaving the dog with you?" Janet continued. "Why would Joanne pass up this opportunity to get her pet back?"

Peggy held off for a minute, as if she wanted to choose her words with care.

"She told me that she didn't want him to have the power to hurt her with the dog again, to use the animal as a weapon."

"Thank you," Janet said.

I had always thought of the law as something academic, businesslike. I could finally see the appeal it had for Peggy. All the things she liked, the constant emotions breaking through polite veneers, the sense of battling for a reason . . . all of that conflict scared the hell out of me. This was my life and there were people I cared about getting battered and bruised for something I'd started. Joanne was the most battered and bruised of all. The Timbros were right. I wasn't worthy of a child. I wasn't even worthy of the people around me.

After Sean and Peggy, the psychologist Janet had engaged, Dr. Akers, seemed like a walk in the park. She said all sorts of nice things about me and Cal—rosy pictures of what great parents we would make. How my teenage rebellion sounded perfectly in line with normal development. I hadn't realized I'd rebelled. I glanced at my mother several rows back. She looked absolutely gray. It broke my heart to think of what this sounded like to her.

Mr. Jackson spent a few minutes assassinating the psychologist and her credentials instead of my character for a change. Then we broke for a recess. Cal could barely look at me and I didn't see Mom anywhere.

THE STATE TROOPER on the stand looked familiar. I had a vague recollection of his face and it didn't bring back any positive associations.

"Do you recognize Mrs. Stevens?" Mr. Jackson was asking.

"Yes," he answered. "I remember her face and her name from her driver's license."

The boat landing.

"Why from her driver's license?"

"I spoke with Ms. Stevens and with Ms. Timbro on two different occasions and I'd seen them more times than that. They were in a car, parked at the Lake Riley boat landing."

"And what made you notice them there?"

"I smelled marijuana and on those two occasions approached the car. Both times, I determined that the smell was coming from the vehicle. I warned them both verbally that they had to cut it out. The second time I told them if I saw them again, I was going to have to arrest them on misdemeanor drug charges."

"And why didn't you arrest them during those times?"

"I usually give people a warning or two, for that sort of thing anyway. They seemed like regular girls, nice people."

"But they came back again? After the first warning?"

"Yes," the officer said. He pronounced this as more of a question than an answer.

"Would you consider this reckless behavior?" Lawyer Jackson asked the trooper.

"Yes," he answered. "I suppose I would."

The lawyer ended there, the officer looking uncomfortable, as if wondering whether to get up or stay put.

Janet stood up and he settled back in his seat. She started immediately on damage control.

"Have you seen the car or the women in the last year?" she asked.

"No."

"Did the two women seem out of control or in any way dangerous to themselves or people around them during the times you spoke with them?"

"No." He smiled. "Just a little giggly."

Janet smiled back. The judge wasn't smiling though. I wondered if he'd already decided I was unfit.

"Thank you," Janet said to the state trooper.

THE LAST WITNESS was their psychologist. The judge asked if we minded going a little late so that we could finish up testimony and not have to come back in the morning. No one objected. No one, with the possible exception of their sadistic lawyer, wanted another day like the one we'd just had.

Led by Mr. Jackson's scripted questioning, the psychologist talked about the kind of person who would ask her best friend to sleep with her husband in order to impregnate her with a child for herself.

"I would have to say that is highly manipulative behavior," the skinny woman managed to say through her very tight lips. "She obviously wouldn't be taking into account the emotional consequences of such a request."

Not the kind of person to be trusted with a baby, the woman implied. Morally vacant, manipulative. I'd started to believe them all.

It went on for what seemed like forever, the psychologist profiling a woman even I wouldn't want to know, much less inflict upon the people I cared for *and* a brand-new baby. Janet got up, looking fresh and ready for late-round sparring.

"Now, Dr. Simpson." Janet sounded disdainful. "Would you mind telling us who is paying for your services today?"

As she said this, I realized the wisdom of trading pro bono work with the psychologist we'd gotten to testify. No hired gun on our side.

"I was retained by Mr. Jackson to evaluate the Timbro family and to review the facts of the case."

"So you are working for the Timbros?"

"Objection! Argumentative."

"Sustained."

"Okay, forget that. Can you tell us how you have come to the conclusions you have just presented?" Janet looked cool, strictly business.

"As I told you, I reviewed the facts of the case and in my professional opinion, Mrs. Stevens has shown a willingness to manipulate others for her own benefit."

"Now, I'm just a simple lawyer, but aren't there tests and other ways to determine a person's traits and characteristics? You know, objective measures that avoid bias?"

"Of course. We use them all the time in custody evaluations."

"Oh, so you administered these tests to Mrs. Stevens and came to your professional opinion objectively? Can we see what her scores were? Just how . . . what was it you said . . . manipulative and self-centered she is? I assume you brought those test results with you today."

The woman looked angry enough to spit.

"Well, actually, since I was retained by Mr. Jackson, I based my opinion on the materials he made available to me—court records, depositions, interviews with Mr. and Mrs. Timbro—it's all part of the public record."

"So you never actually spoke with Mrs. Stevens or administered any objective tests to her?"

"For this case it really wasn't necessary. The family knew her well, there are records of her from school and a few traffic tickets and the like. Her own deposition provided the strongest evidence of her manipulative tendencies."

"So she said, 'I'm manipulative'?"

"Of course not, but . . ."

"But what? Where did you come up with this professional opinion, Miss—?"

"It's Doctor. I have a Ph.D. in psychology."

"Oh, well then, Doctor, I'm sure you've heard of the eyes on rule. Will you explain that to the court?"

"Objection! This is not a jury trial. Ms. Burdette is out of order."

"Excuse me?" The judge didn't care for Mr. Jackson's repeated input on how he should rule. "Overruled. You may continue, Counselor, I'm very interested in the answer to your question."

"Well," she faltered, could see what was coming. "In medicine, a physician cannot diagnose or prescribe treatment for a patient on whom he has not laid eyes. That is, there has to be an actual meeting, with a clinical interview and examination, before he can make recommendations." The woman squirmed in the chair, surely regretted that she had taken the case.

Janet walked in front of her, changed her position so that the woman had to nearly face the judge in order to see her.

"But you're not a physician. You said it was a Ph.D., correct? Does that mean that the law applies differently to you?"

"No, it doesn't."

"Then I'm confused. How is it that you have formed such a strong professional opinion of Mrs. Stevens without ever meeting her?"

"I . . . uh . . ."

"That will be all. No further questions. And, Your Honor, I request that everything that this witness has said be disregarded. And I respectfully request that the court make inquiries about possible ethical and legal violations committed by her in her handling of this case."

Janet stepped back. I couldn't read the judge's face. We'd all heard what she said, and not even I could disagree with most of it. It was hard to unring a bell, so I knew he had to be considering some of it.

Cal looked beaten to a pulp. Before Janet had gotten her turn, Mr. Jackson had even gotten into Cal's dysfunctional family background, which was really a cheap shot. How he was ripe for my purposes. Regardless of Janet's efforts to discredit the woman, I felt like someone who skinned puppies to make fur coats.

As we exited the courtroom, Janet broke into a grin.

"Not bad," she said. "I think we've got it. Impossible to tell for sure, but I feel good about our chances."

"Are you kidding?" I asked.

"I'm going to get the car," Cal said. He looked ill, his color, his posture—drained and beaten down to dull skin.

"What about all the stuff that woman said?" I asked Janet as my husband literally fled down the hall to escape looking at me.

"Psychobabble," she answered. "Some judges go for it. This judge is bread-and-butter facts. We've got the biological father and a history of cruelty in one of the petitioning grandparents . . . I think we'll be fine."

"What about the pot?"

"That wasn't your finest hour," she said, pulling gum out of her purse and offering me a stick. "But you and Jo clearly stopped when the baby was in the picture. I think all the other will outweigh any damage it did."

Mom walked out of the courtroom with Sean.

"Are you okay?" I asked her.

"Not my best day," she said, avoiding my eyes. "But I'm fine. I just want to go home."

She looked like hell, but what did I expect? I could see her needing Daddy. Home was an apartment with her cat and my old keepsakes, the latter only false trappings of somebody she thought I'd been.

In the last few weeks she'd found out that I'd asked my husband to sleep with my best friend so that I could have a baby. Then she has to hear about my pot-smoking adventures with Jo, not to mention my teenage sex life. Pretty rough stuff for the next best thing to June Cleaver. She needed Daddy to tell her that her daughter wasn't a stranger. I don't know if he could have or not. I don't know if I could convince myself.

Sean stayed beside me as Mom turned to go down the hall. Sensing the awkward exchanges that could follow, Janet said she had something to do, she'd be right back.

"I should be with Mom," I said to Sean.

"Give her a little time to sort through all this," he said, looking down the hall where she walked away. "I'll stay with her a while."

"Oh," I said, managing a smile. "So the guy who took my virtue is better than the daughter who let go of it?"

"The collar covers a lot of ground," he said, his eyes gentle. "Seriously, I picked her up to come here, so I'll go in with her when I take her home. Make sure she's okay. You've got wounds to nurse with Cal."

I was grateful that he seemed to still be himself with me. I didn't know how he could be so solid after all he'd been through on the stand.

"I'm sorry about what happened to you in there," I said.

He shrugged. "She was doing her job. I pray and serve the downtrodden. She rips out people's entrails in public. We all have our gifts."

He had a half smile, but his eyes looked sad.

"Are you okay?" I asked him.

He stood quiet. For a second I thought he hadn't heard me. Then he shook his head.

"No, I'm not. Neither are you. I don't think anybody involved here is feeling *okay* after that beating."

"I'm sorry," I said. "I really am."

"Darla, you didn't do it by yourself. We all painted part of that picture in there. Except your mom. She's pretty innocent in all of this. I need to catch up with her."

"Sean?" I said before he turned to go, "Am I that person? The person they talked about in there?"

"I don't think *that* person," he told me, "would worry about the answer to that question."

I hoped he was right, but I wasn't sure.

TWENTY

JOANNE LET ME OFF at the corner. The huge, plastic Santa figure was propped in the backseat like some cheerful hitchhiker we'd picked up on our way back from Austin.

"Can you carry that thing by yourself?" Jo asked, talking to me over the back of the driver's seat.

"Yeah." I hoisted Santa out of the car, could barely fit my arm around his middle. "He's a big guy, but he doesn't weigh much."

"Okay," she said, turning back around. "I'll see you tomorrow."

There was a subtle dig in that last part. She'd been complaining lately that we never did anything at night anymore; that I always spent my evenings with Cal. She was right, but spending time with a boyfriend was a pretty normal occurrence, just not in Joanne's universe. Still, it made me feel like shit when she brought it up.

The Langley house faced the street. I could see the windows, dark against the weak December sun. I wondered if old Edith Langley, Cal's landlady, was watching in one of those spaces. If so, my mother would know about the Santa before I got home.

Cal lived in the garage apartment on the backside of the Langley property. The rental consisted of two rooms—a small bedroom, notable for its lack of a window, and a larger room that was everything else. He had a separate entrance up a steep set of stairs that faced the side yard. I hauled the plastic figure up the metal staircase, stopped on the landing, and knocked on the door. While I waited, I pulled the dime-store price sticker off Santa's boot. The cold wind at the top of the landing offered steady pressure at my back, threatened to launch Santa into untimely flight. I wished I'd worn a heavier coat.

"What the hell is that?" Cal asked when he opened the door. He'd already changed out of his uniform, looked easy in his sweatshirt and jeans.

"Hello to you too." I walked past him, put Santa in the corner of the den, and plugged him in. The red glow coming through the suit made the room look warmer.

"There," I said, while Cal still stood by the door looking bewildered. "That's more cheerful. If we get you a little tree and a box of balls, you'll be all set for the big day."

"You saying I don't have balls?" he asked.

"None you'd want me to hang on a tree."

"Ouch," he said, walking toward the corner that was the kitchen to get two bottles of beer.

Christmas was three weeks away, but from the looks of Cal's living space it could have easily been March or July.

He handed me a beer and walked over to the Santa, tapped it with his finger.

"This is just about the ugliest thing I've ever seen," he said.

He came back and sat down on the couch.

"But thank you for taking charge of my holiday decorations. Somebody had to, I guess." Then he stopped, took a deep breath. "Come over here for a minute, I want to talk to you about something."

The last part registered a shift in tone, sounded serious. Getting-fired serious or I've-been-to-the-doctor serious.

"What is it?" I settled in close to him. The couch was new, a sleeper sofa I'd helped him pick out. The cushions were still firm and I felt perched up high, buoyed by the unyielding springs.

"I was thinking we might go up to visit Portland and Seattle just before or maybe right after Christmas, see my folks."

I hadn't met Cal's parents, but I'd heard all the horror stories—the two-timing father, the bitter, ill-tempered mother . . . It didn't sound like an Andy Williams Christmas to me, but I didn't want to squash any snow-globe fantasies he had in his head all of a sudden.

"Did one of them call and invite us?" I asked, stalling for time. "Are they even speaking to each other?"

He'd gone back once since we'd been dating, a couple of months after we met. He'd visited his mother first, then his dad. It wasn't clear to me that he'd even told them about us.

"No, but we ought to see them." He paused, seemed to be holding back on something. "I want them to meet you."

"What *aren't* you telling me?" I asked, finally, after he'd made a few more failed attempts to speak his mind.

It did seem logical that he'd want to see his parents over the holidays. I just hadn't considered it one way or the other, and certainly hadn't assumed I'd be involved.

"What's going on?" I prompted again. "I mean, it makes sense that you'd visit them, but I might be a surprise guest."

"They know about you." He shifted toward me, touched my cheek so that I would focus squarely on his eyes. "They know a lot."

"What do you mean?" I asked.

"Well, I've told them all about you."

"Oh, and what makes you think you know so much about me?" I teased. I felt myself at the center of the moment, blushed hot under his stare.

"I know all I need to know." His eyes held steady when he said this. "I want to ask you something."

My heart shifted gears, accelerated at the sound of his words. I'd played with this conversation in my head, hoped for it and feared it in equal measure, but it was sooner than I'd imagined. My arms, my legs, every part of me, felt disconnected. I was flying, weightless, tethered to the moment only by keeping my eyes on him, on his face. I could barely breathe.

"I want to marry you," he said. "I don't know how you feel about it, but I'm in love with you. That can't be a big surprise."

The couch, the room, the certainty of his heart . . . everything brought me around to the first feelings I'd had with Sean, over a garage, on a sofa. Feelings I'd had before I let myself doubt, before I saw myself as singled out by God, and later simply damaged. But Cal knew about me already. He knew everything that I hadn't known then.

"You know how it is with me," I said. It had to be said. "When we make love, you know what it's like sometimes. I don't want you to cheat yourself out of marrying someone who doesn't have that kind of—"

"You're the most exciting person I've ever been with." He stopped me. "I love when we're together. Even when you hurt . . . I don't know, I love you more for trying. I'm patient, Darla. We make it work, right?"

I nodded. Tears came instead of words.

"We work through it. That's part of it," he went on. "And when we break through, when it's good for you too, there's nothing like it for me. Honestly."

The large kindness seemed no effort for him and it overwhelmed me. The word itself, *love,* offered ordinary language to something without a real name. But my fears gathered as he spoke. It couldn't be as simple as he made it sound. There had to be a catch. Something I was missing. How could he think I was worth it? That was only part of the real question, the fear that skirted the edges of my mind. I chased it, formed it into a thought. *How could he think I was exciting, with somebody like Joanne around?*

"What makes me so special, Cal? What do you get? Seems like I get everything out of this. I mean, this is a really big decision for you."

"Are you kidding? You really don't know what I love about you?"

I shook my head. I was almost afraid to know, afraid to find out that what he loved consisted of spun sugar, puffed candy that wouldn't last. I saw myself that way, confection that when handed over to time and air would dissolve into nothing.

Or worse yet, what if his feelings had landed among the romantic notions of adversity. That would get really old when dishes and diapers took center stage.

"I need to know you're with me for the right reasons, that's all."

He sat back a little. Glowing Santa looked on with empty humor, oddly unnerving in its steadfast cheer.

"Well, for starters, I love the fact that you listen to baseball on the radio, even when I'm not around."

"Cal, you can't—"

"Hush," he said evenly. "You asked and I'm telling you."

I closed my mouth, sat back against new pillows that smelled of showrooms and storage.

"Instead of listening to that crap on the radio, you listen to Neil Young, the Rolling Stones. You love riverbanks and wet leaves. Hell, you have your shoes off when you come see me at work. Before you even say hello, your feet are covered in mud. You're a kid and a woman, all at the same time."

He was caught up, on a roll. I felt like a character in a movie. But it wasn't really about me; it was about Jo.

"You come up with crazy stuff, like that damn Santa. Convince me it's normal. The time you dragged me off to Galveston for the day, to play the arcades. That was one of the best days I've ever had."

His words were spinning, moving too fast. I wanted to step back and be still. I wanted to tell him he was describing someone else.

"I think you're confused." It was all I could manage.

"No," he said. "I'm pretty clear on all this."

"Cal." I had to say it. Dating was one thing, but he was talking about marriage. It was too big to keep quiet. "The person you're talking about isn't who I am, at least not how I see myself."

It was Jo, he'd described everything I loved about Joanne. Could I hand that over to him? Could I tell him and maybe put my doubts in his mind too?

"All those things you described, the spontaneous person you think I am . . . that's not . . . that's . . ."

"Joanne." He said it. In spite of my worries, I felt relieved. The word. Her name. Putting it out between us seemed dangerous, but the hardest part had passed. It was said. Why wouldn't he prefer her? It wasn't jealousy as much as bewilderment. I was afraid that when he saw it, when I finally brought it to the surface, he would feel foolish for having missed it before. But he said it. He knew.

"You think it's Joanne I see in you." He repeated it. There would be no turning around.

"Jo and I . . ." I fumbled for the words. "We've been friends a long time; it's easy to mistake—"

"No," he said, almost smiling. "I don't think I could ever mistake the two of you."

"But all the things you just said. It doesn't sound like me."

"So you don't like the Rolling Stones?" he asked.

"Sure, I do, but—"

"You didn't want to go to Galveston?"

"Cal, you don't understand."

"No," he said, "you don't understand. I appreciate what she may have brought out in you over the years. I'm sure you've done a lot for her too. But you don't know what I see in you that I never saw in Joanne."

He stretched his arm along the back of the couch. I felt protected, shielded from all my fears.

"I saw you both at the same time, Darla. I saw you both and I wanted you."

"Why? Everything you've talked about—"

"Is you," he said. "Only there's more. The first time I saw you, I knew what you had inside. I saw Jo pretty clearly too."

"What do you mean?"

"I think I knew, even that first day, what she couldn't give. If I had a lousy day at work or if my son-of-a-bitch father called and I felt like hell . . . On a day like that Jo would crack a joke, make it worse somehow. But you . . . Yeah, you can be insane, take me for a real ride sometimes. I love that. But you're more. I need somebody real, somebody I can rely on. Somebody who knows how to love."

"You don't think Jo knows how to love?" I sounded almost defiant, felt nearly at odds with him over his dismissal of her. It was messed up, all my feelings turning on themselves.

"Not the way I need it. You're what I need, Darla. You have to trust me, what I feel. I want you to marry me."

It seemed unreal, to suddenly *know* something was true. Preachers spent lifetimes trying to elicit that single response. Blind belief. Love as an act of faith. I felt part of Cal already.

"I'll marry you," I said, at ease after all. "I love you."

"Do you believe me?"

"Yes, I believe you." That seemed to be the make-or-break part of it for him.

He leaned toward me, his face earnest, holding a question, but the words didn't come. Instead we moved toward each other, drawn into what we had created out of words and air.

He touched me, my throat, my breast, and I held his neck between my hands, guided his mouth to me.

As I gave way, I accepted the raw cry of nerves, a chorus inside me both lovely and sharp. Pleasure pushed beyond its boundaries to meet with pain. He stopped, reading my breath, my eyes, my skin. He stopped to let me choose and I moved close against him.

December wind sounded against the door. But it couldn't reach us. We were safe. My sheltered fears, once exposed, settled as benign thoughts. Simple as it was, I was happy.

JO SLOUCHED BACK on my mother's perfect chintz, a bag of chips resting on her stomach. I'd surprised her. Picked her up at her parents' house well past dark, after I'd said good night to Cal. Her worn denim and ample skin clashed with the distinct patterns of Mom's floral upholstery.

"That's great," she said when I told her my news. "Just fucking great."

I hadn't expected a celebration, but it was worse than I'd imagined.

"You're being a real shit," I snapped back at her, then winced, suddenly remembering that my mother was asleep in the next room.

Jo turned her face away, pulled another chip from the nearly empty bag, and stared at the TV. The late news was on, turned down too low to hear.

The television mumbled, keeping us from total silence. I thought of an expression Peggy's dad had used. *Survivor's guilt.* He'd come back from an aircraft carrier at Okinawa. Had come back to a job and a house and a family when a lot of his buddies hadn't. The phrase ran through my head over and over as I watched Joanne and felt unable to say the right thing.

"I know it's weird," I tried again, "but it doesn't have anything to do with us."

"Bullshit." She took another chip, still didn't look back at me.

That was it. Enough.

"What the fuck do you want?" I kept it to a menacing whisper. "You want us to be old ladies raising hell on the weekends? Don't you want a family someday? If you're going to be an asshole, just take my car and go home."

I got up, cleared our dirty glasses and wrappers off the coffee table and took them into the kitchen. Two wineglasses sat on the counter. My mom had poured one for both of us, to toast my news. At least *somebody* had been happy for me. Minutes passed. I kept busy at the sink, refusing to go back and set myself up again. Finally I heard her move in the other room.

"I'm sorry." She was in the kitchen, leaning against the door. "Really, I mean it."

I looked at her. She seemed smaller than usual, younger somehow.

"It's okay," I said, rinsing a glass under the spigot. "It's all mixed up, I know. It changes everything."

She nodded.

I turned to face her, leaned back against the counter but kept my distance. I didn't trust the change in her just yet.

"I don't have a sister, you know," I said. "I need somebody to get up there with me."

"You gonna dress me up funny?" she asked.

"I'll let you pick."

She smiled, muted but real. The storm had passed. So I walked over, hugged her, and to my relief, she hugged me back.

"Any of that wine left?" she asked, pulling back. She nodded to the glasses on the counter.

I opened the fridge, found the bottle in the door, and poured into the same glasses my mother and I had used. We stood for a moment, holding our wine, then finally drank without toasting.

We would survive. She was scared, didn't know for sure. But I did.

The phone rang just behind me, made me jump. It could only be Cal calling so late. Mom had finally given up, turned the ringer off in her bedroom so that his midnight calls wouldn't wake her. I heard the sound again and went still.

"You gonna get that?" Jo asked, a trace of irritation back in her voice.

If I sounded casual, Cal would wonder what was wrong. But our intimate mumbling would take Joanne right back to square one in the mood department. I didn't have the energy to battle with her again.

"I'll call him back later," I said. The trill ringing set me on edge.

We stood together, listening, not speaking. We listened until it stopped. Then we took our wine back into the den. The room seemed changed somehow. The night had become long. Before we sat down, Joanne turned to me.

"Cheers." She held her glass up in a belated offering.

"Cheers," I said, meeting her glass with an uneasy touch.

"You guys are going to be happy," she said. The sentiment came with such effort.

I felt the weary pull on my own spirit, wondered why both of us should have to try so hard.

TWENTY-ONE

C AL AND I MADE LOVE when we got home from the courtroom. It began more as an act of need than passion. The thin mattress of the foldout couch left our bodies just inches from the hard frame beneath. The metal angles reminded me second by second of where we were, and why. Even though the painters had finished in our bedroom, I hadn't been able to sleep on the bed in there. Cal hadn't pushed me to go back.

"Are you hurting?" he asked just after we started.

At first I thought he meant about Joanne, but then I realized he was talking about my illness.

"I'm fine," I told him, mumbled something about medicine, about it not being bad these days. He seemed new to me and it made me inexplicably shy.

"Tell me if you're not okay," he said.

"Where do you want me to start with that one?" I said, trying to pull off a weak joke.

Even though it wasn't funny, he smiled, then pulled me to him with an urgency, a coarse vulnerability that forced my numb feelings to quicken. For the first time since the days of awkward fumblings with Sean, I felt taken, desired beyond thought or reason.

Cal, his flat hand pressing the small of my back, pulled us to a tight intermingling of nerves, of skin. I caught the rhythm of his need, clung happy and tasted skin and salt, felt his breath on my breast, my neck.

Without the effort I thought it would take, I abandoned the wrong days that had come before, gave everything to the grateful relief and tasted precious oblivion that offered something rare and kept.

In the still minutes that followed, I tried to name for myself what had happened, what had changed. We hadn't talked about what had happened in the courtroom, but it felt resolved.

I had wanted to forget the whole business, but as I lay awake with Cal, finally dozing, I knew that something strong and right shared space with the constant ache over Joanne, with the misery of the day's words and images. It gave me hope.

I hadn't been to the hospital since the court proceedings had started. I had been afraid; afraid that if I saw her, those numb feelings would fade, like painkillers that slowly wear off. I had more than I could handle trying to hold on to the baby. I couldn't go back to missing Joanne. Not like I had. It was a betrayal and I knew it. Without expectation, Cal had taken the weight of those fears, left something in place of it that would hold against the pain.

"Darla?" He was awake, had asked me something, the question had registered somewhere in my head, but I'd missed the words entirely.

"I didn't hear you. I'm sorry."

"Are you hungry?" he asked again.

He'd gotten up, was dressing in the middle of the living room. It was nearly dark outside and the light from the kitchen fell in a line across the pale, blue sheets of the foldout bed.

"A little, I guess. I don't know," I said, sitting upright, and finding my shirt. "Cal, let's go to the lake." The thought and the words arrived at the same time.

"Now?"

"It's a full moon," I said. "We can take what's left of that six-pack in the fridge and sit on the dock outside your station."

It sounded desperate, even to me. Cal never went for my spur-of-the-moment ideas anyway. I waited for him to tell me why this was insane, to tell me why we should eat a bowl of soup, go to bed, and stay there. Part of me wanted that too, just sleep and escape all the words I could still hear in my head.

"I have a better idea," he said. "Come on."

He opened the door, called for Rigsby to get in the truck. I still stood by the couch, unable to process that we were actually going to do something.

"Come on," he said again as he held the door open for me.

We got in the truck and drove, Rigsby hanging his head over the edge in back to catch all the smells. We drove past the road to the lake on the way out, crossed the line into a county that wasn't dry. At the first convenience store, Cal pulled the truck in and left it idling with the radio on. He came out a few minutes later with a bag, but he wouldn't show me what he bought.

"What'd you get," I pressed.

"You'll see" was all he would say.

The duck blind sat at the edge of the water. It looked like a childhood fort, but with hunting season months away had the forlorn quality of abandoned play. Brown leaves and twigs that disguised the frame stood out in the bright night. In winter, it blended with the colors of the season, but on the still-green shore of early September, the hunters' drab lair was not disguised. I could see it up ahead, knew that was where he planned for us to go.

"What do those look like inside?" I'd asked him before, more than once.

"I'll show you sometime," he always said.

Moonlight reflected off the water, covering us with silvery air as we walked the bank to the blind. Rigsby trailed us, intrigued by the rich smells of the river. Cal carried the grocery bag. I could hear the bottles clinking against each other as we walked.

"I can't believe this was your idea," I said, just behind him and slightly winded.

"My idea? You're the one who said let's go to the lake."

"I was thinking of a drive," I said. "This is an outing. God, I'm out of breath. I've got to give up the cigarettes again."

"Let's deal with one major ordeal at a time," he said, continuing at a slower pace so that I could catch up. "I'll help you when this is over."

"Sold."

When this is over . . . It was the closest he'd come to acknowledging the day or that we might come out intact from our courtroom carnival ride from hell.

"What's in the bag?" I asked for the third or fourth time.

"You'll see," he said—again.

Inside the duck blind, the wood-plank floor was covered with dirt and leaves. Cal brushed aside the debris and put down a blanket. Rigsby curled and settled right away. I sat Indian style and Cal knelt on one knee to unveil his mysterious bag of goodies.

"The theme for the evening," he said, "is . . . Quik Mart top shelf."

He pulled out two bottles of red wine with screw tops where the corks should have been, pork rinds, cocktail peanuts, beef jerky, and two four-packs of cigars.

"Oh you've outdone yourself," I said. It felt good to smile without effort. "Two packs of cigars? You must be anticipating a big night."

"Two *varieties*," he said, holding the boxes in the moonlight from the opening that served as a window. "Regulars for me. Tiparillos for the lady."

"You're out of your mind," I said, now in a full grin.

He opened a pack of paper cups and poured the wine, then took out the last item from the bag, a box of Milk-Bones. Rigsby left my side and circled around to Cal.

"Selling yourself for a box of dog treats," I joked. "I thought better of you, Rigsby."

The dog looked up, regarded me, and turned his eyes back to Cal as he opened the box.

The wine, flavored like gum and nearly as sweet, went down in easy swallows until the world backed away from me. Just the barest sense of joy slipped in. I almost didn't claim it, felt I should push it away out of habit, but then I relaxed and let it come. There could be a life after Joanne, just the way there'd been life without my daddy. A different life, to be sure, but full and laced with measured happiness. Fleeting gratitude moved through me, and I didn't know who to honor with the feeling. Cal, for starters, but it seemed beyond him too.

"Your face looks relaxed," he said.

"That's 'cause I'm fairly looped on this Kool-Aid wine you bought."

"No," he said. "It's not just that. We needed to get away from everybody else."

The pork rinds and peanuts offset the sweet bite of the wine with salty grease. Rigsby licked my fingers. Cal kissed my neck. I wanted to stay inside the leaf-and-stick walls forever.

When we were done eating, he lit two cigars and handed the plastic-ended Tiparillo to me. Pungent smoke, common as dust, grew exotic around us, a strange incense that took us far from our known days.

"This is like a kids' hideout," I said, my mind floating from the wine and the nicotine.

"Yeah. That's about what it is. Grown men, you should see them, dressed up in funny combat suits. Only their toys are guns that happen to shoot real shells. But they come in here and act more like kids than they did when they were young."

He poured the last of the second bottle into our cups.

"They drink too much of this stuff," he held up the empty bottle, "and by the time they stumble out, drunk with loaded guns, I have to come out here and be the parent. Haul their asses in and talk to them like nine-year-olds."

"Poor baby," I said, thinking I ought to lie down somewhere; the room was going on a little joyride of its own.

I put my head on his lap, turned on my back so I could look up and talk with him. He was griping about work, but his face was content.

"What's your fantasy?" I asked.

"What do you mean?"

"Your perfect world, as of right now."

He took a deep breath; a breeze through the opened space of a window moved the fragments of leaves that were our walls.

"This place," he said. "A little roomier, but basically the same—a houseboat out in the middle of the lake. We're out there, live out there. I go to work. Come in for lunch. But all day I can see our little houseboat, our own private island, and it's safe and we're happy. No one bothers us."

"Where does Rigsby go to the bathroom?"

"We've got this wooden pier off the back of the house and there's a little hole in it. A net sits under the hole with water purifiers built in so he's not soiling our swim area. We train him to go over the hole."

"Same for us? A hole in the bathroom? Net underneath?" I asked.

"You're getting it," he said, smiling. He rubbed his hand over my forehead. A slight film of moisture covered my skin and when he moved my hair away from my face, it felt cool, delicious.

"How about you?" he said. "Your fantasy."

I looked up at his pleasant features. Still relaxed. Happy. It had been so long since I'd seen it, I could barely take my eyes away from him.

"I'll go with the houseboat too," I said. "It's a night like this. We've been asleep for a little while and the baby starts making noises. Not loud cries, just little waking sounds—kind of I'm-getting-hungry noises. We both wake up and I tell you it's okay, you have to work the next day, I'll get up. I go to the baby's room and sit in the chair by the window giving her—or him—a bottle. We don't even need a rocking chair. The little waves on the lake are enough. It rocks us all the time. And it feels so good, the water moving me a little from side to side, the baby in my arms, you sleeping, Rigsby by the bed . . ."

I was lost in this picture. It seemed almost real and I was frightened to hope that it could be. Janet thought we had a real shot at having the baby legally declared ours. The wanting grew fierce inside me when I let it, so I pulled back, tried to protect myself enough to keep living if it didn't come my way.

I looked up again at Cal's face in the moonlight. The easy ride of the wine stopped when I saw his expression. We were on separate tracks with this fantasy business. His had just come to an abrupt halt.

"What's wrong?" I asked.

"Nothing."

"Cal, it's okay to say that you didn't have a baby on your houseboat. I know you're slower coming to this than I am."

"I'm fine. Really. Let's don't overanalyze what may or may not be in my head. We had a lady doing that all afternoon, remember. And it ain't pretty." He managed a weak smile.

"Cal, are you going to be able to handle all this?"

"I'm doing all right, I said. Just let it go."

"What about after?" I pressed. "What if we really do get this baby? Can you handle that?"

He looked out the opening, toward the bright night.

"I'm not sure," he said. He looked defeated somehow, even saying it. "But I'm trying. As long as we're in this together, as long as we stay strong, I think I can do it. I just can't promise."

"I understand," I said, but I didn't. Not really. I couldn't understand why it wasn't clear to him.

"Are you okay right now?" I asked.

"Yeah," he said. "I'm okay."

"Really?"

"Really."

His face had softened again.

I closed my eyes, could feel him breathing. The world was holding me gently, rocking. Our hideout had become the houseboat again. No one knew where we were. No one could find us—for a while.

TWENTY-TWO

I SAW THE DUST in the driveway before I actually saw Joanne's truck.
She was so mad. It took me a few minutes to figure out that she was
pissed at herself.

"It was stupid," she said, stomping around my front yard.

I had to shadow her pacing, keep at her heels to catch pieces of
the story. Something about the lumberyard. Andy Roman.

"I'm always by myself with the dog at lunch. Except today. Jesus!
I can't believe it. The first time I screw up . . ."

Her shirt rose slightly above the low cut of her pants. The pale
band of skin at her belly suggested a vulnerability masked in all of that
posturing.

"Just tell me what happened," I said.

"It was stupid."

"You already said that."

She stopped, looked at me. Her eyes had a faraway quality that
looked familiar. And when I got close enough, I could smell the pot—
in her shirt, in her hair. She'd called me from the lumberyard office a

little over an hour before; bored, waiting for her lunch break. It didn't take a whole lot to figure out had what happened since then.

"What did you do?"

"I fucking screwed myself, that's what," she said.

"That's redundant."

"Go to hell." She kicked a flowerpot over. The plants were half dead from the heat anyway, so I let it go.

"Let's get inside," I said. "I've got some coffee."

"Do you have any bourbon?"

"I've got some coffee," I said again.

SHE'D BEEN AT WORK at the lumberyard. Her office was in the makeshift trailer in the middle of the yard, the only air-conditioned spot in the whole place.

"I had my sandwich out," she said. She was sitting at my kitchen table, coffee in hand, and she'd managed to settle down a little. "Nobody else was around and I went to the back door to see if Rigsby was there."

"The dog?" I asked.

"Yeah. He meets me at the back door every day and I let him in, give him some food. Then he goes off to wherever it is he lives. Kind of like the rest of the men in my life." A joke, but her heart wasn't in it.

"So what happened?"

"Rigsby wasn't there. I walked out and looked all around the trailer. It's weird, 'cause he always comes around right at lunchtime."

"Skip the dog. Get to the part where you decided to get high at work."

"How did you know?" she asked, looking at me with a little suspicion.

"I can smell, for one thing."

"Oh, right." She pulled part of her hair to her nose. Made a face. "Andy Roman had a joint. He saw me looking for Rigsby, said if the dog stood me up for lunch, he'd be happy to step in. Andy's a good guy. I figured, what the hell. We were sitting out behind the trailer when the foreman comes around and sees us. Like high school, for crissakes. Getting caught out back behind the Biology lab."

"So all hell broke loose?" I pressed her. I could already picture the scene.

"The jerk of a foreman told Mr. Franks, who was mostly pissed that I left the office unattended. They keep some money in there. But they all smelled the stuff, knew what we'd been doing . . ."

She put her forehead in her hands. I'd seen her sorry about screwing up only a couple of times in our whole lives. I didn't like it much. It jumbled my image of her, of myself even. Life seemed a precarious endeavor when Joanne's guard was down.

"So he told you to go home," I said, finishing her story. "Big deal. He'll get over it and you can tell him—*honestly* . . ." I stopped for emphasis. ". . . *honestly*, that you won't ever do it again."

"He already fired me."

"He what?"

"He said he had a dozen girls apply for jobs every year, too many to put up with a mistake like that. Honest to God, he was more upset about the empty office than about the pot, but . . ." She shook her head.

"Hold on," I told her, getting up from the table.

"What are you doing?" she asked as I walked to the other room.

"I'm getting Cal's bourbon."

She stayed at my house all afternoon, took a shower, and put on some of my clothes. She didn't say much more about work. We watched the straight lineup of afternoon soaps and ate ice cream laced with bourbon followed by chunks of refrigerated cookie dough broken straight off the roll.

"I better get home," she said finally, when the television had nothing but talk shows to offer until the news. "I need to tell the 'rents what happened and watch my dad's cheeks turn into a mood ring."

"Can you drive?" I asked.

"I think so," she said. "But if I get lucky, I'll wrap myself around a telephone pole and get the sympathy vote before I get the big lecture. Do you have any gum?" she asked, putting her hand up to her face to check her breath.

I watched her leave. She had just learned to use a stick shift, and her truck, a hand-me-down from her dad's pre–hardware store days, rocked on the incline at the end of our driveway, waiting for cars to pass on the highway. I expected at any moment to see the pickup come rolling back toward my living room wall. But after a couple of nervous seconds when the road had cleared, she lurched onto the highway and out of sight.

"WHAT THE HELL was she thinking?" Cal said over our prepackaged dinner of black beans and rice.

I'd thrown in some sausage to make the side dish look more like a meal; but served alone, the small mound seemed meager fare on our large Fiestaware plates. I made a mental note to put it in bowls the next time.

"Joanne doesn't think," I said, sitting catercornered to him at our kitchen table. "She just *does*."

The table was too large for the two of us. I'd seen us populating the empty spaces with high chairs and booster seats, but that dream had dwindled after about a million visits to the clinic in Austin.

"Jo's a grown-up with a real job now," he said. "Adults have to think about what they do."

"She lives from one impulse to the next. She was bored and the guy had a joint," I countered, as if that somehow justified her decision. "And she *used* to have a real job. As of today, that's history too."

"She's got to settle down at some point," he said, shaking his head, turning his attention back to the island of rice on his mango-colored plate.

He sounded as if the subject was finished, and I didn't mind moving on. Cal tolerated Joanne, liked her for the most part but thought she brought out the sides of me he least understood.

"You want coffee?" I asked, standing up.

"Sure," he said, looking at me.

Sometimes there was something in his eyes, something I couldn't read, but wished he'd just say.

"What are you thinking?" I asked.

He hesitated, opened his mouth, but before any words came out, we both heard the grind of a poorly executed downshift as Joanne's truck came into our driveway.

I saw her through the window. Late summer light still played off of the shiny black of the truck's hood. She opened her door, but didn't get out of the seat right away. She sat, cigarette in hand, and stared at our house. She stared until she saw me at the window, then gave a weak wave and pulled herself out.

I opened the kitchen door for her. She put out her cigarette in the driveway, then walked in without saying anything.

"Hey, Jo," Cal offered. He didn't get up.

"Hey," she answered. Went over and leaned against the counter, propping herself with her elbows behind her.

"He threw me out," she said. Her voice stayed even. A simple statement.

"Your dad?"

She nodded. I waited for more, but it didn't come.

"Jo?" I prompted. "What happened?"

Cal had stopped eating. He sat watching her, waiting. I felt squeezed between them, with no room for comfort.

"Was there an argument?" I prompted when she didn't answer me.

"Oh yeah. You could say that." She walked to the sink. Wet her hands and rubbed water on her face, through her hair.

"It was pretty awful." The hard edge had left her voice. She looked as if she might actually cry.

Silence gathered around us, crowding my thoughts. I wasn't sure what I could offer without talking to Cal, but I didn't want to pull him out of the room for a secret powwow on the situation. I glanced at him, feeling desperate for a clue, any clue, that would shift the moment away from where it held us in limbo.

"You can stay here," Cal said, finally. His voice was flat, the words forced, but offered nonetheless. I felt the room open up a little; looked at him, mouthed a silent "thank you" and he gave a weak smile. She looked from me to him, must have gauged him to be sincere.

"Maybe just a couple of nights," she said, glancing back at me. Her eyes apologized. "Thanks, Cal, both of you. I've really messed things up this time."

Cal nodded.

I walked over, stood close for a second before I offered a hug. To my surprise, she gave in, a rare acceptance of comfort. Her arms, bare outside a sleeveless blouse, pressed damp against mine. Her heart beat fast. She was more frightened than she was showing. I pressed closer, felt the need to cover her, shelter her.

But then she pulled away, unable to sustain herself in the fragile moment. When I turned around, Cal had gone.

AFTER JOANNE FINISHED EATING what was left of the beans and rice, she looked a little more like herself. She said she wanted to take another shower, wanted to be rid of everything that reminded her of the scene at her dad's house. I listened to her, humming while the water was running. The sounds she made echoed richly off the shower walls.

"Can I borrow something else to wear?" she asked coming out of the bathroom.

The towel was barely draped over her and I wondered how she knew Cal hadn't come in. It occurred to me that it wouldn't have mattered to her, one way or the other. Her body wasn't the part of herself she needed to keep hidden.

"Sure, put on anything you want," I told her. "Mi closet es su closet. You know that."

She picked a pair of jeans and a gauzy turquoise shirt that she'd talked me into buying in the first place.

"You can have that shirt," I said. "I've never been able to pull off wearing it."

She shrugged, nodded, and didn't argue. It was true and she knew it. After she dressed she got her pocketbook, fished around for her keys.

"I gotta go back over to the office," she said.

"What do you need from there?"

"I left a bunch of my stuff," she said. "I've still got office keys. They can ask for them if they want 'em back. But I've got to get in there before they do. I left my makeup bag and my thermos, an umbrella and a box of tampons. Anyway, I'd rather get everything when nobody's there. I don't want them all looking at me while I go through drawers."

"You think that's a good idea? Going in there when no one's around?"

"I just want to get my junk and be done with them. Okay?" Her tone implied that they couldn't do much more to her than fire her. I hoped that was true. We hadn't talked about the fact that pot was, sort of, illegal. "You going with me?"

"Sure," I said. "Let's take my car. I don't want to get whiplash from riding around with you in that stick shift."

Outside, I looked up the road for any sign of Cal's truck. I'd let myself relax a little in his absence, then felt guilty when I realized I felt that way. I went inside and left him a note before heading off with Joanne.

THE LUMBERYARD SAT STILL in the early evening, but the dust from the day's activity still hung over the stacks of cut trees, the machines, and the trucks. We drove right up to the trailer. If somebody was around, I didn't want it to look as if we were sneaking around.

"Just give me a minute," she said, implying that I should stay in the car.

"I'll go in with you," I said.

I didn't want to be alone there. The feel of the place gave me the creeps. A huge crane sat off to the right of us. Logs were suspended in midair, giving the impression of a job half done. I half expected it to begin moving on its own, a ghost crane gone mad on two trespassing girls.

Joanne had gotten her things, but the odd collection in her hands didn't look like much. I wondered if she'd had to come back for some other reason, some kind of final punctuation on the incident.

When we came out of the office, the dark had set in, but large lights, mounted on poles, lit up the lumberyard brighter than noon. Jo was locking back up when we heard something, a weak little sound— half yip, half wail. A dog sat slumped near my car. His head hung down. A whole side of him moved every time he took a breath, as if the act of taking in air took the effort of his whole being. Fur matted with blood covered one side of his back half. His tail drooped down, mangled and mostly gone.

"Oh God, Rigsby!" Joanne ran to him, knelt down, and began to pull him to her, but he yelped when she touched his side. We found a big piece of cardboard near a Dumpster behind the office trailer. Jo coaxed him onto it, careful not to touch his back leg. Then we put him in the backseat of my car.

As I turned the car around, we saw a truck turning into the lumberyard off the main road. When it came under the lights, I recognized Mr. Franks inside. He parked beside us, got out and walked over to my car. Joanne rolled down the window in the backseat when he tapped on it. She was sitting by Rigsby, hovering over him, anxious for us to leave.

"Joanne? What are you doing?" Mr. Frank's voice was soft, anything but an angry ex-boss.

"I came to get my personal things out of the drawer," she said. "We found him. He's hurt." She looked down at the dog. "We've got to get him some help."

She started to roll up her window, when he told her to wait.

"Listen, Jo," he said. "Maybe I was hasty. If you want to come in tomorrow, we can talk—"

"That's okay," she interrupted him. "You probably did the right thing. I think it's better if I don't come back."

He looked at her, confused. She didn't offer any further explanation.

"Here are your keys," she said, handing them through the window. "We've got to get Rigsby to a doctor."

Then she rolled up the window, told me to drive.

Rigsby whimpered and Joanne openly wept on the way to Dr. Sanders' house.

"Hurry," she said, every minute or so.

I knew I'd never figure her out. She sat unmoved through movies that had me weak from crying. Stood dry-eyed through showdowns with her father that rocked their house sideways. But something about dogs, a hurt dog, a missing dog, and she'd turn into a total mess.

"Any idea who he belongs to?" I asked as we drove.

"No," she managed. "He wears this collar, but it doesn't have any tags on it."

The animal clinic was already closed, but the old vet never turned away an emergency at his house. His wife came to the door and he rose behind her, still sleepy-eyed from nodding off in his recliner.

"Looks like he got in on the losing end of a fight with a bigger dog—or at least a meaner one," Dr. Sanders said, leaning into my car to look at the animal.

"His back leg's hurt bad," Joanne told him.

"Yeah," he said. "I see that. We better get him to the office."

I followed Dr. Sanders' old Cadillac four blocks over to his clinic.

"Wait here," he said as he fumbled with the keys. He went in and came out with a gurney of sorts, a flat wooden board on wheels with a handle like a wagon.

"Rigged this up myself," he said, pulling the dog up a small ramp and into the building.

It was all I could do to get Joanne to leave Rigsby. Dr. Sanders had bandaged him and given him something to help him sleep. He had him in a pen padded with a pile of old sheets and towels.

"He's breathing okay," the vet said, "and the bleeding's stopped. I think he'll be all right. Just needs to rest now."

Joanne wanted to stay, offered to sleep on a vinyl couch and have coffee ready before anybody came to work the next morning. Dr. Sanders was a bit of a softy and would have given in, but I talked her into going with me, bribed her with ice cream at Dairy Queen. As we drove away, she watched him lock up. I could tell she was worried about the dog being alone, but she didn't say anything. She just stared at the clinic until we'd rounded the corner. Then she stared straight ahead.

"Jo?" I asked. "Back at the lumberyard, why didn't you take your job back?"

"I don't know," she answered. "It just hit me, looking at Rigsby all messed up, that my days in that office don't count for much, not really."

"Most people just go to work, Joanne."

"Yeah, but when they get home, they're raising kids or coaching Little League. Something besides adding up receipts all day and going home and smoking a joint."

I didn't know what to say to her.

"Besides," she said, before I could try and console her, "I didn't want to go back owing them anything—owing him."

"Why? Is he a lech or something?"

"Nah. It's just different after somebody does you a favor."

"I do you favors all the time," I said.

"You're different."

"Yeah, I'm different, all right," I said.

I drove on. The thoughts of what I'd been thinking of asking her to do for me played in my head. But I kept them to myself. I needed more in my life too. But she had enough going on. She didn't need to be dragged into solving my problems. Still, it was there in my thoughts. The question. It was a question that in some ways I hoped I never got the nerve to ask.

We pulled into the parking lot of Dairy Queen, walked in past a poster of soft-serve the size of a grown man.

"There's got to be more to it," she said as we waited in line to order. "Something worthwhile. Like what Doc Sanders is doing."

"You want to be a vet?" I asked.

"No," she said. "But I want what I do to matter, to be important to somebody."

We stepped up to the counter to order. The moment seemed open, ready for me to ask, but instead I said only, "You matter to me." Even that was lost as the young girl behind the register began talking, asking us what we wanted to order.

I stared at the menu, the colorful pictures, but nothing seemed to be right.

"Pineapple sundae," Jo said, sure of herself, as usual.

"Make it two," I said, less sure of anything than I had been an hour before.

TWENTY-THREE

"H EY!" it was Evie's voice on the other end of the phone line.
"Hi, Evie," I said. Her timing couldn't have been worse.

Cal and I were due in court at 10:30. The judge had a ruling ready and Janet wanted us there half an hour early to go over what could happen and what our response would be to each of the various scenarios. Still, I was anxious to talk with Evie about the night Joanne crashed.

"Michael said you'd been by a couple of times looking for me," she said. "I was up at my mom's with the kids. I guess he told you that much."

"Yeah," I said. "He told me. I was just trying to piece together a little more about the night of the accident. I wanted to see if you remembered exactly what Joanne's note said. There are some things that don't make any sense to me."

"Well, you can see it if you want."

"What?"

"The note. She left instructions for Rigsby on it—his doctor's name, what kind of food makes him sick, all that stuff. I put it on my fridge and as far as I know it's still there; nothin' gets thrown away at this house. I'm in the bedroom. Want me to go check and see if it's there?"

"No, that's okay. I've really got to run now, but I need to talk with you. Can I call you later today, maybe come by?"

"Sure. Michael took my car today so he could get the oil changed. I can't drive that thing of his, so I'm stuck here all day."

When I hung up, I looked over at Cal. He stood by the door, waiting for me. I could tell by the look on his face what he thought about my questions for Evie, but he didn't say anything.

The suit made him look older, like he was somebody's dad already. I thought it was a good sign.

"You look handsome," I told him.

He offered a courtly nod. "Thank you." He held the door for me to go out first.

IN THE COURTROOM, the judge, who had said so little while everybody else weighed in with an opinion, suddenly had the only words that mattered. He'd put on his glasses, referred to the paper in front of him. The glasses made him appear less imposing, as if imperfect vision might somehow afford him empathy when considering the shortcomings of others.

"This has been a difficult week for everyone," he started. "These things always are. I hope that, for the sake of the child, all of you can put your feelings into some perspective. You all care about the welfare of the baby, or else you wouldn't be going through this. Try to remember that you have that in common, rather than dwelling on anything that's been said or done here."

He went on a little longer about the need for harmony. I wanted to hit a fast-forward button, to be done with his fatherly advice. I just wanted to hear his answer.

"The Timbros," he said, and my heart dropped, "have attempted to make a case, primarily against Mrs. Stevens, casting her life as reckless, thus making her home unsuitable for a child. While Mrs. Stevens has made some grave mistakes in judgment, and while the method of obtaining this child is decidedly unorthodox, I see no compelling

reason to deny what we presume to be the biological father the opportunity to raise his child, and I think there is no question that the
wishes of the biological mother were that Mrs. Stevens serve as the
child's mother. This judgment, of course, is pending the outcome of a
paternity test after the child is born."

Janet grabbed my hand under the table. There had been so many
words. Did he say the baby was ours? *No reason to deny . . .*

I looked at Cal. He smiled at me, nodded.

Janet had let go of my hand. Her forehead furrowed and she was
listening carefully to the rest of what the judge offered.

". . . the various studies on family and child-rearing point to the extreme increased benefit to a child when extended family plays an active role in early life. Whether you like it or not, Mr. and Mrs. Stevens,
the Timbros are related to this baby. It is therefore my judgment that,
while Mr. and Mrs. Stevens will retain primary custody upon the birth
of the child, liberal time with the grandparents will be enforced, which
will include at least, but not limited to, temporary custody for Mr. and
Mrs. Timbro during two weekends a month. I will leave it to you to
sort out the particulars. If you come to no agreements, we can get the
court involved in that too."

Two weekends? I thought of the baby staying at their house. Any
time under the same roof with Larry Timbro seemed like too much.
He didn't need even that much time to put a kid's ego on the skids.
But still, it was so much better than what could have happened.

The judge was still talking, more general stuff about resolving dif-
ferences.

"What does all this mean, exactly?" I whispered to Janet. "We get
custody, right?"

"Shh . . ." she said. "Let's hear him out. This is good, Darla. Believe me, this is good."

Fifteen minutes later, Janet was shaking hands with the smarmy
Mr. Jackson as if they were drinking buddies from way back. Larry
Timbro kept a stony expression, but Mrs. Timbro gave me a kind look.
Her face was older, but she was basically the same person who'd of-
fered sodas and sandwiches—and kindness. She had been kind.
Maybe she would be able to do more for another child than she'd man-
aged for Joanne.

As soon as the judge dismissed, a rush of bodies surrounded us—all family and friends, including Mr. Romeros and Peggy's parents. The only conspicuous absences were Cal's parents. He'd called them, finally, but not with enough notice for them to get away. It was just as well.

The happy crowd pressed around us, but I felt outside of the moment, as if I was looking on from a slight distance.

"Darla!" It was Peggy, arms wide, coming toward me. I saw her smile and it registered that it had actually happened, the baby was ours. "Hey, little mama!" She took me into a Peggy-sized hug.

The fear that had grown too familiar for me to regard most of the time was remarkable in its absence. A small thread of unease remained in its place, a natural holdover from the weeks of uncertainty, I reasoned. It would fade, and the baby was mine.

I willed away any traces of the old anxiety, took Cal's hand, and allowed myself to relax, to smile even. The relief felt so tangible that it brought tears in the wake of its arrival.

I looked at Cal, tried to figure out what he was thinking, but all I saw was a face that I could count on, not one that I could read.

"Congratulations." Sean came up beside Cal and me, gave me a hug, and shook Cal's hand. The two of them, Sean and Cal, locked for a moment in a casual glance, took my adult history from beginning to present. The only player missing was Jo.

"Thanks," Cal told him, reaching out to shake his hand, but still guarding his enthusiasm.

Cal was on automatic, but as my mom came over to talk with him, I watched him let down his guard, just a little. I saw the eyes behind the smile, the uncertainty. I felt myself standing, mute, trying to own the happiness of the moment, but my eyes kept going back to Cal, to the questions I might have failed to ask. What were his concerns? Really? Whatever they were, they would fade. I would work to make it happen.

"Are you all right?" Sean asked me.

I nodded, wondering if I was after all.

"I'm really happy for you, Darla," he said.

The clock at the back of the courtroom said it was early afternoon. *Had it really been that long since we'd arrived?* Time had skipped beats and left me behind.

"Thank you," I told him. "Thanks for everything you've done."

He put his hand on my shoulder, a touch that still registered more than it should have muddied my thoughts even more. I backed away.

"I've got to get back to the retreat center," he said, as if reading my cue. "I'll call you in a day or two, see how things are going?"

I nodded.

Mom stood near him. Waiting. She looked at me directly, leaned in to hug me and said, "It's all going to be okay now." A mother's chorus that rang true every time.

"I can't seem to focus," I whispered as she lingered close to me.

"It's a lot to take in." She stood beside me with a firm arm around my back. "It'll all settle down."

Over her shoulder, I saw a smaller group standing around the Timbros. Their gathering seemed more subdued, but not defeated. In some ways, they appeared less forced, more normal to me than my own throng of well-wishing. I stepped back from Mom, saw Janet beside me.

"When can we leave?" I asked.

The baby would be coming home with me and suddenly time seemed short. I needed to be ready; I needed to put some things in order. I wouldn't shortchange the baby with unclaimed distractions, so I needed to name them, to face them down before the baby slept one night in our home. I had to learn how to be a mother, a *good* mother.

"We've got to stay just a little while," Janet said. "We'll sit down with the judge and the Child Services people. They'll make their recommendations. We'll have to see if the Timbros plan to pursue any further action. It won't take too long. I know you're eager to go home."

Part of me was. Part of me wanted to go sit with Joanne, but I couldn't say that. I needed to focus on Cal—and home. That's what Jo would tell me to do.

"Come on, guys," Janet said to Cal and me. "Let's plow through the last of this so we can get out of here."

We followed her toward the hall that led to the courthouse offices. I had to pass by Mr. Timbro on my way out. He glanced over at me. I tried to look winning, smug even, but his look connected only with my insecurities, gave them a casual appraisal. Then he looked away and I knew I'd been dismissed.

PEOPLE FOLLOWED US HOME from the courthouse and Cal brought out champagne he'd bought and left hidden in a brown sack in the refrigerator. The Timbros had agreed to their every-other-weekend custody, although the judge emphasized that the process was ongoing and we would go through a short probationary period after the child was born.

Uncle Roger toasted the soon-to-be mom of baby Stevens and I began to ease into the idea that it was real.

"I'm so happy for you," Peggy said.

She'd followed me into the kitchen, where I'd gone to unwrap one of the several plates of little sandwiches that had appeared out of coolers in the trunks of the various cars. I looked down and saw Rigsby at my heels. He was agitated, hiding out in the kitchen from the unfamiliar crowd. I gave him a Milk-Bone and he settled on his pallet in the corner.

"Thanks, Peg."

I looked in the cabinet for napkins. Focused on the task as if it had some reach beyond entertaining my guests.

"You're a little strange. What's up?"

"I don't know," I told her honestly. "I can't seem to hold on to any one emotion for very long; I go back and forth from euphoria to terror. It doesn't seem real that they're really going to give me this baby. I put everybody through such hell. I hope they know how much it means, all the support."

"Have you talked with your mom about all that stuff she heard in there?" Peggy said, cutting through to the point, as usual.

"A little. You know, she loves me, mistakes and all. But I feel like such an ass. A real imposter when it comes to her. I wasn't what she thought I was. Hell, I'm still not. Jo, the baby, how it happened. I think that's been harder for her to take than the business with me and Sean."

"We're all works in progress, sweetie," Peggy said.

"I know, but I let her believe I was exactly the way she pictured me. I didn't prepare her for any of this. I feel like I've betrayed her."

"And that baby will betray you, and you'll love her or him anyway. It's what good parents do. Believe me," she said, smiling. "I know a little bit about the resiliency of parents. Look at my folks in there. I was a hard pill to swallow."

I had to laugh. I'd never talked to Peggy about how they'd taken the news that she'd rather date a prom queen than be one.

"When did our normal family become an advertisement for alternative living?" I asked.

"But look at us, all the love there is in this family, in spite of everything. Joanne's dad never quite got the unconditional thing. He never stopped trying to make her into something else."

"Yeah, like I didn't do the same thing. She wouldn't have been pregnant, out driving in the middle of the night if it hadn't been for me."

Peggy put her hand on my cheek, turned my face gently so that I was looking at her.

"When she agreed to have that baby, she knew what she was doing. For you and for herself. I'd never seen anything make her happier."

"She talked to you?"

"Yeah, more than once."

"I just wish she'd had something more." I stopped, thought about what I meant. "Someone, I guess," I settled on finally.

"She did," Peggy said, looked like she might say more then changed her mind.

"What do you mean?"

"She had all of us," she said. "That's what she wanted. She wasn't the wine and roses type. You know that."

Again, she sounded as if she might continue. I waited, but she pulled back and simply said, "The only thing you owe her is a good life for that baby."

Words seemed to hang in the air until she said, "Let me take those sandwiches in to people."

Even after she left and went back to the others, I felt an odd sense that there was something else I should ask her. But by the time she said good-bye, the feeling had passed.

Peggy was one of the first to leave. It was late afternoon when the rest were finally gone.

"Where can I take you for dinner?" Cal asked when we were alone.

"Like there are more than five choices around here?"

"I'm serious." He came over and put his arms around my waist. "We can drive to Austin if you want."

The windows were open and I could hear cars going by on the highway up the bank from our driveway. People passing by looking at our house wouldn't know that it was going to be a home for a baby. It didn't look any different than it had when we'd left that morning. But everything had changed.

"I can get some steaks and cook out, if you don't want to go out," he said, broadening our choices.

"Why don't I go to the grocery store," I said. "I'll pick up the stuff to grill steaks. I want to run by Evie's anyway."

His face changed. I had hoped to slip that one by, but no such luck. "Not now, Darla. Can't you go there tomorrow?"

"I told her I'd come by. I just want to look at the note Joanne left her. It'll only take a couple of minutes, then I'll get the groceries and be home."

"You've got to let this thing with Joanne go," he said, walking away from me and settling on the couch. "You're not going to know exactly what happened, Darla. No one knows but Joanne. Let it go. Do it for us, for the baby. Hell, do it for Joanne."

"Cal, this isn't that big a deal."

"Then why are you leaving *now*. I'm trying my damndest, Darla, to make this idea of us, *with this baby*, settle in my mind. You've got to work with me, I can't do it by myself."

"I know," I said, settling beside him on the couch. "I'm talking about a few minutes. That's all."

He leaned back, let out a long sigh.

God, I was being an ass. "Never mind," I said. "I'm sorry."

"No, I'm being stupid," he said, sitting back up. "You're right, it's not a big deal, but you're going to be stewing over it all night if you don't go now. Just get it over with."

"Are you sure you're okay with that?" I asked.

"Yeah," he said. "I'm fine. Go."

"Cal, we've been through a lot. I know I need to focus on us, I really do. I promise I'll put all this to rest so we can start fresh *before* the baby gets here. Okay?"

He sat up and pulled me to him. I wanted my mind to stop asking questions. I wanted to give in and forget about why Joanne made her decisions that night. But he was right, I couldn't turn it off.

"I'll try to get past this. I promise," I said.

He kissed me, motioned for me to go.

THE DUPLEX LOOKED DARK in the early twilight that settled on the street. I wondered if Joanne's things were still inside. I wanted to smell her hair spray on the pillow again, look in the cabinets and see the groceries she'd bought. I had to stop. I had to get past the tight grip of mourning that seized me when I needed to talk to her.

I looked away from Jo's porch, looked for any light inside Evie's house. The kitchen was in the back and I could see a small glow in that direction.

I went on the porch and knocked. Immediately, kids squealed and I heard the sound of barking—a puppy, I'd guess, from the high-pitched yip of the animal. They must have gotten a dog while they were away.

I thought of one day soon when all of those sounds would come from my house. The idea sprang up unbidden and presented itself as a gift to heighten my mood.

"Hey, Darla!" Evie had on a sweatsuit with fingerpaint stains low on the front at the very height small hands could reach.

"I'm glad you're here," I said. "I should have called first."

"No," she said. "I told you I'd be here."

I walked through her den. Michael sat at a card table in the middle of the room, putting together some kit made out of balsa wood. An airplane, it looked like.

"Hey, Darla," he said without looking up.

"Hey, Michael."

He worked calmly through the noise of the kids. It reminded me of Sean's house when we were dating. I wondered if it would be the same clutter and activity with just one kid. I hoped so.

"I've got the note in here." I followed Evie into the kitchen.

Their side of the house was a mirror image of Joanne's. She had the note out on the counter for me.

Dear Evie,

I've got to go out of town. I'm not sure how long I'll have to stay. Could you get Rigsby for me and look after him? I know you told me the kids like him a lot. Take good care of him and I'll call you to let you know when I'll be back. There's food for him under the sink in my kitchen and all his information will be listed below.

Thanks so much. I'll be in touch soon.

Joanne

Below, she wrote Dr. Sanders' numbers and lists of Rigsby's favorite treats and what he couldn't eat, all the usual information. Her middle-school scrawl struck me again, the way it had with her note to Mr. Romeros. Some part of her had stayed a kid. I shouldn't have asked a kid to carry a baby for me, to take on such an adult responsibility.

"Like I told you," Evie said. "There's not much in it."

She was right. There was nothing on the note that told me anything new. I thought of Cal waiting for me at home. I'd get back and try to follow his advice, put the questions behind me.

"There was one other thing," she said when I looked up from the note. "I'm pretty sure it was the same night, but I don't think it'll help you with any of your questions."

"What is it?"

"Well, the night before she had the accident was one of those nights when her daddy came by. He couldn't ever stay in there more'n ten minutes before they'd start going at it. Screamin' and all. And that night was a doozy."

"Her dad would come to her house?"

"Oh, yeah," Evie said, encouraged by my interest. "He'd come by once in a while, usually the both of them would come, him and his wife. But sometimes it was one or the other by themselves. He was by himself that night."

"And they were arguing?"

"Screamin' their heads off, both of them. They never did anything else though. And he seemed nice enough when I talked to him. That night—boy, I tell ya! She was doing the most yellin' and it sounded like she was throwing things. I almost called over there, 'cause it was right at the kids' bedtimes and Anthony couldn't go to sleep with all the noise."

"Are you sure it wasn't real late, the middle of the night? She left the house at four in the morning." I was trying to picture a fight and her running out angry.

"No," Evie said. "I hadn't gone to bed yet and Michael was still out over at his brother's playin' pool, so it was just after dinner."

All the notes she left. She hadn't run out in a hurry. Her house when I went in, there was no big mess, like she'd been throwing things. She'd picked up. Maybe Evie was right. Maybe a fight with her dad didn't explain anything about her decision to get in the car hours later. But what if it did?

"Could you tell what they were arguing about?"

"I don't know," she said, picking up a toy car off the counter and running her hands over the wheels. "I couldn't make out any words or anything. Just a lot of shoutin' and the stuff hittin' the walls. She must have had some temper when she got riled."

"You have no idea," I said, smiling in spite of myself. "How long was he there?"

"I don't really know. Not that long, 'cause it all stopped before I got up the nerve to call and ask her to tone it down. Twenty minutes maybe."

"You're positive it was her dad?"

"Yeah, I was out on the porch when he got there. Said hi and everything."

"Did he look mad?"

"No, he was fine. I said, 'Nice evening, huh?' and he said somethin' like 'Shore is,' or whatever. He wasn't huffin' and puffin' or anything like that."

It was an odd piece, too ill-formed to fit into the puzzle. I didn't even know he'd ever been there, much less that the two of them went regularly. Why wouldn't Joanne tell me her folks visited her?

I thanked Evie, made my way through the minefield of toys and blankets in the den. Michael had gotten up from his project and was rolling on the floor with both kids on top of him. I tried to imagine Cal that bonded to our baby, but the Cal I saw in my mind never lost his look of discomfort.

OUTSIDE, I LOOKED at my watch. Nearly, nine o'clock and I still hadn't been to the grocery store. Unless we planned to eat at midnight, I'd have to go right away. But I wanted to sort out what Evie's story meant. I needed a little time and space to think.

I was driving. I hadn't been conscious of turning the ignition or leaving Joanne's street, but my mind kept running over and over the little bit of news Evie had offered and I kept looking for something in it that I'd missed.

I drove past the Timbros', sat in front of their house, wondering if I could get the nerve to go ask him myself. The windows were dark. Even if they were awake, they'd settled in for the night.

I had to talk to Larry Timbro. He was the only one who knew for sure why he'd been at Joanne's, what they'd argued about. Fat chance he'd tell *me* of all people, but I had to try. I couldn't show up at his door and startle the two of them after bedtime. I'd have to wait, but that seemed nearly impossible.

I drove away, checked my rearview just once to see if lights came on as I left, but everything behind me stayed dark.

I was driving on automatic, running through Evie's words, over and over. Was there anything I'd missed, anything that would suddenly snap into place?

I looked at the stretch of highway ahead of me, realized the boat landing would be coming up soon on my left. I'd driven away from town, away from the grocery store, and I'd even gone past the road back to my house. If I turned around, I could pick up Cal and we could go somewhere for food. He'd understand.

But I drove a little farther. *Shouting. Arguing at Joanne's. Just after dinner. An hour, maybe two after she left my house. Six or seven hours before she drove back.*

I crossed the bridge at the north end of the lake, over into the next county. Ten o'clock. Cal would be worried. I'd head back home, let my mind settle down enough to let it go for the night. I didn't want to go in spouting all my questions. I could see his face, his impatient look.

Please, let it go, he'd tell me. It was the same as saying, *please don't breathe* or *please don't blink.*

I pulled off the road, tires bumping on the steep shoulder, bouncing me against the door. I stopped the car, relieved to be free of the road's distraction.

I found a cigarette in my pocketbook. Rolled down the window so I could breathe. I didn't register time passing. I only knew that second to second, the fresh air and nicotine conspired to keep me glued together.

I could see myself sitting there, as if I were a passenger in the car. It seemed clearer when I saw it that way, when I saw everything from outside myself. I wondered if I'd fallen asleep, but the air coming through the window was too real on my skin. Were there any answers from that small distance? No answers, but less agitation. I was Joanne, stone cool, rolling her eyes at all the fretting.

I kept it up minute by minute, until I felt inside myself again, until linear thoughts came without too much effort, until I felt whole.

Time had gotten even further away from me. I felt a panic when I looked at my watch. I started the car, pulled a U-turn back onto the road heading into town. I made a mental note as I made my way toward home that at some point the night had tipped over into morning.

IT WAS NEARLY ONE in the morning when I went in our front door. Cal was on the phone.

"Jesus Christ!" he said. He was angry, slamming the phone in its cradle. All the color was gone from his face.

"I'm sorry, Cal." Words broken with sobs.

He ran to me, grabbed me, and pulled me tight against him.

"Dammit, Darla," he said, holding me so hard that I had to work to breathe. "I was just calling nine-one-one *again,* to see if there'd been any accidents reported. I was scared to even leave again and look for you. I went out before and didn't know where the hell to start. Evie said you left more than three hours ago. Do you know what time it is?"

I couldn't even talk. I couldn't tell him where I'd been because I hadn't been anywhere. The amount of time I'd been gone didn't go with what I remembered.

"I'm sorry, Cal," I said again. I felt numb, resigned to his anger. He had every right.

I tried to make a gesture, to put my hand on his arm. He pulled away, walked into the den, and sat down. I followed him. Even though it was a warm night, I felt cold. I still had on my clothes from the courthouse, gray slacks, knee-highs that cut tight into my calves.

"Were you with the priest?" he asked.

I almost laughed. In any other context, it would be the most innocent of questions; but in our situation, it was loaded and raw.

"I haven't seen Sean since we left the courthouse," I said. "What you're thinking—I wouldn't do that. *He* wouldn't do that."

"I don't know what you would do, Darla. I can't predict from one minute to the next what you'll do. It's like, since Joanne's not around, you have to take her place by being the crazy one. What the hell are you thinking? We got custody of the baby today! Isn't that what you wanted? Jesus Christ, Darla! What's going to be the end of this for you? Our marriage wasn't enough. I figured that part out. But I thought the baby would do it. What else do you want?"

His voice had grown loud. Cal almost never shouted. He wasn't looking for me to answer even. He just needed to get it all out.

"I'm going to get some sleep," he said while I struggled to respond, spouted apologies without any clear answers to where I'd been.

I was still standing, afraid to touch him, calm him. He stood and went past me, into our bedroom, without looking back. He closed the door behind him. We hadn't slept in there since it had been rebuilt, spending night after night on the foldout. He'd been waiting for me to give him a sign that I was ready to move back.

Apparently he wasn't waiting anymore.

TWENTY-FOUR

"I FEEL LIKE AN IDIOT." Joanne held the specimen cup and the over-sized syringe, the end of the supplies I'd "borrowed" from Dr. Adams' clinic on my last visit.

We'd been at it, the "baby project," for several months. Cal said he felt like a sperm factory and Joanne joked that it was better than being the industrial dumping ground. I loved the three of us laughing together. Even though we hadn't succeeded, I'd never been happier.

"Darla, seriously," Jo said. "I think this is a waste of time. I want to do this for you, but—God, there has to be a better way. I'm probably not even doing it right!"

She was in my bedroom. Cal, with considerable encouragement from me, had done his part just before Jo arrived. Then he'd braved an unexpected snowfall, gone to get pizza for us. I had watched Jo down at least three glasses of wine before pronouncing herself ready to "try the damn thing—again." But she was balking, losing patience.

"Come on, Jo. It's not so bad."

She gave me one of her "you ain't been there, honey" looks and I sat down for yet another pep talk. I was a cheerleader for both sides. First Cal, then Jo. I loved almost everything about it: the hope it gave me for having a baby of my own, the time we all spent together when I didn't feel torn between them for a change.

"Joanne. All that can happen is that it doesn't work again."

I sat by her on my bed. She was sprawled out sideways, propped up by her elbow. She had on my pajamas so that she wouldn't make a mess of her clothes and I tried not to dwell on the idea that her body filled them out better than mine.

"Darla, I just can't do this again. Hell, if it was anybody else I'd just sleep with him, but this business of cups and . . . this thing . . ." She held up the syringe, let her face register her opinion.

"Okay, okay . . . listen. Just one more time and I won't ask you to do it anymore."

Even as I was talking, my mind was stuck on what she had said. *I'd just sleep with him* . . . How different, really, would that be? Sure it'd be different, but . . . Maybe I was nuts to even think like that. But . . . It was nuts, that's all there was to it.

While I was thinking, she stood up, paced the length of the room, and began working up to a full act of melodrama. Every word out of her mouth got more outrageous.

"Just get me really drunk, let me pass out, and then you do it for me," she said. The specimen cup in her hand moved at the mercy of her gestures. "I promise you, that'll be better than what I'm doing now. I mean, at least you'd figure out how stupid it is . . . Shit!"

I heard it hit the floor before I actually saw it. The top of the cup had popped off and lay across the room while the cup itself and Cal's contribution to this deal made a mess at Joanne's feet.

"Christ! Joanne, what the hell are you . . . I'm sorry," I said, bending down to see what was salvageable. Nothing. Not a damn thing. All I could think about was Cal. Telling him wasn't going to be the high point of my day.

"Shit," she said again. I half wondered if she'd done it on purpose. Then she went to the bathroom and brought out a towel.

While she was cleaning up, my thoughts moved back to what she'd said before.

"Joanne?"

She stopped, looked up at me.

"What you said before. Why don't you?"

"Why don't I what?"

"Why don't you just sleep with Cal?"

She scrunched her eyes, looked at me as if I'd spoken gibberish.

"It's not so far-fetched, you know," I continued to lobby, as she went back to wiping the floor.

Even as I spoke, the unsettling reality of what I was suggesting gave my stomach a queasy turn. But things were threatening to come to a standstill. I'd invested so much hope in the outcome of our plan. It had to happen.

"Come on, Jo. Why not?"

"Well, let's see," she said, creasing her forehead in mock concentration. "Well, maybe because he's . . . YOUR HUSBAND!"

"Joanne, I'm serious."

"I am too. I don't sleep with married men. Never have. Won't start now. Especially not with the one who's married to you. Come on, Darla! You don't have to go nuts on me . . . And I'm just bitching about all this, but I promise, I'm not going to give up."

"Cal's going to freak out about the cup. It's weird for him, doing that, even when I'm trying to make it romantic. He won't go through this again tonight, and this is the best day for you, right? This is our best chance this month."

The more I thought about it, the more I realized it had to happen.

"You said you might not be doing it the right way, you know, with the syringe thing. Well, you sure as hell know how to get it right the other way. How different could it be from anybody else? I mean, if *I* can get past it, why shouldn't you?"

"I think he might have something to say about it. Don't you? Even if you don't think you mind now, it'll bother you. You know it will."

"I'll be fine, I promise. And as far as Cal goes . . . Jesus, Joanne, look at you. You think it would be a struggle for him?"

"You're underestimating him, Darla." She'd gone suddenly serious. "I mean, you're the one he wanted from day one. He loves you. Hell, he wouldn't be doing all this other mess if he wasn't crazy about you."

"Well, then," I said. "Maybe he'd do this for me too. I've never wanted anything more than I want a baby, Joanne."

"I know." Her voice sounded soft. Almost a whisper.

"If he agreed to?" I asked. "Would you?"

"Darla, you can't be serious."

"I am serious." I heard myself say it, knew that I had to be. If I wasn't 100 percent sure, the two of them wouldn't even consider it. I pushed all the little voices in my head out of range. "I mean it, Jo. This is what I want. It's the best way."

She looked up, green eyes fixed on me, a faint glow from the wine in the clear skin of her cheeks.

"Sure," she said. "If you really want me to. Hell, why not?"

CAL'S HAIR, his down jacket—both damp from the light snow falling outside—carried a chill that followed him from the den to the kitchen. He took the pizza to the table. I'd gone out to meet him while Jo did the cowardly thing and stayed in the bedroom. I followed him into the kitchen and when he saw my face, he stopped, gave me his full attention, and asked, "What's up with you?"

I'd meant to ease into it, but everything tumbled out awkwardly as soon as he asked.

"We had an accident." I told him about the cup. He looked like somebody whose pet had just died. "But we had an idea. Listen, you don't have to do the cup thing again."

He looked sideways at me, could sense something coming. He knew me so well.

"We were thinking, Cal. Jo and I were talking. I mean, you both hate this, the way we're doing it."

"Yeah?" His cheeks were chapped from the weather.

"Why don't you two just . . . you know. Why don't you just sleep together?"

I couldn't read his face just after I'd said it, but within minutes he'd worked up to full-blown indignation.

"Are you out of your mind? You're kidding, right?"

I forced my voice to stay steady, confident.

"It's not a joke. I really think this is the best way."

"No, Darla. You've gone off the deep end here. I'm not like some racehorse. Just forget it. The pizza's getting cold."

"Cal?"

"Darla, you're crazy. I said no." He sounded firm, almost angry.

I backed off, went and pulled out paper plates, and started serving the pizza.

"What do you have to drink besides wine?" Joanne asked, wandering into the kitchen as if she had no inkling of what I'd just said to him.

She had on his blue flannel robe, but it was open in the front, my pink baby-doll pajamas visible underneath.

"We've got Sprite, Tab, and cranberry juice," I told her.

I saw Cal look at her, then turn his head away.

"I'll have Tab," Joanne said, getting a glass down from my cabinet. "Do ya'll need a glass with some ice?"

"Thanks," I said.

"Not me." Cal had pulled a Budweiser out of the fridge, was drinking from the can. He looked pretty rattled, still wouldn't look Jo's way. He hadn't bothered to take off his coat and the nylon shell had gone damp from the melted snow.

"Take that jacket off, Cal," I said. "Try to relax."

AFTER THE PIZZA WAS GONE and I'd served Cal another two beers, Joanne went to the other room and I went back to work.

"Please," I said, cutting right to the point. "It means the world to me to have a baby. You just don't know. And she's getting impatient with this other way, losing hope. We're all losing hope. It's getting to her because of me. She hates to tell me every month that she's gotten her period. Please."

"Darla," he said, leaning toward me as we sat at the table, taking my hand. "Think of what you're asking me to do. Marriages end over this sort of thing. You know? We'll try again another night, the way we've been doing it. I promise, I won't give up. Let's just forget about it tonight."

"Our marriage won't be hurt by this, Cal. My God, just the opposite. We'll start a family. A real family. No one's closer to me than Jo. I trust her. And I trust you. I trust you both enough to ask you to do this. She's beautiful, Cal." I smiled. "Can it be such a chore?"

"That's just the point," he said, his words biting straight into my attempt at humor. "It'd be easier if she was butt-ugly, just plain homely. It just seems . . ."

"Cal. Forget what she looks like—or don't. I don't care, really. Please just do this for me."

"Darla, it'll change everything."

"I know. I want things to change. I want our family to grow. *Please, Cal.*"

With a little too much wine and a parade of infant images in my head—fat baby legs, little fingernails—I succeeded in convincing myself.

CAL SAT AND LOOKED at his hands, ran his finger over the rim of his beer can. When he looked up, his face seemed to have a question for me. But he didn't open his mouth.

"Cal?"

"I don't think I can go through with something like that, Darla."

He was whispering. Just talking about it moved his voice into secret tones.

"Will you try? For me? If you can't . . . if the two of you just can't go through with it, I won't ask again. I promise."

He looked away from me again. I waited. Didn't press with more words. But the silence alone became tense. Finally, he turned back to me.

"I don't know," he said, his voice so low I could barely hear him. "Let me think about it."

"Okay," I said.

My heart was racing at the thought that he might agree. Part of me never imagined that he would. I felt a pull, a deep hesitation. Could I possibly want for them to be together like that? I could see him with her in my mind, both of them so beautiful. I pushed the thought away. It would work. She'd get pregnant. I just knew it.

"Just think about it, okay?" I said. I kissed his cheek, his mouth, his ear, then went to tell Joanne what he'd said.

"IF HE SAYS YES," Joanne asked me, "what are you going to do while we're . . . you know?"

She still wore Cal's bathrobe over my pajamas. She looked like herself, but with pieces of us scattered about her for decoration. We were standing in the den and Cal had gone into the bathroom. I tried to think of an answer for Jo, but nothing reasonable came to mind.

"I don't know," I said. "Drive around, I guess."

She went to the couch and I sat down beside her.

The night seemed strange. Snow, so rare in our corner of the world, had been falling all evening. It put us in an altered place. Somewhere familiar, but new.

"I want this to work out," she said. "The baby, I mean. I really do. It's important for me too."

"What do you mean?"

"Like I told you before, I need to do something worthwhile, something right for a change. I've screwed up so many things."

"We've all messed up a lot of things. Everybody does."

"Yeah, well, I'm the queen of the messed-up lives," she said. "I've wasted a lot."

She seemed to be choosing words carefully. Vague words that didn't say anything. Maybe she meant her dad. Everything bad in her life eventually pointed back to him. Having a baby for me wouldn't touch that problem. I didn't think anything could. But if it settled any of her demons, satisfied something in her, all the better.

Joanne touched my hand with hers, curled her fingers around mine. My wedding ring pressed into my skin, but I didn't want to stop her, to break the moment. I had felt bad, guilty even at times, for pulling her into this. If she could find something in it for herself, it would be perfect, a perfect gift for all of us.

I heard Cal in the other room. He was killing time, trying to avoid talking about it. Outside the window, the night looked almost like afternoon with moonlight breaking through clouds to light the snow. Jo leaned in close beside me. I wanted to hold the moment, the very instant when everything seemed possible to me.

She put her head on my shoulder, broke through the stillness with that small gesture. I felt her breath warm on my neck.

"Jo . . ." I heard myself say her name, my voice strange and outside of me somehow. Gravity shifted. I could feel my pulse, in all the pressure points on my body, could hear it in my ears. She turned her face to me, kissed lightly under my jaw, and I moved my head to look at her. Warm breath mingled in the thread of space between us.

I needed to move back, but my muscles wouldn't connect with my thoughts. I could only register nerves sliding over precarious falls, at once thrilling and terrifying. She touched the hollow of my neck with her fingertip, and I closed my eyes, tried to push my thoughts into order, but they scattered, exploded into fragments, feelings.

I opened my eyes, saw Cal standing over us. A brief fear caught me, fear that he would somehow be angry. Instead, he leaned down, met Joanne's hand at my neck; I felt their fingers against my skin, and my emotions slid into uncharted places.

A warmness inside me dissolved all traces of body or form. I was fluid and felt most keenly that which was absent. For me, pain of some fashion had been married to desire for all time, it seemed. Unclouded pleasure startled me, left me confused with gratitude.

Cal kissed me and with his other hand stroked Jo's hair, an instant that exploded in clarity, as unbearable as it was beautiful. I tried but found it impossible to sustain. My breath, my brain—something vital—threatened to cease.

I willed myself to pull away from the two of them, an act of preservation, nothing less. I urged Cal to move to where I had been. Joanne's eyes searched mine and I nodded. Cal had gone beyond questioning, had turned to Joanne, his breathing fast. Without taking my eyes off of them I found his coat on the chair, slipped out the door to save myself. From what, I couldn't say. Whatever it was, it would have ended me somehow. All I was, all I knew, would have faded to nothing if I had stayed.

THE SNOW WAS LIGHT, settling on the trees, but not sticking to the road. Cal's keys were in the pocket of his coat. I didn't have my purse, but decided I'd have to live without it. Cal's truck had four-wheel drive. It felt solid under me and I took that as a good sign. I didn't know where I could go. Not to my mom's, for certain, but there weren't many other choices. My other friendships had been light and limited. No one could share this with me. I was on my own.

The highway out of town was a random choice, but promised familiar comfort when I found myself at the boat landing. The water was still, snow falling on the clear reflections from the floodlights near the ramps.

I turned off the truck and sat watching the water. At some point, the cab had become cold; I wasn't sure how long I'd been sitting. I wanted a cigarette, wished for the first time in months that I hadn't quit. Instead, I pulled the collar of Cal's jacket higher to cover my ears, took in the faint smell of him tucked deep in the down that kept me warm.

I huddled inside the softness and let my mind go back to where they were. The small space of the truck around me seemed a shield of sorts, making me bold to think of them.

I knew the skin, the familiar bodies. Joanne's had grown with me, while we giggled and compared. Then as we got older, we stepped back from our curiosity, breathless at how we had changed. I saw her as finished, her figure done almost as it started. I took longer and was never sure of the result.

Cal was different. He had offered his physical self to me all at once—love and lovemaking all of one piece to him. That he loved me in all ways was something of a marvel. I wondered how he would feel with Joanne, free of the exceptions I brought to our bed. My discomfort—even the fear of it—a constant partner.

Joanne would close her eyes and make him one of the many, the men whose names fell away like wrappings of candy once she woke to another day.

I could see him bending over her, moving to her. As they closed in together in my mind, the muscles in my belly and down my legs grew useless, gave way to nerves, to something hopeful and strange. I could feel the beginnings of the other too, the ache that was almost pleasure, but would grow to pain. Jo didn't know the odd kinship my illness initiated. Cal knew, and for now could forget.

I couldn't hold it for long, the picture of them together, because of the desperate place it could lead. It started spinning in my head, bringing feelings the language had yet to name. Jealousy was a vague cousin to the fear I glimpsed at the edges of my thoughts. So I veered away, went to the core of all my emotions, the single overriding need. I had to reach beyond the images of them and think of where their time together could lead. A baby. I centered my mind on the baby.

The air had gone solid with cold. I turned the key and the motor complained, but finally gave. Snowflakes gone sideways over the water told me of the shifting wind. I pulled out of the landing, back onto the highway, huddled forward and waited for heat.

I went back toward town, the same way I'd come out, but in the shadows of my mind, I knew the detour I wanted—a small road off of a more familiar one. I slowed down, counted on the intermittent moon, bright off the snow when it appeared, to give light enough to find it.

Joanne had taken me back there once or twice since my daddy died, at various points of sadness or fear. I'd come to accept it as an offering from her, the best of what she knew by way of solace. I'd come to realize she believed in something to be found there. It baffled me, but I accepted it, as I accepted everything about Joanne.

In the night, my eyes searched through the snowy line of trees. I didn't know why I was going there by myself, but I didn't question that I needed to either. When I saw the opening, the dirt road, I turned, drove the short distance, and stopped the truck.

The burned-out church appeared clean with its covering of white, charred walls painted with a crystal shine. The surviving corner of the roof had lost its angles with the soft covering. It reminded me of coming out of the water on that day at the stream, bathed in brightness, looking for Joanne.

I made my way to the covered corner. Sat where we always sat. Her Bible had long been taken to the duplex, where Larry Timbro couldn't rummage and find it, but the empty place beneath the bench still seemed to wait.

Maybe it was the walk from the truck that warmed me, but I didn't feel the cold as I had at the lake. The partial wall kept the wind at bay and the air just around me fell oddly still, though the branches in the woods moved as snow took flight all around. Calm settled inside my thoughts also. Settled and unsettled, as I wondered again if what I'd asked of them was right. I felt a shyness, as if my mind had asked out loud. Answers fell short of conviction and I breathed in deeply to focus the time.

Angles. The image came to me of oddly shaped sketches without a name. Right and wrong had more angles than sides, and even unexpected turns would lead somewhere. I couldn't retrace the choices I'd made, could only follow after them. Regardless of the answer to any question, any doubt, my world was unseated from its former place.

I stood up and stepped out from the shelter, my head down against the wind, or perhaps out of habits unspoken when standing before an altar. As I made my way to the truck, I wondered if I should go home, if I could even. I registered a sense of loss; foolish since I had so much to gain. I decided I'd stop somewhere and call before I arrived at my house—a courtesy of acquaintance delivered to my very own home.

TWENTY-FIVE

THE CANS IN THE GROCERY AISLE reminded me that regular life still existed for most people. Hot-dog chili and green beans. Boxes that needed only eggs and oil added to produce a cake. Normal food, normal errands wouldn't turn our lives back to ordinary. But I tried anyway.

Cal had still been upset when he left for work. I tried to doze on the foldout in the den while he showered, but couldn't relax so I got up before he came out of the bedroom. I made coffee, put out ready-made biscuits and jam and waited.

"I'm not hungry," he said when he saw what I'd done.

He was wearing his uniform. Khaki and olive, standard colors of his workday.

"Eat something," I said. "I'll leave if you don't want to talk to me, if you're still mad."

He walked closer to me, shook his head as if I'd missed something entirely.

"*Mad* comes and goes, Darla." His voice was calm. "*Mad* I would get over with a good night's sleep. I'm scared of you right now. I'm scared to trust you, to count on you, because I don't know what you're going to do next. I can't keep going through the wringer every damn day. I just can't do that."

His hair was still wet and smelled of sweet shampoo. Strawberry-scented. He used whatever I left in the bathroom, never complained.

"I'm sorry, Cal." I didn't know what else to say. "I'm really sorry."

"Sorry? Jesus, Darla! I was one phone call away from having the police out looking for you. It's like now that Joanne's not here to turn your life upside down every five minutes, you have to do it yourself."

He was right. All the gaps Joanne had filled for me, the color she'd added; it was all up to me now. But my late-night outing wasn't about that. I needed answers about Jo's accident, about what she was trying to do. Then I could let it go. I tried to think of a way to explain how I felt, that this was one last push that would put it all to rest.

"Once the baby comes," I said, "I'll be settled. I won't go chasing answers forever."

"Some answers just aren't there for us. Look at me and tell me that you can walk away from all the questions, even if you don't find what you're looking for. Tell me that at the end of the day I'm more important to you than those answers."

"Of course you are," I said.

"Then show me. Right here. Right now. Let it go."

I stared at him. The words were stuck inside me, my heart wouldn't let them out, wouldn't let me say them, wouldn't let me lie.

"Cal, just let me . . ."

I hadn't even finished my sentence before he turned and left for work. I fretted for an hour after he left, couldn't think of who to call. Joanne would have been there for me. The thought of her was too much to handle alone in my house, and the refrigerator lacked milk and soda. So I dressed and went to buy groceries.

The supermarket was nearly empty. More employees than shoppers. I looked at ramen noodles. Instant food, cheap, with little effort. I turned the packet over in my hand. Wives were supposed to fill the pantry with seasoning and flour. Wives shopped in grocery aisles, bought packages of meat, and imagined tables of good intentions that were hours in the making. Effort equaled love. I looked like a wife, stood in the aisle with a cart and a list, but I was an imposter. Even so, I had an errand to run. It could be sooner or it could be later, but the day wouldn't end before I talked with Larry Timbro.

"THE TIMBROS AREN'T HERE," the young guy at the hardware store told me. "They both left this morning. Said they'd be back before I had to close up. I've never closed out the register before, so I know they'll be back before then."

He was somebody's brother, the boy the Timbros had hired. He looked familiar. I could sketch in my mind the twelve-year-old he'd been when I'd seen him last, but I had no name for him, no particular context.

"Do you know where they went?" I asked.

He looked uncomfortable and it worried me. Why would he look like that?

"What's wrong?" I asked him.

"It's just that I know you're her friend, and it's sad. I don't want to make you sad. But they said they have to think about it."

"Think about what?"

"They're at the place, that fellow's shop out off Shiloh Road, where they make headstones. I think they figure it'd be good to talk to him, you know, about Joanne. It takes a while to make one, I guess, if you're custom-ordering."

I stared at him, took in the smells of paint and plastic, wood and insect spray. I thought I might cry, but I didn't feel any tears. My thoughts stayed calm, my eyes dry. I remembered picking out a stone when my daddy died. The boy was right. Daddy's grave lay naked for months while they finished his headstone. I remembered how careful my mother had been in the choosing. I thought of the Timbros looking and hoped they chose well. As far as I knew, it would be the first thing they'd bought her in two years.

"Thank you," I said.

He nodded. "Sure. Do you want to leave a message for them?"

"No," I told him. "No message."

The air outside smelled like fall, just the first hint, but the rest would follow. The season would shift, but with the exception of the baby growing inside her, Joanne wouldn't change. She wouldn't grow older, and it broke my heart. After the baby came, they would let the machines go quiet. I couldn't bring myself to hate them for that. If Joanne saw herself, she'd do the same thing.

There wasn't enough time in life to waste on lies, even the ones you want to be true. There was only time enough to tell the truth. I stopped by the house and put the groceries away. Then I got back in my car and headed for the lake to find Cal.

"HE'S GOT A BOAT out on patrol," Jack Ainsley told me when I asked about Cal. "Over on the north end of the lake, I think. I can radio, let him know you're here."

By the time Cal pulled up to the dock, I had worked it all out in my mind.

"What's up?" he asked, his tone still wary, but less angry than before.

"I just needed to see you." I tried to follow with a smile, tried to ease the moment, but it came out forced, the awkward cadence of second-date conversation. "We need to talk. Can we go somewhere?"

He motioned for me to get in the boat with him. "How about right here in my office." He still wasn't smiling.

I sat down and he put the motor in forward, headed away from the dock.

I hadn't brought a jacket, hadn't thought I'd need one, but the afternoon air on the water was cool and Cal gave me his windbreaker. It said "Wildlife Officer" on the front. He drove out into the main channel, headed south, and pulled into a large cove where the shoreline was owned by the Forest Service. It was free of houses and docks, free of people and gossip.

"I'm not sure what we have to talk about," he said. "You seem pretty clear on what you want to do."

He swiveled his chair around to face me, but his body leaned back, away from where I sat. He needed distance. I didn't blame him for not trusting me. I didn't trust myself.

"I don't know how to make everything right," I said. "Our lives or our marriage. This will end, all these questions I have. Either the people who know the answers will tell me or they won't. But it can't go on forever. There's just one thing that has to be clear before the two of us can solve anything. Cal, does any part of you want this baby?"

He waited. His jaw moved slowly as he chewed his gum.

"I want you to be satisfied," he said, finally.

"That's not the same thing."

"I never said it was."

A fish jumped, sending water rings through the partially submerged branches of a fallen tree. I watched the ripples, breathed in smells of lake and leaves, smells I had known for twenty years or more.

"Do you feel like a father?" I asked him. "Even a little?"

He stared out toward the bank, thinking, considering. Could it be so hard to know?

"I might, someday. Maybe when I see the baby. But the truth is, my thoughts about a baby have always centered on how it will make *us* stronger. I'm just not sure that's the case anymore." He looked back toward me. "When I think of the baby now, I don't feel like a father, I feel like an adulterer. I feel like a younger version of *my* father, and it makes me sick."

"You did what I asked you to do."

"Then I went back to her," he said. He wasn't yielding. "I went back to betray you."

"I've come to terms with that, Cal. I know my part in causing it. I haven't asked you to hold on to it."

"I know, and I could work through it too, if I felt like we were solid, if I knew what I was working for. But I don't know where your heart is right now. It's not with me."

"That's not true," I said, a weak rebuttal.

My head ached from the wind and the talk. I wanted him to understand, but he was missing it. He wanted me to let go of my questions about Joanne and just be with him. I needed to answer the questions *so* I could be with him. So I could be with myself. Part of me—my history and the baby's history—was lost in those questions. Life with our family couldn't move forward until there were answers.

"Look at that," Cal said, his voice a little lighter, distracted for the moment.

I followed his eyes, squinted against the sun to see what was in the sky. Four birds, three small ones, mockingbirds, flapped wildly then dove in pursuit of a full-sized hawk. Urgent calls and frantic wings surrounded the larger bird.

"What are they doing?" I asked. I loved his sense of wonder. It caught him at the oddest times.

"They're getting him away from their nests."

"Aren't they scared? Don't hawks eat rabbits and squirrels?"

"They act on instinct. I don't think they wonder if they're scared or not."

"I guess not," I said.

Two small birds fell away and three new ones joined in as the hawk entered new airspace. The mockingbirds were fierce, unrelenting.

I looked back at Cal. He wasn't watching the birds anymore. He stared off at nothing. It felt awkward to begin talking again. I don't think either of us wanted to go where the conversation was headed.

"Darla," he said, after a minute or so of quiet. "If you can't overcome this obsession with the accident . . . if you can't let go of Joanne . . . how am I supposed to get past what I did, and what this baby's done to all of us? Hell, Joanne's still with us. For God's sake, she might as well be living in our house right now."

We had drifted too close to the shore. He started the motor, moved us to neutral water at the mouth of the cove. Looking out at the main channel, I could make out Darryl's Marina, and across in the other direction, the boat landing.

"Maybe I could come to see the baby as ours," he continued when we stopped. "I sure as hell had planned to try. But not if you can't let go of Jo, of everything that's happened."

I'd always felt pulled in two directions when I was with Cal and Joanne. I thought the baby would change that, bring us all into a perfect circle and make us a family. I'd been so sure that it would happen that way.

"I don't remember a time when Jo hasn't been part of me. I don't remember a time when I ever saw myself as completely separate from her. All those stories about twins. I always thought they sounded like the two of us. Even if she's gone, I have to remember her to begin to understand myself. I don't know how to explain it any better than that. Letting go of Jo would be like pretending—pretending I'm somebody else."

Cal had gotten thinner. A lot thinner. Sitting in the boat with him, I noticed it for the first time. He must have been like that the day before, and the day before that one. How long? How many times had I stared right at him and not seen it?

"This thing with the baby," I said. "It's taking a toll on you. On both of us, but especially you. It's killing little pieces of you, minute by minute."

"It's not just the baby, Darla." His voice stayed low. He wasn't angry anymore. He wasn't fighting anymore, and it frightened me.

"What do you mean?"

"This obsession you have. This need to know what happened. It's making you more like her. Darla, she *hurt* everyone around her except you. I didn't fall in love with Joanne." His eyes were sad. I felt as if we were walking somewhere without making note of the path, without thinking of the trip home.

"You've been so caught inside yourself," he went on before I could speak, "inside your need to make her alive, even if it's just in you, that you've been really blind to what it's doing to the rest of us."

"What do you mean?" I asked. But I didn't need an answer. I could see it in him. All the hurt I'd caused. How could I have missed it just moments before?

"Darla, you've got to have some idea of what I've been going through."

"I know," I said, seeing it clearly for the first time. "I've been blind to what it's doing to everybody, especially to you." Beyond his thin face, the drawn look in his eyes, I saw inside for the first time in months. How I'd changed him inside.

"If you . . ." he began, then stopped. "If we could just start off new . . ."

I shook my head. For the first time in my memory, I wanted to let go of Joanne. I wanted to have that much control over how my life proceeded. But it was too late for me too.

"We're part of everything that's happened," I told him. "Joanne is part of everything that's happened. She's part of this child. For better or worse, she's part of me too. I can't say that isn't true. It'll always be true for me. Loving you can't make that go away."

"So we're at a wall."

I wanted to stop, to retrace my words, even my thoughts. I wanted to tell him we could erase everything else. I wanted to lie and make it right for another day or another week. I wanted to hang on. I thought of the Timbros, walking rows of stones, trying to choose. There wasn't enough time in life to lie.

"You can't live with this, can you? With any of it."

"Not the way it is," he said, his shoulders sloped down. I felt as if I'd changed him into someone else, someone slighter, more fragile than he'd ever imagined he could be. "I can't live with constant re-minders of Jo. I hate who I've been the last few months, even before the accident."

"I asked you to be that person, the person you hate. I wish I could take it all away, everything but you, me, and a baby. I wish I could make everything else disappear."

"But you can't."

"Not if it means pretending Jo isn't a part of it, that she never lived. I could lie to you, but I couldn't do it. I don't know who I'd be if I let go of her completely. You knew that when you met me. You've known it all along."

The perfect circle, all of us joined as a family. What had that been, really? It seemed so clear, even though the thoughts, the realizations, had been with me for only moments. All of it . . . it wasn't for the baby, or even for Jo. It was for me. I needed to have both of them and I tried to make it happen, never considering what it would do to anybody else. I needed both of them and suddenly, it seemed, I would have neither.

A small breeze stirred and I felt the cool line of tears down my cheeks.

"Hell if I know where to go with this," he said, looking away from me, out over the water.

I saw it then. The only move left on the board; an unthinkable de-cision, but one that would end the game we were playing with each other.

"You need to walk away, Cal." I felt myself shaking, a tremble from the deepest parts of me. "Before you hate me. Before the baby ever has a chance to see that you feel that way. The last thing I want is for all of this to turn you into somebody you can't stand to be."

"Oh God, Darla . . ." He looked at me. His eyes mirrored what I felt.

"I love you, Cal." The words had never been so full for me. "I really do love you."

He put out his hand and I took it. He pulled me gently beside him on the seat. The boat rocked at the movement, I pressed close to him, pressed my face to his neck.

"I don't want to be without you," he said. "I've loved you since the first time I saw you. And without me, they'll take the baby." I felt the words in his throat. The sound moved over my cheek. "I couldn't live with that."

It frightened me to think he was right. I refused to follow through with those thoughts, shut them down before they were fully formed. My head, my eyes, even my brain ached from the effort. I sat back, just enough to make him look at me, enough to make him know what I said was true.

"I can't do this anymore, Cal. I can't be somebody who hurts you. If I don't do this the right way, if I drag you through hell and back just to make us look like a family, if I do this just because it's what I need, the baby will know. I'll know, and it will never be right. I'll find some way with the baby, some way to show them that I'm that baby's mother."

I touched his neck, could feel tears that weren't my own.

"But if I'm going to try and be any kind of mother," I continued, "I've got to start with at least this much honesty. And if I don't do it now, I'll talk myself into backtracking, into telling you things that can't be true, even though I want them to be. That's not right, Cal. It's just not right. Not now, when I know what it's really doing to you. I'm sorry I ignored that for so long."

I could feel him against me, strong and familiar. I wanted something to change, some answer to come clear to me before this terrible thing settled into a fact. But nothing was clearer than what we both knew.

The birds had gone and the wind had calmed to nothing. I took off Cal's jacket and handed it back. I waited, wanting him to argue with what I'd said and say he couldn't leave me. But he didn't. He leaned over and kissed my forehead, then sat for a second before he started the motor and drove us back across the lake.

I'D DRIVEN AROUND for what must have been hours after I left the lake. It was dark when I drove up to the Timbro house. The lights were low, but visible through the living room curtains. I didn't want to face them. I wasn't even sure what I would say. I had my questions, but with so much already lost there were still so many things at stake.

Mrs. Timbro answered the door.

"Come in, honey," she said, terms of endearment an old habit even after our bloodbath in court. She was distant, but polite.

"I'm sorry it's late," I said. "I thought we should talk."

I could see him in the recliner in the den. I took in his profile as he watched the TV. He didn't get up, didn't turn to greet me.

"We just finished supper," she said. "We got in late from the store."

I nodded, decided not to mention the headstone, decided not to ask.

I followed her into the kitchen and she got me a glass of tea.

"I've got some pound cake if you're hungry," she said, sitting down at the kitchen table with me.

I shook my head. I tried to think of a way to tell her that I hadn't been trying to hurt her with all of those things in the courtroom, but there were other, more important things I had to say first.

"I might as well just tell you," I said. I hadn't intended to blurt it out so fast, but it seemed the only way. "Cal and I, we aren't going to be together, at least for a while."

She didn't appear to register the news, what it might mean. I thought for a moment that she might offer the usual condolences—a cup of coffee, a kind word.

"When?" she said, finally. "What happened?"

"This has been too hard on him, and I'm still wrapped up in Joanne, the accident. It's causing us to . . . I don't know . . . Maybe I'm just losing my mind."

It was dangerous, talking with her. She was the enemy. The lesser of the two, for sure, but still, it was taking a chance. But she loved

Joanne. I needed someone who understood, who loved her too. Someone else who was hurting.

"I'm sorry, Darla. I don't want bad things for you. Honestly. I never did."

"I know. It hasn't all hit me, really."

He coughed in the next room. It sounded like a growl. I lowered my voice. She was the one slim chance I had to keep my world intact.

"Without, well, if Cal is gone . . . Mrs. Timbro, I need to know if you would try and get the baby again. That court business was terrible for all of us. I need to know what I'm facing here—besides the problems with my marriage."

She sat back. Her hand went to her face, fidgeting slightly.

"This is sudden, Darla. I don't know," she said.

"We could try to work it out ourselves. I don't want to go through that again, do you? Even though Cal won't be with me, he's still the father. We could figure out ourselves what's best."

"I don't see where you have that much to bargain with." His voice startled me. I hadn't heard him get up, but he stood in the door of the kitchen, filled the space and then some with his broad shoulders, his arrogance. "In fact, I can't see that you're fit to raise a child at all, much less by yourself."

"Larry," she said, but then stopped.

"We all went through a lot in court," I said, fighting for calm in my voice. "It seems there has to be another way to do this."

"I don't think there's much to think about. If he wants to fight for the child, that's one thing, but you have no claim to that baby without your husband."

Mrs. Timbro stayed silent. I knew how alone Joànne must have felt, all those days living with the two of them. Joanne had fought with what she had, used anything she could to stand up to him. I didn't have much at my disposal, nothing really, except Evie's story, and a hunch. I was blowing my chance for any civilized answers from him, but I had no choice.

"What happened the night before Joanne's accident?" I kept my voice steady, kept my eyes locked on his.

"What do you mean?" It was Mrs. Timbro asking. I glanced at her, saw her eyes wide, almost frantic. His expression hadn't changed.

"The argument," I said. "What happened, Larry? If you want to go to court, a lawyer can ask you the same thing. They'd wonder why you didn't mention it before, seeing her that night. Why didn't you mention it before?"

Color rose in his face. I wondered if he could be violent. Would she try to stop him if he was? I pursed my lips to keep them from trembling.

"You need to leave now." It was her. She stood up, waited for me to stand and do what she'd asked. "I want you to leave my house."

I looked at him. His face frightened me, the size of his arms, his hands. He could strangle me if he decided to. Never taking his eyes off me, he stepped back, away from the door, made room for me to go by him.

"Listen to my wife," he said, in low, rough tones. "Do what she said."

"We have to deal with this sometime," I said. "I have to know what you're planning to do."

"Please, just leave him alone," Mrs. Timbro spoke again. Her voice had changed, sounded near pleading.

She loved him. I'd missed it all those years. How could she love him? She opened the door, kept her arm raised as if to show me what direction I had to go. The arm was shaking.

I turned back to him. He was watching his wife. I couldn't tell what he thought of her display. He'd pushed his anger back, behind a passive face. He showed no emotion at all. I realized what a trip it must have been for Joanne when she could bring his rage to full boil. Frightening as it was, to have that power . . .

"What did you argue about that night?" I pressed.

His eyes changed and he took a step toward me. My mouth was dry, my breathing off, and I worked not to show it.

"I told her the same thing I told you," he said. "And I told her that baby didn't do a damn thing to deserve it, but if somebody didn't step in, that little thing would end up living, or dying, with her mistakes."

"Larry . . ." Mrs. Timbro spoke his name.

"You knew she was pregnant? Before? You knew?" I asked. I could barely speak, there was so little air. "She told you?"

"She never said anything about what you'd cooked up. This surrogate scheme of yours." I could feel his fury building. "But she couldn't wait to tell me she'd gone and got knocked up. Threw it right in my face. Not a single word about you and that husband of yours. But she did tell me how she was going to walk around, her belly all the way out to Sunday." It seemed he could see her. For a second I almost felt sorry for him. "Said she was going to waltz back and forth in front of my store and I couldn't do a damn thing about it."

He wasn't lying. I knew Joanne. I should have known how she'd use the baby to hurt him. But why didn't she tell me he knew?

"What did you argue about that night?" I asked again. It was getting easier, the asking. I'd keep at it until I knew.

"She said I couldn't do a damn thing about it," he said again, Joanne's taunts stuck in his head, and I wondered if he was listening to me at all. "I told her what I could do. I told her I wasn't going to go through all that mess again. I'd have them take her in, raise that baby myself before I'd go through that . . ."

"Larry, stop it," Arlene Timbro told him. Her voice was firm, louder than I'd ever heard her address him. She still stood at the door. Then she turned to me. "GET OUT! GET OUT OF HERE!"

I stepped back away from her, my nerves rattled by the sound of her voice, the look on her face. Her eyes, frozen on me.

"Arlene . . . Arlene . . ." He'd come out of his rant, stood by her side, coaxing her, his voice gone soft. "Come here. It's okay." He covered her, made his body a shield, protecting her against me. How could I be a threat to her? To them?

"Do what she said," he told me, without looking my way. "Just leave now."

I started to go through the door, then stopped. I needed to hear him say it.

"What did you say to her?" I looked in his eyes, pitted my will against his and felt bolder by the second. "Tell me what you said to her."

His face stayed passive, but his eyes betrayed pain.

"Like I said. I told her she was unfit. By my standards, by the law's. I told her I'd raise that baby before I saw her mess up another life. That's all you need to know."

He told me this calmly. Mrs. Timbro was weeping and he held her, but kept his eyes on me. "Now get out of here," he said. He was done with me, but I didn't move.

"There's more," I said. "What did you use to frighten her, to make her run away?" I could feel myself shaking, but I kept my eyes steady on his face. I needed to read what he wasn't saying.

"It's not his fault," his wife said through quiet sobs. She was clutching his arm as if it could save her, keep her afloat.

I looked at her, then for her sake, regretted what I'd caused. I went through the door and it closed behind me. Standing on the stoop, my thoughts came too fast to hold on to all he had said. I tried to gather them, all his words, collect them in memory so that I could put them in order when I was calm.

I needed a place to go, a place to think. I needed Joanne. I wanted to put my hand on her arm and feel it warm, see the rise of her growing belly, hear the sound of the machines giving her air—giving her life for my baby.

THE NURSES AT THE DESK recognized me, motioned me on, even though visiting hours had ended.

I sat on the bed, fought the urge to curl up and escape in sleep the way I had before. In some ways, sitting there with Joanne was the only time I relaxed, the only time I didn't worry that she would suddenly be gone, taking the baby with her.

I straightened up, took in a full breath of air. I looked at her lying there, wished I could have her back, if only for a few minutes. I could ask her the questions that held me suspended. Why she'd kept so many things from me. Then I could tell her good-bye.

"I know he came to your place that night."

I said it out loud, maybe something in her, her soul, was listening. I ran through the jumble of what I'd heard from him.

"Why the hell didn't you tell me he knew about the baby?" I said it and regretted blaming her. I couldn't question her needs, not after everything she'd tried to give me.

"I'm sorry."

I told her the same thing I told you . . .

I could hear his words, his threats.

She said I couldn't do a damn thing about it . . . I told her what I could do . . . that I wasn't going to go through all that mess again . . .

"He threatened you and you got in the car, tried to come to me. That was right, Jo. You were right to try and get to me. But what did he threaten you with, Jo?"

. . . what I could do . . . I told her what I could do . . . I told her she was unfit.

I could feel her panic. She spent hours in the apartment before she left. I wanted to take that away from her, those last hours of worry.

"The baby," I said to her. "I know he told you he'd take the baby." *You're not fit to raise that baby . . . I told her the same thing I told you . . . I told her what I could do . . .* "But he couldn't do that. No court would let him do that. You knew that, didn't you?"

I saw her. Scared, picking up the mess she'd made while he was there. Picking up books or pillows, maybe broken glass. Running all the options through her mind while she bent down to gather things, put them away. She'd come get me. It made perfect sense. Cal had broken a trust. Cal had tried to betray me. So she'd come get me and we'd solve our problems together. She wanted to keep our baby safe.

"That's why you were out that night." It seemed so clear, so right. "I don't understand everything, Jo, not yet, but you had a good reason, didn't you?"

The fact that it was true—true beyond my blind belief, true because of something I knew . . . It should have eased things, made everything better. But she was still lost to me. Maybe Cal had been right all along. Why did I have to know? What difference did it make?

"You cleaned your house. You wrote your notes. What was going on in your head, Jo? I only wish I'd been there, knew you were okay."

It seemed too hard to think about. I was useless to her, sleeping in my bed while she worked to save our plans—picked up her house, packed her bags.

"He couldn't have done it," I said again. I felt exhausted, too empty to raise my voice above a whisper. But I had to keep talking. While she was here, I had to say it all.

"He couldn't have taken the baby, Jo. But you didn't know that, did you? You thought there was nothing he couldn't do once he decided. What don't I know, Joanne?"

She saw him even larger than he was, larger than anyone could ever be. Was that enough to make her believe he could destroy everything? All our plans?

"It's all falling apart right now, Jo. Cal's going to leave. I'm losing my grip. But I promise, I won't let it happen. I won't let Larry get this baby. They said weekends. Every other weekend. I might have to give him that much. But I won't let him take more. I won't let him raise this child. If I have to, I'll tell them that he threatened you, made you frightened enough to run."

I felt suddenly self-conscious. There were no secrets inside of curtains, and a full overnight nursing staff outside to hear me ramble. I still needed to get somewhere. I needed some rest, some time to think. I needed to talk to Sean. Father Sean. He could help me do the right thing. He could tell me how to build a life worthy of a little baby.

"I'm going to Sean," I told Joanne. If she could hear me, that would calm her. In the end, she trusted Sean. I leaned over her, my hands spread light on her belly. I kissed the blanket that covered her, then raised up, kissed her forehead. "He'll help us. Just like he was helping you. He'll tell me how to make it right."

I closed the curtain behind me as I left. The nurses glanced my way when I walked by the desk. I thought I saw sympathy, maybe even pity. I told myself it didn't matter; I didn't need either one. I could make everything right.

TWENTY-SIX

ALLIANCE, TEXAS—MARCH 1983

I T WAS TWO O'CLOCK in the afternoon. Joanne called me from the duplex, told me to come over.

"Did something happen at work?" I asked.

Joanne had worked in the office at the car dealership for about seven months with no screwups. It was high time something hit the fan.

"No," she said. "I went home before lunch feeling sick. Can you just get over here?"

"It depends on what you've got. Is slacking-off contagious?" I said as I grabbed my keys off the counter.

"Asshole."

"I'll be there in ten minutes."

SHE WAS STANDING at the door when I got to the duplex. She did look pale, her shoulder slumped against the door frame as if she could barely stand. But she was smiling.

"What's up with you?" I asked. "Are you really sick?"

"What's the best answer you can think of to that question?" She made herself stand straight, gathered energy as she spoke. "Huh? Go ahead, take a guess."

"Oh my God! You're . . . Are you?"

"Second try was the charm." She grinned, and I ran and hugged her.

"Oh shit! I ought to be careful." I stepped back, looked for signs that my squeeze had caused some sort of pain or rupture. "Are you okay?"

"Don't get weird on me," she said as she walked to her couch. I closed the door and followed her.

"But you are, right? How do you know?"

She was still smiling, but her rally had run its course. She looked as if she might be sick again.

"The kit thing you bought me is in the bathroom. You can see for yourself."

"Oh God . . . Oh, wh—oh . . . Jo . . . God . . ." My vocabulary had been reduced to sounds. I was standing, staring down at her. Afraid to move, afraid the moment would pass and it wouldn't be true anymore.

"I felt like hell last night," she said. "Was fine this morning, then got sick as shit right before lunch. I'm late, so I figured we'd hit the jackpot. I came home and peed on that thing and . . . sure enough!"

I sat down beside her, couldn't help staring at her stomach. She wore a tight sweater and her belly looked as flat and perfect as it had the day before.

"Why didn't you tell me you were late?"

Her face went serious. No one else ever saw how kind her eyes could be.

"I didn't want to see you all happy, and then have it go away. You know, not be true. I was really tired of disappointing you."

I hugged her again, taking care to be gentle. Her hair felt stringy and tangled. I got up and went to the bathroom, got a cool cloth and her brush and brought them back to where she sat.

"Okay," I said. Settling down behind her I handed her the cloth and started to brush. "I'm officially your slave for nine months. What do you want? Right now. What do you want?"

"Pace yourself," she said, leaning her head back toward me, giving in to the tug of the hairbrush. "We've got a ways to go."

I tried to breathe normally. "You're right. I'll calm down."

After brushing her wavy hair as smooth as it would go, I settled back against the cushions beside her. She took my hand, glanced over, and gave me a grin. She looked happy. Really happy.

"Is this wild, or what?" she said.

My dad used to talk about "snapshot feelings." Moments you want to hold on to, recall with the same clarity, the same emotion time after time. I stared at her, at the room that framed her, made the images into deliberate thoughts, then worked to memorize them.

"I'll think about this every day, Joanne, from now until the last day I live. I'll think about this, about what you've done."

Her eyes became full, tears threatening to spill.

"You better," she said. "My figure's gonna go to hell. And this throwing up is for shit." Then she stopped, looked at me. "I'm hungry."

"Ice cream?" I stood up, postured like a servant awaiting word.

"With sprinkles." She pouted.

"Ice cream with sprinkles it is." I got up and headed for the kitchen, then stopped. "Do you *have* ice cream and sprinkles?"

"No."

"Why didn't you say so?" I asked, still standing.

"You're a smart girl," she said. "You'd figure that part out pretty fast."

"Where do you want to go?"

"Dairy Queen."

"Dairy Queen doesn't have sprinkles," I said.

"I want to go anyway."

I got her coat out of the closet and handed it to her.

"Come on," I said, waiting for her at the door. "Let's go."

HALFWAY TO DAIRY QUEEN, she pulled something out of the pocket of her jacket.

"Shit. It's my mom's birthday. I was going to go during lunch and leave this at the door for her."

She pulled a bottle of perfume out of the bag she was holding. It had a gift tag attached to it, but wasn't wrapped.

"At the hardware store? I can run you by."

"No," she said. "At the house. I don't want to see him. I figured I'd call her tonight. He goes to bed before she does."

"Do you want to get ice cream first?"

"No," she said. "*He* might be home by then. It's Wednesday and they close up early."

"Can you live without the sundae?"

"It'd probably make me puke again anyway," she said.

"Okay," I told her. "Let's go to your mom's."

It seemed strange driving in our old neighborhood. Kids were walking home from school. I felt interchangeable, replaced year after year. We parked in the driveway at Joanne's old house and she left the perfume propped up at the kitchen door, where they would go in.

"Does your mom wear perfume?" I didn't remember any scent that I associated with her.

"Sometimes. She ought to more, but he says it stinks up the car. I told her she should wear it at work, give the customers something to smell besides paint thinner."

We stood on the front lawn and listened to the kids talking as they walked by in groups of two, three, and four. Joanne and I had always been two. Only two.

"Let's go see your old house," she said, taking off toward the back-yard.

I followed behind her, noticed how similar the yards looked, so un-like the days when we lived there.

"This guy keeps a better yard than my dad used to," I said, cross-ing the now invisible line to my old backyard.

"Mom said he got advice from dad on how to spruce it up because they're selling the house. He got transferred to Wichita Falls or some-thing. A woman in my office is friends with the guy's wife. She said they already moved."

"It's empty?" I asked.

"Yeah," she said, then turned and raised her eyebrows. "Want to go in?"

"No. I don't." I stopped in the middle of the yard.

"Come on," she said. She was already stepping up on the bricks where the foundation came out a little just under my old window.

"Joanne," I called to her. "We're not kids anymore."

"Oh but God, I wanna be," she called back without turning around. She was jiggling the window.

"Joanne! You're gonna hurt yourself, or the baby. For God's sake, you're pregnant. Stop it!"

"I'm fine," she called back, laughing.

She jiggled the window a little more. The latch had always been loose inside, so we could come and go whether it was locked or not. If they'd been like us, never bothering to fix it, the window would be a piece of cake.

"There," she said, pushing the frame up.

"Joanne!" I could hear cars, kids all around. I stepped up to support her, keep her from falling as she climbed over.

"Nothing's in here," she said once she was inside. "They've already moved out. Come on. I just want to see it again."

ONCE INSIDE, my mind filled the empty rooms with our old furniture. I could imagine all of it, down to the green candy dish my mom kept on the side table by the couch. We'd moved out so fast after daddy died that I only remembered the house with him in it.

It occurred to me that he wouldn't ever know my baby, a child that had already become part of my frame of reference. I didn't know what my father would think, what he would say about how I'd gone about it, but I knew he'd love being a granddad. I almost cried thinking about it.

"Hey." Joanne's voice startled me. "What's up with you? We're breaking the law. It's supposed to be fun."

"I just haven't been here since right after my dad died." I sat down on the floor in our old den, leaned my back against the wall. "I wasn't through with this place yet. I came back from college wanting to be home. All of a sudden, he was gone, then *it* was gone. I just wanted to be home, but that wasn't even a place anymore. It was just an idea."

It felt the same, still smelled like oak and Old English oil, even years removed from our stuff.

"This was the last place, the only place, that ever felt like home." I was rambling, but she listened anyway. "I shouldn't say that. I mean, my house now, it's home. It's just . . ."

"The baby will make it home, Darla," she said. "Once you have a nursery and baby junk all over the floor . . ." She smiled. "Okay?"

"Okay," I said, took the hand that she offered to help me up.

"Let's go look at the cabinet under the sink," she said, already heading that way.

On the inside edge, behind the cabinet door, the numbers were there—1966—with a *J* on one side and a *D* on the other. I felt better, knowing that something of me had stayed at the house; and I took comfort in the marks and imperfections the baby would leave, hidden in our house—mine and Cal's.

"Oh God," I said. "I've got to call Cal and tell him! Tell him his hard work paid off." I put my arm around Joanne. "He's gonna be a daddy. I can't believe I didn't call him before we left your place."

Joanne braced herself inside my hug. She and Cal weren't the buddies I'd hoped our joint venture would make them. But she nodded, agreed that we should let him know.

"We gotta get out of here anyway," she said. "The 'rents will be home soon, in from a hard day in the hardware business. I'd just as soon be outta here when they come rolling in the driveway."

We locked the window again, left through the front door and locked it from the inside on our way out. No harm done. No trace of us left, except two initials and a date behind an old cabinet in an empty room.

TWENTY-SEVEN

I T WAS LATE by the time I stopped at my house to get a few things before heading out to the retreat center. Rigsby met me at the door, scratched to go out back as soon as I'd greeted him. Cal wasn't home yet, or maybe he'd come back and left. But from the urgency Rigsby had shown running out the back door, I didn't think so.

In the space of twenty-four hours, I had lost all expectations of Cal. Would he let me know where he was? I decided to leave him a note when I left so he wouldn't worry. Then it occurred to me that I ought to give Sean a call before I just landed on his doorstep well after dark. I went to the kitchen phone.

"Is Father Latham there?" I asked the brother who answered.

"Yes, he is, but he's counseling someone right now. Could I leave him a message?"

I told him who I was.

"Would you tell him I'm riding out to the center this evening? I know it's late, but I need to talk with him."

"Sure, I'll tell him." There was no hint of curiosity in the man's voice; he found nothing strange about an anxious-sounding woman who needed late-night advice from a priest. I thought of how exhausting it must be for Sean, to be so close to the raw nerves of people and their emotions—all the time.

When I hung up the phone, I saw Cal standing in the den. I hadn't heard him come in.

"Hi," I said, suddenly shy, self-conscious.

"I came to get some stuff," he said. "I was going to Randy's to stay. I thought it might be better. You should get in touch with your mom. She called me at work. She was worried about you."

"Did you say anything about . . ."

"No," he said. "I figured you ought to talk to her."

I just looked at him, must have nodded or given some response. I walked into the den and stood near him. I could hear the two of us breathing, the room was so quiet.

"Why don't you stay here tonight? I can get my stuff and go to Mom's for a while. I'm . . . I called the retreat center just now. I'm riding out there to talk to Sean."

His face didn't change.

"I heard." That was all he said.

"Cal, I'm not going to see Sean my ex-boyfriend. I need to talk to Sean the priest. I need advice on what to do."

"Darla." His voice had gone softer, more real. "I don't know what you're thinking, but I won't go back and forth on this marriage. This is not an ongoing debate and I don't want Sean involved . . ."

"I'm not going to talk about our marriage."

He stopped. Shook his head slightly to say he didn't understand.

"I saw the Timbros," I told him. "I went there to talk about what's happened with us, to try and convince them to leave the custody as it is."

"And?"

"He said he'd fight me on it, no big surprise there. But when I asked about the argument he'd had with Jo the night before . . . Cal, he exploded and his wife freaked. He as much as admitted that he threatened Joanne that night. He threatened to declare her unfit, to take the baby."

"You're kidding! How did he know she was pregnant?"

"He knew because she told him." I didn't say any more, didn't say she'd waved the pregnancy in front of him like a red cape. "She thought he could really do it. Take the baby. I think she was leaving so that she could get the hell away from him."

Cal went to the couch and sat down. He kept shaking his head.

"What a bastard," he said, then looked up at me. "Did he know why she was having the baby? If he did, he lied to the judge about not knowing . . ."

"He didn't know. She didn't tell him. Even when he threatened her, I don't guess she figured it would matter. She just wanted to run, I think."

"Why was she coming here?"

I thought about not telling him. I hadn't told him before, not after I talked to Tommy Wells at the Quik Mart. Why tell him at all? But things had changed since that night. I'd changed. For the baby's sake, I needed the truth—to hear it and to tell it.

"She was coming to get me. She wanted me to go with her."

He stared at me. I thought maybe he hadn't understood. Maybe he didn't care. But then he said, "Because of me. Because of what I did. That's why she wanted you to go with her."

"In part, I think. She was mostly worried about her dad, I'm guessing, but I believe she felt the baby had to be her first thought, even if it meant straining our marriage. She just wanted to protect the baby."

I sat down beside him. His arms were limp and he stared at the floor. He turned his head slowly to look at me again.

"Would you have gone with her?"

I thought about his question, was ashamed that I didn't know the answer.

"It's hard to know, looking at it now," I said, "but I might have."

He nodded his head, bit his lip—to keep from talking, from crying? I didn't know.

"I might have gone for the baby," I said, trying to soften my admission. "We had distance between us, you know that. Even before the accident."

"We had Joanne between us, the same way we do now," he said.

"It's strange," I said. "But in some ways I feel closer to you now than I did just before the crash. I meant what I said on the boat, Cal."

I needed to give him all of it, more than just the hurtful part—for his sake, and mine. "I really do love you. I'm not sure how much I understood that before. I took a lot for granted."

He watched me, waited for me to finish.

"The more I peel back all the layers of this mess, the more I know that's the truth. I'm not saying we should be with each other. I know we've run up against that brick wall and there's no way through it. But don't ever think there wasn't love in this marriage."

"I never thought there wasn't love," he said. "I just wasn't sure if it was both of us feeling it."

I moved toward him, put my arms around him and, to my surprise, felt his around me.

"I did feel it, Cal. I still do."

I CALLED MOM before I left, told her I'd be by the next day, that I needed to talk with her and that I was okay. She didn't ask what I wanted to talk about. She just said she'd be there. It was after eleven by the time I got on the road. Cal said he'd stay at the house with Rigsby for the night. When I got back, he'd go to his friend Randy's until we figured out what we were doing.

I could make out soft lights through the trees even before I turned off the highway to the retreat center. Lamps burned all night on paths throughout the grounds so that people with restless thoughts could walk to calm themselves.

As I drove to the parking area and looked at the buildings, I realized I didn't know where Sean lived or even if I was allowed to go there. On my earlier visit, I'd been in the dining hall and down by the lake. That was it.

I got my duffel out of the backseat and walked along the path that ran among the buildings. A cross stood high on top of a large, rustic structure that I took to be the sanctuary. I could start there, end there if I had to. There were worse places to spend the night.

The well-oiled door opened and closed without a sound when I went into the large room. Two lamps by the altar gave a dim amber glow, leaving the wooden pews to the descending shadows. Kneeling benches lined the wooden floor in front of each pew and no pillows softened the seating. I considered the long night ahead, then saw the communion rail, circled with thin cushions. Maybe I could crash there. The very thought probably constituted confessional material to an upstanding Catholic. A failed Baptist, my association with pillows ran only to comfort.

"Mass is over." Sean's voice startled me from the back of the room. "But counseling services run straight through the night."

"Hi," I said. "I didn't know where to find you."

"This was a good guess, but I was actually waiting on you in the dining hall. Brother Andrew said you called."

It was like Sean to be thoughtful, watching for me.

I put my duffel down on the first pew, sat down, and waited for him to come sit beside me.

"What's up?" he asked gently.

I started talking and couldn't stop. I found myself going on and on. I'm not sure I said everything in order, about Cal, about Larry Timbro, but I heard myself grabbing pieces of the story from my mind, each piece leading to another.

Sean listened, nodded, and furrowed his brow. He did all the right things, sent all the right signals of empathy and concern; and for the first time since I'd seen him again at Joanne's, I knew him purely for what he had become. It felt good to pass through to the place where he was to me what he'd been to Joanne—a friend, a priest, and a counselor. I needed all of those so much more than I needed a former lover. I had such an urge to tell Cal, then felt the loss of knowing it didn't matter anymore.

"Darla?" He was looking at me, waiting. I must have just stopped, consumed with my inner dialogue.

"I'm sorry. I'm really tired, I guess."

"Well, that's not much of a surprise, considering your day. If you want to stay, there's a room in the house where Katherine, our administrator, lives," he said. "I'll—"

"Sean, wait."

He moved back, put his hand on my shoulder. "What?"

"Why didn't Joanne tell me that her father knew about the baby? I mean, why do you think?"

He didn't answer at first. I'd learned to be patient with him. His opinions rarely came as fast as I wanted them.

"She didn't tell me much about her relationship with him," he said, finally. "It was the hardest thing for her to talk about. I didn't know she'd told him about the baby. But she talked about him more in our last visits, about some of her regrets."

"Her regrets? He was a total bastard to her."

Sean stopped talking. I'd jumped in with my pronouncements, cut off his answer.

"I'm sorry. I want to know what she said."

"Darla, from what I could tell, Joanne had big spaces inside of her, emotional spaces that parents usually fill. She looked to you to cover a lot of gaps."

"I know."

"Did she tell you her father paid off her car for her?"

I wondered if I'd misunderstood his words. Her car. I loaned her the down payment for the car just after she started working at the dealership. They were flexible some months when she had trouble making payments. Her landlord was the same way.

"I don't think so," I managed to say. "I would have heard about that."

"She just didn't tell you, Darla. There were other things she didn't tell you. Mostly about him."

"Why?"

The lamps by the altar seemed to brighten and dim, a pulsing change that ran loosely with the throbbing I felt near my temples.

"If you saw him as anything other than the enemy, as anything but awful and evil, she might lose what she needed from you. I think that's what she was afraid of. She couldn't afford to lose what you gave her."

"She told you this?"

"She told me a lot of things. A lot of it I put together from what she didn't say. But I'm right on this one. I've seen it before."

"Why would she tell you and not me? Why didn't she trust me?"

"She wasn't afraid of losing me. You were the only person she trusted completely," he said. He sounded so sure. "She just didn't trust how worthy she was—of you or the baby. She had too much at stake emotionally to risk letting you see everything. That's how I see it anyway."

I closed my eyes, could still see the pulsing lights. I could feel gravity bending and I tightened my fingers round the edge of the pew, opened my eyes to place myself deeper into the real world around me.

"So her dad paid off her car?"

Sean nodded. "She told her mother that she was having trouble making the rent and her car payments. This was a couple of months before I came back to town, I guess. The next week, she went to ask her boss for some extra time, to ask him not to take the payments out of her paycheck because she needed it for rent, and he told her that her dad had taken care of the rest."

"And you're sure it was her dad, not her mom?"

"Yeah. She told me that it made her mad."

"Mad?"

"She was embarrassed that her dad stepped in, that the people at work saw him do that. She went and told him to stay out of her business."

Joanne had a level of existence just below the surface that I never saw. If I'd found out before the accident, I would have been angry. As it was, I felt betrayed, lost as to what I could do with all the information.

"I still don't understand," I said. "I don't know why he would do that for her. He threw her out of the house, didn't want anything to do with her."

Sean leaned toward me. Inclined his head to look at me directly, to see my eyes.

"He has a lot of flaws, a lot of problems," he said. "I'm not beginning to suggest that he doesn't. It's just that there were shades of gray to his relationship with Joanne. You heard the black-and-white version of every story. Just consider that there were different versions of the things she told you."

"Why is it that you know all of this and I don't? And why are you telling me now and not before?"

"Like I said, she had nothing to lose with me. And I don't know everything. Not even close. There was a lot she didn't want us to know about her, about her father. And I'm telling you now because you're asking now," he said.

"Could you please stop this textbook counseling crap," I said, suddenly annoyed with him.

He laughed. A charming, disarming laugh.

"Well," he said. "It's in the textbooks for a reason. What do you want to know that's not part of the official lesson?"

"Why didn't you tell her to be honest with me?" I asked.

"Who says I didn't?"

"And she just didn't listen?"

"Joanne? Not listen? That's a thought, isn't it?" His eyebrows went high and I laughed even though I still wanted to be mad at him.

"Okay, okay," I said, relaxing a little, trying to push the crowded thoughts into neater spaces in my head. "But he threatened her. He told me as much. I'm not imagining that. It's why she was driving that night. It's why she's all but dead, Sean."

I tried to muster the anger, all of it that I'd felt before. But I couldn't let go of what Sean had said . . . *shades of gray in his relationship with Joanne.* I thought of what I'd heard in court, how her father had called to get her dog back for her. How she'd refused. Shades of gray . . . How gray was it that night? I wanted to go back, to make her trust me. I wanted her to believe that it wouldn't have mattered. Nothing she told me could have mattered.

"We need to get some sleep," Sean was telling me.

"I know."

If things could have been different, if she had talked to me . . . I stopped. Mid-thought, I made myself look at everything I knew to be true. Not yesterday's true, but life as it had become, literally overnight.

"You didn't give me any advice on my marriage," I said as Sean walked me to my room.

"Are you asking?" We were nearing the cabin porch. Locusts kept a frenzied chorus.

"No," I said, climbing the steps with him. The porch light made a circle around us. "I'm not asking. I just appreciate the fact that you haven't made any judgments. At least none that you've shared. Thank you."

He shrugged, gave me a look I couldn't read.

"Second room on the right," he said. "She keeps it made up."

I nodded, mumbled my thanks. Then I left him standing on the porch as I went in.

THE DINING HALL WAS FULL the next morning, various groups of youth and adults from churches in the diocese. The people looked happy in general. One table of teenagers reminded me of myself only a few years before. Did they have issues pulling at them, all the angst I remembered from that time? Were they questioning God? Or themselves? Maybe they didn't lay blame the way I had.

Sean was busy, so I sat with some of the brothers, who ate heartily and talked with equal enthusiasm. I'd always thought of monks as subdued. Perpetually contemplating. The group around me seemed more like a fraternity. A philosophy-debating, nondating sort of fraternity. I finished my breakfast without getting a single word into the conversation, and I needed a cigarette more than air.

Sean caught up with me on the path toward the lake, asked me all the polite questions about how well I'd slept.

"What do you think I should do about the baby if they want to go back to trial?" I tried to cut to the chase. "I'm asking, just for the record. I want your opinion."

We walked in step together. September still felt like summer. I wondered when the season would change, what life would be like when it did.

"This is where I make you crazy and tell you that I can't tell you what to do," Sean said.

"You're not really a therapist. You're a priest and you're my friend. You don't have to stick by all that answer a question with a question crap that we learned in Psych 101."

"I'm not trying to dance around anything," he said. "I just think you should consider the baby. I think this child is going to need a lot, from you and from them too, as time goes on. Figure out what you can live with."

"He threatened her." I didn't want to let go of that, even though I could feel my convictions faltering. *He* was the reason she was dying. I still had to believe that, otherwise nothing made sense.

"Listen," Sean said, the impatience clear in his voice, "you can bring your arguments up in court if it comes to that. Do what you have to do. I'm not telling you not to. It's a powerful thing to have in your pocket. All I'm saying is that you have to filter your decisions through the baby's needs, not your needs, not even Jo's. That's what parents do all the time. It's what they have to do. What does the baby need? It has to be your only question."

A parent. I was a parent, at least for the moment. I had to act like one. Sean saw me as a parent. That gave some weight to it.

"Sean, I meant what I said last night. I know you don't agree with how I made all this happen. Thanks for skipping the lectures."

The sun was in my eyes and I couldn't see his expression. I let it go at that, didn't ask for any more of him. I stopped, pulled my cigarettes out of my pocket and lit one, shielding the match against a nonexistent breeze.

"Hey, Father Sean!" The same woman I'd seen in the boat on my last visit was out again, calling to him, her Irish lilt echoing over the water. She was closer to shore this time, looked younger than I remembered. But she was still dressed ruggedly, like a man.

"How're you doing?" he asked. "Anything biting?"

"Got my line caught in that branch," she said.

I could see a slim branch moving as she pulled. The leafless tree that had fallen into the water some time back lay partially submerged.

"How come you're fishing in a tree?" he called back, grinning.

"That's where the fish are, wise guy," she shot back. "Can you free me up? I can't get close enough because of the bigger branches."

"You want me to get wet?" Sean asked. "I'm in my clothes."

"Come on, Padre," she said. "Help me out. I can't swim or I'd do it myself."

"It's not all the way up to your waist there," he said, but he walked toward the shore, even as he protested.

"Scared to death of anything deeper than my ankles," she told him.

He shook his head, took off his shoes. Though the water near the tree would rise clear up to his hips, he made the futile effort of rolling up his pants. Then he waded in the shallow area closest to the tree. One of the brothers, standing on a ridge above us, looked on with amusement.

There was still no breeze, no ripples other than Sean's fleeting wake on the water. In the hot stillness, I felt the air press close around me. Sweat ran over my temples, under my shirt, and between my breasts.

I looked out at the lake, the cool water seemed a necessity all of a sudden. I remembered the strange light off of the surface when I'd been there before, the feeling that a presence, larger and most surely benign, had been inside the vision, maybe just inside my head. It didn't matter. I thought of Jo, how she'd lived her life, following feelings rather than thoughts. Drawn by feelings I wouldn't try to name, I stood up, slid out of my sneakers, and moved toward the shore.

The thick mud felt like Play-Doh between my toes. The water, warmer at the shore, became cooler as I waded in. Sean looked over at me, so did the woman. I imagined the brother, standing on the ridge, wondering if I'd lost my mind. But no one spoke. I looked up at the sun and it felt good, full on my face. I let go of my cigarette and it moved slowly, floating away with an unseen current.

Even with the weight of the water soaking my clothes, I felt lighter and lighter as I went deeper in. When the lake reached my waist, I stopped, laid back, and let it hold me. I trusted the water. My body, nothing, slight as powder floating on the surface—the weight of my thoughts diffused by all that held me.

From just under the water, my ears picked up the drone of a motor. A motorboat, moving slowly toward me, the sound carried through the water. I could feel the sound through the length of my body, could feel it stronger as it approached. The vibrations peaked as the boat passed, and I opened my eyes slightly, saw the two men looking my way, and then ahead to where they were going.

I closed my eyes again as the sound of the motor grew fainter. Waves from the boat's wake began to rock me slightly, moved lightly against my cheek. The waves built, growing larger, and I held my breath as they came high against my face. I released my muscles, through my fingers, my toes, felt the gentle submersion as a wave washed over me.

Then, again, there was light and sky. I felt the bright sun dressing me, my damp cheeks cooling as they met the air. Eyes still closed, I registered a shadow covering me, opened them to see Sean standing beside me, his head tilted a little, his face calm.

My breath quickened. Something had altered, although nothing outside had changed. I looked at Sean to see if he knew. He nodded, a small, almost imperceptible movement of his head, and I wondered if I'd imagined it. He put his hand out and I took it so that he could help me stand. His other hand supported me lightly, until I had firm footing.

We walked to shore together and I noticed that the rowboat and the woman were gone. Time had passed, but the day seemed new, an odd perception of morning, regardless of the hour.

TWENTY-EIGHT

I CALLED MOM from a gas station on my way home. She said she'd have a sandwich for me when I got to her place. Sean had offered lunch before I left, but I wanted to get back. My old life had been stripped down to framework and studs. I needed to start building again.

"I've been worried about you," Mom said, as I walked into her apartment. "You're here and you're there. Cal sounded strange when I talked to him, and I can't get an answer out of either one of you about what's going on. We hear that you've got custody and suddenly—"

"Mom," I interrupted. "Sit down for a minute and I'll explain. As much as I can anyway."

We sat on her couch—chintz, all flowers and green, all new since Daddy had died. I'd hated the couch, the room, the whole place; thought it was a betrayal of him somehow. But sitting there I understood. She'd built what she had to in order to survive his absence. For the first time, I admired her for it, loved her for it even. For the first time, I let go of my resentment and thought about what she'd gone through after he died.

She settled beside me, put her hand on my arm and rubbed it, a gesture absent of anything but love.

"Mom, Cal and I, we've decided to separate."

Divorce seemed too harsh to say in front of her. She shook her head, started to speak, but I kept going.

"Hold on, please," I said. "It's going to be okay, I think. We're both going to be all right."

I must have talked for an hour, explaining, apologizing, opening doors to rooms that had never seen light. At some point, we moved to the kitchen to eat sandwiches she'd prepared. I saw the care she'd used, crusts trimmed, lemon in the tea. I watched her, not as her daughter, but as a pupil. I needed her lessons to be what I wanted to become.

Over sandwiches and cookies, I told her about my life with Joanne, the parts she'd heard about in the courtroom that must have confused her. Things in my life she'd never heard about and that I had imagined she never would. I told her about my time with Sean, then and now. How I'd loved him. How in my warped logic, I'd left him to save Daddy, to save myself. How it hadn't done any good. And I told her an abbreviated version of Jo and Cal. The pregnancy and my part, my insistence in the grand scheme. What I'd planned for it to be and what it had become. I told her how I planned to see it through, how in the last twenty-four hours, with everything falling apart, how so much had become clear to me.

"I'm telling you all this, Mom, because—first, I think you deserve to know; but also, I need you. You built a life after Daddy died. You had to do it by yourself; God knows I didn't help you much."

"Darla . . ." she began.

"I know, it's okay," I said. "I don't plan to beat myself up anymore. But you did it, after Daddy. I've got to do it now. I've got to figure out how."

"Life after Cal?" she asked, her eyes looked tired, sad somehow.

The honesty of the room, Mom's simple kitchen, kept me from simply nodding, agreeing with what seemed obvious.

"Yes," I said. "And life after Joanne," I said. That was the whole of it. That was the truth.

"YOU'VE GOT NO CAUSE to be here," Mrs. Timbro said. She stood in the front aisle, as if she wouldn't let me pass if I came forward.

Customers turned to watch her, then glanced at me, wondering what menace I might cause at the hardware store in the middle of a workday.

"I need to talk with you," I said. I kept my voice reasonable.

"I've told him to leave it be. You've got what you want. I won't have you dragging him through that last night with Joanne, not again. Not here and not in court."

"I don't want to drag him, or you, through anything anymore."

"I've always liked you, Darla," she said. "I don't hold to all that they pulled up in that courtroom, about you and Joanne, and that poor priest. But it didn't hurt you the way it did Larry. You can't see it, but all that mess nearly did him in the last time. I won't watch him go through it again."

"Mrs. Timbro—"

"No, you listen to me." I'd never seen her so on fire before, never seen her stand up for anything the way she was standing up for him. The old fear in her eyes was absent. "He was doing it for me. Do you understand that?"

"What?"

"It nearly killed me to see Joanne like she is. He thought, he still thinks, that the baby would be better off with us. But mostly, he thought it would be something for me. Something . . ." Her voice trailed off to nothing.

The store had cleared. People who had come for nails and wood glue didn't expect an emotional display. They found the door pretty fast.

"But I won't sacrifice him to have that. I want you to just go. Leave him alone. He's been through too much already. Like I said, you got what you want." It was a last effort, a final push to get me to leave. She was nearly spent. I felt bad for her. All of that was unnecessary, given what I'd come to say.

"I don't have what I want," I said.

She moved over to the counter, suddenly small, with her back to me.

"What I want," I said, "is what you want. I want Joanne back."

I felt my tears and I didn't try to hide. I walked to where she could see me when I spoke. She still didn't answer, but her eyes changed, got back a trace of the kindness that I'd known before.

"I can't have that," I said. "None of us can have that. And on top of everything else, it's cost me my marriage. I think too much has been lost. I want to stop it before we all lose even more."

I stopped and considered what I had to say. The world my baby would know rested on how well I chose my words.

"I know that your husband isn't an evil man. I didn't know that yesterday, but I know it today."

She settled back a little, relaxed, at last willing to listen.

"Joanne pushed him. Kept pushing every time she saw him. She needed his anger. I don't think I'll ever understand that. I'm not sure she understood it either. And she kept a lot of it from me on purpose for her own reasons."

I looked around the store. I looked at what the Timbros had built together. It appeared to be a normal life, running a store that served everyday needs. But their daughter was in a coma, carrying my husband's child. Even before that, she'd been anything but normal. All the things that had drawn me to her had tormented them.

"I've started to believe that she wanted it to end, the awful cycle of fighting with her dad. She can't end it now, but I'd like to try."

Arlene stepped toward me, stopped at arm's length.

"You're right." Her voice came in a whisper. I strained to hear. "He made a lot of mistakes, but she did too. And I did. The things she told you, they were only half the truth."

"She needed for me to think that it was all him. I wish she'd let me see all of it. But she didn't. She was afraid she'd lose something from me if I saw. She wouldn't have. I wish she'd known."

"Why now? How do you know all this now?" She still had her suspicions. Was I making it up, pretending so that I could have what I wanted? Her question was clear.

"I talked to Sean last night. She shared more with him about that than she did with me. She had some regrets, he said. Part of me feels disloyal even saying that some of this was her fault. But I've got to get past that. For the baby, I think we've all got to get past a lot. She couldn't bring herself to make it right. Sean thinks she wanted to. Then she got scared. She thought she had to run away to keep him from taking the baby."

"She called me," Arlene Timbro said.

"Who? Joanne?"

She nodded. She looked like a nice little girl who'd been caught doing something bad.

"When?" I asked.

She walked toward a small room off the back of the store, the place where they had outdoor furniture displayed. Then she turned, gestured for me to follow her to a small patio table. The umbrella that grew out of the table's center shielded her from fluorescent light. She sat down in one of the matching chairs and I walked over to sit beside her.

"When did she call you?" I asked again.

She leaned forward, rested her elbows on the aluminum surface. The bell on the front door signaled that someone had come in. She started to get up, but the young man who worked for them called out to her that he was back from the bank.

"Okay," she answered, then turned back to me. "She called me that night. The last night before . . . before he got home from her place."

I felt myself trembling. I took in air slowly. With her skittish nature, she could stop, retreat at any second.

"What did she say?"

She didn't answer at first. I wondered if I should speak again, ask again. Then she shifted a little in her seat, leaned slightly my way.

"She sounded calm. She sounded okay. It's the only thing that's gotten me through these last two months." She broke down, spoke between small sobs.

I was crying too, but it didn't matter. All that mattered was that she tell me everything Joanne said.

"She told me that he had just left. That they had argued something fierce. And she told me what he'd said, about . . . you know, saving the baby from her."

She sat up straighter, pulled a tissue from the pocket of her pantsuit jacket.

"It wasn't like you thought. Like it sounded the other day. He didn't just go in there threatening this and that. He never did that, regardless of what she told you. He went over there because he was worried about her. She'd told us about the baby, but she wouldn't tell us anything about the father, what she planned to do."

I watched her, amazed that she'd kept all of this inside for so long. She seemed younger, calmer, just saying it all out loud.

"She wanted him to suffer over it, Darla. I know you don't want to believe that about her, but she needed to hurt him. I don't know why. It hurt me too, but that was secondary to all of it. He asked her if the father planned to step up and help. He asked her again to tell him who the father was."

"What did she say?" I was almost afraid to ask. It pained me to think of her using the baby to get back at him.

"She said she didn't know." She looked down at the table, away from me. "Maybe the yard guy, she told him. That Mr. Romeros' nephew. She didn't, couldn't, know for sure, she said."

"Oh God." I couldn't think of anything to say. The worst part was I knew what Joanne's mother said was true. Joanne lied just to hurt him.

"Larry hit the roof. Told her she couldn't possibly raise a baby on her own. Told her she wasn't fit to. He did say that, but you have to understand, she drove him to it. There's so much more that you don't know, things I don't think Joanne ever told you."

"Well, you tell me, then," I said, my face a mess of tears. She reached out and laid her hand on top of mine. It was a kindness I didn't expect. "Please tell me."

"I can't," she said. "I've never talked about it with anyone but Larry. We don't even talk about it anymore."

She pulled her hand back, bit her lip to keep her own tears under control. She looked toward the door to the main room, as if she thought help might arrive, someone might come and save her from my questions, her words.

"Please, Arlene," I said again.

She took a deep breath, turned her eyes back to me.

"Arlene," I said, keeping my voice low, gentle. "I need to understand. I need to know the truth."

She nodded. Her eyes never left mine.

"Something happened," she said. "It was during that time you were away."

"Away?"

"That year you went away to school."

I wondered what could have happened then that would still matter. I stayed quiet, let her talk.

"Larry got a call. That friend of hers, that *Lindy,* she was on the phone. Crying, nearly screaming into the phone. I could hear it across the room."

"What was wrong?" I asked, part of me didn't want to hear.

"They were in Mexico. The three of them. Joanne, Lindy, and . . . and *that boy.*"

That boy? I tried to sort out what she meant. It was so long ago.

"Conner?" I asked.

"Yes," she said. She wiped her sleeve against her cheek. "Joanne was in a bad way, you see. She'd planned to have it. We found out, heard her talking about it and found out. Larry was furious at first. But then we all talked. We talked about what we could do to help. It was a terrible time, but we'd worked it out."

She stopped to catch her breath. I had trouble piecing together her meaning. They planned to help Joanne? Help with what?

"But then she panicked," Arlene continued. "You were coming home. She didn't want to tell you. And she got it in her head that something would be wrong. That she'd done things that would make it all go wrong."

"What are you talking about?" I could feel my heart racing. "Go wrong with what?"

"The baby, Darla. She was going to have a baby. Back then. She was pregnant before."

My nerves went numb. How could that be true? Before I'd as-sembled the pieces in my head, she started talking again.

"That boy. That Conner. He'd gotten her pregnant. But by the time she found out . . . Well, she didn't love him anyway, but when she knew it was true, about the baby, he was doing terrible things. Putting drugs in his arms with needles. The girl too. It scared Joanne."

"Oh my God." I hadn't been there. She'd gone through hell and I had been at school, feeling lonely and sorry for myself.

"But she came to see me at school. She came that January. I would have known she was pregnant, wouldn't I? She would have told me."

Arlene shook her head. I could hear the hum of the air-conditioning.

"She didn't want you to know. She was so afraid of losing some-thing. You thought so much of her. It meant a lot to her, what you thought."

I'd let her down in so many ways. I'd failed her, failed to let her know that I would be there—through anything.

"So what happened?"

"Like I said, she panicked. Decided she just couldn't go through with having the baby. She told me later that she was terrified—of being a mother, of the power a baby would give Larry over her. I don't know, so many things. I think she'd done some things too, while she was carrying the baby. She didn't say exactly, but . . ."

I thought of Joanne in my dorm room that weekend. Getting high with the girls down the hall. What was she thinking? Maybe that she could make it go away if she just forgot about it.

"Then they told her, those friends told her they knew of this place in Mexico . . ."

"And she went," I said, more to myself than Arlene. I could have told the rest of the story myself.

"We didn't know, didn't know where she was until we got the call. Joanne was in a terrible way. Her friends were scared she might die, and the baby . . ." She stopped, began to sob.

I put my arm around her, tried to calm her. All the images of Joanne sick, Joanne scared; it was too much for me. I waited until Ar-lene collected herself, then sat back while she continued.

"The baby, they saw it. I think even Joanne saw it, but she was so sick, I don't know what she remembered. It was more than they expected. It already looked like . . . Oh Darla, it was a little girl."

I felt the air collapse around me. The image came to me and I fought to get it out of my mind. A girl. A little girl.

"Oh God no," I said. I felt the room tighten. "Oh . . . God . . . How far along was she?"

"That was the thing," she said. "That was the worst part of it, the reason they drove to Mexico to start with."

I waited, didn't really want to hear what she would say.

"The baby was nearly seven months along. I think it was illegal, what she was doing."

"And Larry still went to her?"

She nodded. "He went right away, drove to Austin and got a flight out. He found her sick, burning with fever, had to get her across the border to a hospital. He had to make arrangements . . ."

"What?"

"He paid somebody in Mexico to bury that child."

I could see it. The little body. It tore at my heart. My hands on the table in front of me shook, shook as if I were freezing, but the room was warm.

"I see him thinking about it sometimes," she said. "I see a certain look and I know he's thinking about handing money to some stranger, so he'll go and bury that tiny baby."

I pushed it all through my mind, rushed the thoughts so that they couldn't linger, couldn't fester into the torment he must have felt. I tried to think logically.

"What did that have to do with the night of the accident?" I asked, forcing myself to move on. "What did that have to do with her running?"

"He brought it up that night, told her he wouldn't go through that again. He told her if he had to, he'd have her declared unfit, tell them all what she'd done before. He said if it came to it, he'd get them to lock her up before she could change her mind again, until he had it safe to raise himself. He couldn't go through that again. Don't you see?"

I thought of Joanne, thought of the wild panic that must have gone through her. He was going to take the baby. My baby.

"She must have been out of her mind to get away," I said. "What else did she say to you?"

"Like I said, she was calm. Calmer than you'd think. She told me everything he said. He still hasn't talked about it, doesn't even know she called me. But by the time she talked to me, she'd calmed down. She said she was tired. Just exhausted from fighting with him. She said she didn't want it to be that way anymore. That she knew how much of it was her fault. Honestly, Darla. She said that to me."

"I understand," I said. "I know you're being honest with me."

"He hadn't come home yet. But she told me how mad he was. What he'd said. She said she was afraid it was too late to go back, to tell him the truth. I asked her what the truth was, and she said it didn't make any difference. She had to leave."

"Did she say anything about me at all?" I asked.

She nodded. "Yes."

"What?" I could barely speak, my voice caught, as images of her on the telephone played clearly in my mind.

"I was worried about her taking off alone, pregnant. From the way she sounded, I knew she wouldn't do it again. You know, run off and panic. But I was afraid for her to be alone. She said she couldn't tell me, but she knew where she was going. Had some place to go. She said she was going to get you to go with her. She was sure you'd go with her. That eased my mind a lot."

She stopped, handed me a tissue, and waited for me to get myself together.

"I asked about Cal, how you could just leave him, and she said that she couldn't explain, but that he didn't deserve to have you there with him. She said you'd be better off coming with her."

The room seemed quiet. Outdoor furniture, set up indoors, gave an odd misplaced quality to the scene. The clerk in the next room talked in normal tones with a customer, oblivious to the emotions just a few feet away.

"Did she say anything else?"

Mrs. Timbro smiled.

"She said that she loved me. That she'd be in touch when things settled down, but for the time being, she just had to get somewhere and make sure the baby was okay. She wanted a favor from me. Could

I keep him busy, keep him away from her until she had a chance to get off to wherever she planned to go? I think she planned to leave the next day, but she must have gotten worried or something, afraid he would come back. At any rate, she decided it was best to get started for *some* reason. I don't know."

"But both of you were at the convention? That's where they found you. How could he have gone to her place that night?"

"When he got home, he was a mess. Darla, you just don't know how it hurt him to go through something like that with her. In the pocket of his coat, there was a check he'd made out to her. A check for four thousand dollars. He'd gone there wanting to help her and it had turned into something so awful. You just can't understand."

"I'm starting to," I told her. "But . . ."

"The convention, I know. Honey, it wasn't much of an act to tell him we should go to Houston after all. We'd decided not to. It'd been going on for a couple of days already. But there were two days left. I said we ought to just get in the car and go. He argued with me about closing the store; we hadn't hired Ray yet." She nodded toward the other room. "I said we both needed to get away. Have a little time off. He gave in. I put a few things in the suitcase and we left early the next morning. They found us later that day. Told us . . ."

She didn't need to tell that part of the story.

"I know," I said. "I know it from there. It must have been awful. And you never told him she'd called?"

"No." She shook her head.

"Why? It might help him to know—"

She went rigid again, her body suddenly taut.

"To know what?" she interrupted me. "To know that he'd been just a few words away from turning things around maybe? To know for sure that he was the reason she got on the road that night? He can talk himself out of that right now. He needs to. But if I told him . . . Please don't you go and tell him that. I wouldn't have told you if I thought . . ."

She was terrified she'd made a mistake trusting me. I could see her expression go from worry to panic.

"I won't," I said, leaning toward her, putting my hand on her arm.

"You can't tell anyone about all this. About what happened before either. He still has dreams; it tortures him to think about it. Paying somebody to . . . to take care of that little body."

She was crying.

"I promise." I put my arm around her. "I won't say anything. Not ever."

She calmed down a little, but it would take time before she believed a promise from me was any guarantee.

"I know that you don't know this yet, but you can trust me, Mrs. Timbro."

"Arlene," she said. "Please call me Arlene."

We sat for a moment and it seemed like a natural close to our talk, but I had one more thing to tell her. It was the part I was most afraid to ask, to get into. I'd made my promises, but I needed to trust them, the two of them.

"Arlene," I said before she could stand. "This baby . . ."

"I told you the truth, Darla. He was going through this for me. I've told him I won't go back to court."

"I'm alone, Arlene."

She settled back, looked squarely at me.

"I'm scared of all that I have to be. I don't know how to be a mother. I need help. And I think the baby needs us. Needs all of us. Will you and Mr. Ti—will you and Larry work with me? Help me raise this child?"

For an instant, I thought she might pull away, say she didn't want anything to do with me, with the baby. In that moment, I felt I'd failed Joanne. Failed a last request somehow, though I'd never heard her voice it, to me or to anyone.

My fear gave way when Arlene moved toward me, leaned over, and put her hands flat against my cheeks as if I were small and needed my attention focused directly on her. She was crying again, but smiling through the sobs.

"Nothing could make me any happier. Nothing. We'll do whatever you need."

"What does she need now?" He came through the door from the main store area. His tone continued directly out of our last conversation. Hard and suspicious. All the progress of the conversation with Arlene seemed tenuous at best.

"Larry." She was up and beside him. "She knows. She knows it wasn't all your fault. All the things that happened with Joanne. She understands that now."

"She understands she needs to get us in line so she can hold on to that baby. Now that her husband doesn't even want her anymore."

I sat. Nothing I said could outweigh her influence on him. I knew this, understood this for the very first time. I wished she'd been able to intervene more with Joanne, but I was nearly certain she wouldn't make the same mistakes when it came to her grandchild.

"It's not like that, Larry. It's not like that at all. She wants our help."

"Help?" He spat out the word. "Money?" He looked at me. "Is that what you want? Money?"

I shook my head. No, I didn't want money. I felt insulted and small. The pressure rose in my chest, the anger and humiliation. I hated him. All over again, I hated him.

I sat back, forced myself to think. This is the point where Jo made her mistakes, this is where she decided she had to cut him down. I could almost feel her, all her emotions, only they were magnified in her from years of struggle with him. She wanted it to change. She would want me to succeed where she failed.

"I don't want any money, Mr. Timbro. I'll put that in writing, if you like." I kept the words soft. It took all the effort that I could call. I didn't want to hand him any satisfaction, but I continued. "I talked with Sean."

His look was blank.

"Father Latham, the priest."

He shrugged, obviously unimpressed with Sean's holy credentials.

"He'd been counseling Jo, Mr. Timbro. She opened up to him with things that she didn't tell me."

"Such as?" He wasn't yielding.

Arlene stood by him. "Listen to her," she urged him in a small voice.

"He told me that Joanne regretted fighting with you. She regretted needing to do it. Over and over. It hurt her the same way it must have hurt you."

"He told you that?" I saw it, faint but definitely there. He was hoping, clearly wanted it to be the truth.

"Yes, he did. I talked with him yesterday."

"And what is it that you want now. Besides the baby, what do you want, if it isn't money?" He attempted to hold his ground, but I saw his weakness. His weakness was caring what Joanne thought, what she'd said.

"I want your help." I kept my eyes connected with his, determined to meet him on equal ground. "I want you to be in the baby's life, to help me raise this child. I want the baby to know that there are grandparents there to count on. If you want to go to court, I'll work out terms that you can live with. I'd rather work on trust. I trust you. You trust me."

Then I waited. The jingle of the door in the other room gave a frivolous note to the gravity of the moment. Arlene watched him. I don't think she was breathing. I'm not sure I was.

I wondered if I'd heard him at all when he gave a nod, simply said, "All right." It was all he could offer, still reeling from his years with Joanne. But it was enough. I looked at his eyes, the set of his jaw, and I believed him. With all that rested on our agreement, I still somehow knew that he meant what he said, and I accepted it as an oath, a promise I would call on and expect the best.

TWENTY-NINE

I WOKE UP on the foldout—except for Rigsby, alone in the house. The season had finally cooled, changed from summer to fall. But I still felt temporary, rendered a guest by my self-imposed exile from our bedroom. But with Cal gone, I could find even less reason to try and move back in.

I needed to get dressed. I let Rigsby out, put coffee in the filter and set it to brew. Peggy was coming over for the morning. She had an afternoon appointment in Alliance, said she'd hang out with me until she had to go to the meeting.

I'd been using the guest bathroom to shower every day. I'd venture to bathe in my own bathroom. That would be a small step toward pulling my life back in order.

"Come on, Rigsby," I said, letting him in from the backyard. "How about keeping me company while I shower, okay?"

He trotted through the bedroom just ahead of me. It was just a room, a nice room at that, but just inside my heart beat faster. Why did I feel anxious? Paint fumes still lingered. I told myself the smell could account for it and I almost believed it. When the doorbell rang, I registered a certain relief, turned around, and followed the dog to the front door.

"ANY LUCK WITH A JOB?" Peggy asked, after I'd poured us a cup of coffee.

She'd brought cinnamon rolls from the grocery store and put them in the oven.

"Not yet," I said. "Most places are looking for full-time people. I don't want to work more than three or four days a week when the baby's here. With what Cal's going to send every month, that should be enough for us to get by, if I can find reasonable day care. There's so much to think about."

"Yeah, I know. Finding three days a week with benefits is going to be hard," she said. "If Cal ends up going back to Portland, it may mess up medical coverage for you and the baby."

The mention of Cal's move, as if it were an everyday topic, brought the reality of it into focus. *Cal is leaving. Jo is dying. Life has to become something new.*

"Darla?" Peggy said. "Have you thought about insurance?"

"No, no . . . I need to think about so much. He's decided to go back there. Some days it's clear to me why he's leaving, others I can't figure out how we got to this point."

"Did it change anything for the two of you, now that the Timbros aren't on the warpath. I thought that was the biggest stress."

"No," I told her. "It's Joanne's part in this, his problems with Jo and my closeness to her. He wants it all to go away. But the baby will be hers too. That's only become more clear since I settled things with the Timbros. Cal's still reeling. I can't say that I blame him. I've had a hard time making myself think about everything, but I'll sort it out."

Peggy sat down beside me at the table. She lit a menthol, offered me one. The pull seemed unbearable, but I shook my head.

"I don't want to smoke around the baby," I told her. "I figure it will be easier to quit again now, rather than after . . ."

"I'm sorry," she said, and put her cigarette out on the ashtray that sat on the counter behind her. She reached over and put her arm around me.

"You've got about a month," she said. "To get ready for a baby and to say good-bye to Jo. I'm not surprised that you're having trouble coming to grips with everything."

"As it gets closer, it's on my mind a lot. It's like I don't have any right to look forward to the baby, because . . ."

"You're trading one for the other. Joanne for the baby."

"It wasn't supposed to be that way," I said.

She sat back. "I know."

She got up and took the rolls out of the oven, put them on a plate, and poured us some more coffee. I still wore my bathrobe. She had on a gray wool suit and was acting like a waitress in my own kitchen. The picture seemed a little absurd.

"Are the Timbros behaving?" She had doubts about my newfound truce with Joanne's parents; but for my sake, she was coming around.

"They're not bad people, Peg. He's a real bastard sometimes, but mostly when he's provoked. Joanne knew all his crazy buttons. I know some of them, but I've stopped pushing. It's going to be okay, I think."

She didn't respond one way or the other.

"Where will you set up the nursery?" She changed the subject.

"I guess I'll pick one of the two little rooms, fix it up," I told her.

"And you'll move into the other one," she said, raising an eyebrow as she took a sip of her coffee.

I glanced over her way, didn't answer. She didn't expect one. She was right, the baby and I could be guests together in our own house. Peggy could come and be the hostess to both of us. I had to get my nerve up and move back into my own damn room.

"I'll come help you with the nursery when you decide," she said, not pushing the issue any further.

AFTER BREAKFAST, Peggy was gathering her things together to leave, when the doorbell rang.

"That's probably your mom," she said over her shoulder as she sorted through her briefcase. "I talked with her this morning and she said she was going to get you out of this house and do *something* today."

I walked through the den, thinking up excuses to get out of shopping or whatever Mom had in mind. When I opened the door, I saw

Ray, the young guy from the hardware store, standing there. He wore a short-sleeved knit shirt and blue jeans, a green work apron over them. He had no jacket, stood shivering in the cool, fall air.

"Ray?" I said, motioning him into the house. I closed the door against the air outside. "What are you doing?"

"They told me to come," he said, out of breath. He put his hands in his pocket and pulled them out again. "They asked me to get you. It's . . . they called from the hospital about Joanne. The Timbros are there now."

"What is it? What happened?"

"I don't know exactly. The nurse said there was a blood clot. They took her to the operating room."

"Is she okay?" I asked. It was a ridiculous question. She hadn't been okay, would never be okay again. "What about the baby?"

"I think it's the baby, they're . . . I think the baby has to be born."

Peggy was beside me. She held my wrist with her hand. I could only stand there, shaking, unable to move.

"Darla," she said. "You need to get dressed. We have to do this. Darla?"

"Your meeting?" I could only think about details, mindless information, Peggy's meeting, Rigsby needed a walk. "I haven't showered." Peggy guided me and I felt myself moving "What about . . ."

"Darla." She stopped just inside my bedroom and turned to me. "Honey, do you understand what he's telling us?"

"Joanne . . ." I felt the tears. They weren't enough. How could it be as simple as tears? When a soul rips open, isn't there more? "Is Joanne dead?"

I thought maybe I had it all wrong. Maybe I misunderstood. But Peggy was crying too. She put her arms around me as I sobbed. When she finally pulled away, she brushed wet strands of hair from my face.

"It's the baby now," she said. "We have to worry about the baby. Come on."

She led me to my closet.

"Oh God, the baby." I turned, suddenly stricken with the thought.

"Let's just get to the hospital," she said, shaken but still calm. "Just get dressed and I'll drive."

The curtains were open to Joanne's cubicle in the ICU. Her bed was empty, made up new. Taut, white sheets. The nightstand had been cleared of the cards people sent. I'd read them all to her, read the old ones again when they stopped coming.

The room was waiting for someone else. Joanne's name had been erased from the board behind the nurses' station. For nearly four months I'd found some part of her here. Now that they'd taken her away, I didn't know where to go looking.

"Where are the Timbros?" Peggy asked a nurse at the desk.

I didn't recognize her, but she seemed to know who I was; she directed her answer toward me rather than Peggy.

"They're in the neonatal waiting area," she said softly, without the enthusiasm that would have normally been appropriate for such an announcement. "They said to send you there if you came here first."

She gave us directions and I hoped Peggy took note, because my mind wouldn't hold the details of floor numbers and which way to turn down the blue-coded hall.

"What about the baby?" I asked, almost afraid to hear.

"The doctor will fill you in," she said. "But I heard things went fine."

"And Joanne? She's really gone?"

She put on her kindest face, shook her head, and said, "The doctor will tell you about everything."

I didn't need details from a doctor.

IN THE WAITING ROOM, Arlene sat in a sofa chair. Her eyes looked like a doll's eyes, wide-open, but blank. Larry was in the chair beside her.

"How's the baby?" I asked him.

"He's fine," Larry said. "Real little. They're gonna have to watch him. But he's okay."

He. My son. I have a son. I steadied myself on the arm of a chair, sat down beside him.

"Is Arlene okay?" I asked Larry as softly as I could. She still hadn't looked at me, acknowledged my presence.

"They gave her something." That was all he could manage by way of explanation.

Peggy went to Arlene, put her hand on the older woman's arm. Arlene shifted the direction of her head, but her eyes didn't change, didn't focus.

"Where is he, the baby?" I asked. I needed to see him, to see for myself that he was safe.

"They're still running some tests on him now," Larry said. "They'll let us know when we can go to him. It all happened pretty fast. They had Joanne in the operating room when we got here."

"Did you see her?"

He shook his head.

"And she's gone. You're sure?"

"Yes," he said. "She's gone."

I didn't know what I'd expected, what other outcome there could have been.

"The blood clot," he said. "She died almost immediately. They just had minutes to get the baby . . ." His voice broke. My hand shook as I raised it to his arm. He looked at the floor, his shoulders heaving as his grief took form.

Then the room fell quiet. Peggy got up to make phone calls—to Cal, my Mom.

"Call Sean. Jo would want him in on this," I said. "And I do too."

"Do you have his number?" she asked.

I went through the scattered jumble inside my pocketbook, found my wallet and the piece of paper with his name scrawled at the top, the number below it. I handed it to her and she left.

Arlene didn't seem to notice that Peggy was gone and I moved to sit beside her.

It somehow felt easier with just the three of us. I was grateful to have them, Joanne's parents, their pain keeping company with my own. It was comfort I hadn't anticipated.

I looked across the room at Larry, his elbow resting on his knees, his gaze down. The weight of his anger, and Jo's anger toward him, had made him look older than fifty-four. I hoped my son, her son, could give him ease.

THEY HAD MOVED Jo to some nameless place. A place where no one who loved her could gain access. The people who loved her shouldn't be burdened by the sight of sterile, gloved hands handling her body. I imagined them touching her so with little regard for what she had been, beautiful and alive.

"Where will she go?" I asked.

"They'll pick her up and take her to the funeral home," Larry said. "They take care of everything from here on." No need for doctors any longer, he implied.

I wasn't sure where I fell in the grand scheme of funeral etiquette. If they would even let me be part of it.

"I'll need your help," Arlene said to me, as if answering my question. "I don't know what she would want to wear."

I thought of Jo's closet at the duplex, scanned my memory for something remembered, something right. *What she would want to wear . . .* It sounded like a decision for the prom or some big party. My mind's eye could see her only in blue jeans, her bare feet white below the boot-cut hem.

I opened my mouth, tried to say that I'd do what I could, but there weren't words to show for my effort. I nodded, hoped she understood.

THEY TOOK US to the viewing area where premature babies have monitors and watching eyes to protect them around the clock. I saw a clear box, the card at the end read "Baby Timbro." The little bed was empty inside and my heart raced at the thought that everything might be lost after all.

"Timbro," Larry was saying, making his mouth large and exaggerated so that they could read his lips.

The nurse wheeled a smaller, more shallow bed toward the window.

"We're moving him now," she said, with equal contortion of her face.

Before she transferred the baby to his bed, she wheeled him right over to the window.

I looked down. Like a smaller version of the contraptions by Jo's hospital bed, machines trailed him, attached to his body by tubes and tape. He had a tiny, plastic piece hooked to his nose. Patches followed the life inside his little chest, while the IV and monitor trailed him like a strange, robotic entourage.

But unlike Jo's machines, I welcomed every gadget that connected him with the world outside himself. Machines kept Jo from dying. Machines helped him to live.

My baby. And then the thought came, unbidden. *Cal's baby too. And Jo's.*

"Hey, hey there, fella." I talked through the glass. "I need to call Cal," I said, pressing my forehead against the clear barrier, wanting to change the angle of my view, to be so near him I could hear him breathe. "I love you, little guy."

I'd lost concern that anyone was around. Beneath the plastic and gauze attached to him, he looked perfect. Fine strands of hair grew from his tiny scalp. I made note of the color that would deepen as the thicker strands grew. Auburn. He would be beautiful.

I turned to the Timbros.

"Look at his hair," I said. "Just like hers."

Arlene raised her eyebrows, touched the glass in a gesture of wonder.

Larry smiled. He looked at his grandson and smiled.

THIRTY

THE TIMBROS FOLLOWED ME along the old path until we saw the church through the trees. The air was cool, but the leaves hadn't started to change. The walls of the burned-out sanctuary, turned green with vines, seemed familiar, comforting.

"She came out here?" Arlene asked. She was looking around, probably trying to picture Jo.

"All the time," I said. "She brought me here when Dad died."

Heavy rains all week had left the stream high. I could see the play of sun and shadow on the surface through the trees, could hear the rushing.

Larry hadn't said anything. He moved around from place to place as if walking the property for potential use.

"We have a church, you know," he said, finally. "We already talked to the preacher at First Methodist."

It was a simple statement, but the tones rumbling underneath said more than the words themselves. Joanne would hear the tones, react without listening. I understood; I wanted to do the same thing. I wanted to fire back that Joanne hated the Methodist church on the one occasion a year that they decided to take her there. But I waited, took a breath and, before I could say anything, Arlene walked over to him, took his arm as if they were on a stroll.

"It's pretty here," she said. "Don't you think it's pretty, Larry?"

His shoulders relaxed. He sat on a splintered pew, near the aisle. She followed and sat beside him.

"What do you want to do, Mama?" he said.

The term of endearment, the same my dad had used with my mother, took me by surprise.

"It's unusual," she told him. "But Joanne was unusual."

He smiled at her, put his arm around her shoulder.

"Your friend," he said to me, "the priest. Could he do the service?"

I went and sat down in the pew behind them.

"He can say a prayer, maybe offer a blessing. I don't think he can actually do the service unless the person is Catholic."

Larry nodded. I waited, hesitated to bring up the next subject too quickly. But the time was right.

"There's a preacher," I said. "He used to preach here. Joanne knew his grandson. She told me she met the man, the old preacher, last spring when she came here and he was out walking. She talked with him a long time, sitting here. She liked him."

I stopped. Waited. I couldn't sell it any better than that, so I just stopped.

"You want to ask him to preach the funeral?" Larry glanced back at me. Again a simple sentence delivered as a challenge. Talking with him required constant negotiation.

"I think Jo would have liked for him to."

He kept his arm around Arlene. Didn't say yes or no to my suggestion.

I could hear cars out on the highway. Through the trees it wouldn't be that far. But the church felt like a world removed from pavement and billboards.

He turned around to look at me. Up close, the skin under his eyes sagged. I'd never seen anyone look so worn-out. I wondered if Joanne had ever noticed he was getting old. I wondered about the last time she kissed his cheek; when had that been? Would she even remember if I could ask her? He was another species in some ways from my own dad; in others, not so different.

I missed my father in ways that I hadn't thought about for years, and in an impulse beyond any hope of reason, I leaned forward and touched Larry's cheek. His skin was warm and softer than I would have guessed. I pulled back, embarrassed. He looked startled, but not upset.

"I'm sorry," I said, without explanation.

Arlene smiled slightly, took control of the awkward moment by saying, "Don't apologize. We're all feeling her loss just now."

He didn't respond to me or to her, but his expression had softened, making his eyes benign, almost kind.

"Do you mind talking to this fella?" he asked when the silence became noticeable.

"Who?"

"The preacher," he said. "Will you speak to him about the funeral? We need to get it settled today."

"I'd be happy to," I said. Then it occurred to me that Larry didn't know anything about the preacher, or Joanne's friend, the grandson.

"Larry," I said. "I should tell you. This preacher . . . well . . . he's black. I don't know if . . ." *If what? If you're a bigot.* I felt as if I were in a hole, looking for a way out. Larry Timbro gave me a way back to clear sky.

"I don't blame you for wondering about me," he said. "We've had our opinions of each other, not always good. But I don't know any good coaches who are racists. I said *good* ones, mind you. I was a good coach."

He paused. Let his words sink in, then he went on. "If you know where to find this fella, I'd appreciate you talking to him for us. That okay with you, Mama?"

Arlene nodded.

It dawned on me that they were treating me like family, allowing me to play a role in Joanne's final days. I'd done all of the same things with my mother when my daddy died. I'd felt the burden of it then, but not the privilege. This time was different.

"Thank you," I said.

"For what?" Arlene asked.

"For letting me be part of this," I told them. "For letting me grieve with you. I don't think I could let go of her by myself."

"Well," Larry said. "You're not by yourself now." His voice, the emotional tone of it, surprised me. "That boy is waiting for you at the hospital." Then he added, "I think you two will do fine though."

I managed to say "Thank you," but lost all other words in the swell of tears that grew in my throat. I wiped my eyes on the sleeve of my shirt like a little kid, then stood up, hoping a full breath would steady me.

We walked the path back to our cars in silence.

PREACHER LANGSTON'S HOUSE didn't look the way I expected. I had imagined it deep in the woods, worn-shingled and small. Something Snow White might pass en route to the dwarves.

Not so. It sat just off the highway. I'd passed it a thousand times without taking notice. It was brick with a small cement porch taking up a third of the front. A metal glider faced the highway, ready to observe the comings and goings of the town. Around the L-shaped wall from the glider, the front door discreetly faced the woods to the side of the house in the direction of the old church.

"Hello," he said when he answered the door. His smile opened his face, a guileless soul. "Can I help you?"

He was thin, and very tall, had the vague stoop of age battling natural good posture.

"I'm Darla Stevens," I told him. "I'm a friend of Joanne Timbro."

"Oh yes. I know your name," he said. "Joanne's spoken about you. It's nice to meet you. Come in. I'm just finishing up a little lunch with my daughter."

"I don't want to interrupt you. I can come back later."

"No, no, no. We're all finished. Come on in."

The door opened directly into the living room. The word *parlor* came to mind. It looked like a comfortable sitting room. I thought of our den, mine and Cal's. The foldout bed that hadn't been a couch in weeks.

"This is my daughter, Maureen."

He introduced me to a slightly plump woman in a silky blue jogging suit. She was a little younger than my mother. Her temples were gray, but her skin looked as young as a girl's. Although different in almost every respect physically, she had his face. Open and kind.

"Hello," she said, extending her hand. The other one held a dish towel. "It's nice to meet you."

Neither of them seemed surprised that a young white woman had just shown up at the door unannounced.

"I'm done in the kitchen, Daddy," the woman said. "I'll need to run on."

"Okay," he said, picking up her purse from a chair in the living room and handing it to her.

"Are you Thomas' mother?" I asked, a little too bluntly I realized after it was out.

"No. Thomas is my nephew," she said. "My brother's boy. He's with me a lot though, when he's in town, but I haven't seen him in a while. Is he a friend of yours?"

I just nodded, not feeling the need for further explanation. I don't know why I asked. I wanted all the living connections to Joanne I could find, even a relative of a sometimes friend of hers seemed comforting.

After she left, I waited in the living room for Mr. Langston to bring out coffee. He sat beside me on the couch, apologized that the coffee was instant.

"Since my wife passed on, I don't bother with things in the kitchen much. I gave my coffeemaker to Thomas for his apartment in Dallas."

"What's he doing?"

"He's a police officer, believe it or not." He chuckled at the thought of it. "All that boy put us through, and then he goes off and applies to the police academy. He's on one of their special teams. Doin' real well."

"I'm glad," I told him.

I liked the room. Framed pictures hung in clusters along the walls. No rhyme or reason to the groupings. Some color, some black and white; five pictures in one group, three in another. They reminded me of the way people gather in the churchyard after a service.

"I'm here about Joanne," I said. "You know about what happened to her?"

"Yes, I do," he said. "I'm so sorry. I was up to the hospital two weeks ago after I heard."

His words surprised me. I hadn't thought about him seeing her there, seeing her belly. What did he think?

"She was . . . pregnant. Did you know?"

"She talked to me about it before the accident. In this very room, she sat with me." He spread his arm out in an open gesture to the room.

"She was here?"

"Twice," he said. "I saw her at the church one afternoon, told her to come by anytime. She came twice after that. When I didn't see her at all for a couple of months, I called Thomas. He'd heard from a friend what happened to her."

I sat with my hand on the couch beside me. He put his hand on top of mine.

"You needn't worry about her," he said. "She'd made her decisions." Made her decisions. Packing her bags, a note about the rent, one about the dog . . . Of course she never meant for things to end that night. She meant for them to begin.

"She claimed her peace with God," he went on. "You needn't worry at all."

It was such a standard preacher thing to say, but it had the ring of truth, coming from him, a certain comfort. I thought of what Sean had told me, that she'd considered working for the church in New Mexico. With her father, with Sean, and with the old preacher, she had a life outside of the one I saw. I couldn't let myself be too hurt by that. There was so much hurting inside me already, I had no room for more injury.

"When her time comes," he was saying, "and I feel like it won't be too long—"

"Preacher Langston," I interrupted, startled by his words. "She died yesterday."

He stopped. His face changed. He felt something about her death, even though he'd seen her only a few times, and I was grateful for that.

"I'm sorry," he said. "The baby?"

"He's premature, a little over a month before his due date. But they think he'll be fine. He has to stay at the hospital for a while. His lungs need to get stronger."

I saw him in my mind. Tiny with restless limbs. So like Joanne. Not holding him. That was the hardest part. Joanne gone and glass between me and my newborn son.

"So he's gonna be all right?" Preacher Langston repeated my words.

"Yes."

"Well, that's a blessing for sure. He'll need a lot of love from you and your husband."

I'd tell him about Cal later. I needed to get to the part about the funeral. I felt the need, urgent and clear, to do my business with the preacher and to get back to my place at the glass, as near as they would allow me to my son.

"Preacher Langston? Jo's parents and I were hoping that you would consider preaching her funeral."

He didn't look surprised at my request.

"She loved it out here," I told him by way of explanation. "It was really the only church she came to."

"Well," he said. "I haven't spoken from a pulpit in a long time."

"You don't have to say much. There won't be that many people who will come, I don't think. In spite of what a lot of people think about her, she was a good person, a wonderful person. I'd like for you to say that about her."

"She told me she was baptized," he said.

"Yes," I said. "We were baptized together."

"People can think what they want. Anybody who ever sat willingly in my church and prayed is somebody I count as one of the good. Only God judges hearts. Don't apologize for her. There's no need."

"You're right," I said.

That part of the conversation seemed over. I thought he had agreed to my request, but I wasn't sure. Then he spoke again.

"You ought to know that we meet at the community center about a half a mile from here. It's full of the Lord when we get together, but it's not much to look at otherwise. Just cinder-block walls and folding chairs. They'll do a nice job, setting it up for a funeral service, but—"

"I meant have her funeral at the old church."

"In the woods?" he asked.

"That was her church, the only one she attended."

He sat back, nodded to himself as if he needed to respond to some internal conversation he was having.

"Well, that's not something I would have thought of. But if that's what you want, I guess if the Lord Jesus didn't need four walls around Him to preach, then I don't either."

I told him I'd have the Timbros call him with the time. He talked with me more, a half an hour or so. Took some notes and offered to pray with me.

"I don't do that well with prayers anymore," I said.

"Well, if you're not one for praying, I'll just pray for you. Any objection to that?" His smile took over his face again, took over the room and everything in it, including me.

I said no, no objection. Then he got up to walk me out. The pictures lining the walls to the door offered a benevolent chorus of eyes that sent me on my way.

THIRTY-ONE

*J*OANNE HAS HER FINGERS *tight around my wrist. She squeezes and I feel my pulse strain against her hold. We've waited for this. Our first Communion Sunday after baptism. We will take the drink and the bread from the trays when they are passed, and no one will send scolding eyes our way.*

First, the ushers bring the round trays of bread, miniature squares of loaf bread that women have cut up in the kitchen before the service. Jo and I have skipped Sunday School to watch my mother do it. The women laugh and talk while they work. The bread pieces are so small that a single slice yields thirty or forty squares, like the fishes and the loaves.

I take a square and pass the tray on to Joanne. She takes one, starts to put it in her mouth, but I touch her arm, shake my head, no. She hasn't seen it our way before. We wait until the preacher says, "Now take, eat." I give her a little nod. Hands throughout the sanctuary rise in unison.

Then ushers pass the heavier trays of tiny glasses. The trays are made special with holes where the glasses fit. Little brackets on our pew backs have holes the same size, so we have a place to put them when we are done. The women, my mother among them, will collect and wash them after the service. The glasses hold grape juice, Welch's. They are larger than thimbles, but not by much.

Jo doesn't drink hers. She knows now to wait.

"Now drink the blood of our Lord Jesus Christ," the preacher says. I tell myself over and over it is just Welch's, so that I can swallow without thinking about the blood. The juice is sweet, not salty like blood, and I am relieved. It feels cool as it moves inside my chest.

Jo and I put our glasses in the seat-back holders. Grape juice is left at the corner of her mouth. I make a motion to tell her and she leans her head down sideways, wipes it on the shoulder of her white Sunday dress.

The stain is small, but I can't help staring at it. Through the rest of the service, I can see it out of the corner of my eye. I think of the preacher's words. "Marked as God's own." I wonder if she has been chosen; if she will leave me behind.

THE DREAM CAME so close to my senses that I could taste the bite of the grape juice when I woke. For a moment I forgot the day ahead. When it came to me, I wanted to crawl back into sleep, to dream our lives over from that point and change the outcome that led to Jo's end. Instead I got up and dressed, a nice pantsuit for the funeral and not a dress. We had warned people the church sat in the woods and they had to walk through brush to get to it.

The Timbros offered to have me ride in the family car from the funeral home, but I wanted to stop by the hospital on the way and see the baby. Cal said he would pick me up. He said he'd stay as long as I needed him around. In that case, he'd never leave. I wanted to tell him this, but I didn't. Our split had been hard on him, but he looked like himself again. Even I saw it, and I didn't want to. His easy laugh had come back.

Still, he'd put off his move back to Portland until I got through the worst of things. It made me calmer, just knowing that much.

In typical Cal fashion, he arrived early to pick me up, said he wanted us to have plenty of time.

"Don't you want to go up with me?" I asked. The car sat at the curb near the front door of the hospital, the motor still running.

"I can't, Darla. The baby, he's . . ." I waited for more. He shook his head, held both hands in the air, palms up, like a minister imploring God. The words weren't there.

"It's okay," I told him, touching his arm. "I'll be right down."

He'd seen the baby once. I'd hoped for some change in him, a miracle of bonding that would set us all right. But he had stayed only a few minutes and said almost nothing. As far as I knew, he hadn't been back.

"I feel defeated when I see him," he said, finally, as I was getting out of the car. "There's no right way for me to handle this."

I didn't understand exactly, but it represented his best explanation, so I leaned back in, hugged him.

"I'm just glad you're here today," I said. "I'm grateful for that. Honestly."

He nodded, seemed relieved to let it go.

I went in to see "Baby Timbro." I didn't want to give him a name, not yet. I didn't want to take him away from Joanne any sooner than I had to.

The nurse rolled him near the window. He looked calm, unbothered by all the noise and lights. Asleep and with glass between us, he looked like a framed picture. I wanted him to wake and reassure me that it wasn't like Joanne had been, that he wasn't just breathing until he died. They kept telling me he was doing fine but wasn't "out of the woods yet." I wanted to hold him.

He was still asleep, but in answer to my worry, he raised his small hand, spread his fingers and curled them back again. As if to tell me he would live and grow, would someday smile and run.

As CAL DROVE OUT of the hospital lot, I looked around. It was a day that presented itself in grace. The weather easy on the heels of a southern wind. The dirt of the cemetery beside the church would be soft from recent rain. My heart nearly suffocated in the benevolence of Joanne's good-bye. But for her it was a gentle exit; a day that she deserved.

The funeral director had asked us to arrive early. I could see Cal's confusion at the choice of location. I'd told him about the church, but he hadn't seen it before. The funeral home had put up a big tent on the far side of the church, in case it rained. They had folding chairs at the ready. The setup gave the impression of the circus come to town, or at the very least, a revival. Jo would have been cracking jokes right and left.

Under the tent, they had her casket. Since we'd had no formal visitation, they wanted to give us, the people closest to her, the chance to say good-bye before others arrived.

I walked under the tent; the Timbros stood by her. Larry held his wife and she was crying. I hadn't seen him cry, but I suspected that he did when he was alone with her. It was a thought I wouldn't have entertained a few weeks before.

The funeral director and his assistant stood on either side of the coffin, both of them looking off into space. It was their job, not to notice, but rather to *oversee* grief. They were good at their work.

I wanted to join Jo's parents, but felt frozen at the edge of the tent. I'd seen my daddy, his body anyway, and the sense of his absence nearly killed me. I didn't think I could do it again.

"Darla?" Cal came up behind me. "I'll walk with you if you want me to."

He all but carried my weight as I leaned on him. We made progress. As I got closer, I could hear Arlene's small sobs.

"I can't do this," I whispered, but kept moving forward.

I saw the dress first, the twilight blue empire waist she'd bought for a friend's wedding in June. She selected a style she could wear through the pregnancy. I told the Timbros it was her favorite. Then I saw her hair, more perfect than she'd ever had the patience to achieve. Auburn strands had started to grow back over the injuries. The funeral home had arranged curls near her cheek to disguise scars left on one side of her face. Between the hair and the makeup, they were barely visible.

Regardless of their best efforts, it was just as my father had been, the body no more than a figure of Joanne.

I felt myself crying, but the tears were old, recycled grief that had lasted for months.

"I found this when I was clearing out her things." Arlene was talking to me. "Do you think I should put it with her?"

In her hand was the Bible, the Bible that had lived in the back pew of the burned-out church, the Bible my mother gave Jo when we were kids. I took it, thumbed through and saw her large, loopy scribble in the margins. Words, circled, highlighted. I handed it back to Arlene, nodded that I thought it should stay with Jo. Words wouldn't come, but she understood. She laid the Bible on Joanne's chest, near her hands.

I wanted to touch Jo, but couldn't bear the idea of how cold she would be, so I put my fingers to her hair, slipped them through the shiny strands. Underneath the coating of hair spray, the hair was softer than I'd imagined. The feel of it took me by surprise. I stepped back, unable to see through my tears. As they closed the lid, I told her I loved her, over and over in my mind I said it. She'd always been able to read my thoughts. I hoped that wasn't lost to us now.

Cal walked me to the edge of the tent and Sean met us there. He wore his habit, a robe of simple brown wool tied with a rope belt. His only modern concession came in the form of hiking boots, just visible at the hem.

"Here." Cal held out his handkerchief to me.

I wiped my eyes, mascara and rouge smeared across the white cloth. I could only imagine how my face was faring. Cal moved away to talk with my mother. Sean stood by me, and I looked at him with eyes that felt like balloons.

"You okay?" he asked.

"No."

"Anything I can do?"

"Tell me something good about her. Tell me she's still somewhere," I said.

"She is," he said. "I saw it in her, heard it in her voice. She's all right."

"Yeah? Well, maybe she was the lucky one after all. I let go of all that faith business a long time ago. I'm not sure I'll ever find it again. Too bad. It would sure come in handy right now."

My voice was thick, a register lower than it should have been.

"Maybe it'll find you," he said. "Come on. They're waiting."

The Timbros were standing by the front pew. Sean took my elbow gently, directed me toward them. I saw Peggy walking toward the church, my aunt and uncle just behind her.

"I want a cigarette so bad I'd walk over glass to get to it," I said.

"Just hang on," Sean told me. "You'll get through this."

The pianist, on a stool in front of the portable keyboard, started in with soft music, the cue for people to begin settling into the weather-worn pews. The funeral home had put vinyl cushions on the seats. It almost felt comfortable. Men in suits, Cal among them, brought Joanne's coffin to the front of the church, near the altar, then he came and sat beside me. Looking at us, no one would know we'd become two separate people again.

We'd decided we wouldn't make the service long, citing Joanne's lack of patience as our excuse. Just a few words, then the burial in the adjacent cemetery. Jo would join the former members of the church, the slaves and children of slaves who rested there. She'd like the company, her white skin not an issue in the afterlife.

When the music stopped, Sean got up to read a scripture passage that the Timbros had chosen. Something about throwing off old apparel, new garments, new robes. I could only imagine old-timey Bible clothes that Jo wouldn't have worn on a bet. But it meant something to the Timbros—the idea that in death she could be herself, but changed. Maybe they imagined her as someone who would accept their love without such a struggle.

We sang. Thin strains of the portable keyboard competed with the sounds of the stream and the breeze. *Shall we gather at the river . . .* A mimeographed program with copies of the words had been passed around. The song was my idea. We'd sung it at our baptism. Then Sean got up and said a prayer. His pastor's voice hit notes that echoed like memories through my emotions. He really was a priest.

I turned around to see where Mom was sitting. The large gathering behind me took me by surprise. I hadn't been aware of so many people arriving, but they were there. A group from the car dealership, Mr. Romeros' family, Peggy and her parents, and Janet. I saw Evie and Micheal near the back, and a whole crowd of people Jo had known in high school. The pews were nearly full.

After Sean sat down, we sang "Whispering Hope." The melodies of the old songs were woven deeper in me than I imagined. As we sang, I looked at the casket, pushed away thoughts of her closed up and alone. She wasn't alone. She wasn't there.

Preacher Langston got up. He'd been sitting near the pulpit in a kitchen chair someone brought for him. He went and stood behind the pulpit, waited a moment before he spoke. It was impossible not to regard him standing there, tall and silent. I was eager for comfort, wanted him to begin. Feelings stirred in me, naïve feelings that should have been extinguished by now, but they were there, waiting to grab hold of his words.

"Hello, friends," he said.

From there, I gave in to the cadence of his voice, followed as his sentences flowed like a song. I followed his voice until I heard my name, then I stopped, listened as he spoke about me and Joanne.

"When Joanne left us this week, she didn't leave a husband, or a family of her own to grieve. She left her parents. Two people who sit before us with broken hearts at the unspeakable sorrow of burying their only child.

"Joanne also left a special friendship, one that filled many places in her life. That is why I ask you what she would have asked of you. Support Sister Darla as she works to raise the tiny boy that Joanne left in God's hands and in our care."

He paused. I don't think anyone was breathing.

"Many of you knew Joanne. You knew she had a tendency to turn the rules upside down. She had a tendency to twist them into knots and bows, then untie them all over again. If that worries you, brothers and sisters, if you are concerned about Joanne . . . rest easy tonight. Through a winding path that makes sense to only God himself, she has found her way to Heaven. On this day, she lives with God. As it is set down in First Chronicles . . .

" 'God chose the foolish things of the world to shame the wise; God chose the weak things of the world to shame the strong.' "

"God chose Joanne, my grieving friends. And that is her redemption. I know this because of time I passed with her. I know what I saw. Make no mistake about it."

Then he prayed. My eyes wide while others' were closed, I looked at the light. Rays of sun marked the open sanctuary, bright on me. Flesh to light and back again. I remembered it so well. I was nothing and everything all at once, and Jo, a kindred creature of that day. Something, once vague, came nameless and clear. Of the twins, one lived. I lived, but changed by what Joanne had offered. She had saved me from a danger that I had yet to name; rescued me with fierce love and a tiny child.

People were standing, holding off-white programs as their hymnals, and singing "Amazing Grace" without the help of the keyboard. Naked voices from an open church. As we sang, we filed to the cemetery, Jo's casket was carried by the men and put on a contraption that would ease her into the soft earth.

Ashes to ashes, dust to dust . . .

Before they lowered her, Preacher Langston read verse after verse from scripture. Verses I had once memorized, and long ago lost. His final prayer dismissed us, and I stood but couldn't go. Cal and the Timbros had moved on, expected me to follow.

Joanne, I can't leave.

"You can." Preacher Langston was beside me, heard what I must have spoken out loud. "You've got work ahead of you."

He held out his arm and waited until I was ready, until I could walk away from her grave, her casket, until I could leave her deep in the moist red dirt. That same earth splattered as I stepped, stained my clothes as I moved away from the cemetery, away from Joanne.

THE TIMBROS ASKED ME to ride in the funeral car with them.

"You were her family too," Arlene said. Cal said he would follow in his car.

Arlene sat between Larry and me. Larry slumped forward, elbows resting on his knees. There was ample room around him, but the space still seemed too small for his pain—an old coach, who'd just suffered the loss of a lifetime.

"Why don't you tell her your idea, Larry?" Arlene had her hand light on his shoulder, urged him to come out of his sorrow.

He turned his head and looked my way. Nodded to his wife.

She sat back against the seat so that I could talk with him.

"What is it?" I prompted when he didn't speak.

"She's not Joanne, Larry," Arlene said to him softly. "She'll accept this if you give her a chance."

I tried to fashion what he would say. Couldn't imagine what he could give me that would matter, now that Joanne had been taken from all of us.

"There's some insurance," he said. "Joanne had a little policy at work and I had a policy from years ago. I near 'bout forgot it until they got in touch with me this week."

"I don't want money from Joanne," I told him. The thought of cash in my hand that came directly from her death . . . "Please Larry, I appreciate it but—"

"Hear me out," he stopped me, but his voice was soft. "I've arranged to spend it, the part of it that's mine anyway. The policy from work had you listed as the one to get it."

Joanne had me on an insurance policy? I'd never known. There was so much I'd never known.

"I was hoping you'd want to put that in with mine on a down payment."

"On what?" I asked.

"On a house," he said. "On your old house. I don't know if you knew, but the people have moved. They're still trying to sell it."

I saw Joanne, newly pregnant and fearless, crawling in my old bedroom window. The house, empty. Rooms, familiar, but new, waiting for a family to fill them again. The baby had been there already with Joanne, just barely formed, but loved from those first days. He was in the world now and my home could be his home.

"Darla?" Arlene spoke my name. She and Larry were waiting, taking a chance and hoping to be spared more hurt. "We can help you if we're close like that, living right behind you. We don't want to take anything from you, honestly. You're that boy's mother. But we could be a real family. You're gonna need—"

"I know." Again the tears were overtaking me, flooding my words and my thoughts. "I want that. I want to raise Joe in that house. I really do."

"Jo?" They said it at once, thinking I'd gone off the deep end, confused.

"Joe. Joseph," I said. I hadn't realized I'd used the name, the name I'd thought about as I stood, looking at my baby boy through the glass. "Joseph Timbro Stevens. Is that okay?"

Arlene's eyes went wide and Larry's face changed to a smile. They kissed each other and she leaned over and hugged me. As I pulled away from her I looked in his eyes.

"Come here," he said.

I leaned forward, over Arlene. Waited to hear what he wanted to say. Instead he met me there in the middle, kissed my cheek.

"Joseph," he said before he sat back and nodded his approval.

I felt his strange kindness lingering on my face. It was a kiss Jo should have had, but so much of her had been a part of me—maybe she felt it after all.

I made myself think of the day ahead. We'd go to the hospital together, the three of us, and tell them Baby Timbro had a name. He had a name and a home, and two backyards; two yards that for a second generation of childhood would be like one.

EPILOGUE

ALLIANCE, TEXAS—JULY 1988

I WATCH THROUGH THE WINDOW of Joe's bedroom, my old room. Any
minute Arlene will send him out her kitchen door, across the yard,
and home to me. She does this every day when I get in from work. Joe
has asked me to let him do it by himself, travel the length of two backyards to his home. I know he's big enough, so I said yes. But he's still
little to me, so I stand to the side of the window and watch—just to
be safe.

My life is safe now. Arlene looks after Joe while I'm at work. I'm
back at the newspaper, only I'm not in the print shop anymore. I run
the front office, once again know the stories before they are news.

Some days Mom helps Arlene, and she keeps Joe when I want to
go out at night. She likes coming back to our old house. Memories of
Daddy linger for her, but the colors are muted and give her some
pleasure now.

Through the window, I see Joe on the Timbros' kitchen stoop.
Arlene is wrapping something, a cookie or biscuit most likely, in a
napkin for him to bring home. He waits, listens to whatever instructions

she feels the necessity to offer. *Don't eat this before dinner* or *Have your mama heat this up.* He'll disregard what she says and eat it as soon as he hears her door slam. But it's the listening that's the key. He's figured that part out.

He listens to Larry too. Joanne's flesh and blood will listen to instruction and mostly obey. It's confounded all of us in the nicest possible way. He loves the hardware store. Spends entire afternoons there. Larry lets him climb on the lawn mowers and play with the cash register. I'm tempted to intervene when I hear Larry building steam over some minor infraction. "Dammit, Joe, I told you not to play with the tools and leave 'em in the aisle!" Joe sits on the floor, tools littered about his legs and feet. "I've got to sell those things, boy. I've told you a thousand times!" His voice is working to a boil and I move to intercede, to tell him he's overreacting, expecting too much of a boy who has yet to turn five. But before I speak, I hear Joe's giggle.

"Granddaddy, you're the biggest ol' bear sometimes!"

And I see Larry's anger settle to calm, laid low by the boy's love.

I worry sometimes that Joe doesn't have a father with him. But there's Larry, a yard away. And Sean, who comes in on Sundays to help with Mass at St. Elizabeth's. He picks Joe up for Sunday School on his way. Lately I've been dressed to go with them when he gets here. Sean has never said anything about my decision to go. He just opens the car door for me and starts his usual chatter with Joe.

While Joe's in Sunday School, I sit in the back of the service, try to follow the kneeling and standing and sitting and kneeling again, as I marvel at the aerobic nature of Catholic worship. But it calms me, and without realizing it I've come to look forward to the liturgy, to the songs and the humbling notion of bowing to something out of respect, not grief.

Joe is all too comfortable at St. Elizabeth's. He started morning preschool there two years ago, and between Sean and the nuns has achieved the status of parish darling. Larry's come to terms with the idea that—to our utter bafflement—we are raising a Catholic.

"Well, if I buried my daughter in a black cemetery beside a burned-out church, I guess nothing much is going to surprise me with her boy," he said. But he was smiling when he said it. We can smile when we talk about Joanne now. That's not trivial to any of us who loved her. In his way, Larry loved her. I believe that now.

I peek out from my hiding spot to see Joe's progress across the yard. Rigsby has made his way out to where Joe is bending over, inspecting something in the yard. Rigsby is struggling on arthritic legs to muster playfulness at Joe's arrival; but Joe, too little to know why, understands anyway. He sits in the grass and lets the dog settle beside him, feeds him a bite of whatever Arlene wrapped in the napkin.

He knows that Cal is his father. Cal sends money every month and visits when he can. He's visited more often this year, and has spent more time with Joe when he's been here.

He came last weekend, and after taking Joe to a baseball game in Houston, he brought him back to the house and asked if my mother could keep Joe while we went to dinner. It felt really good to be out with him. His talk of Joe's afternoon with him was easy and full of smiles. I have to see hope in this, but I'll allow myself only so much.

And hope ventures only so far. I won't ask myself why he wanted to take me to dinner, or why I enjoyed myself so much. All I can say is that I went, and both of us seem glad that it happened. I won't apologize for being Joe's mother. It's the one part of me I won't yield. Not to anyone. But Cal hasn't asked me to—and all that said, I did like seeing him across the table. There's no denying it.

I send thoughts to Joanne all the time. I still try to explain to her that her daddy is a hard man, but not a bad one. Not like she thought. If our souls are really wiser than ourselves, and Sean tells me they are, she already knows this.

When Joe prays, he sends messages to her care of heaven. Sean assures me that he's sending them to the right address. Sean believes she's with God; believes it the way most people believe an ambulance will come if you call. For now, I take him at his word; someday, I may believe again for myself. I'm not ruling out anything. Not anymore.

I take Joe to the burned-out church and we sit with the air around us and feel how close the day can get to our skin, to our breath. Then we walk to the cemetery.

I tell him stories about Joanne. I tell him that I'm his mama, but Joanne is too, in a way. I tell him how much she loved him. I tell him that she gave him his rich copper hair and his good name.

Mama Jo, he calls her, like she's some grandmother he's loved for-ever. But she's young in my memory. Fresh and forever alive in an oc-casional expression on my son's face, in the promise of green in his beautiful eyes. It's not all I'd hoped for, seeing her only through him. But most days, it's more than I need.

He's up now, walking toward the house, moving slowly so the dog can keep pace. I leave my place by the window so he won't know I've been watching. I go to the kitchen so I can be there the instant he walks in, before he even calls for me.

Any moment, he'll be inside. I'll kneel down to hug him, let his small arms claim me, name what I am with no words at all.